Littoral Magic, Book One of All Oceans Aglow

A Norton Place Publishing Publication

www.nortonplacepublishing.com

Copyright © 2024 by Aaron Mason and Leslie Ann Moore

Cover artwork by Bear Pettigrew of Crossroad Art

Additional artwork by Neil D'Monte

Interior design by Norton Place Publishing

ISBN:978-1-7358330-1-9

PRINTED IN THE UNITED STATES

First Printing: March 2025

NORTON PLACE
PUBLISHING

BOOK ONE OF - ALL OCEANS AGLOW

In Memory of

Tony N. Todaro

1946 - 2023

Rest in Power

CONTENTS

"Gitxsanimaq-Ookl-Thipuuntzn-Tyypara-Mataxiae-
Haqipenxurn-Elludeenthi..."

"...Great Ookl dreaming in The Blue, whose Ink colors the night sky;
whose Eye always watches from the deep; by Your Will alone all obstacles
shall be removed, and Your Garden Effulgent restored..." *

* An imprecise ideogram-to hijna-to English translation of the scrawled
Ulurii sand prayer (*Eemsura*) pictured above

CHAPTER 0

A DIRE PREDICAMENT

*S*leek ran for his life.

Almost there... *the young river otter thought, breathing hard. He struggled to swallow in a parched throat. His lungs burned and wheezed.* Just a little further now...

Sleek wanted to stop. Only a few blessed seconds to cool his smarting muscles.

But he dared not —

From the blackness came a reverberating noise, like boulders grinding each other into grit. Fear brought bile into the otter's throat, and fresh adrenaline surging through his limbs. Risking a backward glance, Sleek glimpsed the six-legged hunger hunting him with a singular intent. Its fury, indivisible from its personality, seared like a bloody star in the smothering cave-darkness.

This fury had many names: The Cruel Dweller. That Which Devours. Death By Rending.

The Voracious.

"Oh...yurch," Sleek cursed, as the crimson light radiating from his enemy's fiery viscera settled on his ashen fur. The profanity didn't make him feel any better.

Redoubling his efforts in a desperate bid to outdistance his pursuer, Sleek ran faster than he'd ever thought possible, even with an injured hind-leg. His four callused paws made short work of the topple of cold boulders he was doomed to scale. Up, up he went, climbing higher and higher still. As Sleek limped and labored, the fateful decisions that led him to this dire predicament replayed in his mind.

It had held so much promise, the beginning of this theft ...

PART ONE

THREE TRIBUTARIES

"In chambers deep,
Where waters sleep,
What unknown treasures pave the floor?"
Edward Young (1683 – 1765)
***Ocean*, Stanza 24**

CHAPTER I

WHERE THINGS GET DARK

F irst Tide nearly ended by the time Sleek got a chance to slip into the restless Blue and make for his objective. *It's now or never*, he thought.

It required stealth to ensure no clan members saw him leave. A tricky feat, considering all the watchful eyes among the river otters, or *Lontra*. Sleek knew to be cautious. Binding blood-treaty with the *Lutris* — the rival tribe of sea otters that dared claim all local waters as their own — designated entering The Cave and returning to the surface with its coveted treasure as *aijeer*, forbidden.

As dawn approached, the crafty river otter put his plan into motion.

Misdirection and the pretext of a solo hunt presented the perfect cover. With his trusty *ynth* — a four-foot-long fishing-pole shaft spear — in webbed paws, Sleek swam from the towering crags of High Split Rock, the ancestral *Holt*, or home of his mustelid tribe, and headed in the opposite direction of the revered Cave.

All adult Lontra enjoyed solitary hunting as a needed reprieve from the constant noise and bustle of Holt life. The vast Blue allowed them a chance to frolic in a world of constant motion. It was a place where they could lose themselves amid the verdant tangles and perpetual undulations of the vast kelp forests, stalking prey esteemed or meager according to their whims.

Sleek could be gone until nightfall, three full tide cycles, before anyone would miss him. But only fools hunted alone after dark. The last thing he needed was the Den Sire, his father and Alpha — or *Eehr* — of the Lontra, sending out a search party.

When he'd reached a safe distance from home, Sleek changed course, sticking close to the tangles of swaying kelp rising from the verdant sea floor. Using them, and their accompanying emerald shadows to hide his movements, he swam for *The Cellum*, a wood and metal shrine revered by both Lontra and Lutris. In reality, this 'place of prayer' and contemplation was the wreckage of a human fishing boat wedged tight into the coastal cliff wall, across the cove from High Split Rock.

Accident did not ground the vessel, but divine intervention.

Or so the story went ...

Lontra legend attested that, uncounted seasons earlier, Old Father Fathom, in His inky wisdom, conjured a mighty storm to run the offending boat afoul of the upthrust rocks, thus concealing The Cave's opening from those creatures wishing to exploit it. Sadly, over generations, the once glorious testament to Great Ookl's preeminence had decayed to little more than a symbol. A sacred place now foreclosed by the whims of a hostile invader possessing no dignity, no couth — just blind appetite.

Sleek felt his Holt's patron deity should intervene to rectify the situation. Yet, season after season hidden *Liminal*, the blessed *Garden Effulgent*, remained an occupied paradise, its once easily accessible miracles now beyond reach.

Apparently, their Old Father had more pressing concerns than the wellbeing of His subjects. *Sadly...* Sleek thought *...such are the whims of imaginary beings.*

The young river otter arrowed through shallowing coastal waters toward his destination. Handsome by Holt standards, tiny ears, sharp golden eyes, and an arrowhead-shaped nose wreathed with sensitive whiskers graced a streamlined head the same diameter as his neck. Beneath his lower lip a one-inch white turritella shell — a decorative *alcq* labret piercing both otter tribes kept custom — signified his hunting prowess, bravery, and lineage. Nineteen tiny patches of vivid blue fur adorned the dark-gray pelt of his right forelimb. Short, powerful legs propelled him while a tapering tail, half his six-foot body length, stabilized his movements.

Ahead, a ceaseless procession of foam-crested waves arose from the Pacific and dashed against a barricade of massive boulders. Jutting jagged and guano-stained like the broken teeth of a great, earthen monster, these unyielding stones split the punishing waves into foam and mist.

Sleek, as did all river otters, felt more comfortable swimming with his head exposed above the water while using the three or four-legged paddling style of casual surface travel. But time couldn't be squandered. So, he chose the faster — and more taxing 'hunting stroke' — the hind-leg and tail sweeping technique that kept his five-fingered forepaws, and the spear it held, free and ready. Sleek dove, his nostrils and ears closing to keep water from entering them, and with all haste slipped into the frothy tumult of immolating waves.

Competing currents jostled and buffeted the young otter. But Sleek, being a strong swimmer, soon passed unscathed through the saline gauntlet.

Beyond, an inner row of rocks loomed, smaller, yet far more numerous than the megalith vanguard. Carpets of thick kelp along with countless tufts of lush sea grasses and dulses further tempered the incoming swells. As a result, the wide inlet they protected had a calmer, almost wistful, surface demeanor.

The brave otter swam across this shallow cove of gentle waters and fertile tidepools.

On shore, the mysterious Cellum awaited as reward.

To Sleek and his mustelid kin the shipwreck seemed alien in both design and purpose. Gifted by a deity every bit as enigmatic and unfathomable as the human-built vessel — a strange place of straight lines, sharp angles and forced unions of wood and substances harder than stone — this foreign 'thing' conveyed more questions than answers.

Still, for all The Cellum's secrets and ambiguities, Sleek held a begrudging respect for it. Untying the knot of its *true* nature would never be easily accomplished.

It's just one of the mysteries The Blue dares us to understand, he thought, then winced. *Yurch. I sounded like Father just then.*

The young hunter scurried out of the lapping waves and onto the partially submerged stern of the boat. His wet, charcoal-gray pelt glistened. Hundreds of empty crab shells, pincers, feathers, and tiny fish bones littered the weather-beaten deck in abstract patterns and symbolic mounds. For Sleek, these *ghaydn* — reverently fashioned talismans offered as either prayer tokens to Old Father Fathom or banishment effigies meant to drive away The Cruel Dweller — were little more than superstitious trifles used to mollify the simple-minded devout.

Sleek chose a niche amidst a cluster of rusted crab cages to hide his prized ynth. The two tail-length silver and blue fishing-pole, shorn of eyes and spindle, boasted a stone-flattened metal hook tightly lashed to the tip with scavenged polymer line. In his paws, it proved both a versatile tool and princely weapon. It had slain countless fish, both great and small, harmless and deadly, during Sleeks ownership. Among his kin, only the hereditary spears of the Den Sire and Suckling Mother were superior.

But in the test to come, all weapons were useless. Nothing but speed mattered, and Sleek would need all four paws free for that.

The sneaky Beta, or *Saia* in his tribe's tongue, crossed the sloping deck of the wreck towards its upturned bow. He squeezed through a slender gap between cliff wall and wooden hull and entered The Cave proper. Like a shadow in the water, he swam the one hundred tails of the low flooded tunnel to the boulder that sealed the deeper cavern from the outside world. Present, not by accident but evil design, the gouged and chipped limestone mass had been torn from its original resting place in the earthen depths and hauled to the surface by The Cruel Dweller.

Sleek saw where boulder and wall merged. The sheer power needed to dislodge, drag, and wedge this colossal rock into its current location outstripped his understanding. The boulders' presence daunted. Yet, Death By Rending, for all its raw might, lacked a need for perfection. It should have seen, and sealed, the slit between boulder and ceiling.

The stealthy Saia felt determined to exploit this oversight.

Sleek scaled the coarse surface of the boulder and wiggled into the slit. Caught in the taper, he exhaled, flattened his supple body, and pushed. Cool stone scraped his back and belly as strong limbs propelled him through to the other side.

Hmm... Easier than expected, he thought and jumped to the passage floor. *If my luck holds out, this theft will be just as simple.*

A beam of muted sunlight speared the boulder crack, breaking the perfect gloom of the passageway. Sleek scanned the shadows ahead, sniffing and listening with a hunter's focus.

Nothing awaited but more rocks and puddles. The coast was clear...

Sleek scampered onward, confidence bolstered by the simple conquest of the boulder. Outside light faded rapidly, then, abruptly, the tunnel floor fell away into darkness.

Sleek crept forward and peered over the edge. In the feeble light, his keen predator-eyes spotted a multitude of jagged places upon which to twist an ankle, break a limb, or snap a spine.

One careless misstep and his thieving career would end before it even started. The thought of tumbling head-over-tail down the slope, cracking his face and teeth against each rock as he fell, sent a shiver down Sleek's back.

Fear would not deter him, however. Resplendent treasures that would cement all his romantic hopes and dreams awaited discovery somewhere beyond this subterranean midnight.

Sleek steeled himself — *Ready or not, Liminal, here I come* — and began.

Carefully, the Lontra scrambled down the treacherous slope of barnacled rocks, the soft glow from the blue *ureola* on his wrist the sole rebuke to the crushing darkness. The living bracelet, woven from a rare species of bioluminescent soft coral, attested to Sleek's Beta status among the *romp*, or clan residents. As the sole child of The Holt's ruling Alphas, he inherited all the privileges and responsibilities accompanying that rank.

The wan glow of the wristlet struggled against the murk, illuminating two tails in all directions. Only four meager feet, yet it could still mark his position to hostile eyes. Sleek considered removing it... but decided against the idea.

I'll be in and out before Death By Rending even knows I'm here, he thought with confidence. *I won't make any mistakes.*

Sleek's acute predator nose twitched at the fetid tang of rot wafting up from the shadows. Somewhere far below, flesh decayed to liquid. The odor offended the otter's sinuses and made his golden eyes water.

A lifetime in the sea had acquainted Sleek with the myriad smells of death. Though pervasive, he never got used to them. And how could he? They were a constant reminder of how The Blue would never grant a painless demise.

This stench evoked the terrible promise of ten thousand different agonies.

The distressed Lontra shivered. *Which agony will finally claim me?*

After an hour of careful descent, Sleek reached the bottom of the slope. To his relief the passage leveled out and vanished into aphotic mystery. Only his breathing and the *plink-plink* of icy water dripping from the ceiling broke the profound silence.

Sleek took just three steps into the subterranean drizzle before the glow of his wristlet revealed the source of the reek — skeletons. Dozens, maybe hundreds, all heaped and piled from years of accumulated tragedy.

Worse still, scattered amongst the bones lay the remains of recently dead sea otters, bloated harbor seals, and the withered forms of gulls and fulmars that had blindly dashed themselves to death against the walls. All the carcasses lay strewn about in macabre, postmortem sodality. Though the odor of decomposition hung heavy, no buzzing *myzee* — the ubiquitous and bothersome kelp fly — were present: they could never travel so far below the surface to reach this putrefying banquet.

This grim sight chilled Sleek's heart. These animals, had they but reached Liminal, would have evolved in splendor, and discovered their True Names. They could have told their own life stories, found their own voices, sung their own unique songs.

Their deaths represented ambitions unrealized. Dreams unfulfilled. Potentials wasted.

And, to add insult to injury, an unglorified grave.

Once, not so long ago, the bodies would have been reverently collected and set adrift into The Blue where current and tide would decide their final resting place. But this courtesy had ended with Liminal's theft. Now, this aggregate death did but one thing... offer a warning:

— Beware those who seek the Light. Turn back while you still can —

Sleek tugged his whiskers in customary respect for the dead. *Poor, poor Monoah*, he thought. *They'll never know the joys of speaking or thinking. What a shame.*

In those earlier days of his education, the first lessons were the simplest.

Three domains divided the world: the ocean, called The Blue; the sky, named The Above; and the land, known as The Still. All life began as *Monoah*, or the 'Unaware.' Sleek was taught Monoic animals were blind to any larger reality outside the 'kill or be killed' hunter-prey relationship.

"Yet The Garden Effulgent we call Liminal is the great healer of blindness," Suckling Mother instructed her son and his milk-brothers Swims

Past, Nimble, and Watches in the teaching den. Sleek hung on her every word, but only when he wasn't play-wrestling with the other kits. "By partaking of its gifts are the lucky afforded the chance to climb out of the darkness of ignorance and into the light of awareness," continued Suckling Mother. "And what do we call those who achieve this ascension?"

"Envorah!" Sleek and his milk-brothers shouted together, when they stopped their rumpus long enough to listen and learn.

"Excellent, children. And what does Envorah mean?"

"We Who Speak!"

"And what do we call those Garden Blessed who've eaten from Liminal proper?"

"Aanandi!" the kits proclaimed.

Sleek smiled at those memories, gleaned from a carefree time when only spirited lessons and mirth mattered. Sadly, those bright days were long gone.

As the lessons continued, Sleek was taught that for many creatures inhabiting The Blue, including the Lontra, being Envoric provided a common foundation. It defined who and what they were; each mind unique, yet sharing a singular, empathic unity.

It took but a single particle of Liminal's light to uplift an animal above the shoals of skittish Monoah. Just a nibble. Merely a taste of the magic.

Envoric animals were often (*but not always*) larger, stronger, faster, and longer-lived. Evolved minds pondered abstractions, discerned symbolism. Bronzed eyes radiated emotion. They shed tears. Digits lengthened and became dexterous. Air-breathers enjoyed greater lung capacity. Lontra and Lutris hunters often held their breath for over fifteen minutes.

This elevation increased in direct proportion to the amount of magic ingested. Sadly, it did not last forever. Without regular consumption of Liminal's magic the enhancement dwindled, leaving in its wake a sorrowful awareness of what the animal had lost — like the salts of an evaporated tidepool; a sad residue of what was once alive and thriving.

This intellectual waxing-and-waning — the 'Tides of Awareness', or *Kleaa* — permeated all aspects of Holt life. It started in the womb as a 'carryover essence' gifted by their mothers and deepened through suckling. Ebony irises changed into bronze as a kit developed. Once weaned, only direct pryzoic ingestion allowed an otter's mind and body to continue to progress.

But this evolution, once a common right, was no longer guaranteed.

Since the Garden's capture by The Cruel Dweller, and the magical drought that followed, all Envorah knew the sorrow of gradual physical and mental decline. Other than death or crippling injury, all fears underscoring their lives were subordinate to a waning Kleaa. And some few Lontra, Sleek among them, considered a painful demise a distant second to any lost sapience.

Sleek glanced back up the hazardous incline, taking a moment to appreciate the scope of the obstacle he'd just conquered. The cloud over his heart lifted as the young otter reveled in his surefooted skill.

Mourning the dead could wait. Sleek still lived and had a theft to perform.

The next challenge waited deeper in the darkness — navigating the labyrinth known as *The Winnow*.

CHAPTER 2

A VERY LONG DRIVE

"Are we there yet?" Ayana Outerbridge groaned.

She purposely soured her voice with that annoying *brat-tone* she knew Mother hated. But Ayana didn't care. Not today. She wanted to spread her misery far and wide, like heaping shovelfuls of petulant manure. She felt it her right as an angry thirteen (soon to be *fourteen*)-year-old.

"For the umpteenth time — *no!*" Hayley snapped, glaring in the rearview mirror at her cantankerous daughter. A silken, teal scarf wrapped her meticulously — and quite expensively — straightened hair whenever she drove with the windows down, lest the wind mess it up. And that was a strict fashion no-no. "I told you: *not* until six PM at the earliest. More like seven. And that's if we don't stop for lunch and eat in the car. We're not even close. Stop asking."

"We've been in this stupid car, like... *forever.* "

Ayana knew this trip would take at least twenty hours of steady driving. Trapped in a wheeled rust-box for a full day (...*God, this is pure misery...*) chewed on her soul. She couldn't resist complaining. Besides, what else could she occupy herself with? Pleasantries and idle conversations with her mother?

Not this year. Or the next...

Or — maybe never.

Ayana grumbled. "It's like they live on the moon, or something. It's ridiculous."

"You've said that. More than once."

Summer vacation of 1984 had arrived two days prior... and with it, the tenth consecutive annual visit to Ayana's grandparents' homestead on the rugged Pacific Northwest coastline. Lost somewhere between the densely timbered border of Oregon and Washington State, it was a soggy domain of briars and berries. An evergreen world of mold and mildew and misery —

Deep, deep Sasquatch territory.

Ayana didn't remember *exactly* where on the map they lived, although she had ample time to learn. *Why bother?* she wondered.

Her grandparent's house always seemed like an abstraction. Geographical coordinates were unimportant. Only the fact Ayana had to spend *three solid months* exiled there, hundreds of miles from friends — or, more precisely, the few friends she still managed to keep — mattered.

True, they'd celebrated birthdays (both for her and for Father) and even Independence Day. But Ayana had no say in the matter, and this year felt like a punishment instead of a vacation. Familiar pleasures of salty sea breezes, sandy beaches, woodland hikes, and slippery tide pool rocks did not blunt the isolation she felt. Nor did it compensate for the mediocre cooking, the lumpy beds, and the tedium of endless chores.

And, worse than all that: constant reminders of a happier decade never to return.

Those sweet-turned-sour memories splattered Ayana's soul like a cow-flop hurled by a demented circus clown. Everyone was laughing about it — everyone but her.

Ayana stared out the dust-speckled window as bucolic scenery rolled past.

Lazy cows grazed within wire-fenced pastures of green and gold (...*boring...*). Live oaks and the occasional lonely farmstead studded the dun hillsides beyond (... *pfft, so stupid...*). Flyspeck towns with silly names and modest populations flitted past, seen, pondered, and promptly forgotten (...*just like my life...*).

"It's too damn hot back here," Ayana groused. "I'm literally dying."

Early-June weather steadily pushed the border between 'tolerably warm' into 'melting-into-your-couch hot'. To make matters worse, the aged station wagon's AC had once again gone on the fritz. If the car deserved a name, it would be 'Fritz', hands down. Yes, *Fritz*.

"Just stop," Hayley's voice cracked in warning. She had been subsisting on strong, sugar-sweetened black coffee from a thermos for the last six hours, and neither her stomach, nor her nerves, could contend with her daughter's attitude. Her frustration grew equal with Ayana's belligerence.

"For Heaven's sake, if you're hot then roll down the window. God. You're driving me bonkers."

Ayana landed a frustrated kick to the back of the front passenger seat. Her scuffed, navy-blue Keds snagged the duct-taped hole in the brown upholstery. She cursed under her breath (that certain F-*dash-dash*-K word that drove her mother into a killing frenzy.)

"What was that?"

"Nothing," Ayana lied, then cranked the handle and lowered the dusty window. Warm wind found her tawny-brown face and ruffled the curls of her fawn hair. She blinked the rush of incoming air from hazel eyes.

"Now, was that so hard?" Hayley asked.

Ayana scowled and sucked her teeth. "Yes."

Hayley threw a frustrated gesture at the slow-moving dairy truck plodding ahead of them. "Oh, come on." She angrily mashed the horn four times. "Give. Me. A. Break!"

They'd been stuck behind this automotive tortoise for the last forty miles. Its logo — a piebald cow painted across the rear doors — taunted her with a cheerful, anthropomorphic grin and a ridiculously inflated udder. The driver must have thought going ten miles *under* the speed limit somehow safeguarded the delicate cargo of milk and cottage cheese. The pace put a severe crimp in Hayley's schedule — until, after another ineffective salvo of horn honks, the salvation of a passing lane appeared.

"Yes. Thank you." Hayley flicked the turn-indicator. "About damn time."

She checked the side mirrors and hit the gas. Fritz accelerated past the truck, overworked engine laboring. Hayley kept an anxious eye on the temperature gauge. The jalopy tended to overheat at inopportune moments. Two extra jugs of coolant stashed in the trunk served as necessary insurance. The dairy truck shrank in the rearview mirror.

Satisfied with her new momentum, Hayley eased off the gas. "That's better."

The mottled black and white fur of the absurd bovine mascot mouthing its lame corporate slogan ("It's *udderly* fantastic!") as it passed stirred a sour reaction in Ayana. Gaze settling on a bare right forearm, she sighed at the procession of nineteen white splotches speckling the top of her hand all the way towards her elbow. The first started between her middle and ring fingers, and then in a haphazard pattern, crept up, up, up for all the world to see. *Focal Vitiligo*, a "depigmentation condition in her epidermis" was what the doctors called Ayana's affliction *(What the hell do they know, anyway?)* She just called it *cruel*.

From an early age her parents tried convincing Ayana the 'milk drops' on her arm were special. Magical, somehow; even when they itched. And thus, by inference, she was somehow exceptional. For a while, the ruse worked. Her vitiligo were the Kisses of Angels or Faeries or Pixies. As she aged, these milk drops were rechristened 'dew drops', which seemed even more special and cherished.

But once Ayana entered the public school system, and her peers caught a glimpse of her enchanted dew drops, what had once been special became torture. The name changed once again, and not for the better. Kids were mean; always had been, always would be. The 'dew' devolved into 'glue', and though Ayana pretended the hurled insults held no venom ("Nice Elmer's-arm," or "Did a bird poop on you, or what?") they secretly smarted like the bee sting that could threaten her life.

A fatal trait potentially inherited from her father...

Ayana heaved a sigh, *tap-tapped* each glue drop with her left thumb and index finger, and quietly counted to nineteen. She found herself engaging in this childish game whenever stressed or bored.

Hayley heard the dissatisfied exhalation. Her deep brown eyes found Ayana's tetchy reflection in the rearview mirror. "Why don't you read a book?"

"If I read in the car, I'll puke." Ayana snorted at this clueless suggestion. "Is that what you want?"

"Fine. Then count cars. Or look for birds. Or take a nap. Just do something, *anything*, instead of complaining."

A desired arrival to the Grandparent's by suppertime had forced them to leave home at the unholy hour of 2:13 AM, and by then they were already thirteen minutes behind schedule. Nothing but vampires and insomniacs were up and about at that hour. Luckily, Hayley packed Fritz and filled the gas tank the night before. Ayana had dragged herself, zombie-like, from her warm-bed and slid into the cold backseat of the station wagon, its rumbling engine-lullaby coaxing her back to dreamland. When she awoke one hundred miles later, the dashboard clock read 4:36 AM.

Now it said 8:36 AM. Exactly four hours *(...that's so weird...)* had passed.

Ayana had been awake every tedious minute, and mile, since. She stretched, elbows popping. A lingering exhaustion now swept over her like a wave. Her drooping eyelids felt like lead weights. Mom had deduced her condition and managed a decent suggestion.

Ayana laid her head against the back seat cushion. "That's once in a row," she mumbled and shut her eyes.

Ayana woke, yawned. She glanced at the dashboard clock through gummy eyes — 10:28 AM. Hunger bit at her stomach.

"When can we have lunch?" she asked the back of her mother's scarf-wrapped head.

"Another two hours," Hayley answered. "Once we make the interchange and stop for gas. You hungry?"

"No. I asked because I'm *not* hungry."

Hayley ignored the snide reply. "I packed apple slices in the cooler."

Apples? Pffft. How original.

Ayana reached into the trunk, found the old green Coleman cooler, liberated the apple slices from the zip-locked bag within, and munched away. Tart, crunchy, and oh-so-cold, they refreshed. Still, she did wish them sweeter. "Could use some cinnamon and sugar."

"Plain is better." Hayley's tone carried the whiff of an impending argument.

"Whatever."

At least two more hours until the coast (*...my sad excuse for a life ticking away in this stupid car...*) and Ayana felt morose. To pass the time, she tallied roadkill as they whizzed by at a steady sixty MPH. Some animals she could identify — skunks, raccoons, opossums, the occasional unlucky farm cat — but most were pulverized into anonymous meat, left to ripen under a merciless sun for clouds of hungry flies.

Ayana felt sorry for the poor critters. They should've stayed inside their woodland burrows, instead of trying, like the chicken of that tired, dumb joke, to cross the road.

The world, she recently learned, or perhaps *relearned*, loved nothing more than ending life. Mother Nature's perpetual chore of *making* life inevitably concluded with the perpetual *taking* of it. Ayana read all about it in National Geographic: a mass death here, an extinct species there; environmental disasters — both natural (and more frequently, manmade) — everywhere. A staggering ninety-nine percent of all earthly life had already gone the way of the dodo. The roadkill Ayana idly counted proved the world had a billion years to perfect this passion.

So, what did her life matter in the grand scheme of things?

What did anything, really? *Pretty dark stuff*, she mused.

A memory rose, unbidden, and presented itself before her mind's eye: a man in a red flannel shirt and baseball cap sitting beside her on a shady park bench. The man was her father. It was summer, she was six, maybe seven years old, and wailing at the top of her lungs after seeing a baby bird, dead in the grass.

C'mon, Pipsqueak, Father cajoled, but gently. *Don't be sad. It'll be all right.*

"Will it, Dad? Will it really? I don't think so."

Though she spoke the words aloud, Ayana barely heard them leave her mouth...

But Hayley did.

She glanced at the rearview mirror, saw her daughter — eyes locked somewhere in the middle-distance — hold a silent, one-sided conversation. *Ayana's doing it again*, she thought. She tried, unsuccessfully, to ignore the little spasm of worry in her belly.

The grief counselor Hayley insisted Ayana see once a week for six weeks — it was all the therapy she could afford — had assured them both that imagining a dead loved-one, and talking to them, was perfectly normal: 'It's simply a manifestation of Ayana's grief and regret,' the counselor said with a clinically indifferent demeanor. 'A coping mechanism. When she has sufficiently processed her grief, she'll stop.'

Hayley sighed as her eyes returned to the road. She had to have faith the counselor was right. After all, she'd paid the woman an exorbitant amount. There was no point interrupting and questioning her daughter during one of her 'quiet banters.' She would only deny, deflect, and then go silent. *Just let it be.*

Miles and minutes ticked by. The station wagon sped through a grove of eucalyptus trees. Ayana wrinkled her nose at the sharp, menthol cough-drop smell wafting through the half-open window. As she watched the trees zip past, amber bark peeling from creamy trunks in long strips, Ayana decided — then and there — that she didn't care much for trees.

Or rocks. Or woods. Or beaches.

Yesterday she did. But no longer.

She concluded the act of enjoying something (or anything, really) was inappropriate now that Father was dead. Filling the void left by his passing felt somehow... disrespectful.

Thirteen months had come and gone since a tiny insect killed the strongest person in Ayana's world. The balding, bespeckled doctor at the emergency room decreed with an almost antiseptic detachment how Father had succumbed to "...a severe allergic reaction to bee venom..." A flaw in his physiology no one knew about — until it was too late.

But did the reason even matter? No. Not really.

One minute, Ayana had a father. The next —— *POOF!* —— she didn't.

And the World? It didn't care a single, solitary iota.

Ayana looked at her nineteen glue drops, subconsciously double tapping each one. *And why should it?* she thought. *Aren't people just bugs to be crushed? Or bees to be swatted?*

Fritz sped past a roadside sign displaying the distance in miles to the Podunk towns of Jarvis, Valley Creek, and Clementine. None had populations greater than five hundred... but at least they *were* towns with grocery stores and sit-down restaurants. Maybe even a movie theater or video arcade.

Not like where Ayana's grandparents chose to live. The Outerbridge family farmstead sat along an isolated stretch of wooded, coastal road at the end of a twisty, mile-long gravel drive, marked only by an old-fashioned metal mailbox on an innocuous wooden post. Their home, a throwback to an early retirement-world almost devoid of modern technology, boasted no VCR, no cable box, and no gaming system. Their closest neighbors lived twenty minutes away. By car.

The nearest town — the rustic flyspeck of Grovert, population a whopping two hundred and six — lay a full hour north. Every other Sunday, Grandma and Grandpa would make the trip to the Grovert American Legion post for their 'Big Night Out' — an all-you-can-eat seafood buffet and heated Bingo binge.

Once upon a time Ayana looked forward to visiting her father's parents. Their remote woodland kingdom became, after the chores were done, a veritable playground where she could climb trees, explore tide pools, fly kites, and horseback ride. It all seemed to last forever.

Now, everything felt small, gray, and fleeting.

Everything except her anger.

For thirteen months it had burned big and bright like a fiery briquette lodged in her chest. It hurt to keep it locked away, but she didn't know how to let it out safely — and so it remained there, scorching her soul, slowly cooking her from the inside out.

She often felt like exhaling that smoke. She wanted to fill the car with it. Choke the world with it. But she kept the soul-fumes to herself, like a dormant volcano fighting back eruption. Outside, another roadside smear of fur and bone, the latest example of the world's deadly plan, caught Ayana's eye as it sped past.

"That's seventeen," she sighed, and then saw *yet another* carcass. "Eighteen."

CHAPTER 3

WILLFUL DISOBEDIENCE

For Gloss, the chill morning offered an exciting promise.

Little more than a shadow flitting between the leafy spires of the emerald kelp cathedral, she stalked the Lutris hunting band — or *graehl* — at a discreet distance. She used all her natural guile and time-honed skill to avoid detection.

Her thick pelt of ashen fur kept a thin layer of warm air trapped against her skin. An outer layer of clinging air, the *shuuhl*, danced across Gloss' streamlined body, slippery and mercurial. The bevy of silvery bubbles it dispensed in her wake was the only thing that might expose the young sea otter in the tangles of current-jostled kelp.

This *uja*, or female — a true beauty among her Lutris tribe — moved when the graehl moved, surfaced for breath when they surfaced, stopped when they stopped. Gloss used the water's natural aquamarine murkiness and shoals of knotted seaweed to mask her silhouette from any curious eye. She'd tucked her lambent ureola into one of the natural pouches formed from loose skinfolds under her forelimbs as a precautionary measure. The wristlet's amber light, signifying her humble Epsilon, or *Loyc*, status amongst the Lutris as an unmated female, would give away her position like a beacon.

Gloss knew well the twin imperatives of stealth and camouflage. Being a "simple uja" meant she could not openly swim with any graehl, let alone hunt with them. She could not wear the hunter's alcq (although her lower lip, secretly pierced many seasons earlier, filled her with defiant pride), nor even touch a spear that had taken prey. The rigid gender-caste laws, hereditary and almost instinctual, governing the behavior of the entire Lutris population, called *The Raft* by friend and foe alike, made such rebellious acts forbidden.

Getting caught would earn her a painful, disciplinary ear or nose-bite.

Or perhaps something far worse...

The graehl — comprised of six streamlined, ureola-adorned *uju*-males of various ranks armed with calcified baleen lances and wearing shark tooth lower-lip piercings — remained unaware of Gloss's presence. The keen-eyed sea otters were too busy searching the *Oorum* for suitable prey. The optical verge, where dappled green light and water turbidity diffused all objects into a single blur at the edges of vision, played a vital role in the existence of every marine animal. Not just a perceptible vanishing point, the Oorum marked a threshold where the seen transitioned into the unseen, where the real and imaginary whispered secrets to each other — where the living and dead coexisted one final time.

The Lutris scanned the subaquatic terrain in earnest, their bristly whiskers feeling for any change in water pressure that might discern nearby quarry. To their frustration, the expanses of rainbow-hued corals and the ubiquitous tufts and tangles of leafy *nooree* — the Envoric catch-all word for all species of seaweeds, grasses, dulses, algae, and kelp — hid nothing worth pursuing.

Still, they kept hoping. And, with their keen bronze or golden eyes, kept looking.

Several days earlier, a brief summer downpour washed many land-locked nutrients into The Blue, invigorating the plankton and krill which drew hungry shoals of smaller fish. These in turn brought larger prestige game — giant sea bass, tuna, ocean-phase salmon, goliath groupers, and the "blood drawn" *aorxa,* or deadly shark — all graehls preferred to hunt.

Yet today those chosen prey remained hidden from the spear toting Lutris.

Gloss' impatience for a kill far outstripped that of the males. They hunted because they could. She hunted because the rules declared she couldn't. And though she must follow the graehl in secret, by taking the risk she not only honed her stalking skills, but she also positioned herself to slay any prey flushed from its hiding place by their mustered lances.

The ynth she wielded with such proficiency held a special place in her heart. Crafted from calcified whale baleen by the paws of Fearless, her father and Eehr-Alpha of the Lutris, the rigid shaft had belonged to her older sibling Grabber, before he went missing over two hundred tides earlier. This spear, shorn of bristles and boasting a stone-filed, serrated point, had on its first outing skewered a hundred-pound tuna.

Now twice as sharp, it could easily do so again. Gloss longed for the chance to try.

What good is the ynth if you're never allowed to use it? she mused.

The graehl halted. Their collective body language suggested something alarming. They drifted in a tighter formation — back-to-back-to-back — raising lances in a defensive posture.

Something's coming, Gloss thought with a twinge of unease. She ducked behind an algae-softened boulder crusted with orange sea stars and peeked around its curve to watch.

Soon, three shapes materialized from the Oorum like aquatic ghosts. They swam towards the graehl, their outlines clarifying into a trio of proud *Irounga*.

Two piebald harbor seals, earless and doe-eyed — each a full tail longer than the largest adult sea otter — dutifully followed a massive black sea lion. Lacking the proper anatomy, they carried neither ureola nor spear nor net. The Lutris looked like pups in contrast.

Seals, regardless of their species, were considered Irounga, or 'free swimmers'. Yet all were subservient to their colossal master, the immigrant southern elephant seal known as Diuun Dunn. As robust as even the black sea lion appeared, he was little more than a child when compared to the immensity of his corpulent liege.

Gloss watched the seals glide towards the sea otters. *These are* our *hunting waters,* she thought, tightening the grip on her whale-bone lance. *Irounga know better than to come here!*

The Envoric seals ranged at great distances from their remote island rookery. They patrolled vast stretches of coastline encompassing their territory, whose boundaries hemmed the shallower littoral regions occupied by their otter rivals. Preying on the same fish as the Lutris and Lontra, conflicts between the species were inevitable.

The three Irounga slid past the cautious graehl. They appeared un-concerned at the spears pointed towards their sensitive, whisker-wreathed snouts. The seals flicked their leathery flippers in unison, gracefully altering their trajectory, and began circling the huddled sea otters. After two full orbits, the Lutris males lowered their weapons, piquing Gloss' curiosity even further.

They're not attacking. What are *they doing?* she wondered, straining to see with little luck. *I need to get closer.*

Forsaking the cover of the boulder, Gloss swam along the bottom, using the verdant kelp shadows and feathery corals to cover her movements. When she spied the ritualistic bite scars on the Irounga's necks, inflicted with due ceremony by the pampered females of Diuun Dunn's harem, she halted. Any closer approach risked detection.

From behind a tussock of rubbery red algae, Gloss' keen eyes appraised the situation. It appeared as if the seals and sea otters were having a conversation, although she couldn't detect their *hijna,* the 'Shared Voice', from her present location.

Not all mouths allowed for vocal speech, and not all discourse occurred above the waves. The Garden's gift of hastened evolution removed this limitation, allowing the myriad species of Envorah direct mind-to-mind communication. Each animal tapped into a unique wavelength, all running like rivers of consciousness along different courses — yet these tributaries fed into the pool of collective sapience, the ocean of True Speech. The ocean of hijna. Whether fish or fowl, otter or seal, turtle, or crab; no matter how alien the mind or diverse the anatomy, all spoke a common language with fellow Envorah.

Gloss picked out snippets of conversation, but nothing solid on which to hang a conclusion. "*Ulurii*... hidden... Lontra know...we offer *pryzoa*... Blubber Snout hungers..."

On rare occasions Lutris and Irounga traded foodstuffs for simple tools or ornamentation — pretty shells, woven kelp bands, feathers, tiny bones, and other baubles — for the females of each species. The desire for beautification, it seemed, struck a common chord among the Envorah. Yet, Gloss couldn't shake the feeling that a darker, more dire purpose underscored their meeting. It sounded suspiciously like a plot.

Once, the venerated Ulurii, also known as octo-snails, had been a numerous tribe. Considered sages of the sea, their wisdom had devised, among other things, the common lexicon used by all Envorah. Now, just two survived in all The Blue, and they dwelled under the protection of the Lontra's many keen spears.

Why would the Irounga want our graehls to help find them? Gloss wondered.

Curiosity aside, the slow burn in her lungs could no longer be ignored. It demanded she surface to snatch a cool, refreshing breath. And besides, whatever schemes were unfolding between the Irounga and the graehl did not involve her. Yet.

With a sharp kick of her hind legs and swishes of her long, graceful tail, Gloss propelled herself like a furry bullet back up through the tangled nooree towards the sparkling surface. She did not realize a pair of gold-within-gold eyes witnessed her departure — and their owner was not pleased.

A quarter tide-cycle later found a green-speckled lingcod — the *atiqah,* or 'hungry thief' — swimming among the seaweed-bearded rocks on the sandy ocean floor as it searched for food. Little more than a cavernous mouth and spiny fins, it ate anything it could fit into its maw.

The graehl either missed or ignored the meaty, delicious fish — but not Gloss. Always anxious to make a kill, feed her kin, and prove her skills *yet again*, she trained herself to strike whenever the opportunity presented itself.

A lethal shadow, Gloss stalked her prey from behind, taking extra care to approach at just the right speed; moving too fast would trigger the fish's instinctual flight-cues. Once she could see the cod's individual scales, she set the base of the ynth against the tip of her muscular tail and, with steady paws, aimed the shaft.

She had one shot. One chance.

Gloss slowed her heartbeat, centered, and prepared to cast her Hunter's Eye —

The lingcod's attention remained on the slimy rocks below.

With a quick twist of her body, coupled with a dexterous tail-slash — Gloss hurled the lance with an accuracy that would have shamed most Lutris males. The needle-sharp barb impaled the unwitting fish in the sweet spot behind its gill slit.

The atiqah bolted like a shot, heedless of direction, blood streaming in its wake. Gloss followed the wounded lingcod into the leafy kelp. The protruding spear became entangled in the fronds, slowing its frantic flight. Soon, its death spasms stilled, and the fish went limp.

Gloss retrieved her prey and admired its beauty. A fine kill worthy of even the most skilled graehl member. At two tails in length, almost as large as Gloss, the well-muscled atiqah would fill the bellies of many hungry Raft members during the communal evening meal.

Exhilarated, Gloss reveled in her accomplishment. This is what she lived for, what she did better than anything else! Her true calling, her true passion, her true self —

"Stop!"

The authoritative hijna-shout slew her triumph quicker than her ynth had the lingcod.

Gloss saw the graehl of six males floating above her. Backlit against the glittering surface, they glared at her with angry eyes, their wire-thick whiskers bristling like their spears.

"What do you think you're doing?" the large male, Sharp Tooth, asked. As leader of this hunting band, his piercing Aanandic gold-within-gold eyes and oversized canine tooth, coupled with a prominent shark tooth alcq piercing, evoked an intimidating aspect. He wore the blue ureola of Saia-Beta, similar in knot-design to Gloss' wristlet and symbolic of an elevated status.

"Just hunting," Gloss hijna-replied innocently. "I wanted to do my share."

"You know hunting is forbidden to females," Sharp Tooth barked. "Those are the rules of our Raft. How many times do you have to be told?"

"As many times as it takes to sink in," Gloss answered defiantly. "And it hasn't. Yet. Sorry-not sorry."

All five graehl members took instant umbrage with her answer. Their whiskers flared, chisel-like teeth rasping in agitation. Hijna-curses followed. If Gloss were the child of anyone besides their Alpha, they would have bitten her as penalty. Many females were disciplined in this manner, ears and noses torn and disfigured as testament to their disobedience.

As it stood, they only dared report Gloss' behavior to her father, their Doyen. He would punish her accordingly. Maybe...Sharp Tooth couldn't hide the disappointment in his hijna. "You're a proud, willful uja, Gloss. Far too stubborn. Far too contrary. And far too..."

"Yes, yes. I've been told," Gloss interrupted with casual defiance. "More than once."

"Give up your kill. Now," Sharp Tooth ordered. "Harvest the uboorl with the other females like you're supposed to do. As our Doyen's daughter, you need to set the example."

The sharp twinge of competing venoms — anger and resentment — stung Gloss' heart. Anger that her kill would become the trophy of anoth er... but ultimately resentment hurt the most because her skills were always dismissed. She could match the ability of any male in The Raft. She knew it, her father knew it, and even the assembled males knew it.

But would they ever recognize it? Never. They detested the truth, and by law only pups or the sick could eat the fish she caught.

Gloss put her webbed foot against the lingcod's scaly body as leverage, and with a defiant tug, yanked the spear out. A gout of blood came with it. Before the lingcod drifted to the bottom, a lesser-ranking graehl male skewered it with a keratin lance.

Sharp Tooth held out a webbed paw. "And I'll be taking that ynth."

Gloss bristled at his presumption. Her lance, a gift from her beloved brother — the very Beta Sharp Tooth had replaced before he went missing — defined her personality as much as her rebelliousness. She did not intend to relinquish her weapon to Sharp Tooth or anyone else.

She would rather pluck out her own whiskers.

"No," Gloss answered, her hijna offset by a low growl. "You will *not*."

Gnaw, one of a small number of fifth-ranked Loyc-Epsilon males among the Lutris, so-named from his habit of chewing off the fingers and ears of rivals, could not hold back his disgust. His hijna sounded as sharp as the teeth he bared. "No? No! Uja do not carry the ynth! Uja do not cast the Hunter's Eye! That's our Doyen's decree! You fling spraint on our customs with your disobedience. You should be bitten and put in your place!"

"I'll never be unarmed in The Blue!" Gloss shot back, defiantly pointing her ynth at Gnaw. "No pup or Raft-sister of mine will *ever* be prey because you can't accept a spear in the paws of an uja. I will defend my Raft just as you do. *Better* than you do. I know it, and you know it. So, get over it."

And with that, Gloss spun about, insolently flicked her tail at Sharp Tooth and the seething graehl and swam off into the acres of emerald seaweed. The males growled, their whiskers twitching with anger. But they did not pursue her. Too much hunting and patrolling needed to be done; as males, that priority superseded all others.

Gnaw fantasized of witnessing Gloss' discipline at the teeth of her father. *I hope Fearless humiliates her before the whole Raft. That'll put her in her place.*

The graehl continued with their as-yet unsuccessful hunt. Sharp Tooth took the lead, a bubbly shuuhl leading the other males as they fell into rank-assignment behind him.

Gnaw brought up the rear. As he swam, the hatred of his fifth-rank status, and the Lutris who put him there, twisted like a shark tooth in his gut. Only the crippled, sick, or — worst of all — unmated females were relegated to Epsilon.

Why couldn't Fearless see that everyone Gnaw bit, down to the last helpless pup, deserved to feel his teeth? Turning a blind eye to this fact invited weakness into The Raft, thus endangering everyone. Discipline through naked aggression — just as The Blue intended.

Yet the Doyen's warning of any further biting offenses would find Gnaw forever lowered to the rank of Omega, or *Nihl* — he who could, no *should*, be a primary Saia-Beta! — rankled. Demotion to Nihl meant forever wearing the crimson ureola of shame.

Galling as it felt to be bringing up the rear of the graehl, the threat of having to wear the red wristlet, and never rising in status again, made Gnaw want to grind his teeth until they split. Instead, he chewed the base of his keratin spear, adding fresh bite-marks to the countless others marring the baleen shaft. Gnaw's need to bite when distressed bordered on the pathological.

Someday I'll wear the alcq of the Alpha and wield his weapon, Gnaw thought. *Someday I'll rule The Raft, and on that day, I'll bite everyone. Some of them more than once. Like Gloss. I'll bite her beautiful face clean off.*

CHAPTER 4

THE URCHIN HARVEST

G loss inhaled and dove for the fourth time, her dense, silvery fur protecting her from the water's chill. She grasped the needle-sharp ynth in webbed paws — but what good was a spear when harvesting urchins?

After swimming several fathoms, she reached the waving fronds of a thick kelp forest. Her agile body allowed her to maneuver with ease through the tangle of rubbery blades. Visibility dropped to less than a tail-length amongst the increasing numbers of brown and green stalks. Gloss wasn't concerned. Direct attacks from predators seldom occurred in the thickest parts of the seaweed, where a Lutris could hide and mount a counterattack with a lethal spear.

In an area of the intertidal sea floor, beneath a dense canopy of unfurled nooree blades that diffused sunlight, changing the ocean blue into green, lay Gloss' objective: food — *uboo* — or, the ubiquitous sea urchin.

Hundreds of red and purple sea urchins competed for space with a medley of starfish, rubbery sea cucumbers, and immobile, white-plumed anemones. The spiny invertebrates grazed mindlessly upon the root-like holdfasts anchoring the kelp to the rocky substrate. Large urchin multitudes like these, known as *uboorl*, served as the cornerstone of the sea otter diet.

Depending on how a Lutris used the word, uboorl could either mean "inexhaustible food" or "without end." Yet, for the sea otter female, it simply meant, "work" — tide in and tide out. No time for play or adventure, and certainly no time for any of the 'higher' martial pursuits the males enjoyed, like hunting, combat, or expanding territory.

Gloss reached the murky bottom and chose a nearby clutch of languid urchins for harvest. *This tide was made for hunting,* she fumed. *Not stringing uboo.*

Setting aside the spear, Gloss reached into an underarm skin-pouch and removed a *plijet*. This length of nylon line — one end affixed to a discarded, stone-sharpened toothbrush, the other a bit of driftwood — provided females with a useful tool.

Gloss plucked an urchin off a rock. With a repetition-honed skill first learned as a clumsy juvenile, she jabbed the toothbrush shaft through the creature's tiny oval mouth and out the back of its prickly shell, threading the cordage through the animal. The driftwood wedge kept the urchin from sliding off.

I hate this, Gloss thought as she threaded a second urchin. *This is a waste of my time and talents. I'm stuck using a plijet instead of the ynth.*

Boring, yet necessary. Without predators to keep them in check, the uboorl could breed uncontrollably and become a ravenous plague-front sweeping through the seaweed, devouring every holdfast in its path, and setting entire forests adrift. With the nooree gone, so went the prey fish, for the ensuing urchin-barrens held little more than swarms of inedible feather stars and the sunflower starfish feeding on them.

For generations, sea otters kept urchin populations stable, and Lutris females did the vital, if unenviable, work of gathering that food. While the balance continued, uboorl-plagues remained a thing of the past.

Gloss threaded a third uboo, then a fourth, all the while chafing at the notion that, if she'd been born a male, then as a pup of the Doyen she would be Beta... which meant deference from others and giving orders, *not* taking them.

Yet, in the eyes of privileged males, she was 'just an uja' — a mere Loyc at the bottom of the Lutris social order, along with all her unmated Raft-sisters. She could never wear the hunters alcq, or openly cast the Hunter's Eye. And only through the bestowal of a mate's rank could she, and all Lutris females, rise in status.

Of all the beings in all the Blue, Sleek alone treated her as an equal — and she loved him for it with a deep and true passion.

My dearest Sleek. How I miss you. In a few short days they would reunite at the Oyster Shell for the short span of Fourth Tide. The anticipation made Gloss want to purr.

She strung a tenth uboo, then slung the spear back over her shoulder. Weighted down with all the urchins she could manage, she kicked up towards the sun-sparkled surface, strong legs and sweeping tail propelling her through the swaying columns of emerald seaweed.

Leaving the sooty depths behind, she pinpointed her destination, silhouetted against the brighter waters — the *ghossn*, or driftwood carryall.

The buoyant construct, lashed together with kelp strands and lengths of salvaged fishing line, bobbed on the gentle waves. Six slender branches radiated from its crisscrossed center, each draped with several plijet-wreaths laden with threaded urchin — prior hauls of other females. A shoal of tiny fish darted through the ghossn's latticed shadow to nibble on spilled uboo innards.

Gloss swam up beneath the logs and hooked her urchin string upon a suitable limb. The added weight pulled the makeshift buoy a fraction lower into the water. Surfacing, she filled her lungs with fresh air. *Four more bundles and I'll be done for today,* she thought with a sigh. *If I'm lucky I'll be able to sneak away tonight and go hunting.*

Gloss slid onto the driftwood welter to inspect the stability of the urchin wreaths. She didn't want any coming apart and felt happy to find none needing attention. The sun warmed her backside, and for a joyous moment, all problems vanished. She fancied enjoying a quick nap.

Nearby her Raft-sisters, Follows and Shines, floated on their backs like lazy flotsam. With their webbed feet folded onto their torsos to conserve body heat, they happily munched on sweet Dungeness crabs for breakfast. Their tails, festooned in tight strips of nooree, colored shells, delicate feather stars, and other scavenged adornments, were in strict keeping with the current fashion trends. While they drifted and ate, they gossiped. Yelps, barks, coos, and other vocalizations punctuated their hijna-conversation.

"So," Follows said, "I told Splendid there wasn't enough time in the day to help groom her tail." With her sharp teeth, she cracked open a still-moving crab leg and ate the tender meat inside. "Her tail isn't the only one in The Raft, after all."

"Oh, I'm sure she didn't like hearing that," Shines added as she cleaned the last bits of roe from a bisected sea urchin. "Deshi-Oad's Fluke, I think she believes we're here to keep her looking pretty."

Follows nodded as she munched. "That's my point. I have my own tail to worry about, thank you very much. It takes a full tide to decorate it properly. Sometimes longer."

"And none of our uju's appreciate it." Shines rolled in the water to wash the bits of urchin shell off her soft auburn fur. "We go out of our way to look attractive for them, but they're always in a rush. They notice nothing but their spears and their bellies."

"You must put in the time. But try telling Splendid that. Besides, if you ask me, her tail is too fat. She should eat less and swim more." Shines discarded the last uneaten portion of crab leg and nibbled on a second. "All her pups are fat, too. It's disgraceful."

For Gloss, seeing her Raft-sisters piddling their time away undercut her desire for a well-earned nap. While admiring the subtle rebellion of their idleness, she also despised said idleness. Especially when hungry mouths waited to be fed.

Gloss, herself, never decorated her tail. To do so would connect her to deliberate indolence — and one couldn't be a successful hunter with a cluttered tail.

But, for now, a much more pressing matter loomed. Shines and Follows were supposed to be watching Cries Often, Gloss' older, mentally hindered sibling.

"What do you think you're doing?" Gloss demanded.

Follows jolted in surprise. "Oh, Gloss. I didn't see you there. You scared me."

Shines didn't startle so easily. "We're eating. What does it look like?"

"Where's Cries Often? You're supposed to be watching him."

"Don't be angry," Shines replied. "He wanted to go swimming by himself."

"We told him 'No', but he refused to listen," Follows said. "If the Alpha's last remaining son wants to swim unattended, then I'm not going to interfere." She offered Gloss a ruby-hued crab claw. "Here. Have some crab. They're sweet today."

"Did he surface?" Gloss asked. "Please tell me you at least saw that!"

Follows shrugged. If she felt any guilt about slacking off in her duties, she didn't show it. "Nope. Didn't see a thing. Sorry."

"But he's lame. Slow. He's helpless without me! Xaad could get him!"

Follows rolled her striking bronze eyes and shook her head. "Deshi-Oad's Stone Teeth, Gloss. You worry too much. Cries Often isn't a pup. Besides, Xaad doesn't swim in these waters. He's probably following a graehl and scheming for scraps."

"How do you know?" Gloss leveled her baleen spear at Follows. "That vile barracuda could be watching you this very instant, just waiting to bite your over-groomed tail clean off. Or maybe it'll just take one of your feet instead."

Shines gasped and worriedly tugged on her whiskers. "She may be right."

Follows looked around nervously. The thought of Xaad circling below her, menacing her with its toothy maw, sent a shiver of panic up her supple spine. "You really think so?"

"Yes, your tail *is* over-groomed," Shines agreed.

Relieved, Follows giggled and flicked water at Shines with a webbed hind-foot. "Oh, shut up, Shines. You had me going."

"You're both impossible," Gloss snapped, losing patience. Her so-called 'Raft sisters' took nothing seriously, except keeping their bellies full. "You shouldn't be so careless out here in the open Blue. The sooner we finish the harvest the sooner we can get back home. Then you can lounge about all you want and stuff your faces."

"The uboorl isn't going anywhere," Shines stated. "So why chase it?"

Follows munched on the crab claw she'd offered Gloss earlier, savoring the translucent flesh within. "Besides, who says we want to go back? This time away from the ujus and pups is nice. They're always so needy and helpless. All they do is take, take, take."

"We deserve some much needed us-time," Shines declared. "Period."

"Chookzl," Gloss swore, gripped the ynth, and slid into the water without a ripple.

Shines shook her head in frustration. "Gloss acts too much like an uju for her own good. Always barking orders. Acting important. Throwing her weight around. It's going to come back and bite her on the nose."

"If anyone needs their tail decorated, it's her," Follows agreed. "And in a hurry."

Gloss streaked towards the swaying thickets of emerald kelp. All concern for urchins, lazy Raft-sisters, and her unfair, gender-biased predicament vanished.

Only the fate of her sibling mattered now.

He could be trapped or wounded with no way to surface! Gloss fretted and swam faster. *I'm coming, Cries Often!*

Though considered an adult by virtue of age and Raft law, in the eyes of many, including Gloss, he would forever be an adolescent — and a helpless one at that. It didn't matter he had two full seasons on her. Every Lutris knew of Cries Often's difficulty swimming because of his lame right foot and how he could neither hunt nor fend for himself. Any strong current could sweep him into the open Blue, where he might drown. Or worse.

From the verdant nooree, a black surfperch darted across Gloss' path. She ignored the prey. The need to find her brother overwhelmed her hunter's impulse.

— an impulse warning her Xaad could be nearby, stalking prey in the briny gloom.

The rapacious barracuda claimed a section of Lutris-territory, and with his arrival, many of the prized fish sea otters hunted had fled. Measuring almost six tails in length, Xaad was twice the size of even the largest Monoic barracuda. Having never eaten from The Garden-proper, the loathsome animal had nonetheless devoured enough enchanted life as either flotsam — or other Envoric prey-animals — to spark his intelligence past all evolutionary norms. His malice increased to match, and over time, he chased off or killed all rivals, including most sharks. He could barely hijna and enjoyed nothing but slaying and terror.

For now, Xaad claimed the title as the most dangerous predator in the region.

Gloss swam deeper, sensitive whiskers stiffening in the currents as her sharp, golden eyes, extra keen to the ultraviolet spectrum, scanned the constantly swaying shadows. She found nothing but thriving aquatic forests, a constellation of purple and orange sea stars, and algae-encrusted stones.

But that didn't mean danger wasn't lurking.

She caught a fraction of movement among the tufts and tangles of leafy kelp; just a flutter of gray and then it vanished. Another surfperch? Xaad preparing to strike?

Hunting skills kicked in as Gloss assumed an attack posture. The tip of her almost prehensile tail pressed against the notched base of her lance, in preparation for a throw.

Show yourself, Gloss demanded. With taut muscles readied, and a steady heartbeat, she waited. No prey emerged. No hidden predator appeared to challenge. Doubt crept into her mind. *Great. Now I'm seeing things.*

Just as Gloss lowered her spear and turned away, a shape barreled towards her from a thicket of caramel-colored nooree. She twisted to avoid the collision, kicking as she swerved.

Though boastful of her speed, she still wasn't quite fast enough.

"Aaargh!" Gloss's scream escaped in a torrent of bubbles.

She froze for an agonizing instant, something a true hunter would never do. *Xaad has killed me,* she lamented.

"Ha-ha! I scared you," Cries Often proclaimed. "I got you, Gloss!"

"Yurch!" Gloss swore. Her hijna rang out, sharp with fright and annoyance. "Cries Often! You shouldn't sneak up like that! It's not nice!"

Cries Often's simple, grinning face crumpled. His thin whiskers drooped. "Oh...uh-oh..."

Gloss regretted her harsh reprimand. "Yes. You got me, Brother. You got me." Her rapid-fire heartbeat began to slow. It hadn't been the murderous barracuda. Just a prank from her slow-witted brother — though not so slow that he didn't catch her off guard.

"Sorry, Gloss." Cries Often rubbed his blind eye, a permanent bother, and flashed her a jagged grin, shark tooth alcq wobbly in his lower lip. Three winters past, he'd broken two of his incisors biting into a rock he'd foolishly mistaken for an oyster. The gums around the stumps always looked swollen and red. "I wanted to play."

"It's all right. I'm sorry I yelled. You had me worried. Why'd you swim off on your own like that? I asked you to stay with Shines and Follows."

"They're boring." Cries Often looked both sheepish, and defiant. "I wanted to hunt with a graehl, but Father wouldn't let me."

"I know the feeling," Gloss replied. "But, even so, you can't just go off alone like that. There's too much in The Blue that can hurt you."

Heedless of Gloss' concern, Cries Often snatched the spear from her paws. He jabbed a nearby kelp blade. "Look at me!" he crowed. "I'm the greatest hunter ever! Look!"

Gloss' exasperation evaporated in the face of her brother's carefree enthusiasm. "Yes," she agreed. "You're a fine, fine hunter."

As she watched him play, a cold sadness washed through her. Gloss feared her simple brother's life swam inexorably towards a terrible end, and she could never stop it.

The Lutris suspected, but didn't understand, the damage Cries Often suffered in the womb derived from the two-legged, Still-dwelling *Penuree* — may Deshi-Oad forever curse their clumsy, hairless hides! They used The Blue as a dumping ground for all manner of foul pollutants, poisoning both waters and shoreline with their never-ending filth. Countless animals succumbed every season, most suffering a slow, wasteful death. Gloss had no doubt the Penuree were somehow responsible for the infirmities afflicting her brother.

Lutris elders taught that Deshi-Oad, The Whitest Whale, directed all things towards a greater purpose. Gloss never discerned His purpose in her brother, made lame and helpless through no fault of his own. She detested the way others harassed Cries Often, whose sole offense was being less than they. Even his name functioned as a persistent reminder of his reaction to their constant cruelty.

As the Doyen's offspring, Cries Often held the rank of Saia-Beta —— but only if Fearless cared enough to pay attention, which he seldom did. Most times, The Raft treated him as an *Nihl*-Omega, the least-of-the-least.

Fearless knew of this slight. Yet, he tolerated the situation to maintain stability.

Nepotism bred resentment, and leadership challenges often followed. Bloodshed and death resulted, inevitable as the next tide.

Gloss loved Cries Often with all her heart. She understood her father's keen disappointment in his eldest child, yet she suspected a spark of love still burned, albeit a well-hidden one, somewhere in his calloused heart.

There has to be... she hoped. *There'd better be...*

So, with each new tide, Gloss resolved to guide and protect her brother at all costs, and against *all* foes, both within The Raft and without. "Let's go home." She held out her paw. "Can I have my ynth back, please?"

Cries Often finished slaying the kelp blade and handed the lance to his younger sister with reluctance. "Will you make me one, Gloss? Long and sharp like yours?"

"Later. Let's take the uboo home." With a strong kick, Gloss swam towards the sunlight.

Cries Often fell in behind, his lame foot dangling. "When I get my ynth I'll slay Xaad once and for all. You'll see. Then I'll be the best hunter there's ever been. The best in all The Blue. Won't I, Gloss? Won't I?"

"Yes, Cries Often. The very best." Gloss put her arm around her brother's skinny shoulder. "And maybe we can go hunting together."

Cries Often nibble-kissed Gloss' nose, a show of affection among otter-kind, more so between brother and sister. "I'd like that. Together then.

CHAPTER 5

TERRA INFIRMA

S leek wandered through the perpetual midnight of The Winnow for a full tide-cycle. Its complexity never ceased to amaze him. In spots, the choices were easy: a simple fork in the passage versus a long, snaking shaft. In others, it fractured into a sieve of passages or jagged rents dividing the limestone and granite substratum into a maddening riddle.

Yet this riddle harbored a luminous answer deep in its heart.

Only the occasional drip of water, the clatter of a paw-loosened rock, or Sleek's breath broke the pervasive silence. He welcomed the noise. Too much darkness and quiet could become oppressive, and he didn't want his thoughts straying down even darker paths.

The atmosphere, devoid of most everything but the redolence of chilled earth, offered one tantalizing clue: the faintest hint of... sweetness. The luxuriant scent — not produced by Liminal proper, but that interim border between worlds — awaited somewhere in the darkness ahead.

Just follow your nose, the Beta thought, sniffing. *It'll lead you in the right direction.*

As Sleek traveled deeper, he recalled how, as a freshly weaned youngster following his parents through the subterranean confusion, the darkness and silence frightened him. Too inexperienced to use his nose to divine a path, he'd trailed the beacons of his parents' royal ureola, shining like twin constellations in the void.

Sleek's lip curled with embarrassment at the memory of his youthful fear.

Inch by rocky inch, The Winnow revealed itself in the bracelet's soft blue glow. Now and again, Sleek discovered the leathery, desiccated cadaver or partial skeleton of an animal sprawled on the cold stones — evidence of another failed Liminal attempt.

Sadness bit his heart with each grisly find. But, where they failed, he would succeed.

The passage delved deeper through the bedrock, and with each passing stride Sleek crossed millennia of stone-locked time. The Saia had no reckoning of The Still's vast geologic age. The Envorah had never developed concepts for numbers so large. Yet, The Garden he sought somehow resided at the heart of it all, timeless and perpetual. That much he grasped.

Though the fragile glow of his wristlet struggled against the darkness, its cerulean halo illuminated patterns on the bedrock wall.

What is that? Sleek wondered.

Standing on his hind legs, the young Lontra raised the ureola above his head for a closer inspection. What looked like odd patterns were, upon a second glance, revealed as fossilized bones of long-dead animals dispersed within the rock.

The sections of prehistoric anatomy jutted at all angles from the walls, adding to the ankle-twisting topography. It reminded Sleek of the drift-wood hillocks piled ashore after a storm, branches and barnacled trunks protruding from a hundred different directions.

Now the trunks were bones. The branches — horns. The barnacles: teeth.

Sleek touched the gaping mandible of a tyrannosaur skull, its eye sockets large enough to pass his head through. He marveled at the lethality of its dagger-like fangs, far bigger than any shark tooth. Columns of flanged vertebrae rose from the floor like a breaching whale, while the sweeping ribcage of an enormous, long-necked sauropod adorned the wall.

Was Liminal open to the sky when these creatures lived? Did they look for it as I do now? Sleek wondered. *Did they have names? Were they Envor—*

The *crack* of splitting rock echoed through the tunnel, snapping Sleek's attention back to business. He froze, resisting the urge to flee as a jolt of adrenaline quickened his pulse.

Golden eyes searched the darkness around him, keen ears, nose, and whiskers straining for clues. A faint tremor tickled the soles of his paws, like the purr of a contented kit against his chest. It persisted, a mere whisper at first. By slow degrees, it grew and grew until climaxing into a scream, as if all the rocks were complaining at once about their position in the earth.

The walls wobbled. The floor convulsed and began to buckle. The rolling motion threw the Saia-Beta onto his side. Quickly, he scrambled upright and leapt off the juddering floor onto a nearby rock, sharp claws scratching for purchase.

What's happening? his mind screamed. *Why is The Still moving like this...like The Blue?*

In answer, Sleek's rocky sanctuary lurched forward, as if pushed by invisible paws. "*Kex!*" he swore and leapt again to save himself.

He watched in amazement as the rock he'd just abandoned rolled away, bouncing this way and that. An instant later, a great noise heralded the collapse of a granite wall into a flood of gravel and grit. At the same moment, a curtain of rough-hewn rock burst from the floor in an earth-grinding tumult, impaling the ceiling and bisecting an empty section of passageway. All about, freshly exposed stones clattered and rebounded into new configurations.

Sleek had heard older Lontra whispering that the Winnow sometimes rearranged itself without warning. If caused by the will of The Voracious, or just proximity to the reality-bending nature of Liminal, only Great Ookl knew for sure. Sleek always dismissed the rumor as nothing more than a foolish notion used to frighten the kits at bedtime.

Until now —

Sleek clung to his rock, helpless in the earthen dervish. He watched for the next peril; feet primed to jump. All about him, pebbles skittered and collided like shoals of blinded fish. Boulders fought for new positions in the darkness. The fossilized bones toppled, spun, and protruded like petrified quills reconfigured from ceiling to floor.

Walls buckled and heaved into fresh angles. The noise deafened his sensitive ears.

Then, abruptly as it began, the chaos ceased. The maze settled.

Silence and stillness reigned once again.

Sleek could not comprehend the nature of what he just witnessed. He had no reference points. He sniffed the damp air, detecting the scents of churned earth, pulverized stone...and yes, the growing sweetness of Liminal, unchanged.

Still, the confidence Sleek owned moments earlier now lay as upended as The Winnow. *I can find my way out if I leave now... maybe,* he thought. He looked behind him, then shook his head. *No! Going back is admitting defeat. The Garden Effulgent ...my prize...is forward.*

"I can't give up," he declared to the darkness with a resolute hijna.

The Lontra lingered until his heartbeat settled and cautiously climbed down off the rock. He pressed on, more determined than ever to complete his quest.

The Winnow twisted, branched, turned, forked, and twisted some more. It climbed, leveled out, dipped, and climbed again. Sleek marked his path at intervals by scratching a 'X' upon a boulder with his *acuur* tool — a flake of sharpened, multi-purpose stone, bone, sea glass or sharks' tooth every adult Lontra kept ureola-sheathed for easy access.

Believing he'd made timely progress, Sleek came upon a boulder that already bore a mark — his own cynosure crosshatch. "Ookl's Ink!" the Saia cried. "I'm going in circles!"

He started off again. And then again. And then once more. Each time Sleek picked a new course. And, each time, the Winnow foiled Sleek's innate directional sense. The pain behind his eyes grew with his frustration. Finally, after what seemed like an eternity of false-starts, Sleek discovered a slender vein of luminescent rock, no wider than a kit's whisker, twisting through the substrate.

He fingered the delicate filament. Cool to the touch, its gentle, flittering light beckoned him to follow. And so, he did. Soon, one light-vein became two. At the spot where they converged, a tiny sprig of life grew, like a water droplet frozen in mid-splash. Pulsing with soft light, its delicate bell, stem, and roots oscillated through a gamut of colors. Hints of its finer anatomy — a whorl, pistil, and filaments — glimmered and danced within.

It stood as a beautiful, prismatic rebuke to the crushing cave dark.

Kholo, Sleek thought. His heart skipped a beat. *I'm almost there!*

High Polyps always grew wherever The Garden's enchanted fauna resided. Sleek took this discovery as a good omen. Bravery and luck had guided him through The Winnow to Liminal's very threshold.

His heart raced. Radiant veins pulsed in the cold rock, urging him onward.

Epochs receded with Sleek's lengthening stride. Casual centuries passed under each dexterous footpad. He was, with each step, going back in time. The rock-jutting dinosaur fossils transitioned to squat amphibians and then armor-plated fish. Carboniferous trees, giant ferns, Zygomycota fungus followed. All around, slabs of mineralized amber dense with insectoid inclusions sparkled under the geo-luminescence.

The glowing filaments twined into brilliant arteries that sent the shadows fleeing. The sparkling strands in turn threaded the bedrock like cables of sunlight, leading Sleek towards their timeless, incandescent source. The fragrant aroma of hidden miracles intensified with his pace.

The young Lontra ran and ran, nimble paws heedless of the treacherous terrain. Segmented trilobite, Permian crinoids, and fossilized nautili mosaics heralded Liminal's proximity. Kholo thickets flourished on floor, wall, and ceiling. Bristling fibers and feathery knots tickled Sleek's face and stomach as he raced through the rainbow tangles. Under his paws, scattered everywhere like discarded gemstones, lay blown-glass seashells of all shapes, sizes, and colors — the semi-translucent scraps of meals devoured many seasons earlier. Their heady scent mixed with the kholo, producing a mixed odor somewhere between sweet summer flowers, rare bird-bartered honeycomb, and freshly cleaned fish.

Sleek's mouth watered. Yet, he knew the *true fragrance* of Liminal waited just up ahead.

As the Beta hurried to his goal, memories of lazy outings with the romp at Liminal's threshold flooded his mind. Recollections of languid meals and prayer-worship to Great Ookl with his parents; frolicking with his milk-brothers and playing hide-and-hunt amongst the rainbow kholo thickets; spying on, and giggling at, adults engaged in secret couplings in secluded grottos.

Concealed among the crush of prismatic tufts, and unseen by Sleek as he struggled forward, dwelled the bleached bones of many long-dead Lontra and Lutris warriors — the casualties of a failed bid to reclaim Liminal. Though kholo-shrouded, and beautiful in a macabre sort of way, the broken and brittle skeletons offered a woeful reminder of the high price paid for threats ignored and chances squandered.

But Sleek didn't care about the past. His only goal: push ever forward.

The Saia's senses yearned for the dazzling wonders calling from around the next corner. They tugged his whiskers like a ghostly paw. Sleek couldn't reach them fast enough. The cunning Lontra had gambled his life on a foolhardy wager to find magic — and soon, it would be time to collect his reward.

Sleek skirted a final, rocky junction, leapt upon a boulder threaded with mineralized nematodes, and cried out. He wanted to say something profound, something suitably poetic and worthy of a miracle rediscovered —

— but a profanity worked just as well. "Oh...

CHAPTER 6

A Morsel of Magic

"B *ishq!*"

Sleek almost choked on his gasp.

At first glance, this riddle of light replacing the midnight Winnow appeared alive, independent of the earth... and perhaps even self-aware. Sleek got the impression Liminal *might just be staring back at him.*

With the second glimpse, the vista swirled and collided like shoals of crazed luminescent fish fighting against a jostling, sunlit surface. Swimming in opposition faster and faster still...

The third glance threatened to topple Sleek off his four paws.

The pure radiance of *Liminal Gheelindreeliah* — this oblique realm of *'Life by Liquid by Light'* — felt like electric sand swept on a warm breeze. Even the bedrock was saturated with energy, its substance more like fiery glass than granite. To the young Saia it seemed as if some celestial paw had sown every star in the night sky in this one spot, the resulting yield a million times brighter, and mysterious, than the heavens themselves.

The topography affronted natural law, at least nature as Sleek understood it. Few words in his clan's limited vocabulary could fully describe the experience of gazing into The Garden.

Impossible might serve, as would *unbelievable*.

Try as he might, Sleek could think of no others.

From his boulder-perch, the young Beta watched the radiant atmosphere, which appeared equal parts liquid and light, coalesce into droplets that ignited as gravity took hold. Much of the luminous rainfall filled countless rock pools... but whether the shower flowed up, down or sidewise, Sleek couldn't tell. The ceiling and floor seemed to changed positions, as if at random.

Yet a part of this downpour, via a series of fractal expressions, underwent a spasm of creation manifesting into parodies of krill or zooplankton that dispersed in the aether and formed the underpinning of Liminal's marvelous ecosystem. This entire evolutionary process — eons of sluggish time reduced to energetic milliseconds — was an exquisite madness to behold.

Below the skittish swarms: vast carpets and thickets of riotous Garden-life competed to fill every speck of exposed bedrock. Snail or limpet, anemone or chiton, flatworm, mussel, sea star, or coral, their organizing principles were fashioned by a mingling of congealed light instead of water and mundane earthly elements. Tiny biologic sigils, the flame-as-liquid *cyr,* flickered over the enchanted animals as symbolic expressions of their rudiment personalities.

These creatures — the *pryzoa*, or 'First Life' — were not 'real' animals as Sleek understood the notion, but high-energy approximations conjured by The Garden itself. And these were merely the humblest specimens lingering on Liminal's periphery. Who knew what organisms dwelled in its vast middle reaches? To say nothing of the mysteries existing at its very center. Could even venerable Great Ookl guess what lurked at the foot of the mysterious Golden Barnacle, that inaccessible spot where, according to rumor, light existed as a stone-solid thing, and reality churned, bubbled, erupted, and subdivided into potentiated froth?

Despite the topsy-turvy confusion, with all the questions and contradictions it elicited in Sleek's mind, he couldn't dally. Little time remained to harvest what magic he could. And he knew other, hungrier eyes besides his lurked in this realm.

So, the love-compelled river otter looked down at his paws, mustered his courage with a steadying breath, counted to three... and stepped towards the threshold.

Like a line etched in the rock, the colorful kholo tangles abruptly ended.

Sleek had just crossed the barrier — and pierced the membrane between two vastly different worlds.

As soon as he did all natural demands on his senses of smell and hearing escalated to an almost unbearable degree. The aroma of Liminal-proper went beyond just stimulating his nose. It tickled all his instincts reveling in easily dispatched, and overly abundant, prey. A long-forgotten memory struck Sleek then: as a kit joining the romp in a banquet of countless beach-stranded grunion — except the metabolic urgency he now felt was amplified a thousand-fold.

Yet it was the sound of the Garden, or perhaps the *vibration* of it, that overwhelmed the most. Sleek not only heard the noise, but felt it: against his footpads, across his whiskers, over his tail, through his eyelashes. Echoes of busy Holt life, hunting prey, circling gulls — of all subtle things comprising his auditory world — were contained in those vibrations. But so much more: waves hissing over sand; rain pelting stone; currents sighing through kelp groves; gurgling puddles; seafoam fizzing on gentle swells. All these sounds fed and resonated off each other.

Sleek seemed to be perceiving the mighty hijna of Gheelindreeliah itself.

"Ookl's Ink!" The Beta staggered as if he'd imbibed too much fermented *oixrd* beverage.

He squeezed back tears. Delicate senses, conditioned for a slower life in the sea and nocturnal hunting, felt overcome by the totality of the experience. The small headache burrowing behind his eyes like a grub flared with fresh pain.

His brain, struggling to process the bombardment of information, failed.

Sleek covered his ears, shut his nose, and buried his head in the crook of a fore limb —

His father's cautionary words, spoken to a kit dealing with this topsy-turvy realm for the first time, returned: *"Never look directly into Liminal, son. There's too much for the eye to behold in this place, and it's racing in too many different directions at once. But your mind sees it all. And hears it all. And smells it. That's why you get lightheaded. So, don't drink it in all at once. Take little peeks, like sips of water. Look down at your paws if you feel dizzy."*

"I will, father," the inexperienced kit had replied. *"Little sips."*

Sleek turned back to the light and peered into The Garden Effulgent through squinted, tearing eyes. "Little sips of water..."

He forced himself to attune to the crush of Liminal's light, sound, and aroma.

"...little sips of water..."

Focusing on his paws, he stepped cautiously — yet deliberately — into The Garden.

"...little sips of water..."

And he was soon striding once again with confidence.

Ookl, no! Sleek thought. *The ruin!*

The Beta couldn't deny what his eyes confirmed. The horror was too great —

Entire swatches of Liminal had fallen prey to the unforgiving appetite of *Vile Chaac'Xib,* The Voracious. Relentless pincers had sheared the lucent, life-teeming groves down to bare stone, leaving behind a tattered carcass of its former glory.

Even the very rock underfoot was gouged and chipped. Sleek's heart sank at the devastation. In his mind, he imagined The Garden crying out: "*Save me!*"

Cold fury raged within the river otter.

At that moment he pledged to make the monster pay. One way, or another.

The Saia-Beta scurried deeper into the marred paradise. With great relief, he discovered many of The Garden's wounds were already healing. A vanguard of tentative sprigs and runners crept back into the injuries, scabbing them with light. The surplus of life, forever renewed, thwarted The Cruel Dweller from consuming it all.

Sleek sneered. *It seems even a bottomless pit can be filled.*

Liminal's radiance doubled, then doubled again. Soon it would be far too bright for his eyes to tolerate. Yet, among the confusion of lights, Sleek found a clutch of jeweled topsnails grazing on a patch of ember-algae fixed between a colorful coral ridge and a colony of silver-veined tube worms. The ruby-shelled creatures glowed with an inner fire.

The young Lontra couldn't believe his luck. He'd half-expected to search The Garden for a full tide-cycle before finding the right pryzoa to fill both his romantic need and his salivating mouth. But instead, he found a veritable treasure trove of otter-sized morsels waiting for him.

I'll eat just one, he thought. *Any more could be risky. But, which one?*

Sleek selected his prize — a fiery whelk. With dexterous fingers, he pried the shell free and devoured the plump snail inside. He did not treat this as *Celimner*, the sacred meal-sacrament his romp demanded. There would be no stacking of empty, glass-like pryzoa shells in pious ghaydn mounds. Nor any of the *nibble-prayer-nibble-worship-nibble-plea* reverences that often took an entire tide to complete.

Just bite, chew, swallow, and repeat as fast as one could —

Each mouthful renewed Sleek's mental clarity. It felt like emerging from a tide of squid ink. The sensation proved overwhelming. Electric euphoria tickled his spine, stiffening his whiskers. Senses surged into overdrive.

Sleek saw his breath curl from his nostrils like wisps of rainbow light, heard the deafening, nonsensical chattering of the jeweled topsnails in his mind. Liminal's life-giving heartbeat — *thud-THUD-thud-THUD* — pulsed through the very stones, pumping liquid-light deep into the earth and the spaces beyond.

From snout to tail, every hair on his body bristled. The delicate tissues of his sinuses quivered. Even the liquid within his eyes vibrated.

And the flavor! Far sweeter than he remembered. Sleek felt he would burst with pleasure.

The sensory overload to his pryzoa-charged brain blinded the river otter to the presence that now turned its dark focus upon him. A nightmare, bloated out of all proportion to any creature found in The Blue, claimed these enchanted grottos as its own.

Two crystalline stalks — wider and taller than two full grown Lontra — emerged from beneath an adamantine-dense carapace leached to transparency by The Garden's perpetual light. Each armored stalk ended in a blister holding a single eye, large as Sleek's body and darker than the blackness shrouding The Winnow. The absence of light lurking behind those ocular cysts bespoke of boundless greed and appetite.

Rage smoldered in the gluttonous mind of the beast as it watched Sleek wolf down the pryzoa. By right of its formidability, it claimed *all life* within Liminal as its food.

Great, black-tipped pincers rubbed together in anticipation. Scimitar-like maxillae limbs fringing the gruesome mouth twitched with the need to kill, dissect, and devour the intruder.

The coiling entrails of That Which Devours burned red-hot, illuminating the surrounding viscera with a noxious sanguine backlight. With the sound of cracking rock, it unfolded six thick limbs as it lifted itself from its resting place. Flakes of pryzoic detritus fell away from its body as it moved towards the thief in its lair.

Oblivious to the danger, Sleek remained focused on his quest — to find the perfect pryzoa his romantic plans demanded. Exquisite in their crystalline glamour, no two were identical. This made the selection process even more difficult.

Drawn to a field of blown-glass rainbow snails, the lovesick Beta studied their flickering cyr-haloes. *Gloss will love these*, he thought. *No one has ever given First Life as a courtship token before. But which do I choose?*

Sleek touched a glassy shell, delighting in the mild static tingling his fingertips. He plucked two jeweled topsnails free *(...one for Gloss, and one more for me...)* and secured them within inner cheek pouches. The sweetness they promised washed over his tongue.

Feeling greedy, Sleek lingered to collect a third pryzoa — just as his newly heightened senses tingled: *Imminent danger!*

Sleek instinctually leapt aside a split-second before lethal pincers sliced the air a mere kit's-whisker from his nose. *Snip!*

The scissoring blades had nearly cut the otter in half. A gush of adrenaline propelled him like a shot through the glowing orchards. *Vile Chaac'Xib!* Sleek's mind screamed.

The Saia darted in frenzied flight through the shoals of First Life, heedless of direction. The enraged Voracious scuttled towards the otters retreating heels like a multi-legged avalanche.

Ookl's Ink! Why was I so careless? Sleek thought. *I shouldn't have risked a third pryzoa!*

In a moment of wild despair, Sleek realized he didn't know which way to run.

The exit vanished in a kaleidoscope of lights. Sleek, now faced with predation, realized this verdant place of uplifting magic now showed a more sinister nature — one of chaos and madness. A memory of Gloss' beautiful face flashed across his mind's eye. It both calmed and spurred him onward. *No! I will get away! I must see her again!*

Sleek wrung a burst of speed from protesting muscles, leaping from floor to wall to ceiling and back to the floor, but Liminal's bizarre, opposing gravities played havoc with his inborn directional sense and equilibrium. What should have been an easy leap from one boulder to another instead sent him tumbling rump over snout.

He landed hard on his side, sharp pain exploding in his right hind leg.

"Yurch!" Sleek scrambled upright.

He glanced at his leg — and found a deep cut leaking blood into his fur. With no time to catch his breath, let alone tend a wound, Sleek cut an irregular course hoping to confuse his pursuer. His magic-stoked metabolism granted him extra speed. And he would need all of it...

On frantic paws, Sleek splashed radiant puddles, disturbing nearby pryzoa and causing their cyr-haloes to flicker out or flare in irritation. Swarms of phosphorescent zooplankton, evolved seconds earlier from a fiery downpour, scattered at his approach.

The chaotic terrain offered no hindrance to The Cruel Dweller. It toppled or pulverized the glassy boulders blocking its path. The First Life tangling Sleek's feet it simply crushed. Any pryzoa clouding the otter's vision it violently swept aside.

Lethal pincers clove neon corals, lambent tubeworms, and crystalline stalagmites with equal ease. All things succumbed to their wrath. The din of the crab's pursuit rivaled the stone-churning tumult that rocked The Winnow earlier.

Serrated appendages reached for the fleeing otter...

CHAPTER 7

VILE CHAAC'XIB

There! Over there!

A prismatic thicket of kholo marked the exit. With a sudden backward leap, Sleek altered course. The move sent a stab of pain through his wounded leg. Hissing in discomfort, he shored up his courage and darted between the stomping pylon-like legs of The Voracious.

The swift maneuver caught the great beast off guard. Not as agile as its Lontra prey, the ponderous armored body careened into a cluster of phosphorescent megaliths with a thunderous crunch. The cavern shook with the collision. Hundreds of minuscule pryzoic invertebrates, no two identical, scattered into the maddening grottos as the glassy pillars toppled, casting angry sparks as they fell and shattered into electric shards against the bedrock.

Capitalizing on this clumsiness, Sleek escaped through the jungle of tangling kholo in the precious few seconds it took Vile Chaac'Xib to re-orient itself. The void-black eyes of the monstrous crab spied the tip of the otter's tail just as it vanished into the rainbow thicket.

Within its transparent shell, The Cruel Dweller's already crimson-hot innards flared brighter than a blast furnace. Enraged, it charged after the river otter, armored limbs clattering like a landslide.

Sleek wove through the dense kholo patches and past the bones of his long-dead kin hidden there. A tiny hope blossomed in his chest that he just might get away. His strides lengthened with his confidence. He chanced a backward glance. Fresh fear constricted his throat as The Voracious scythed through the polychrome fields, implacable and unforgiving.

The number of High Polyps thinned the further Sleek retreated from The Garden, until at last, he managed to clear the kholo. Footpads touched bare rock once more. Optical echoes of the Liminal's majesty danced behind his eyes, slow to fade. He tried but could not blink them away.

The sound of fracturing stone echoed behind him as The Cruel Dweller scrambled forth. No longer hindered by kholo, Sleek found his footing and pulled away.

Sleek located the glowing arteries that first guided him towards the Garden Effulgent and followed the sparkling cables until they unraveled into their constituent filaments and branches. Their light faded until, at last, it was extinguished.

Crushing darkness descended as Sleek reentered The Winnow proper. Frigid air wafted against his cheeks once more. Only the cool blue glow of his ureola remained to guide him now.

The Beta intended to retrace his earlier route, but The Winnow's confusion of passages, walls, openings, and junctions stymied him. Fear The Voracious was still out there hunting him intensified.

Sleek now teetered on the verge of *The Scare*, an instinctual — though restrained — 'call to flight' still present in the Envoric soul. Even the added clarity of the ingested pryzoa couldn't mute it. He had to get away while he could still think.

Before blind fear made all his choices for him —

If The Scare took hold, as it did with his poor Holt-brother Diver, he might never regain sapience. His precious Kleaa would be at its lowest ebb, his Envoric condition all but gone.

He would be no better than Monoah. An inchoate beast.

Beautiful Gloss would never want him then! The thought of her tender nibble-kisses stemmed his panic.

Relax. Breathe, Sleek! You're letting your imagination get the better of you, he admonished himself.

Sleek forced his lungs to comply, willed his heartbeat to slow. His whiskers drooped.

Finally, The Scare, like the tide, receded. Calm returned.

Don't think about what's behind you. Let it stay in the dark where it belongs. Find your way out!

Sleek pressed onward, determined to escape the labyrinth. As he rounded a rocky corner and mounted a boulder, something caught his eye — and he froze.

The armored, six-legged nightmare filled the passage, blocking his way.

"Yurch," the Lontra hissed. In his blind circling, he'd blundered up behind his pursuer!

The Cruel Dweller's glowing entrails threw horrid crimson light across the cold cave walls. Ten tails away, Sleek could still feel the wretched heat of its body against his face. He wanted to hide, but his legs refused to move.

Though exposed, he sensed he'd be safe so long as he remained still. And didn't breathe. Or blink...

The crab crouched with its back to Sleek. Pitiless eyes considered several openings through which a Lontra might squeeze. Great pincers, like hungry jaws, opened and rasped closed in frustration.

Sleek watched, terrified yet curious. *What will it do?* he thought. *Which path will it take? Does it even have enough brains to understand it has a choice?*

Sleek sniffed — then wished he hadn't. The monster's natural odor should speak of death and insatiable hunger. And yet, Death By Rending reeked of rampant life.

And life meant food! *But how is that possible?* the otter wondered.

The answer, in all its horrible irony, rattled Sleek. He realized The Voracious camouflaged itself *with what grew within* Liminal, like a crude pryzoic pelt. The fertile aroma promised a full belly — yet threatened to stall him just long enough for death to snap shut.

Not just death, but slow digestion as well.

Sleek eased off the boulder he had climbed, trying to be as stealthy as possible —

Clink-clank.

— a dislodged pebble bounced off a larger stone and hit the tunnel floor. In the silence of the labyrinth, such a tiny sound jarred as much as a crashing wave.

Bishq. Sleek winced. *Ookl's Ink. How many mistakes am I going to make today?*

The eyes of The Cruel Dweller swiveled around and fastened on Sleek. Hunter and prey recognized one another. As the young Lontra gazed into those soulless orbs, his Aanandi-shade — that aspect of his evolved psyche capable of leaping beyond logic and into the realm of abstractions —

convulsed in horror. It recognized a bottomless appetite, and an equal desire to inflict pain, lurking behind those eyes.

The Voracious' innards flared with light, washing the granite walls in blood-glow and heat. The Scare made a crashing return through Sleek's bones, threatening to scatter his wits once more. In desperation, the Lontra sank his teeth into his own wrist. The sudden pain snapped The Scare's hold, wrenching him back from the brink.

I need a distraction, he thought. Casting about, he glanced at his ureola. *Of course. Yes!*

Slipping it free, he tossed the woven ornament behind him. The Cruel Dweller's focus whipped to the glowing circlet as it sailed across the cavern and landed amidst a heap of knobby boulders. The monster swiveled its tectonic mass to follow.

Using the sudden shadows as cover, the otter dove into a crevice to hide. Death By Rending trundled over Sleek's hiding spot, tree trunk legs knocking aside adjacent stones. Its mighty pincers pulverized the rock into rubble as it searched for the elusive Lontra thief it associated with the blue ureola.

Sleek bolted like a shot down the corridor. The bloody illumination of The Voracious faded, but not before Sleek found an 'X' he'd earlier scratched onto a boulder.

At least, for now, he could be certain of the right direction.

Two more steps and all light vanished. Sleek employed his pryzoic-heightened faculties to reach into the darkness and navigate the terrain using sensitive whiskers, paws, and nose.

Lontra were visual hunters by nature. Regardless of how his other senses might have compensated, without the use of his eyes, Sleek felt hobbled. His speed reduced to a crawl. As he crept across the jagged, slippery rocks, an unpleasant sensation began impinging on the Lontra's stressed awareness — *pain* — and it centered in his mouth. His gums were irritated by the glassy mollusks stowed in his cheek pouches.

Sleek spat the topsnails into his paws. The relief brought a revelation — the pryzoa shone, bright as twin stars! The magnitude of Liminal's aggregate magic overwhelmed their individual lights, but here in the darkness they cast thrice the light of his lost ureola.

I'll use a pryzoa like a kholo-torch.

Returning the smaller pryzoa to his cheek pouch, Sleek pushed deeper into the maze. He held aloft the larger glowing mollusk in one forepaw for light. Pain stung his wounded rear leg with every step. After limping past two more 'X's scratched into marker stones, Sleek felt renewed confidence in his directional instincts, which raised his spirits.

Somewhere behind him, The Cruel Dweller's search continued unabated, like the din of a distant avalanche. The Lontra's keen ears distinguished each sound the creature made — the grinding mouthparts, the hiss and bubble of fetid breath, the *snip-snap* of terrible pincers that displaced the air like thunderclaps, the crack of moving joints like shattering bedrock. In The Blue's acoustical environment, Sleek would have no trouble pinpointing the location of the beast. Yet here, deep within The Winnow, the confusion of echoes made it impossible.

Sleek felt confident he'd given Death By Rending the slip. *Too slow, you kexxing —*

No sooner had the thought formed in his mind than another earthquake shuddered through the cavern.

— Ookl's Ink! Not now!

The Lontra froze. For an instant, The Scare once again threatened to paralyze his mind. He banished it with a series of slow, calming breaths, and regained control of his limbs.

Holding fast to his precious pryzoa, Sleek scrambled atop a boulder, hoping to ride out the upheaval while the maze settled into its new configuration. The floor began swirling and swelling, like water churned by a storm. Rocks tumbled and collided, ricocheting into new formations.

Sleek's perch bobbed within the chaos. Stones and petrified bones ground and churned to meal. Suddenly, a wall sank into the floor, opening a yawning chasm like a hungry mouth. The fearsome glow of Vile Chaac'Xib's fiery innards washed over Sleek again — the monster lurked in the very next chamber!

Sleek squeaked in terror, and The Scare rushed back with full force.

The monstrous crab spotted the fiery pryzoa in the otter's paw, its merciless eyes covetous. The beast advanced, pincers snapping. Ropes of black saliva dangled from its horrid mouth, scoring the cold floor like acid.

But The Winnow had its own agenda...

The beast could not find purchase amidst the swirling quagmire. Its legs slipped and wobbled on the restless rocks. Still, it struggled forward until its primitive brain realized its prey could not escape.

So, it hunkered down to wait.

As the boulder Sleek rode hurtled towards The Cruel Dweller, the creature's body heat made the river otter's golden eyes water. The Scare howled in his brain like wind whistling through fissured bedrock, commanding Sleek to leap off the boulder and run, heedless, in the opposite direction.

Get away! Flee! NOW!

The Beta's muscles tensed, prepared to obey the primal shriek of survival instinct —

Stop!

A flicker of self-control broke through the panic.

Relax...Breathe.

Jumping meant death. But wouldn't remaining on the boulder prove just as perilous?

Back or forward, either way spelled painful doom.

The pincer of The Voracious lashed out in a sweeping arc, clipping the boulder and missing Sleek's head by a hairsbreadth, showering his ears with pebbles. Sleek squealed and darted to the opposite side of his rocky mount, almost losing his grip on the lambent pryzoa. All three unencumbered paws clung for dear life, sharp nails digging into the stone.

A second pincer reared back for another attack —

In a roar of sound, a section of earth beneath The Cruel Dweller's legs gave way. The monster toppled sideways. With a mighty crash it pitched headlong into the hollow. A split second later, the crevice cinched closed, rendering half of the crab's body useless. One pincer and three thrashing legs thundered against the bedrock as it tried to free its entombed bulk.

Sleek found the sight both horrifying and amusing. Laughter bubbled up from his chest, but fear stalled it in his throat.

"Serves you right, monster!" he muttered. "I hope you never get ou—"

Without warning, Sleek's precarious perch heaved upwards, tossed him flailing through the air to land with a *thud* atop Vile Chaac'Xib's slanted back. Slicked with pryzoic algae, the shell offered no traction. The otter's feet shot out from under him, sending the Lontra slipping across the glassy armor of the great beast. His free paws scratched and clawed to arrest the slide, his one forepaw still clutching the pryzoa. A moment before toppling over the side and onto the killing floor, the Saia hooked a cluster of glittering barnacles festooning the monster's shell.

As he dangled a whisker-width from death, chest heaving in exertion, an intriguing thought struck the young otter: *Is Liminal turning The Voracious into a pryzoa?*

Sleek hauled himself onto the shell before he found the answer.

Onyx eyes rotated in time to witness the Lontra re-secure the stolen pryzoa into his cheek pouch. The beast wildly swung its free pincer. But its armored anatomy hindered it from reaching its intended target. Legs and claws flailed. Coiled innards flared in impotent rage. The burst of unnatural body heat singed the Lontra's already tender footpads.

"Ouch!" Sleek cried, prancing a manic rhythm. "Hot, hot!"

Abruptly, all sound and motion in the passage ceased, save for the rocks pulverized by The Voracious in its attempts to wrench free. Seizing the opportunity, Sleek sprinted across the monster crab's shell and leapt clear. The tip of his tail delivered a *snap* — a much-enjoyed parting insult — to one of the creature's eye-orbs. The oculus recoiled in pain and a retaliatory pincer lashed out, snapping shut just shy of the mark.

Sleek hit the ground running, heedless of his direction, so long as it took him *away* from the armored monstrosity. The fearsome sound of The Cruel Dweller's frustrated movement sped the Lontra's steps.

By the time Sleek's paws detected the distant vibrations of shattering stone, heralding Vile Chaac'Xib's imminent escape, he was well on his way towards the exit and the waiting Blue. Luck had evened the odds. The weak defeated the strong...

This time.

CHAPTER 8

SOMEWHERE ALONG HIGHWAY ONE

Interstate I-80 finally met the Pacific Coast Highway. Cool, salt-scented air offered a welcome relief from the incessant inland heat. Six or seven hours of Hell left to endure, and Ayana's torment would finally be over... at least the initial 'getting there' phase.

The real ordeal would begin on hour eight.

Sporadic traffic along the coast kept the old station wagon moving at a brisk speed. Thick stands of pine trees hugged the right side of the road. To the left, the immeasurable vastness of the Pacific flickered with billions of sun-kissed waves. Seagulls and pelicans floated lazily on warm thermals. Here and there, Ayana spied people on surfboards — appearing as mere specks in the water — some waiting to catch a massive wave; others fearlessly riding frothing crests towards the rocky shoreline.

It's all fun and games until someone breaks their neck. Ayana grinned. *Or a shark eats 'em, like in that movie. No thank you.*

An hour beyond the Highway One junction, a squad of burly, bearded, beer-bellied bikers — adorned in leather vests with the stylized emblem of a snarling hound — overtook Fritz. They held back for a moment, engines belching raw horsepower; then, one by one, veered into the opposite lane and rumbled past.

Ayana stared, transfixed at the roaring two-wheeled chrome parade. Noise from the choppers rattled windows and eardrums. They were, without a doubt, the loudest things she'd ever heard; both terrifying and fascinating.

It would be awesome to ride one, she thought. *Ride and ride and never look back.*

Frowning, Hayley raised the windows to prevent the pungent exhaust fumes from choking them. She avoided looking directly at any of the bearded faces as they rolled by. Eye contact could invite a hundred different troubles.

One biker kept pace with the car for a short distance, his mirrored sunglasses fixed on Hayley's profile. Her grip on the steering wheel tightened.

Look forward. Just pretend he's not there, Hayley thought, mantra-like. *He's not there. Not there. Not. There...*

Finally, with a clattering roar, the chopper put on a burst of speed and flew ahead to join the rest of the squad. Hayley relaxed and let out a slow exhale. As the bikers dwindled down the road her heart slowed its panicky thumping.

"Was that an outlaw biker gang, Mom?"

"Don't know," Hayley answered. "About the 'outlaw' part, I mean. They could've just been a club."

"Yeah, a club called 'The Hellhounds,'" Ayana retorted. "You think they'll come back?"

"No. You don't need to worry about them."

"I wasn't worried," Ayana lied. "Geesh." She laid her head back against the seat and closed her eyes. *She thinks I'm a scared little girl. I'm almost fourteen!*

Another hour of driving brought much-needed salvation: Berkley's Diner & Mini Mart. Equal parts grocery, gas station, and greasy spoon, the diner sat tucked in a large, semi-paved clearing surrounded by dense evergreen trees. A slew of mud-splattered big-rig trucks sat in a gravel lot off to the side, smaller cars in the oil-stained parking spaces out front.

Berkley's offered relief, and not a moment too soon: Fritz's gas tank flirted with empty, the temperature gauge, for the last hundred miles, had inched dangerously close to the red. But, more importantly: Hayley had emptied her coffee thermos and had to pee — badly.

Hayley steered off the road and slowed her speed. Fritz sped past several dead opossums lining the driveway like furry, tire-squashed tomatoes, and guided the station wagon towards the diner. Its red, white, and blue color scheme of faded and chipped paint matched the row of eight vintage gas pumps that looked like props from the set of a 1950s war movie: pretend patriotism on full display.

Ayana leapt from the back seat almost before the tires had stopped turning. She stretched her stiff legs and aching spine. Odors of gasoline and pine groves rode an ocean breeze, while the stomach-taunting smells of frying potatoes and grilling meat filled her nostrils.

Yet, it was her water balloon-sized bladder threatening to burst that commanded all the attention. Ayana hadn't used a bathroom all day. The very notion felt like child abuse.

"I really, really, *really* have to find a bathroom."

Hayley cranked the emergency brake and killed the engine. It rattled and Fritz fell silent. She fished around the inside of her brown-fringed suede boho bag, retrieved her wallet, and plucked out a ten-dollar bill. She handed it to Ayana through the open window. "Eight on pump six. Use what's left to buy two sodas. Diet."

"*After* I pee." Ayana snatched the money and quick-stepped towards the mini-mart.

Hayley reached under the steering wheel and popped the hood-release lever. "Remember: pump six," she called.

"I heard you the first time."

Hayley opened the door and slid from behind the wheel. She stretched, felt the insistent pressure in her bladder. A post-caffeine lethargy wobbled her knees. An hour-long nap would set her right; two, even better. But they couldn't afford the delay. Sleeping in a motel with Ayana would be both expensive and frustrating. Better to cinch up her big-girl pants and push through.

Hayley felt under the warm hood for the latch, pressed, and propped it open. A gust of heat, mingled with the telltale odors of burning motor oil and coolant, wafted upward. She surveyed Fritz's tired mechanical guts, examining all the grimy hoses, wires, and connections she knew could cause problems. She had become something of an amateur mechanic during the last thirteen months. *I'll need to check the oil and top off the radiator*, she thought.

Yes, this stop was all about the filling, and removing, of fluids.

Twenty minutes later, with the gas tank full, the oil and coolant levels topped off, and both bladders blissfully emptied, mother and daughter climbed into their faithful orange wagon and hit the road. Ayana unpacked the cooler. Lunch consisted of chicken salad sandwiches and a slightly green banana — and for dessert, three soft-batch chocolate-chip cookies. Yummy.

Ayana popped open her soda and counted the opossum carcasses scattered along Berkley's driveway. "Thirteen." She took a swig of cola. Cold bubbles danced in her mouth and burned her throat. She burped. "Unlucky."

"Let's make some time, kiddo." Hayley felt a gust of rejuvenation when she hit the gas, feeling Fritz respond the same way.

The station wagon merged back onto Highway One. Hayley turned on the radio and changed the station from the soft rock she'd been enjoying. She dialed through buzzing static, until she found a news channel.

About time, Ayana thought. *I hate that Seventies stuff.*

A male voice, scratchy as if tempered by scotch and cigarettes floated out of the single speaker: "*...this warm, wet summer storm should make landfall by ten PM tonight. Expect one to two inches of rain and forty mile-an-hour wind gusts. But it should blow itself out by six AM as it moves further inland. We'll keep you updated on all coastal weather. And now, Huell Horstmann with sports...*"

"We should reach Grandma and Grandpa's house before then," Hayley commented. "It'll be close. Keep your fingers crossed there's no traffic jams." She accelerated until the speedometer hit sixty-five. "I'm glad we left when we did. Aren't you?"

"Whatever," Ayana said and hungrily finished the last of her sandwich. Meal devoured, she fished out last years prized birthday present: a silver and black Walkman cassette player.

Ayana unzipped a faux-leather satchel holding her mix-tape collection and slipped in a selection of brooding New Wave songs championing her dour mood. Tunes of loss and misunderstanding set to swirling synthesizer soundscapes shared their wisdom. Tracks of unfulfilled dreams and paranoia tied to staccato drumbeats hinted at bitter truths. Ballads of anguish and unrequited love filled her soul in easily digestible three-minute anthems.

Ayana hummed along as the outside world sped past the dusty window. But she didn't notice it, nor the passing cars. Or her mother. Instead, Ayana's imagination focused on the music videos highlighting her favorite bands, each lip-synching to the camera with painted faces and mascara-smeared eyes. Her mind swirled with images of wild costumes and outlandish haircuts.

Resigned to her fate of hours-long boredom in the sweltering car, all Ayana could do was bear it with a catchy tune and a smile.

Actually... she thought *...forget the smile.*

In the dream, Ayana stands beside the old station wagon.

She watches as Dad inserts the gas nozzle into the tank. The air smells of gasoline and drying flowers. Dad turns to her and smiles. It's a smile Ayana recognizes from the mirror, or photos of herself.

So much of her face belongs to Mom; the eyes, the cheeks, the nose and chin. But the smile is something Dad alone gave her.

Tiny laugh lines appear at the corners of Dad's blue eyes. He lifts a faded green and yellow baseball cap off his head and rakes a hand through sandy-blond hair.

"We'll be home soon, Pipsqueak," *he says. And she believes him...*

Just then, the air feels thick and heavy with foreboding. Something is coming for Dad, something tiny and terrible. Ayana opens her mouth to warn him, but her tongue has turned into a chunk of wood, her lips cement.

A droning noise grates in her ears, startling her and causing her to stare up at the sky.

Don't look into the sky. Don't look into the sky. Don't look into... Don't look... Don't...

Too late. She looks.

There, like a tiny helicopter coming in for a crash landing, a lone honeybee descends out of the sun, only to land on the back of Dad's neck, just above the collar of his red-gray flannel.

Dad winces at the sting. He swats the honeybee with a wild palm.

Ayana screams, but all that comes out is a sound like sheep bleating.

Dad clutches at his throat, fingers raking the skin. His beautiful, blue eyes bulge. His knees buckle and, in exquisite, painfully slow motion, he crumples to the pavement.

Ayana continues to scream. "Baaa! Baaaa! Baaaaa!"

She wants to help. She wants to save Dad. But her limbs are frozen.

Dad's eyes ask one final question his constricted throat can no longer vocalize.

"Am...am I...dead?"

Ayana can't even nod. "Yes, Daddy. You are," *she would say if only her mouth worked.*

"I'm sorry for dying today, Pipsqueak. I'm so, so..."

Then those eyes, blue enough to rival the summer sky, slowly dim to a dull wintry gray. And then his skin. And then his hair. And then he falls.

Ayana can't move. She can't look away. All she can do is keep screaming.

"Baaa! Baaaa! Baaaaa — !"

— Ayana awoke with a gasp, the jerk of her head tugging the headphones from her ears. In the adjacent lane, a mud-splattered truck kept pace with their station wagon. The tread of its oversized tires made an odd noise against the road... like the bleating of distant sheep.

"You okay back there?" Her mother's voice sounded more preoccupied than worried.

"Fine," Ayana mumbled. She put away the Walkman, AA-batteries now dead. Her left-hand *tap-tapped* the glue drops without noticing. Ayana decided not to tell her mother she'd had *that* dream again. She couldn't deal with the inevitable, "Oh-my-god-my-daughter-is-still-having-night-mares-about-her-father's-death" meltdown.

Not now. Not today. She was too hot. And too bored.

And far, *far* too angry...

CHAPTER 9

TANGLESAFE

"Hrmmm...that looks like the perfect place to land," Pijper said to the breeze, as if in casual conversation with it. "Or does it?" The great pelican wrestled with the verdict for another indecisive moment. "Has the time come to descend? Or maybe I should wait a tad longer, hrmmm? Yes, yes, I think the time has arrived."

The bird shifted russet-hued, four-tail long wings. The feathers caught just enough wind to bring Pijper down to a soft landing on a spot of calm water.

Most seabirds found one patch of water much like another. However, things were seldom so simple for Pijper. When it came to settle upon The Blue, the envoric pelican applied his own obsessive logic to the 'art' of the marine landing. He would hover for hours upon a thermal, circling the same spot, watching, and waiting, until conditions were perfect.

There couldn't be too many waves, or too few. They couldn't be too big, or too small. Even the surface sparkle had to be 'just so' to appease his neurotic preferences.

Other Envorah birds mocked his behavior. "Land already, crazy-beak!" they would hijna-shout. "Just do it," or, "It's easy. Stop being so foolish."

Their admonishments never worked. The dignified brown pelican was too much in thrall to his mental foibles.

Pijper did not emerge from the egg enlightened. He lived the first year of his life as a benighted *Lhuuni*, or the "Skittish Ones" — the collective Envoric name for all Monoic birds. Like the rest of his feathery kin, pure instinct governed his life. He spent his uninspired days riding the winds in the search for food, eating, and defecating.

A simple existence for an even simpler mind.

Until the day the adolescent bird chanced upon a scrap of pulpy matter floating on the currents. He fought off four other pelicans to claim the morsel and devoured the silvery flotsam in one gulp. Instant change followed. His mind electrified, as if waking from a long slumber. Thoughts purified and tickled the edges of abstraction. His pale, ice-blue eyes gained an inquisitive bronze patina as a new, hitherto unknown reality revealed itself.

Once he'd achieved enlightenment and decided on a proper name, Pijper — or, *Noble Seeking Wing* as the Ulurii defined it — found he could no longer relate to his fellow pelicans. They had no names, were incapable of speech, and lacked all imagination or understanding. So Pijper left the flock that hatched him and set out to find others like himself who could speak.

Once discovered, he would cohabitate with these new friends and learn their language; and they would come to appreciate his poetry and clever ponderings.

At first, he sought only birds for companionship. But when he discovered other Envoric species, many of them (...*most* of them...) owned no wings at all.

Just like his dear friends, the Lutris, whom he'd come to call upon today.

Pijper's landing — graceful even for a pelican — made no ripple. The dignified bird's wings collapsed into the 'rest' position upon his feathered back. On the surface nearby, he spied the weft of drifting leaves and fronds marking a thick nooree forest. He paddled his black, webbed feet towards it.

The pelican enjoyed relaxing among the canopies of verdant seaweed, buoyed by their gas-filled pneumatocyst bladders floating among the nooree like aquatic acorns. This kelpy domain, by far the thickest and most protected known to Pijper — and he knew them all — encompassed the Lutris home known as *Tanglesafe.*

Aptly named, Tanglesafe's prodigious density of caramel and emerald seaweed deterred most predators larger than a rockfish. Any enemy foolish enough to venture inside the Lutris domain either drowned from quick entanglement or were dispatched by a volley of whalebone and calcified baleen spears from many sea otter hunters. Thus, all sea birds, including Pijper, could paddle worry-free while visiting Tanglesafe.

With no fear of subsurface attack, Pijper put his erudite mind at ease. Gentle waves, a warm afternoon sun, and the tickle of nooree upon his ureola-adorned ankle set his musings free.

"Days like today were made for birds, both water and sky. We are the masters of current and thermal. Hrmmm, perhaps I should compose a poem?" Pijper cleared his throat and opened his great beak. "My ode to The Blue: Upon the waters I soar, upon the sky I swim; tides sway the weak and the strong, while the current moves everything along; to dive is to challenge the deep, yet the circling thermal makes me keep..."

"Hey! Hey!" an excited hijna cried from the kelp dividing Tanglesafe from the open sea.

The exclamation broke the pelican's concentration. "Oh, what is this?" Pijper grumbled. "It's not every day I feel inspired for poetry. Bother, bother!"

"Look, Pijper, look! We're back from the uboorl with food!" shouted Cries Often. He stood to his full height, waving to the pelican from atop the driftwood ghossn propelled by the tired legs and tails of Gloss, Follows, and Shines.

Pijper waved back with a russet wing. "Splendid to see you, my Lutris friends."

The three Lutris steered the spindly carryall to Tanglesafe's knotted periphery and stopped. They were grateful to catch a breather before the final push inside.

"Dearest Gloss, dearest Follows, dearest Shines," Pijper gushed. "You all look so radiant today, and your tails are extra, extra lovely."

"Oh, thank you, Pijper. You're always so kind," Shines replied. She exposed more of her bauble-decorated tail, attempting to garner another compliment. None came.

Cries Often's whiskers drooped. "What about me? Aren't you glad to see me, too?"

"Oh, of course, Cries Often, my dear boy. Who could forget you?" Pijper added apologetically. He didn't want to see the simple Lutris weep over an innocent slight.

Cries Often's vibrant smile returned, exposing his broken teeth. "I'm a great hunter. Right, Gloss? Right?"

"So, you *finally* decided to land?" Gloss chided the pelican. "I thought you'd spend all day and night waiting for that 'perfect' patch of water."

Pijper turned his elongated head towards Gloss and fixed her with a wise, bronze-irised eye. "Yes, yes. I've heard all the wisecracks before, my wee Lutris. Hrmmm, we all have subtle issues to work out, yes?"

"Subtle?" Gloss replied with faint sarcasm. "Of course."

Cries Often tugged his sister's arm. "Hey! Tell Pijper I'm a great hunter, Gloss." His simple mind craved recognition, especially from visitors. "Tell him."

"Sorry, sorry. Yes, you are," Gloss lied, and then to Pijper. "Yes, he is."

Pijper understood the nature of this appeasement game and nodded in false agreement. "Of course, Cries Often. That's what I've always said. You're the very best."

Shines and Follows rolled their eyes at Cries Often's childish requirements. "Deshi-Oad's Spume," Shines murmured, her reticent hijna accompanied by a soft hiss.

"So, will you be staying for the evening meal?" Follows asked. "We have lots of juicy uboo. I'll clean and prepare some for you if you'd like?"

"Thank you. That's kind. I may do just that," Pijper replied, always keen for a free meal. Yet, he did have other priorities to consider besides his stomach. "I came to speak with Fearless, but I must confess, it would be an easier thing to be fed by friends then to find my own food. I'm lazy like that."

Pijper cultivated many special relationships with both the Lutris and Lontra over the seasons, familiarizing himself with the many grievances between the species and acting as a buffering liaison. Numerous, and potentially bloody, feuds had been averted due to his tactful peacekeeping. The icy-blue diplomatic ureola, snug on his right ankle, testified to his status.

Gloss wondered if another potential conflict brought the pelican emissary to Tanglesafe. "What do you need to speak to my father about?"

Shines and Follows gasped. They would never dare such a request. Among the Lutris, an unmated female inquiring over the business between the Alpha and his guest, more so if the guest was a visiting dignitary, invited a painful ear nip. Gloss' kinship to the Doyen exempted her from such reprimands.

"Gloss, you know I can't tell you that," Pijper reminded. "Only the Eehr may know. But I'll let you field a guess."

"I know!" Cries Often raised his furry arm over his head. "I know! It's about, about, uhm... about, uhm... about The Glow? Right? Am I right?"

Pijper lowered his head, impressed, and ruffled his ample wings. "That's a clever guess, Cries Often. And I must leave it at that."

"Fair enough," Gloss conceded. "If you can't say, you can't say. Now let's get this food inside." She brushed her amber wristlet against one of the countless kholo fronds that, with the seaweed, defined the undulating perimeter of her submerged home.

At the heart of Tanglesafe, hidden deep within its intricate structure, scores of incandescent pryzoa sensed the contact between ureola and kholo. A heartbeat later, a spectral circuit — established by the two species unique kinship — translated pryzoic instructions to the High Polyps. The threaded kholo fronds, and connective kelp stipes tangled amongst them, twitched, wiggled, unwound, and retracted into a watery passageway leading to the very heart of the mighty Lutris kingdom.

Pijper never tired of watching this marine phenomenon up close. The magic of the squirming nooree tickled his brain in so many pleasurable ways, making fodder for future musings. Poems were sure to follow.

"Yes, yes," Pijper murmured to himself. "These Lutris are crafty. So very crafty indeed."

To Envoric birds, collectively known as *Vialae,* or 'Winged Allies,' the common notions about how The Above behaved — and, by inference, the rest of the natural world — failed to explain the impact of pryzoa upon the oceanic environment. Clearly, Liminal Gheelindreeliah's enchantments proved to be aquatic only. It seemed Vialae, as denizens of The Above, lacked the necessary faculties to grasp that mystery.

It brought to Pijper's mind the ancient Ulurii axiom: "*In water, all things are possible.*"

"Ok, ladies" Shines said. "One, two... three!"

Heaving and grunting, Follows and Shines used their strong limbs to swim the urchin-laden carryall into the magic-made canal. Cries Often chose to rest on a rickety branch, too lazy to lend a paw. "Go, go!" he urged. Excitement flared his sparse whiskers. "Faster!"

Gloss lingered a moment while the others swam out of hijna-range. She had private matters to discuss with the wise pelican. "Any word from Sleek?"

"No. I'm afraid not."

Gloss didn't try to mask her disappointment. "Oh..."

Pijper unfolded his right wing and draped it around Gloss' shoulders, a tender show of support from one friend to another. "Then again, whenever I visit High Split Rock, I speak with the Den Sire or Uuvaloo exclusively. There's little time to for anything else, hrmmm?"

"I understand."

"And when I'm not there I'm exploring The Blue. There's so much of it to see."

"I wish I could go with you," Gloss confessed. She gracefully spun her body in the water and resurfaced. "I'd love to get away from here and see new things."

"You and Sleek will see many wonders together, once all this conflict nonsense is resolved. This I'm sure of."

The notion warmed Gloss' heart. "I miss him so much it hurts sometimes." "He misses you, as well," Pijper assured.

Gloss' ears pricked, her whiskers splayed, and her golden eyes lit up. "He does? Really?"

"Oh, yes." Pijper smiled in pelican fashion: a crinkled brow accompanied by the sway of the fibrous, gular pouch hanging from his lower mandible. "I have it on good authority you're all he talks about. Even more than things he should be thinking about, like the Glow or reclaiming Liminal. If I didn't know better, I'd say Sleek was obsessed. And, believe me, I know a thing or two about that." The noble pelican folded his wing back into a rest position. The two halves of his beak clopped in hungry anticipation. "Now, what was all that talk about dinner, hrmmm?"

The waterway Gloss created with her ureola wound through the kelp canopy like an earthworm through soil. The conduit closed behind them, kholo threads compelling the nooree to re-entwine and fortify them against the perils of the open sea.

Cries Often rode the ghossn's top branch, fascinated by the variety of birds flying over or swarming among the seaweed. Most were skittish Monoic gulls, Northern fulmars, or wayward cormorants enjoying the safety of Tanglesafe. The Lutris tolerated them because they dined on the krill, kelp-clinging invertebrates, and tiny forage fish infesting the kelp.

A fraction of Vialae boasted the bronze-within-bronze eyes of the Envorah. These birds held personal relationships with the Lutris, visiting day after day to pass the hours sharing gossip, food, and laughter. Their cries mingled with the barks, yelps, and other vocalizations from the hijna-conversations between bird and sea otter issuing from every corner of Tanglesafe.

A trio of startled seagulls took wing and flew over Cries Often's head. He reached out to touch one but missed.

"Look at the Luuhni, Gloss. And pretty, Vialae!" he giggled. "They can swim *and* fly!"

The feathered bodies, pointed beaks, and odd anatomies of all birds delighted him. Their ability to escape the sea's embrace and fly away seemed like magic to his simple mind. Shines and Follows held the view that fascination of this sort should belong only to pups.

Shines grumbled, her weary legs and tail frothing the water. "I wish Gloss' brother wasn't such a lazy *nataaq*."

"No other uju his age acts this way. It's pathetic," Follows added with venom.

Gloss bit her lip. She glanced at nearby Pijper, who paddled beside the urchin-weighted ghossn. The diplomatic pelican acknowledged he'd heard the jab with a soft shaking of his head. It wasn't his place to intervene or take sides.

Gloss held back a snappy retort, but thought: *They're complaining that someone else is lazy? That's the puffer fish calling the uboo prickly.*

On either side of the waterway, floating on their backs with their rear feet above the waterline, were the gender-divided Lutris. Each animal lashed itself in place with kelp to resist the currents. Mingling of the sexes outside of mealtime wasn't condoned, although pups played freely between the segregated enclaves. The sea otters' dense fur ranged from gentle auburn to smoky black; the head, throat, and chest being lighter in color than the rest of their bodies. Long, coarse whiskers draped each animal's triangular nose like bristly combs, while bronze and golden eyes glinted with varying intelligence. Sunlight muted the natural glow of the ureola each adult animal wore. Only at night did they shine, twinkling like a rainbow constellation in Tanglesafe's darkness.

"We're back!" Cries Often shouted, interrupting his Raft-mates' private conversations and unaware of his rudeness. "We brought lots of uboo for dinner. Come and see."

"Shut up, Cries Often!" or, "Can't you see we're talking?" The dismissive barks were far from the enthusiastic reactions the young otter expected. Still, they continued... "Don't speak unless you're spoken to!" or, "Stop yelling, you idiot!"

And worse of all: "You bring uboo because you can't hunt like a proper uju."

The hurled rebukes stung worse than the spines of the urchins. Cries' Often's body twitched, tears sliding down his whiskers into The Blue. "Why are you all so mean?" he bawled.

Lutris viewed urchin harvesting as the labor of females, or lowest-ranking males, and therefore unworthy of boasts. Gloss's heart ached for her sibling, but she reserved comment and kept swimming. Now wasn't the time to respond. All too soon, another opportunity would arise. Love compelled her to defend her sibling every tide. Today would be no different.

CHAPTER 10

UNWELCOME ADVANCES

Within Tanglesafe's center resided a gathering pool. Five ghossn already floated in the middle of the kelp-free space like driftwood snowflakes, their urchin-heavy branches fastened together with knotted strands of nooree. Gloss, Shines, and Follows swam the last few tails to the wooden mélange, relieved the toughest part was almost ended. When the branches of the various carryalls touched, they shared a collective sigh.

"Deshi-Oad's Fluke," Shines grumbled. "These things are too heavy for just three." She looked at Cries Often perched and weeping on an overhead branch and thought, *The Eehr's son is a complete waste of fur.* Aloud, she added: "I wish we had more help."

Follows stretched her aching spine. "If wishes were uboo, life would be *so* much easier. But, alas, they're not. Let's get this ghossn tied up. We've pups to feed and mates to tend."

As tired females lashed their carryall together with kelp strips, a bevy of youngsters gathered about. "Come and play, Cries Often," they shouted, excitedly splashing the water with their tails. "Play with us!"

The Beta's tears ceased as fresh euphoria bubbled within his simple heart and soul. All thoughts of the earlier taunts evaporated. "Yeah! Follow me! I know a game we can play!"

He slipped into the water. With renewed vigor he led the eager pups on a wild chase through the acres of kelp thicket. In the eyes of the cynical adults, Cries Often behaved like an undisciplined pup. Yet, to the pups of both genders, he was the most accessible — and, by far, the most fun — of all adults. The boisterous group would cavort through the seaweed, chasing and hiding and tail-tugging, only to return, tired and hungry, to their family units for supper.

For the remainder of daylight, The Raft stayed active with work and chatter. Three more crews of weary females paddled their urchin-festooned carryalls into the central pool, adding their prickly cargo to the collective haul. After all the ghossn were lashed-secured, the urchin sorting and claiming began.

Within sea otter society, a female's social position was determined by the status of her spouse. Mates of the Doyen's Saia-Beta inner circle would choose their portions first, followed by the unpaired males and the mates of lower caste ujus, in order of descending rank. Widowed and unmated females — the lowest caste, save but one — would choose second-to-last from the dwindling leftovers.

Gloss proved the lone exception. Though unmated and still a Loyc, as the Doyen's sole daughter, she enjoyed a Beta's privilege and chose as such.

The highest-ranking females, Gloss included, swam to the ghossn, and inspected the harvest. They pulled the uboo from the laden plijet, and judged them on size, weight, color, spine count, and other characteristics. Accompanied by pups old enough to help, the females combed through the dangling wreathes of spiked echinoderms and selected the juiciest specimens.

As she'd done since the death of their mother, so many years earlier, Gloss selected food for both herself and Cries Often. Though Saia, and capable of choosing his own food, Cries Often allowed Gloss to perform this duty. Not only would she acuur-crack the urchins, but she would also take the time to feed him the flesh and roe — just as a mother would a weaning pup.

The remaining Raft-members waited their turns, hungry and with growing impatience. Growls and irritated yelps accentuated their grumbling bellies. Squabbles resulted, with bites and curses. Only after the premier rank-group made their choices did the next-ranking group swim forward and select their meal. This urchin-claiming continued through the Lutris ranks.

Last to choose were the pawful of Omegas, the lowest of the low. Their own antisocial and often violent behaviors banned them from elevated Envoric society. They had only two choices — either risk death by hunting alone, or to accept scraps — all the while hoping to fight off starvation for another tide.

As the final Nihl-Omega slunk off to curse the Raft in the darkness, a single small urchin clutched to his chest, the first hunting graehl returned empty-pawed from the open sea. Three more returned in short order, also with nothing to show but disgrace on their whiskered faces.

Gloss knew hunters often passed on the chance to seize smaller prey. In Lutris culture, the size of a catch reflected a graehl's skill, and by extension, the male's personal potency. Returning home bearing a small fish would only draw ridicule from the females.

"*Tiny fish, teeny spear, tiny tail, teeny skill...*" they would chide in common insult.

So, males preferred to enter Tanglesafe empty-pawed. Without an inferior prey-fish to symbolize their failure as both hunter and provider, at least a shred of their dignity could be preserved. "The best fish were gone," they could say in preemptive vindication; or "Deshi-Oad willed The Blue emptied." The common excuse of, "There was nothing worth hurling my ynth at," was met with open mockery.

The shamed males would then slink away, clutching their spears like sad comfort tokens; their honor bruised and bloodied — yet still intact.

Gloss smirked at their discomfort. *Serves them right*, she thought. *Weak warriors.*

Sharp Tooth led the last returning graehl. Unlike the other hunting bands, they swam in bearing food — a handsome, green-speckled atiqah: the selfsame lingcod Gloss had killed earlier. Though of a fair size, it wouldn't feed the entire Raft. Only the Doyen and his inner circle of Saia-Beta's, and their immediate family-units, would eat from it.

Gloss watched the graehl brag about their hunting prowess to gathering females cooing over the plump lingcod. Sharp Tooth and the lesser ranking males sensed the anger in her critical eyes. They all knew she'd succeeded where they hadn't. So, they looked away and pretended not to notice. Females witnessing Gloss' disrespect traded worried whispers about what would happen if she persisted in her willful disobedience; secretly, each wished they could do the same.

The Raft settled into its usual contentious mealtime routine. Family units moved to their preordained orbits in Tanglesafe's kelpy wheel: the higher a family's rank, the closer their proximity to the central communal pool. Otters at the bottom of the social order were relegated to the outer fringes. The Lutris equated the idea of 'the center' with Deshi-Oad, the mythological Whitest Whale who dwelled at the center of all things. In this worldview, centrality meant balance, and balance meant power.

And in The Blue, *power meant everything.*

Under darkening skies, the urchin feast began. Adults cursed and quarreled while divvying food between themselves and their pups, who mimicked their parents' behavior. Angry barks and yelps filled the air. Hurled insults often led to quarrels and biting.

Gloss and Cries Often never bickered over food. The siblings took their place amongst the Betas, peaceably dividing their meal and ignoring their neighbor's snarky comments.

The *tap-tap-tap* of hundreds of acuurs splitting urchins filled the air. Each Lutris floated on its back while dining on the sweet and tasty innards, the uboo's prickly shells resting on the dense fur waterproofing their bellies. Arguments raged and laughter pealed across Tanglesafe, while flocks of greedy sea birds flapped about, squabbling over the scraps.

As an honored guest, Pijper floated amongst the Saia-Betas. True to her word, Follows fed him after her own family dined. Halving several urchins with her stone tool, she scooped out the messy innards and dropped them into the pelican's gaping mouth.

His own meal finished, Cries Often swam over to join in. Feeding the bird gave him immense pleasure. "O-o-oh, it tickles," he giggled as Pijper, careful not to hurt the young otter, gobbled the food from his paws.

Watching his brother play comforted Gloss. In the company of a genuine friend, he could, at least for a time, be free of torment. Her heart swelled with gratitude for Pijper's kindness, and simultaneously ached at Sleek's absence.

Supper concluded, and night alight with stars above and ureola below, Gloss, tethered to the seaweed canopy, floated supine, and performed her evening toilette. All around, kholo threaded the length and breadth of Tanglesafe like webs of glowing gossamer, only visible now that darkness had fallen. Layers of subsurface nooree shown in their soft light, their fronds swaying in the currents.

Above the kholo-glow Gloss fluffed and cleaned her elegant, silvery pelt. A loosely articulated skeleton granted her the suppleness to groom every inch. Nimble fingers attended each waterproof guard hairs that hampered the frigid waters from touching the dense undercoat keeping an insulating layer of air next to her skin.

Nearby, Pijper waxed poetic about his travels. Waving his wings about for emphasis, he filled Gloss' mind with wondrous imagery as he detailed the marvels witnessed over land and sea, both natural and Penuree-wrought. Oh, how she longed to see those things for herself!

"The shore is just the first sliver of what awaits," the pelican said. "It extends far beyond the horizon, my dear Gloss. Farther than even the strongest and swiftest Lutris can swim, even though he might try for many tides to find its end. Why, there are places within The Still that have never even touched or seen The Blue."

"Never touched The Blue? Never seen?" Gloss gasped at the lunacy of the idea. "Impossible."

"It's true," Pijper assured. "I swear on my beak. I've seen such places with my own eyes. And by Deshi-Oad's Spume, don't get me started on the Penuree!" The pelican clacked his beak. "They are *everywhere*. There are more than all the shoals of mackerel you've ever seen. Filthy, deluded, ugly creatures. They destroy all they touch. But — and I'm a little ashamed to admit this — I just *love* their food. You'll never taste the like. Fatty and salty and delicious."

"Welcome, wise and noble Pijper," came a hijna greeting from the darkness.

Both Gloss and Pijper turned to see Sharp Tooth swimming towards them, spear in paw.

The Saia acknowledged the renowned pelican with a respectful nod and whisker tug. "I didn't realize you were dining with us this evening. It's been a long time since you've visited Tanglesafe."

The eccentric bird nodded in return. "True, true, Sharp Tooth my friend. Exploring all there is to see in The Blue and beyond takes so much of one's time, hrmmm?" He shook his wattled throat, then added, "I come with news for Fearless. Would you tell him I'm here?"

"Of course." Sharp Tooth looked at Gloss, who resisted a strong urge to swim away. "Hello, Gloss. I was wondering...if I might... have... a moment of your time? Only if you're not too busy?" He'd abandoned his earlier attitude — that of the disciplining male — for one much more courteous.

Gloss didn't buy this ploy. She'd guessed his intent. "Well, actually Sharp Tooth, Pijper was —"

"— just leaving," the Envoric pelican interrupted.

"Wait!" Gloss protested. "I want to hear about your adven..." her hijna trailed off as Pijper paddled away, not wanting to intrude between two eligible, unmated adults.

"So..." Gloss forced a smile and fidgeted. "...here we are."

Twice as nervous as Gloss, Sharp Tooth regretted his curt behavior towards her earlier. An awkward silence hung in the air between them. He nervously scratched his shark tooth alcq.

Finally, the Beta reached into an under-arm pouch and removed a shard of emerald sea-glass. "I found this." Almost the size of his paw, it had originally formed part of a Penuree bottle. Decades in the ocean shaped and smoothed it into a crude jewel. "I want you to have it. Add it to your collection. Maybe make another acuur from it? Like the one you have now. I always admired yours."

Gloss took the fragment, examined it. "Thank you, Sharp Tooth. It's lovely."

The Saia's smile accentuated the oversized canine tooth that informed his name. In combat, with the promise of blood in the water, it made him look fierce and distinguished. But here, within the safety of home, it proved more of an embarrassment.

"I'm glad you like it. It's the nicest one I've found yet." Sharp Tooth's smile sagged as he nervously scratched his cheek. He'd rather face down Xaad without a spear than ask what his heart demanded. "I'm wondering...well hoping that... that, maybe..."

Oh, no, Gloss dreaded what would come next. *Please, Deshi-Oad, don't let him ask what I think he's going to!*

Only when Sharp Tooth closed his golden eyes could he find the words. "Would you allow me the honor of courting you openly?"

Gloss sighed with pent-up frustration. She wanted to scream her rejection in Sharp Tooth's face, to let him know — in no uncertain terms — that her affections belonged to Sleek, and him alone. Allowing any Lutris male to court her wasted both her time and his. Sharp Tooth offered her nothing save binding custom and rigid ownership. Her Aanandi-shade wanted to swim freely, hunt openly, love, and live with unrestrained passion.

And only Sleek could share these necessities with her.

Gloss expressed none of those things. Could not. At least, not yet.

"I'm flattered you'd even consider me, Sharp Tooth," she began. Her rejection must be worded in the softest possible manner. "You're my father's principal Saia," she continued, her hijna even and cool. "His second in command. His most loyal. Any uja would be lucky to be claimed by you. But... the truth is... I'm not ready for a mate."

Sharp Tooth frowned and his golden eyes darkened. "*Not* ready? Still?"

"I need time to find my way in The Blue as my Aanandi-shade directs me," Gloss explained. "For now, it tells me I must remain alone." She offered the sea-glass shard back to Sharp Tooth. She could not accept his courtship gift. "I'm sorry."

"I ask you to reconsider, Gloss," Sharp Tooth pleaded. "We would be unstoppable together. Our pups would rule Tanglesafe and The Blue. We make perfect sense as mates."

"My answer is no. Please respect my decision."

Whiskers drooping, Sharp Tooth reluctantly plucked the emerald fragment from Gloss' paw. "This is about Sleek, isn't it?" he growled.

"It's about many things," Gloss corrected him. "Sleek is just one of them."

Sharp Tooth tossed the sea-glass away. It landed with a *plop* amongst the surface kelp. "Unbelievable. You'd rather couple with a filthy Lontra than with your own kind. Admit it." The Beta's hijna crackled with disgust, his oversized canine now menacing under a snarl.

Gloss turned away. She had neither the time nor patience to fend off his clumsy advances. "Goodnight, Sharp Tooth. For the sake of peace in The

Raft, let's pretend this conversation never took place." She swam off before anger made her do something foolish.

"But it did take place," Sharp Tooth hissed. "Sleek will curse the day you gave him your heart. My ynth will make sure of it."

CHAPTER II

A MEAL BY MOONLIGHT

*W*here is that cursed exit?

The exhausted river otter climbed for what seemed like hours in total darkness.

Abraded paws scrabbled for purchase on slippery rocks. Terror-fueled exertion sapped all the immediate benefits of the ingested pryzoa from Sleek's system. His mental faculties were still sharp, and his Aanandi-shade still resonated with potential — but his body felt diminished and *so very* tired.

Sleek only wanted to stop this grim race for a few restorative seconds. He dared not.

The incline seemed steeper than Sleek remembered from his first descent. Far above, a whisker-thin moonbeam shined past the great boulder wedged into the cave's throat. Barely visible, the silvery light nonetheless held the promise of escape. The Blue's cold vastness waited beyond the boulder, where a swish of his tail and a brisk current would propel Sleek faster than he could ever run. The Beta smelled enticing ocean salts, even deep in the dank Winnow.

The luscious aroma coaxed his exhausted muscles onward.

The two glowing topsnail pryzoa, nestled in his inner cheek pouches, would dispel the dark. But exposing them was risky. They could become flares for the Cruel Dweller to follow.

I'll climb blind. So be it.

Like all adult Lontra, Sleek hunted in nocturnal waters with his graehl. Acute hearing, a keen nose, and sensitive whiskers often made up for his lack of sight. Often, but not always.

Suddenly, the muscle in Sleek's right hind leg cramped into a hard ball under the skin. He cursed and stumbled to a halt on a precarious rocky outcropping. Hissing from the pain, he worked a palm into the knot, kneading the agony away. The blood seeping from his wound slicked his nimble fingertips.

Muscle soothed, Sleek stretched the injured leg, wishing he could lie down and sleep. As his eyelids grew heavy, and fatigue swaddled him in a false coziness, the Beta's mind wandered down foolish paths...

Can I fall under death's shadow, and not be touched? Yes, I can. It's slow and I'm the fastest Lontra alive. It'll never catch me.

The whimsical thought piqued Sleek's natural courage — until the clash of grinding stones jolted him back to the moment. The hairs along his spine stood on end.

Arrogance curdled. Excitement fled.

The Voracious still pursued, tireless and undeterred. It stormed up the boulder-strewn slope, coiled innards radiating a deadly promise in the darkness.

If I had The Skynth *right now, then I'd be the one doing the chasing!*

Sleek shook off this ridiculous notion. His only real hope lay in speed, not in a fabled power. The Skynth promised a pelt aglow like the sun and all the powers of Oussia in one's paws. But the promise was a false one. It existed only in the whimsical shallows where playful kits frolicked.

Adults were forced to swim in the deeper, and far colder, currents of reality.

Sleek rallied his strength. With protesting muscles and numbing paws, he pushed on.

Up he climbed. All four limbs fatigued, on the verge of failure.

Up, up he went. His lungs burning now, as if inhaling fire.

Up, up, up —

Cresting the steep passage, Sleek paused to catch his breath. Once more on level ground, the pain in his body eased. He sighed with relief.

Ahead in the dark — just a short sprint away — freedom awaited. The river otter arrowed towards the boulder and hauled himself up the barricade.

Almost out! Almost home!

As Sleek found the gap between boulder and cave wall, a crimson glow fell over his ashen fur. The terrified Saia watched as The Voracious scuttled over the edge and, without hesitation, launched itself at the fleeing river otter.

The tunnel shook with its reckless approach. Yet the attack proved clumsy: headlong momentum careened The Cruel Dweller into the boulder with an earth-shattering impact. The edges of the shifting rock gouged the cave's walls.

Sleek offered a Holt-prayer, one his mother would sing to him while he was still a blind, nursing kit. She claimed it held power to chase away monsters lurking in the shadows —

"Great Ookl dreaming in The Blue, let me hide in Your Coils until the danger is past; keep me safe in the Bubbles of Your Breath..."

He flattened himself, wiggled inside the gap... and got stuck.

The impact had caused the slit to narrow to half its prior size. The Scare once again threatened to rob Sleek of sanity.

That Which Devours recovered from its collision, and closed in. Sleek hissed with terror, exhaled all the air from his lungs and pushed...

Excruciating pain, as if his every rib and vertebra were being crushed, made him want to scream — but he had no breath to do so. Blood surged in his neck and behind his eyes as he struggled forward. Every inch felt like a losing contest.

Please, Father Fathom, he pleaded. *Let. Me. LIVE!*

As if in answer to his silent prayer, the gap widened a whiskers-width. Then, a bit more. With a final push, Sleek slithered out. After a second of harrowing free-fall, he landed with a splash in the partially flooded channel beyond the boulder. The Scare's awful crescendo faded as seawater soothed his wounded leg, the salt bringing a welcome sting to the injury — it proved he still lived.

Sleek surfaced, oxygen-starved lungs filling with sweet air. The Blue's fragrance washed away the cloying stench of The Voracious from his nostrils. Ahead, beams of moonlight filtered through the fractured timbers of the beached crab boat concealing the cave's entrance.

The Lontra checked his tail to make sure no pieces were missing.

Perhaps Great Ookl came through, he thought. *Or... perhaps I did all the work.*

A *crunch* — followed by the splash of rocky shrapnel — turned Sleek back to the shaking boulder. The Cruel Dweller punched through the gap he'd just escaped from, its serrated pincer backlit by the sanguine glow of its infernal gut.

A triumphant smile bent Sleek's handsome snout. Rare were the encounters where one escaped The Voracious with both life and limb intact. Even if it dislodged the boulder to renew the chase, the rising tide would whisk Sleek away from its vile claws.

"Too slow, monster!" the Beta crowed. "Too slow by half."

The pincer *snip-snapped* one final time, and then withdrew. The fiery glow beyond the boulder dimmed to black as That Which Devours scuttled back to its stolen paradise.

Defeated for now, yes — but by no means vanquished.

Sleek had gambled and won... this time.

Yet he feared the dulling of his intellectual grace. To experience and ingest Liminal's gift, and then suffer the slow stripping away of it... *Ookl's Ink!* Sleek shuddered. He'd sooner pluck out his own whiskers or gnaw off his own tail. In time, the inevitable loss of Kleaa would compel Sleek to tempt fate again, return to the Cave, conquer the Winnow, find The Garden...and confront the terror residing there.

The young Lontra shook his head. *I'll worry about that later.*

For now, he could eat his reward — without the fear of being eaten himself.

Sleek swam towards the cave entrance, the Scare's debilitating cry silenced. He entered through the gaping hole gouged in the keel, climbed up a splintered support timber, maneuvered through a maze of cobwebbed joists, and squeezed through an open hatch onto the grounded crabber's moonlit deck.

The Beta's cherished ynth still lay hidden among the rusted crab cages. Retrieving his spear, Sleek sat amongst the clutter of puerile banishment effigies and spat the two pryzoa into his webbed paws. The topsnails' inner fire washed The Cellum in a claret glow.

Sleek examined their surface details. With no competition from a biome of other resplendent wonders, these cold-fire treasures appeared even more exquisite. Their glassy perfection sparkled unchallenged, like twin stars fallen from The Above to nestle in his paws. Proof-positive rewards of his courage and tenacity.

As Sleek basked in delicious pryzoic light, the enormity of his deed struck like an unexpected spear in the belly. For a few heartbeats, he couldn't breathe. It felt as if the boulder trapped him once more.

I've broken the Liminal Pact, he worried. *I've brought out* living *pryzoa.*

Sleek knew the gifts of First Life to amplify mind and body — as well as manipulate The Blue (and possibly The Still and The Above) — were coveted. They could be used to change the sea into a weapon... if one knew how. So, hoarding them meant authority over others with lesser amounts. To challenge this authority, by its very nature, brought bloodshed.

A binding treaty, the *Liminal Pact* — ratified through pain by his father within the sacred grottos of the Council Pool — had been enacted to quell potential violence. Bringing out living pryzoa was aijeer. The balance of power within the Envoric world, and the relative peace it now enjoyed, rested on this law.

Far better to eat them under the earth than allow them to touch the open Blue.

Punishment for this transgression: banishment, which meant death in the sea's wild currents.

Sleek had knowingly — and with forethought — broken this foundational edict. But wasn't true love worth *any* risk?

To the young Saia-Beta, the answer was a resounding: "Yes."

It's only a crime if I'm caught, he reasoned. *And I won't be. Not this Lontra.*

Sleek took a steadying breath. Plenty of tides remained to worry about politics. Its presence loomed constant in Holt life, as obvious as the sun or moon. For now, his empty belly took precedent.

I should only eat one, Sleek thought. He knew the rules; had heard the etiquette for pryzoa consumption since his first visit to Liminal as a kit. *Any more than one will send your mind down strange paths, either sleeping or awake.* He recalled his father's hijna: *'An eaten pryzoa can harm or heal, if one isn't careful to respect the light it holds. A restrained Celimner nibble is safer than a greedy mouth. Never risk the 'sharp bite of sudden memory' that will follow should if you only seek pryzoa to fill your belly. The scithma-snaag is a warning from Great Ookl. Be wary.'*

Sleek bounced the two pryzoa in his paws, gauged their weight and heft. *But I'm starving. The Old Father will forgive me.* He set aside the larger snails. "You're for Gloss."

Under a waxing moon the color of a shark's belly, the cunning Lontra tossed caution aside and devoured the tender meat of the smaller pryzoa. He savored each juicy sweet bite of his second magical meal. The unsurpassed flavors bathed his tongue, made all the richer now with the salt of

The Blue perfuming the air. Sharpened faculties honed to an even keener edge with each swallow of the intoxicating pryzoic elixir.

How simple for his eyes to now discern the countless nooks and pits of the boulders protecting The Cellum from the waves. Extra-sensitive ears picked out every slosh and gurgle of the surface kelp as it heaved and dipped in the placid cove; and beyond, the sigh of distant winds. He sensed the muscles in his limbs, back and tail recharge and tighten. And it felt as if the heart hammering in his chest could power an entire hunting graehl.

Sleek's fatigue vanished like a fast wave receding from shore. Even the throbbing pain from his gashed hind leg diminished until gone.

The Beta finished off the glowing snail, licked his fingers clean, and discarded the shell, now matte as old sea glass. It tumbled down the sloping boat deck, bounced once, twice, and landed in a coil of weatherworn rope.

The Lontra sniffed the promise of rain in the air. Angry black clouds gathered on the horizon. They spat lightning, coughed thunder, and rolled inexorably towards him. By Fourth Tide's end, the storm would arrive to lash the local waters and timbered hills beyond.

If only he could dawdle a while, dream of exquisite Gloss, and watch the weather unfold.

But he could not.

Sleek had to hide his forbidden prize, then return to the Holt before the worst of the storm hit. He both expected — and dreaded — what would happen there. The whole romp would know of his escapades. They'd smell its success on his breath, see the victory by the burnished gold sheen in his eyes.

The younger and more impressionable Lontra would offer discreet praise for this daring accomplishment undertaken by a privileged rule breaker. *I deserve it*, Sleek thought.

Yet many more would be jealous. Gossip would follow. Questions could be avoided. Accusations dismissed. But envious eyes could not.

In the meantime, more immediate issues needed resolving — like hiding the pryzoa intended for Gloss. A scheming smile lit the handsome otter's face.

And I know the perfect place.

The young Lontra tucked the fiery topsnail back into his cheek pouch, grabbed his spear and slipped into the gentle cove water. He swam with renewed vigor past the protective boulders and the violent waves they sundered and crossed into The Blue's midnight expanses — a single shadow flitting amongst multitudes.

Far below, frigid currents jostled the pillars of emerald kelp that tickled Sleek's body. Above, moonlight strained through gathering clouds to dilute into the sea, where nocturnal turbidities resisted the light's presence. Yet, compared to the cave dark of The Winnow, these shadows seemed like midday sun to the Beta's sharp golden eyes.

As he ventured into deeper waters, Sleek's mind struggled to unknot, like a snare of sticky seaweed, the many problems in his life. They seemed to press in from all sides.

He understood why the Holt, including his parents, frowned upon accessing The Garden. The Alphas' pain in forging the Liminal Pact — agonies endured on behalf of all Envorah after the blood-stained *Cuursuurq* — compelled allegiance from the instinctually submissive romp.

Still, it had never been outright forbidden for those courageous enough, or foolhardy enough, to try. Outside of direct immersion into The All-Light Ocean itself, dining on First Life within Liminal's boundaries proved the closest any creature could get to experiencing Oussia's purest essence. Since all creatures yearned to evolve, all had the inherent right to attempt this heightening from common Monoah to speaking Envorah, and then onward into rarified Aanandi.

But for one Holt-resident, crossing Liminal's border, even to partake in a sacrament, hovered on the edge of insult. Uuvaloo, the Den Sire's wise octo-snail *tharuuspex*, felt entering The Garden not only endangered the romp, but also disrespected Great Ookl.

As Sleek sped through the inky currents, his senses tuned to every fish and frond, he could already hear the Ulura's devout bubblings in his ear: "If all speaking creatures would renew their unquestionable devotion to Old Father Fathom, then, through His Inky Intervention, would Liminal Gheelindreeliah be liberated, that most sacred place of *Light by Liquid by Light*. But they don't, so He allows our misery to continue. To circumvent Great Ookl's purposeful obstruction, manifested in the pincers of The Voracious, is to engage in gravest transgression."

Transgression? Unquestionable devotion? Liberation? Sleek thought. The ideas made him want to throw his spraint. *Superstitious nonsense. The Cruel Dweller is an opportunistic thief, plain and simple. We were lazy and slow, and paid the price.*

Once, not so long ago, an endless harvest of First Life awaited those with the will, and stamina, to conquer The Winnow. But no one took the idea of an invader occupying The Garden seriously. Complacency festered. Warnings went unheeded, for tide after tide.

By the time anyone realized how dire the situation had become, The Voracious had entrenched itself... and the chance to *successfully* dislodge it was squandered.

They had tried, of course. How could they not?

Sleek, too young, and far too inexperienced to join in the battle, recalled the grim tales of the first, and last, attempt to extricate The Cruel Dweller by force of spearpoint. He remembered the injured and dying limping back inside High Split Rock, trailing blood, and tears. He never forgot their groans issuing from the sick den. So many brave Lutris and Lontra fighting — and dying together — in droves. That bleak and bloody tide, afloat with the severed limbs, and severed dreams, had crippled and disenchanted two entire generations.

The ruinous collaboration supplied the initial grit of discord, calcifying over the many seasons into the bitter pearl of hate between the two tribes. All the missed opportunities since That Scathing Tide made Sleek grind his teeth in frustration. The foreclosure of Liminal by The Cruel Dweller, and the resulting scarcity of pryzoa, made all this strife possible —

And, through its long-overdue demise, it could all be unmade.

But how? Sleek wondered.

The combined might of every Lutris and Lontra spear failed to dispatch their adversary during the Cuursuurq. Even with the help of the Irounga, the armor of Death By Rending proved far too thick, its pincers far too lethal. History taught an undeniable lesson: trying to remove the beast through brute force alone was impossible. Any successful plan to free The Garden would also require a thousand tides worth of strategy and full cooperation among *all* Envorah — those found both in the sea, beyond it, and above it.

What are the odds? Sleek wondered, though he'd already guessed an answer.

The Voracious leaving on its own accord seemed likelier than that.

Great Ookl appearing out of The Blue unannounced seemed likelier than that.

High Split Rock crashing into the sea seemed likelier than that.

Sleek stabbed a kelp-frond in frustration as he swam. Himself, his romp and all Lontra kits yet unborn, were forced to pin their hopes for liberty not on practical, well-thought-out plans and cooperation, but through rescue by the rarest of phenomenon.

The Glow.

Unlike the wild idea of Old Father Fathom's existence, or of Him taking an interest in His adherents, this flood of radiant substance from The All-Light Ocean was as real as the gathering storm clouds overhead. No one knew exactly *how* The Glow found its way out of Oussia and into our material world, only that it gushed from Liminal, bubbled through the twisted Winnow, and, from there, rejuvenated every drop of The Blue on the planet.

For Sleek, and the wider Envoric world, far more important than the *how* was the *when*.

No one knew exactly. Not even wise Uuvaloo. For all the tides spent omen-diving, deciphering enigmatic pryzoic signs, and etching pious sand-prayers, it seemed only fair Great Ookl let His octo-snail disciple in on His timing.

Per usual, the tentacled sea deity remained silent.

Sleek swam on, comfortable with the 'hunter's stroke' speeding him forward. Many leagues slipped past. He held his spear loose yet ready. Swaying nooree blades caressed his belly as his imagination wandered to a long-gone tide when he'd experienced his first Glow.

As an weaning pup, Sleek couldn't recall specifics, just feelings and general impressions: The entire Holt assembled in silent awe about The Cellum; every hair on his body tingling with the emerging power of Oussia; the rumbling of the earth like a hurricane underground; the sweet smells heralding Liminal's dislodged habitat, now swept along like so much enchanted flotsam; light gushing from The Cave like a water jet; the sea brighter than the sun for three full heartbeats; the orgy of sapience, and euphoria, that followed...

Then, like now, every animal waited for someone, anyone, to claim the Skynth.

Yet it never came.

Wanting and waiting, Sleek thought. *It seems like my whole life has been hunting one and hiding from the other. But if I claim the Skynth... Ookl's Ink! If I possessed that, then no obstacle could stand in my path. I'd end the war with the Lutris, set The Garden free. And Gloss as well. My lovely, lovely, Gloss.*

Sleek had no doubt Gloss would choose him, if given the right of a free choice. To claim her affections would be an honor even greater than claiming The Skynth itself. Together they'd start their own Holt, the progenitors of a new tribe of Aanandi: a blending of river *and* sea otter.

With the Skynth — a clumsy shortening of the Ulurii concept *Skynthuuhrnymlex*, "Wielding the Cleaving Ynth and Shuuhl of Oussia" — nothing would be impossible.

Nothing in, on, or under land, sky, or sea. Nothing.

Someday soon, Sleek thought. *Not today... but someday.*

PART TWO

TERRITORIAL WATERS

"It's a funny thing coming home. Nothing changes. Everything looks the same, feels the same, even smells the same. You realized what's changed is you."

F. Scott Fitzgerald (1896 – 1940)

CHAPTER 12

SETTLING IN

"**G**et up, sweetie." Hayley gently nudged her snoring daughter. "We're here."

Ayana, sprawled across both backseat cushions, sucked in a deep breath as she awoke. "Hmm...? What?"

"We made it." With a heave and grunt Hayley placed the twin suitcases on the ground.

Pushing her mop of unruly bed-head curls from her eyes, Ayana twisted around and saw her mom wrestling their suitcases from Fritz's trunk. *God, all I did today was sleep,* she thought. *That's twenty hours of my life I'll never get back. Pathetic.*

Beyond the open hatch, a two-story A-frame house stood cozy and inviting, amber light spilling from its many first-floor windows. Ayana always imagined it dropping out of a Norman Rockwell painted Saturday Evening Post cover, deposited by a black-and-white tornado conjured by the wizards at Better Homes and Gardens, it's flower-wreathed foundations crushing the Semi-Wicked Witch of Modernity.

It was too idyllic to be real. Too calm to be inhabitable by anyone other than those in the grandparent-caste. Yet there it lay: peace and tranquility personified in brick and wood.

I can't stand this place, Ayana groaned on the inside. *How can anyone live here?*

The adjacent garage and barn, epitomes of that serene retirement mentality, were hidden out amongst the three acres of shadowed pasture stretching behind the immediate homestead. Ten more acres of dense coastal woods sprawled beyond, its jagged canopy black and featureless against the night sky. Approaching storm clouds, partly obscuring the countless stars, brought a cool, gusting wind that carried the promise of a torrential downpour.

Ayana slid from the wagon's back seat and stretched. Her spine cracked like dried pasta. Fritz's cooling engine ticked an odd drumbeat. The night smelled of wet grass, pine trees, and with just a hint of salty sea air: all the odors Ayana associated with once carefree youth. She subconsciously touched her glue spots and retrieved her suitcase — a smaller, scruffier version of her mother's — from where it sat on the gravel beside Fritz's rear left tire.

Hayley closed the car's hatch with a *thud-click* and started up the pink chrysanthemum-bordered walkway towards the house. Ayana's grandparents lingered at the front door, framed by the den's inviting light. They looked exactly as they did last summer, and the summer before that... and the one prior. Though deep lines etched their kindly faces, and both had thick silver-white hair, to Ayana they somehow stayed both ancient yet ageless.

"Oh, Hayley. Ayana. It's so good to see you," Grandma greeted, her calming voice hovering above a giggle. The same faded blue, seashell-print apron she always wore covered a pine-green dress, hinting she'd been toiling in the kitchen. Rosy cheeks crinkled when she smiled, her pastry-enhanced figure jiggling along with her joy. "Oh, how I've missed you both."

"You're right on time. Get your keesters up here and give us a hug," Grandpa demanded with genial gruffness. Stout with Greatest Generation muscle, and old-man strong, he wore denim coveralls and a soft brown sweater — a Christmas gift from six years earlier. Old reading glasses hung from a lanyard around his neck, and on his feet, soft leather moccasins.

Ayana climbed the four white-painted steps and rushed into her grandmother's waiting arms, snuggling into her ample bosom. "It's good to see you, too," she said, her words and smile sincere. Grandma's embrace always seemed to sweeten the bitterest pill.

Smelling of lavender and Aqua Net, she planted a wet smooch on Ayana's cheek and fluffed her granddaughter's tight curls. "Oh, heavens, you've grown," she remarked with wonder. "You're a lovely young lady. And your hair's longer, too. I love it."

Her gaze settled on Ayana's glue drops. Grandma meant no disrespect. She loved every inch of her granddaughter, from her curly brown locks down to her dainty pinky-toes. Still, Ayana moved her arm away as politely as she could. She didn't like anyone staring at it, not even her grandmother.

Hayley gave her in-laws a kiss on their cheeks. "Eugene. Martha."

Grandpa's strong, calloused hands took Hayley's in a gentle grip. "We're so glad you've decided to stay, honey. We've missed you both. Truly, after the funeral, were afraid we'd never see you again."

Hayley had spent only a handful of days with her in-laws after Jake's death, and those were occupied with hospital, insurance, and funeral business, allowing little time for communal grief. All they'd shared were the immediate financial concerns that came with the closure of a deceased loved one's affairs and the numbness that pushed everything else aside.

Hayley faulted no one. She knew her in-laws loved her and Ayana deeply. They needed their season to grieve, and on their own terms. Still, she felt it wise to soften the truth.

"Sorry. My new job starts the last week of August, and there's been so much I had to do. And figure out. We needed to visit while we still could. Once I start working, well... You don't mind, do you?"

"Don't be silly, dear-heart," Grandma exclaimed, the love she exuded as powerful as the smells of cooking food beyond the threshold. "Of course, we don't mind. We told you that over the phone. You are still our daughter-in-law. You are *always* welcome here."

"What'cha say to some supper?" Grandpa rubbed his hands together in hungry anticipation. "Grandma made her world-famous meatloaf."

"Great." Ayana followed the adults inside, outwardly smiling yet cringing within. Grandma's 'famous' meatloaf recipe included carrot, onion, and bell pepper. Meatloaf should be just that: meat — and *only* meat — in loaf form. Period. *It not called 'vegetable-loaf' for a reason,* she thought.

Ayana entered the living room. As expected, nothing in the elder Outerbridge household had changed — it was a home trapped in emotional amber. Countless black-and-white and sepia photographs of ancestors and distant relations hung on every wall, static eyes watching. A pair of chintz-covered couches, a cushioned footstool, and a worn leather recliner occupied the center of the living room. A collection of sand dollars, each the size of a dinner plate and gathered over thirty years, sat prominently on a shelf filled with a library of books Ayana had no intention of ever reading.

Trinkets and baubles, mementoes from a lifetime of vacations and holidays rested on each shelf, niche, cubby, and sill.

Mingled aromas of sweet pipe tobacco, old wood, baking hamburger, and unwashed dog scented the air. And, beneath it all, the faintest hint of cinnamon. Once, this familiar perfume evoked feelings of whimsy and freedom and self-worth.

But now the house had become a shrine to the recently departed.

Pictures of Father from every stage of life — infant, toddler, boy, teenager, young man, family man *(...I can see a bit of his face in mine...)* — hung in commemorative frames. Everywhere Ayana looked, her dead parent smiled back from within 5"x7" glossies, as if he longed to share the grave worms' last joke — a joke whose punchline she already guessed.

As Ayana moved through the house, a toast-brown, gray-muzzled Labrador retriever crawled from a fleece-lined doggy bed by the unlit fireplace and tottered over. "Hey Shep." Ayana bent to scratch the dog behind his ears. Shep's warm, wet tongue licked her forearm. "That's such a good boy." Her nose wrinkled at his musky odor.

Okay. You need a bath, she thought as the lab's tail thudded the floor. *Like, yesterday.*

"Take our suitcases upstairs," Hayley ordered, "and then come help set the table."

"What? Am I a slave?" came Ayana's retort — and she instantly regretted her tone.

Hayley raised an eyebrow. "What?"

"Nothing," Ayana replied with false cheer. "That's just the name of a song I like."

She grabbed both cases by their handles and started up the stairs. They bumped against each carpeted step as, with begrudging enthusiasm, she lugged them to the second floor.

The smell of dirty canine hung extra thick in the stale air of the narrow upstairs hallway. Ayana's room was the first one opposite the stairs, as it always had been. She dropped her mother's suitcase before the door at the end of the hall, then headed back to the tired old room she'd occupied every summer for the last decade.

With a resigned sigh, she pushed open the door. Darkness *(...my old friend...)*, replete with an aged, wood-grain perfume, awaited within. Ayana groped her way to a yard-sale lamp with a water-stained shade resting on a little table and pulled the chain switch. Soft light revealed a creaky twin bed against the wall, topped by an old green comforter and two white, pancake-thin pillows. A faded picture of a bluebird hung above the headboard. On the opposite wall stood an antique dresser covered in a thin layer of dust. Beside the bed, a threadbare red throw rug covered the scuffed floorboards.

"God, I hate this room." Ayana tossed her suitcase on the bed, eliciting a squeak of protest from the old springs. "I hate this bed. I hate this house."

She crossed to the window and peered past the faded yellow curtains. Darkness obscured the encircling woods sloping towards the distant shoreline. Overhead, agitated storm clouds continued to brew.

Twelve weeks stuck in the butt-crack of nowhere, she thought. *God. Kill me now.*

"Ayana!" Hayley called from the foot of the stairs. "Dinner!"

She remembered her father's teasing admonishments about his mother's cooking. *You can't pull off the mystery-loaf any longer, Pipsqueak. You know it's better than starving, right?* he'd say, his grin acknowledging their shared opinion of Grandma's culinary skills, or rather, lack thereof.

That smile made her feel special.

Now, it was no more than a mind-conjured fantasy, another sad echo of a prior life.

Ayana let the curtains fall, and, resigned to her fate, she left the bedroom and headed downstairs.

Despite her lack of enthusiasm for the menu, Ayana's stomach growled the moment she reached the living room. It sensed food was near and demanded to be filled. Grandma and Hayley worked in the kitchen as Grandpa sat at the dining room table reading *Time* magazine.

He glanced at Ayana. "Storm'll be a doozy," he said and went back to reading.

"Can you please set the table?" Hayley asked. It sounded more like an order.

Ayana stifled a sigh and entered the kitchen. She retrieved silverware and napkins from a drawer, careful to avoid the meal preparation, then took them to the dining room, and laid them on the table. Next, she set four azure glasses from the cupboard beside each place-setting.

"We're in for a proper soaking." Grandpa offered, looking up from his magazine. "Had a brief rain last week. This one will be good for the garden. It's been a dry year overall."

On the *Time* cover: the President and his cheerful wife waving to an unseen audience. To Ayana, the First Lady's smile looked faked, as if she really would rather be somewhere, anywhere, else. The president used to be an actor, sharing the silver screen with a chimp, or baboon, or some other primate. He didn't look much younger than Grandpa.

"Here it is," Grandma said proudly as she entered the dining room, carrying a porcelain serving tray with lid. "Hope you're hungry."

"You bet," Grandpa replied. "It smells wonderful, honey."

Mother followed with a pot full of coarsely mashed potatoes. "There's plenty."

Ayana pulled up a chair as Grandma removed the lid. A cloud of savory steam escaped. As predicted, the trio of hated vegetables riddled the meatloaf.

God. Bell peppers? Ayana thought. *So gross.* Still, she was famished, and enough ketchup made most anything palatable.

The family joined hands and Grandpa led them in prayer: "Our benevolent Heavenly Father: We thank You for this delicious meal; we thank You for Your mercy; we thank You for Hayley and Ayana's safe journey..."

And so, it went — a string of gracious platitudes and humble appeals to invisible powers that Ayana heard none of. Words like "benevolent" or "mercy" or "safe" rankled. *Tell it to the dinosaurs. Or all the poor animals smashed into the asphalt,* she thought. *Tell it to Dad.*

She didn't know much about God, even less about the Apostles. But she understood natures violent proclivities well enough. There was no room for wishful thinking or fairytales. The supernatural was tricks of light and shadow. And magic absolutely, positively, did not exist.

With prayer concluded, the meal began. To Grandma's disappointment, Ayana slathered her food with ketchup. But it did the trick, and she inhaled her supper. *This isn't so bad...*

Catching-up chitchat — stories of home repairs, garden upkeep, and mechanical headaches went around the table. Moans and groans about the state of the country, and the world. Grandpa's comment about earthquakes rumbling the property — "We had two earlier today" — was the only topic that grabbed Ayana attention.

Two? Is the Big One coming? she mused with a dry smile. *Wouldn't surprise me if it did.*

Shep made his rounds. He circled the table, watching and waiting with a dog's patience for the gift of a scrap. When Ayana offered him a piece of food, Grandma warned: "Shep's on a special diet, honey. We keep people food to a minimum. We don't want him getting any fatter."

Ayana withdrew the morsel. "Sorry, boy." She looked into the dog's mournful brown eyes and silently promised to make it up to him later.

A scoop of vanilla ice cream concluded the meal. Leathery and freezer-burnt (who knew how long it had been incased in ice?), it still proved better than no dessert at all.

Ayana cleared the table as the adults retired to the living room. She took the dishes to the kitchen and filled the deep, chipped porcelain sink with hot, soapy water. In defiance of Grandma's edict, she let Shep lick the plates before washing.

"Enjoy," she whispered. The dog's tail thumped the floor mat as his long, pink tongue swept up every speck of food so thoroughly the plates hardly needed cleaning. *I should put them away like this and see if they notice*, she thought mischievously — but decided against it.

Soon after, Grandma came in and busied herself with spooning instant decaf coffee into three cups and setting an old teakettle to heat on the stove. "Let the pots and pans soak for now, sweetie," she said and scooted back into the living room.

Ayana cleaned the plates and silverware, leaving the pots and crusted baking pan to soak as instructed. She put away the dishtowels. In a drawer filled with bric-a-brac, she found four old AA-batteries and pocketed them for the Walkman. With a sigh, she joined the adults in the living room. Hayley and Grandma sat side-by-side on one of the couches while Grandpa relaxed in his recliner. Clouds of sweet tobacco smoke collected on the ceiling as he puffed on his antique, beechwood pipe.

Ayana plopped on the couch. The forced smile she wore made her cheeks ache.

"So, honey. What sort of things would you like to do this summer?" Grandma asked.

There's nothing to do, Ayana thought. Aloud, she replied: "Go to the beach? I guess?" She shrugged, prune-wrinkled index finger tapping a glue drop. "That's sort'a fun."

"You can take Cinnamon and Nutmeg for a trot," Grandpa suggested. "Those nags hardly get any exercise these days. I should've sold 'em after Jake passed. But, they're family."

Hayley's eyes sparkled. "That sounds wonderful." She'd loved horseback riding the woodland trails with Jake. She looked at her disinterested daughter. "What do you say, honey? Come horse riding with me?"

Ayana didn't give a flying fig about horses. But she didn't want to disappoint her mother. "Sure, Mom," she said, hoping her lukewarm tone went unnoticed. "Whatever."

Hayley's smile faded. "Only if you really want to."

Grandma cleared her throat. "Tell us all about your new job, dear."

Hayley shrugged. "It's bookkeeping for a small construction company. Part time. Thirty hours a week. I've been out of the work force since Ayana was a baby. But it'll supplement the insurance money. Stretch it a few more years." She paused. "When Ayana finishes high school... maybe I'll go back to college? Get a degree? Swing for the fences? Shoot for the stars?"

"That's a dynamite plan," Grandpa replied. "And you can count on us to help."

"You can even move in with us, if you need to save money," Grandma added. "All you need do is ask."

No, no, NO! Ayana screamed inside. *God, please, anything but that!*

"I know. Hayley smiled graciously. "And *we* appreciate it. But only as a last resort."

Ayana squeezed her eyes in frustration. *We? We, nothing. Speak for yourself, Mom.*

The teakettle's sharp whistle catapulted Grandma from her seat. "Oh, oh!" she sang, and rushed to the kitchen. "Water's boiling!"

Grandpa rolled his eyes. "Your grandma must think we're all deaf," his tone a mix of exasperation and affection. "The horses heard that kettle."

Grandma soon returned with three steaming cups balanced on a painted wooden tray. Accompanying the cups were a tiny milk jug, sugar bowl and three spoons. "Here we are. A little pick-me-up." She set the laden tray on the coffee table.

Ayana gritted her teeth in annoyance that Grandma didn't bring a cup for her. True, she preferred tea or cocoa to coffee (*...especially the instant junk passing for coffee around here...*). But she still could've asked. It was clear Grandma, much like Mother, considered Ayana a little girl — even with a fourteenth birthday looming.

While the adults sipped their coffee and chatted, Ayana excused herself to the den, and turned on the console television. The old set didn't have a remote; even worse, it was black and white! She clicked through the channels. Half received no signals, just snowy static; of those that did, most were hopelessly distorted. Only two channels proved watchable, and neither broadcasted anything the least bit interesting: news and home shopping.

"Great," Ayana grumbled. "A whole month without TV. Can this get any worse?"

She flicked off the set. Her reflection in the blank screen wore a deep frown. Ayana decided the best thing she could do was to go upstairs and listen to her Walkman. She could stare at the ceiling, lose herself in music, and plot an overdramatic and excessively complicated harikari accompanied by a full orchestra with an audience of weeping spectators.

That dour thought made her smile.

Ayana went over to where Shep reclined in his doggy-bed and gave him a belly rub. The old mutt groaned in delight, tail thumping and rear leg twitching with gratitude.

Ayana paused on the bottom step and glanced at her elders absorbed in conversation.

I wonder if they'll notice I'm gone? she thought. "G'night, Mom. G'night, Grandma. Grandpa." None answered. Ayana started to call out louder... then decided against it.

Let them chit-chat about adult humdrums. She didn't care. She was perfectly capable of entertaining herself. She could spend the evening alone with her favorite bands and plot an emotional revenge. Foot-dragging upstairs to her room, Ayana unpacked her suitcase, brushed her teeth, changed into her goldfish pajamas, and collapsed onto the squeaky bed.

Replacing the Walkman's dead batteries with fresh, Ayana donned the headphones and pressed Play. Familiar music flowed into her ears — revelries, laments, crafty blends of both — but her teenage angst went unassuaged. Reaching into her suitcase, Ayana fished out a stack of well-read teenage magazines: Seventeen, Tiger Beat, Creem, Bop.

She flipped through the glossy pages, disregarding articles about fashion faux pas, make-up tips, and banal relationship advice. After Father died, she just couldn't muster up any ambitions towards popularity, couldn't care less about the clothes on her back, and ignored make-up entirely. And boys... well, boys (at least the ones she knew) were altogether alien with petty loin-driven motivations and personalities about as exciting as a limp carrot.

None gave her the time of day, so she returned the compliment.

No, it wasn't the *words* in the magazines Ayana sought — but the *images*.

Pictures of beautiful people with beautiful personalities wearing beautiful clothes and cavorting in beautiful locations. Ayana didn't need to know the facts behind the photographs. Her imagination easily filled in the blanks. The privilege of celebrity — like a golden skeleton key *(...skeletons, something we're all destined to become...)* — made her grin. Ayana could spend, *had* spent, hours combing through her magazine pictures: absorbing every detail, every head-tilt, every flashbulb illuminated smile.

After a while, even wistful fantasies of living a jet setting life bathed in the bright lights of adoration lost their allure. Still, she yearned to escape being a small-town girl with a dead father, a distant mother, and clueless grandparents, while facing a summer vacation slightly less fun than drowning in a tarpit.

Ayana cast the magazines to the floor. Sighing, she stared at the cramped four walls and reacquainted herself with old roommates: knots in the wood paneling overhead; the chess-board pattern of dents on the floor tiles; a chipped ceiling beam; the lurking dust-bunnies.

In the corner of her eye, where thickening shadows gathered, Ayana imagined a familiar silhouette wearing a flannel shirt and denim pants. "Sweet dreams, Pipsqueak," the paternal shape said with her voice.

Ayana *tap-tapped* her nineteen glue drops. "Goodnight, Dad. See you in the morning," she whispered and fell asleep listening to music.

A full bladder prodded Ayana from her nocturnal soundtrack.

She groaned, peeled off the headphones, and dragged herself from the cuddling bed-warmth. The digital clocked glowed: 10:28. Ayana staggered to the bathroom and relieved herself in the dark using memory and touch. Flicking on the light would be a mule-kick to her night-adjusted eyes.

As Ayana shuffled back to bed, glow from the downstairs living room light caught her sleepy eye. Muffled voices drifted up the stairwell.

Why are they still awake? Ayana slunk to the top stair.

Crouching on hands and knees, she peeked between the banister rails down into the room below. From her vantage, only one couch was visible. Upon it, Hayley sat huddled between Grandma and Grandpa, shoulders slumped, hands hiding her face. A pile of wadded damp tissues filled her lap. On the coffee table: empty wine glasses and a drained chardonnay bottle.

Ayana couldn't see her mother's tears. But she heard the sobs — high and raw like a wounded child's — and saw the anguished jerks of her body as loss wracked her soul. Hayley clutched a framed photo of her husband, the glass splashed with tears. Grandma and Grandpa held their daughter-in-law tight, stroking her hair. They, too, were crying.

"God. Oh, God. I miss him," Hayley moaned. Her cry tore the very air. "I don't know what to do. What do I do without him? Jake, oh... Jake."

Ayana couldn't hear all that was said, but she heard enough. Her cheeks burned with guilt over this eavesdropping. Secretly watching adults cry felt somehow forbidden...taboo. The display of unfiltered emotions unplugged something in Ayana. Her eyes misted, and the lump in her throat couldn't be swallowed away.

As the sole parent, Hayley made herself into the rock Ayana needed. Let the wide world rage and wound and put low — Hayley would remain steadfast and immovable. A foundation of stone. A perpetual harbor in the tempest. And while Ayana instinctually sensed her mother's emotional fragility, she had seen no actual sign of it.

Until now.

Ayana wanted to join in the communal sorrow. She yearned to slip between the loving arms and add her own tears to the healing framework — but sensed her elders needed time to grieve in private.

I love you, Mom, she thought. *And I miss Daddy, too. Every single day.*

Ayana tried to project affection at her mother, to make her broken heart reach out in whatever awkward way it could. A beacon of support from child to parent, connecting one and healing both. But Hayley would never hear it. Couldn't hear it.

Hard reality traded in only two currencies: cruelty and indifference. The ultimate bully, it had no patience for piffling notions like the love between a parent and child. Otherwise, it wouldn't send clumsy honeybees to kill unsuspecting fathers at gas stations.

Wiping away tears, Ayana tiptoed back to bed. She slipped under the thin blanket, folded the pillow into a wad, and cried herself to sleep.

CHAPTER 13

HIDING TREASURE

As harrowing as the ocean could be during daylight, nightfall brought its own shoal of unique perils. Nocturnal hunters lurked in every layer of The Blue, from its restless surface to its crushing, lightless depths. Rather than eyesight, most predators employed other senses at night — smell, touch, sound, and vibrations — to find quarry.

Quarry, that sometimes included wayward river otters.

Darkness served as an indiscriminate cloak. It hid, not just toothy hunters, but the myriad species of prey fish boasting their own, sometimes poisonous, defenses. An unexpected encounter during the night-tides could lead to injury, or potentially, death.

Despite these hazards, Sleek swam with confidence. For a Lontra in the prime of life, The Blue served as both hunting ground and playground. A bane for the careless and weak, the sea — a world of kelp and kinesis, of wave and wrack — proved a boon for the ambitious and strong.

Armed with heightened senses and a sharpened fishing-pole lance, Sleek surface-swam for his clandestine objective. *The water feels wonderful after so much running*, he thought.

To any hungry eye, his ashen-dark pelt made the Beta just one insignificant shadow flitting amongst countless others. Those predators lucky enough to spot him often chose not to attack — an adult Lontra, armed with a spear, made for difficult, and often lethal, prey.

The Blue offered far less hazardous pickings.

A flash of lightning drew Sleek's attention to a black-upon-blacker horizon where mustered storm clouds clotted in the sky. Thunder rumbled over waves agitated by belligerent night winds. The distinctive ozone-smell heralding rain hung thick in the air.

This storm'll be a wild one. I must get home fast.

Sleek swam on but struggled to keep his pace at the surface. Angry swells and howling winds contested his progress. For every tail he advanced, the sea pushed him two tails back.

Finally, the river otter relented and dove —

Ten tails down, almost twenty feet, Sleek noticed a unique deformation in the movement of tangled kelp fronds. He chanced upon a *xhooja*, a ribbon of 'quicker-water' — those rare undersea slipstream-currents snaking through The Blue — and, after considering the possible course of the flow, he risked entry. With an exhilarating burst of momentum, Sleek was whisked along at thrice his top swimming speed; and, best of all, he didn't have to exert himself. Not even a paw flick or casual tail swish.

I'll let this quicker-water do all the work, he thought and relaxed. *Conserve my strength.*

The bigger xhooja — mighty courses that could accommodate and move dozens or even hundreds of Lontra deeper into pelagic waters — flowed faster. Sometimes much, *much* faster.

This minor current, colder and saltier than the surrounding sea, and with a diameter less than Sleek's length, followed the contours of the rough seafloor. It undulated and rolled, sweeping the young otter to-and-fro as it mirrored the nighttime terrain.

Difficult to find, to discover a xhooja conduit here, now, spoke of supreme luck.

Perhaps it's my own luck? Sleek mused. *Or the luck belongs to the pryzoa in my mouth.* Regardless of this blessing's ownership, to the young Saia-Beta, it felt like The Blue smiled on his illicit errand and chose to help. *It's carrying me towards The Gnaarl. At this rate, I'll be there in no time.*

As Sleek let the xhooja carry him along, he noticed a bubble forming against the cheek holding the pryzoa. This wasn't the normal fur-adhering shuuhl.

This was something intentional. Something inexplicable. Something.. .magical.

The bubble grew to the size of Sleek's paw. Deformed by the xhooja's sweeping momentum, the bubble was soon swept away — only to be replaced by a new bubble seconds later. It shared the same fate as its predecessor, as did its successor.

Sleek recalled elder Lontra discussing (more like quarreling) over the pryzoa's curious propensity for *pushing aside* seawater. The tiny bundles of First Life didn't care for The Blue, and, if left to their own devices, banished it.

None in the romp understood the *how* or *why* of it. Not even wise Uuvaloo. But one thing they all agreed on: with practice and patience, disciplined minds could direct the pryzoa's water-bias to their own ends — and make the ocean their plaything as reward.

Sleek regretted not having a mind gifted with such a rarefied discipline. Father did. Mother, also. The Lutris Doyen could, as well as the Ulurii, of course. And scant few others.

But Sleek had no time to ponder this mystery. A flutter of light — like a thread of sparks that shone, vacillated, and went out — caught the river otter's eye.

A knot of cold dread twisted in his belly. His paws tightened on the spear shaft.

There! Again! The Saia fretted as another series of lights danced in the darkness.

Worried at the implications of these flashes, Sleek sculled against the xhooja's wild current. The motion spat him from the submarine speedway and back into languid waters.

The Beta's momentum slowed, and he came to a complete stop in a swaying nooree thicket. Now hemmed by a tangle of kelp fronds, his ynth poised and ready, Sleek's sharpened senses reached into the aquatic darkness... straining, probing for clues —

The lights pulsed again. And, again, they winked out.

This time Sleek recognized the flashes for what they were: the biolumi-nescent signal-flash patterns of a hunting — and now all-but-extinct — Ulurii.

Dread filled his heart. It could only mean one thing...

Father's graehl!

Several faintly glowing circlets of light emerged from the nocturnal Oorum and trailed the biochemical light emissions of the octo-snail. At first, Sleek couldn't tell if the hunting party approached or receded. Until...

Yurch! They're coming this way.

Sleek had to hide. And *quick*!

Not even familial ties would save the wayward Saia from the direst of penalties if the pryzoa in his cheek pouch were discovered. With all the speed he could muster, the young Lontra darted twenty tails down towards the holdfasts anchoring the kelp thicket in place, and hid behind a sea anemone-encrusted boulder —

— and not a moment too soon.

The Ulura materialized from the darkness. Sleek recognized the unique octopoidal-like silhouette of Cixtindi, his friend, teacher, and peer — the skirt of light-discharging fibril; sensitive eye-bulbs mounted atop flexible stalks sprouting beside a pair of smaller, secondary sensory-feelers; anterior and posterior siphons; six snaking tentacles with undersides adorned in creamy white and silver suction cups; and lastly a pair of longer, suc-tion-cup free, arm-like tendrils each ending in a boneless, twenty-fingered 'hand'.

A graehl of nine Lontra glided purposefully behind their soft-bodied companion. Keen otter eyes scanned the water for prey, their shuuhl trail-ing like wisps of silvery-black bubbles. Equipped with sharp spears, and sharper intellects, the river otters feared little while in a group.

Unlike the sea otters' — "every Lutris for himself for honor and rank advancement" — ultra-competitive hunting style, Lontra chose to hunt in cooperative units. The lethal javelins of a well-coordinated graehl, hurled from multiple directions simultaneously, could dispatch far larger prey than any lone river otter ever could. This allowed river otter hunters to regularly take prizes such as the bluefin tuna, the giant grouper, coastal sturgeon, swordfish, and shark.

The sort of prey singular minded Lutris often struggled, and failed, to harvest.

Quick Tail — the Den Sire, Eehr-Alpha of High Split Rock and all Envorah, and Sleek's father — led this graehl. A head-length larger than his companions, he wore the hereditary white alcq of leadership: the spiraled shell of a Spirula ram's horn squid. An elaborately woven, torc-like ureola glinted bright about his neck like a ribbon of violet stars, denoting his undisputed authority. An asymmetrical patch of white fur emblazoned the senior Lontra's once rich amber pelt — now faded to a sandy brown from lack of ingested Liminal potency — from his bristly chin to his taut underbelly. His nimble paws clutched a kingly ynth made from the long snout of an *Ompax*, the regal black marlin, attached to a white carbon fiber Penuree fishing-pole shaft. Four large metal hooks pounded straight and lashed tight with glowing kholo filaments tipped the formidable weapon.

The other eight Lontra were an equal mix of males and females. The four *Vlis*, or Gammas, wore emerald wristlets, turritella-shell alcq, and carried spears akin in stature to the Den Sire's, yet none with the blade-like Ompax nasal-bone of leadership. The four Deltas, or *Dyah*, with their glowing yellow ureola wristlets, held the corners of a large patchwork *majl*, or net. Made from foraged twine, nylon line, and strips of twisted seaweed, the knotted mélange of this 'hunting weave' had been skillfully tied by the cartilaginous 'fingers' of boneless Cixtindi.

Driven to the brink of extinction by relentless predation — all carnivores in The Blue prized Ulurii flesh the highest — Cixtindi, and his spawn-brother Uuvaloo, were the last of their kind. Sleek recalled the grim day several winters earlier when they came to High Split Rock injured, starving and seeking refuge. In exchange for protection, the octo-snails pledged loyalty to the Lontra. Over the subsequent seasons they'd provided a host of indispensable skills and services to the Holt, one of which Sleek now observed from behind his rocky concealment.

Attracted by Cixtindi's yellow and white chromatophore flash-displays, a school of tiny opalescent inshore squid, known as *keerth*, some smaller ones just half-a-tail in length, appeared out of the murk. Keerth were a delicious staple of the Lontra diet. From day one of their patronage the river otters employed the Ulura's natural light-producing abilities to catch these squid. The hungry cephalopods mistook the octo-snail's displays for food, and when they swam in to investigate, the river otter's lethal spears would dispatch them.

From the look of the Den Sire's prized net, the graehl had been hunting for hours and had enjoyed much success. It bulged with squid and small fish destined for The Holt's evening feast.

The keerth drew nearer. The graehl hovered behind Cixtindi, spears at the ready.

Abruptly, a large keerth two-tails long realized the ruse and veered away at the last moment, releasing a cloud of ink in its wake. Not to be denied this trophy, the Den Sire gave chase. Sleek watched in dread as the frantic squid cut a zigzagged course through the kelp fronds towards his hiding place, the Den Sire hot on its tail.

The young otter's gut lurched in fear. *Oh, no, no, no! Father will see me for sure!*

But the predation dance ended almost as soon as it began.

The Holt leader used the tip of his long, muscular tail — and a quick twist of his flexible body — to hurl the javelin through the water and skewer the fleeing cephalopod through the center of its body. Impaled upon the lethal tines, the dying keerth squirmed for a few heartbeats, then went still.

As Den Sire retrieved his ynth and prize, whiskers bristling with satisfaction, his hunter's intuition warned of another presence close by... watching.

Could it be more prey? Or a predator attracted by the smell of blood? Or a rival Lutris or Irounga hunting party?

Den Sire signaled the graehl with a distinctive tail twitch. Instantly, the river otters protectively encircled Cixtindi, then turned their attentions (and spears) from the hunt and began scanning the dark waters for any hint of threat. Even the octo-snail, who knew hunting signals as well as any graehl member, lent his hypersensitive eye-bulbs to the task.

Quivering with dread, Sleek flattened his body against the sea anemone-softened stone, the only thing separating him from certain discovery — and the pain to follow. *Father can sense the pryzoa*, he thought. *He's looking for it!*

He closed his eyes and tried to clear his mind.

Just then, the air bubble clinging to Sleek's furry cheek dislodged. The Beta's golden eyes snapped open in time to watch it float over the top of the boulder towards the surface. Sheer terror caused Sleek's heart to skip a beat. That bubble might just be his undoing.

Yet luck swam with Sleek once again. The bubble continued its upward journey, unnoticed. Convinced his senses played him false, the Eehr returned to the graehl. He gestured, and the hunting party resumed its trek back towards High Split Rock with the fish-bulged net, rubbery Cixtindi taking the lead.

Sleek remained frozen. To any passing eye, he looked like an otter-shaped lump of rock. He dared not move so much as a whisker.

The Beta peeked out from behind the sheltering boulder when his lungs began to ache. He looked about and found himself alone. Weak with relief, he sagged against the rough stone for a few heartbeats, thankful for the luck clinging to him like shuuhl.

Finally, with a tail swish and a kick of his hind legs, he arrowed upwards for the sky. A thunderclap greeted Sleek as he emerged and filled his lungs with fresh air. The storm, in all its raging splendor, gathered overhead like some ravening beast. More lightning struck the horizon, followed a second later by another rumble of thunder.

It seemed as if the sky chastised him for negligence.

I know, I know, Sleek thought in reply. *I can't afford to be so careless again.*

The encounter with the graehl had shaved several tides off his life. It seemed unbelievable that Sleek's fate had almost been sealed by the whim of a single bubble!

He risked greater troubles if he lingered. He needed to hide the pryzoa, and fast.

Forsaking the xhooja, Sleek hugged the coastline to avoid any further encounters, and swam as fast as his legs and tail could propel him. Storm-riled waves dashed themselves against the primordial rocks, their incessant collisions echoing across The Blue.

The swells were rough, but Sleek's adrenaline kept him moving at a brisk pace through the choppy water. Before long, another lightning flash revealed his destination. There, flanked by stony crags and scalloped tide pools, a ribbon of sandy beach awaited.

The Gnaarl! Sleek thought as he paddled for the shore. *I made it!*

Lontra legend claimed that, long, long ago, ages before the first generation of Monoic river otters even found the open sea, Old Father Fathom desired to test His strength. Emerging from the uttermost benthic abyss in an ink cloud darker than midnight, He reached into The Still with a mighty tentacle, uprooted a gigantic Sequoia redwood tree many hundreds of tails tall, and pulled it into The Blue.

Some elders suspected He'd used the tree as a bludgeon to defeat Deshi-Oad, his divine counterpart and eternal rival. Others thought it functioned as the sea deity's *acuur*.

Whatever the reason, eventually the tree was discarded. It drifted in the ocean for untold decades, circling the globe more than once. Over time, its mighty trunk fractured from the incessant actions of wave, wind, and salt. Eventually, its thick tangle of roots became encrusted with the ubiquitous barnacles that, sooner or later, adorned all things residing in The Blue.

Only portions of the trunk survived, but the immense root-ball remained intact. It washed ashore, where time and tide secured it with a steady deposit of sand and pebble. Now, most Envorah regarded The Gnaarl, or *Ookl's Knot*, as a sacred place of meditation where one could wander among the confusion of sprawling roots and, if listening closely, commune with the gurgling wisdom of Old Father Fathom.

But Sleek wasn't interested in legends or spiritual nonsense.

He'd ventured to The Gnaarl many times during his life, both alone and supervised.

Never once did he feel his Aanandi-shade call to him, nor did he witness a phenomenon or miracle he couldn't dismiss upon later, objective reflection.

According to Uuvaloo's ultra-righteous interpretations, this stemmed from a profound "failing of faith." *Perhaps*, Sleek thought. *Or... perhaps it's just an old, sand-locked tree.*

Tonight, Sleek did not require revelation. His needs were more ordinary — the abundance of nooks and cubbyholes in and amongst The Gnaarl's many tangled roots.

Sleek slid out of the cold ocean onto the stony shore. Leaving the waves behind, the Lontra scampered over the algae-slicked rocks to where barnacled stones transitioned to sand.

Beyond this, the wrack zone of old seaweed and dried dulses changed to dryer deposits of driftwood scraps and tide-heaped branches heralding Ookl's Knot. The shrine loomed above Sleek in all its weather-scoured majesty, a thousand twisted roots jutting in all directions like great wooden urchin quills.

Leaving his spear outside, he crossed the tousled threshold and entered the evergreen labyrinth. *The second maze today,* Sleek thought. *Hopefully, there won't be a third.*

He ventured deeper inside. The air within smelt musty with the aroma of decaying timber that crumbled under the Saia's paws. Light dwindled. Five steps later darkness reigned. The ancient wood pulp deadened all noise. Even Sleek's breath and footfalls went silent. To the young otter, it seemed as if Ookl's Knot sustained itself by devouring sound as sustenance.

The sieve of eroded crawlspaces grew ever tighter. The Beta flattened and squeezed his supple body deeper into the wooden confusion, scrabbling ever forward with confidence even without the benefit of a ureola. He'd memorized the route to this hidey-hole long ago.

Finally, in the furthermost cul-de-sac deep in the bowels of Ookl's Knot, Sleek reached his objective. Three winters earlier, the crafty Saia discovered the tiny hollow and decided it would make the perfect place to squirrel away whatever precious thing he fancied. From a piece of driftwood, he acuur-fashioned a screen to cover this hole roughly the diameter of his head. It set so well over the niche as to be undetectable, even to the sharpest eyes.

Sleek pried back the panel to reveal a salvaged Penuree cola bottle of clear glass sealed with an old cork. He plucked the radiant pryzoa snail from his aching cheek pouch. Its luminescence, like a miniature star in Sleek's paw, filled the narrow tunnel and struck shadows from each splinter and knot.

Ah-h-h. That's better, Sleek thought as the pain in his cheek subsided.

As he gazed at the First Life, a strong urge to devour the fiery morsel seized him. He brought the topsnail to his nose, sniffed. The sweet aroma set his mouth watering. Sleek wanted to lick the pryzoa. He wanted to bite it, to chew it, to swallow it. He wanted to feel the flush of heightening energy course through him, setting his Aanandi-shade on fire once more.

It would be so, so easy —

No. No! the Beta thought and shook his head to clear away that greedy spell. *I've already eaten two. That's more than plenty.*

Sleek uncorked the bottle and shoved the pryzoa inside. Its shell proved a snug fit through the slender neck, but a hard push with his thumb solved the problem.

"You belong to Gloss," Sleek said. An exciting thought followed: *I'll offer you two days from now at the Oyster Shell. If that doesn't prove how much I love her, I don't know what will. I'll raise her Kleaa, and we'll be together forever.*

He corked the bottle, wedged it back into the cubbyhole and replaced the false panel. The burrow plunged into darkness once again. Sleek smiled at his cleverness. The pryzoa would remain safe, hidden under the very eyes, and noses, of the devout until he returned to retrieve it.

It'll be the only real *magical thing in The Gnaarl,* he thought.

The Saia threaded his way back through the redwood maze. The storm's first sporadic drops plinked on the overhang of jutting roots above his head. He could smell torrential rains looming close behind. Another lightning flash lit the world just as he emerged from the corpse of the ancient Sequoia.

Sleek paused to blink the afterimages from his eyes as angry thunder shook the sky. Retrieving his spear, he crossed the beach and slid back into the choppy ocean. Pryzoa-granted strength still coursed through his body. His limbs and tail felt taut with energy as he swam.

As Sleek sped for the Holt, he worried over the romp's reaction to his enhanced state. They would know the truth of his deed as soon as they saw his eyes or smelled his breath.

He needed a cover story. Something to deflect the inevitable questions.

I should bring back some food, he thought. *Yes, that's what I'll do. A tasty fish'll be a good distraction. And, hopefully, I can find a xhooja to get me home quicker.*

CHAPTER 14

UNDER ELIHUUL'S LIGHT

Lutris believed the sun submerged each night beneath The Blue, destined to surface at dawn like a breaching whale, alive and burning bright once again. As the horizon darkened with storm, moist evening winds triggered the instinctual cues of Monoic sea birds to wing away from Tanglesafe back to their nests.

Twilight also brought out *Helquru*, the 'Night Patterns,' shining overhead in all their scattered glory. Symbolic in shape, they inspired and mystified the Lutris. *Tsunnth* the spiny lobster; *Zimzala* the sea hawk; and the harbor seal *Socoroo* were but three of the named constellations competing for space in the heavens. Many Envorah suspected the stars were pryzoa clinging to the sky, enigmatic and forever out of reach.

Though the sea otters appreciated the Helquru's beauty, to them the astronomical motifs were pagan. They recognized just one celestial object worthy of veneration — the moon. Called *Elihuul*, the brightest light source of the nocturnal world also lent its name to the nightly adoration of Deshi-Oad. Lutris believed the moon belonged to the ancient Whitest Whale and symbolized His function as the 'Divine Impetus' coursing through The Blue, unstoppable and unchallengeable. The moon and the whale were, for all intents and purposes, one and the same.

Deshi-Oad split the waves, shattered the ice, and churned the water to froth. Deshi-Oad made all *living* things either bend to His will or flee from His great maw.

The Lutris revered the implacable ferocity of their deity. It encapsulated their desire to dominate the entire aquatic world from the surface to the abyss. Elihuul did the same in the celestial realm, returning each night to overpower and scatter the Helquru like shoals of frightened fish.

Tonight, the impending storm brought towering clouds pregnant with rain. Though their bulging silhouettes blocked beloved Elihuul from sight, The Lutris could instinctually feel The Blue react and swell as the moon reached its zenith — and when it did, Deshi-Oad's nocturnal veneration could begin.

Only Fearless, their dominant Eehr-Alpha, could initiate this worship.

But tonight, he wasn't on the surface...

Sharp Tooth dove below the flotilla of ghossn carryalls drifting within Tanglesafe's central pool. He left a wake of silvery shuuhl-bubbles as his long, flat tail propelled him with lithe speed through the kelp-free waters. Far below in the inky night Oorum, the Beta's keen eyes spied a cluster of pale lights. As Sharp Tooth swam, the jagged silhouette of a large, submerged structure began to manifest. Haloed by schools of fish and swarms of mindless jellies, a familiar hodge-podge of driftwood timbers, disarticulated Blue Whale rib-bones, and scavenged Penuree plastic debris defined a roughly spherical structure over one-hundred tails in diameter.

This was fabled *Gwelth* — the 'Center of the Circle' — and pride of the Lutris raft.

If Tanglesafe was envisioned as a great wheel, then this sunken bastion of the sea otter hierarch, generations in the building, would be its hub. To Fearless and his Beta quorum, it served as both counsel and meditative chambers. And, with the waxing tides of war and woe soon to be visited upon all The Blue, a stronghold. Sharp Tooth always thought Gwelth's discordant symmetry bore a striking resemblance to a vast sea urchin — daunting and formidable.

Leafy ropes and hearty lattices of glowing kholo coiled in and through the Lutris fortress like some symbiotic organism. These snaking polyps not only anchored Gwelth to the stony seabed but also spread outwards in all directions, knitting Tanglesafe's kelpy density into its circuitous, phosphorescent web.

Sharp Tooth arrowed towards one of many gaps in Gwelth's architecture functioning as crude windows. Clouds of algae-cleaning fish living among the timber and bone patchwork scattered at his approach. The Beta slowly pierced the great bubble of air trapped within the submerged sanctum. Miraculously, it didn't burst. Deep within, the collective presence of forty-one pryzoa maintained the bubble's delicate water-repelling integrity. Lutris exploited this trait to trap air, allowing the entire Raft to stay submerged, tide-after-tide, day-after-day.

The same membrane that repelled the ocean whisked the remaining water from Sharp Tooth's thick brown pelt. He shook his body (a force of habit) and sniffed the fusty air. Sensitive nostrils discerned numerous odors coloring Gwelth's atmosphere: mildewed wood, rotting seaweed, wet fur, spraint, spoiled fish, and the lingering bouquet of fifty thousand breaths.

And, behind this aromatic medley: the unmistakable sweetness of pryzoa. This odor, above all others, hinted at a banquet of magical promises to Sharp Tooth's Aanandi-shade.

The Beta loped down several rutted passageways towards Gwelth's hidden nucleus. Feathery strands and blebs of radiant kholo wound through the timbers and whale bones to light his way. The scent of First Life intensified with every step, and Sharp Tooth's instinctual desire to eat the pryzoa grew in tandem. With practiced discipline, however, he mastered the urge.

His rank — indeed, his very life — hinged upon this restraint.

By the time Sharp Tooth reached the central cavity, enclosed behind a heavy partition of High Polyps, his hunger had been leashed. The glittering curtain quivered at the proximity of his blue ureola. The tangles of dangling kholo split down the middle and furled inwards, retracting like living theater curtains.

Sharp Tooth slipped past them — and into a chamber of wonders.

A single spectacle dominated the space, and the Saia-Beta's eyes were drawn towards it. Forty-one incandescent mollusks — the living anchor of the Lutris' power base — meandered on a pair of interlocked Penuree tires, levitating like a rubbery figure eight above a rainbow-hued thicket of iridescent kholo. A rickety partition of orca bones encircled this growth. As the pryzoa scrawled their hidden wisdom upon the barnacled surface of the tires, enigmatic cyr-sigils guttered above their bodies like cold fire candles.

Sharp Tooth had heard that, generations earlier, Ulurii sages taught the first Doyen how the future could be divined via the movements of the fiery snails. Data gleaned from their aggregate motion, sometimes called 'the broad current,' could, if deciphered correctly, yield a wide range of predictions. Forecasts offered strategic advantages when it came to hunting prey, preparing for natural (or *super*natural) disasters...or when to sharpen ynths for war.

Unfortunately, the language of understanding this symbolic broad current, sometimes called Omen Diving, was not intuitive. It took the guiding tentacles of Ulurii to properly read.

Luckily, there were other, and simpler, ways to glimpse tides yet unborn.

Forty-one mirror fragments, inserted at odd angles within the web of kholo strands, rimmed the chamber walls. Gleaned over the years, these slivers caught the pryzoic radiance. Gazing long enough into this refracted light revealed future events along the viewer's specific tideline — or 'the narrow current' — and guided the Doyen's personal divinations.

Sharp Tooth did not understand all the mind-bending details, nor was he expected to. His duties required his attention be focused elsewhere, mostly upon the tip of a spear.

He only held the rank of Saia-Beta, after all.

Tearing his gaze from the pryzoa — *how easy to get lost in their light and forget all concerns for self or The Raft,* he thought — Sharp Tooth crossed the chamber to a mound of Penuree life preservers and frayed rope heaped in the corner. Afterimages of light lingered on his eyes, and he blinked them away.

Upon the soft throne rested Fearless, Eehr-Alpha and Doyen of the proud Lutris. Largest and heaviest of his clan, Fearless ruled by not just formidable size, but an equally formidable intellect. From his lower lip, a Great White Shark tooth alcq sharpened his already formidable countenance. As Aanandi, he understood simple mathematics and could think in abstractions. He counted himself in rare company among the Raft's population. Not long ago most Lutris possessed such skills, but attrition via predation, disease, old age — and the generation maiming Cuursuurq — left alive a mere talented few.

That dire reality, more than most, besieged the evolved Doyen's mind.

Above the royal bedding, mounted prominently on two whale vertebrae protruding from the wall amidst the skulls of long-dead orcas, lay the ceremonial *Eehrynth*, or 'Alpha's Lance.' Lutris lore boasted the first Doyen carved the spear generations past from a rib-bone of Deshi-Oad Himself. Sea otters believed it to be the first tool ever crafted by an Envorah of any species. Hundreds of scratches and bite marks — the personal signatures of prior Doyens — covered the length of the ancient lance. Sharper and more rigid than the calcified baleen spears used by later generations, the weight and unwieldiness of the Eehrynth relegated it to an esteemed prop symbolizing and augmenting the Doyen's authority.

But, in the Alpha's dexterous paws, it could slay — and had. Many, many times.

Sharp Tooth approached Fearless. In keeping with his subordinate status, he dropped to all fours and tugged his whiskers in respect, thus offering the traditional Beta-to-Alpha greeting.

"*Kooarii*, Doyen. Elihuul has arrived."

Fearless remained silent, unaware of the Saia's presence. The narrow focus of his gold eyes on the pryzoa told Sharp Tooth that his Eehr rode a current of deepest concentration. Worries, like swarms of buzzing myzee kelp flies, occupied Fearless' mind — from the general health of The Raft and availability of food resources to the forthcoming Glow and The Cruel Dweller's occupation of Liminal.

For eleven full tide-cycles, the Doyen watched, forsaking the surface, companionship, or swimming in the open Blue. He drank sparingly and ate even less.

After a while, Sharp Tooth dared to ask, "What do you see, Doyen?"

"Everything... and nothing," Fearless murmured, more to himself than to the underling. In his concentration, he'd already forgotten Sharp Tooth hunched nearby.

The sea otter ruler searched for a solution on how to best oversee the growing animosity between his clan and the Lontra. The Lutris were the older species: noble, proud, and descended from indigenous Monoah ancestors who had lived in the sea since time immemorial. On the other paw, the upstart Lontra were usurpers birthed from some freshwater cesspit deep within The Still, the salt of The Blue inherently alien to them.

Indefinite coexistence was out of the question. Pure and simple.

Eventually, if the Lontra refused to relinquish what they stole, then the Lutris must force the issue. Yet, options to accomplish this goal without bloodshed were limited.

Advice from Fearless' nine-member Beta quorum could be distilled into one word:

War.

Fearless knew that, if Lontra possessed more pryzoa than any rival, including the Lutris, then by Aanandic decree any direct challenge to the Den Sire's preeminence proved unlawful. Designed to save the lives of both combatants and innocents, this law — in a strategic sense — proved prudent. War against High Split Rock would be glorious, with many sea otters becoming heroic warriors reveling in pitched battles and the spilled blood of the enemy.

Yet, by the end of the campaign, war with the Lontra would also be a colossal failure.

River otters were smaller and weaker, but also quicker. Plus, their spears outnumbered those of the Lutris, along with the attending warriors to wield them. Spears alone did not concern Fearless as much as the pryzoa. With more First Life came a greater command of the sea. The Den Sire may be an imposter as High King, but he wasn't a fool; nor were his Ulurii allies. The fluidic powers they controlled, capricious as the waves, could not be countered by ynth alone.

Fearless knew the answer to his quandary: he needed one more enchanted mollusk — *just one* — to balance the tactical waters between Raft and Holt. Then the Lutris could challenge the vermin inhabitants of High Split Rock for ownership of The Blue, with proximity to the sacred Cellum and, ultimately claim The Garden Effulgent, as their just and rightful reward.

One more pryzoa. Just one...

This solution would be impossible unless they defeated The Voracious and expelled it from Liminal. Then all scores could be settled, and Quick Tail finally dispatched.

And so, for now as well as tomorrow, the stalemate would continue.

As much as Fearless wanted, *needed*, a razor-sharp acuur-of-an-answer to solve this problem, to his dismay all the divination-currents pointed to bloodshed. *Perhaps war is the only answer*, the Doyen thought. *Maybe The Blue must turn red before we can finally....*

"Eehr!" A bark accompanied Sharp Tooth's hijna. "Are you well? Do you hear me?"

The Beta's harsh call snapped the Doyen from his pryzoic trance. Awareness of the outer world returned to his golden eyes and with it the two-fold discomforts of weakness and hunger. "What is it?" he growled. "I ordered no disturbances."

Sharp Tooth lowered his head in submission. "Forgive me, Doyen. The Raft has gathered. Elihuul is almost upon us."

"Elihuul was just here." He waved a paw in dismissal. "Come back tomorrow."

"Doyen... with respect.... it *is* tomorrow."

With great effort, Fearless turned away from the pryzoa. He stretched the ache from his limbs, back, and tail. "No wonder I'm so hungry." He yawned, exposing a mouthful of sharp teeth. "Bring me food. Fish first, then uboo."

"Of course, Doyen. Right away. Also, Pijper is here. He wishes to speak to you."

Fearless closed his tired eyes and scratched his fuzzy cheeks, then under his shark-tooth alcq. Afterimages of glowing snails danced behind his lids. "It'll be nice to have a fresh hijna in Gwelth. There's much to discuss. You will be part of the conversation, Sharp Tooth. You'll be Eehr someday. If you live."

A surge of pride warmed Sharp Tooth's furry breast. "It would be a privilege."

"Did you find any sign of Grabber?" Fearless asked, yet he already knew the answer. It didn't surprise him when Sharp Tooth shook his head 'no'.

"We found no hair or track of your son, Doyen. Neither have the Vialae or Irounga."

"He may have been struck with The Scare and is hiding," Fearless said. "Increase your patrols to include the periphery of Abundance. Double the uboo reward as well."

"With respect, Doyen, but that is far from our normal hunting grounds. If the Lontra..."

Fearless cut him off with a raised paw. "The Treaty of Abundance is spraint. If Grabber lives, he could be drawn to the food there. And so, there you will search."

Sharp Tooth ducked his head. "Of course, Doyen." An accompanying tail flick indicated he understood the orders. "I'll see it done."

Fearless once more turned his attention to the hovering tires. On sluggish, weak legs, he dragged himself closer to study the broad currents hinted in the pryzoa's languid movements. A piece of grit lodged within the rubber treads caught his eye. He pried it free with a sharp claw and flicked it away. "Deshi-Oad willing, maybe you'll catch some thieving Lontra exiting Abundance. If so, kill them."

Sharp Tooth smiled at the thought. "Yes, my Doyen. A pleasure." He tugged his whiskers, then turned to leave. The kholo curtain parted at proximity to his ureola. Before exiting, the Beta paused and looked back. "We caught Gloss hunting. Again. She took an atiqah with Grabber's spear. I thought you should know."

Fearless shook his head in disappointment. His thick whiskers drooped. "Deshi-Oad's Stone Teeth. She simply won't *listen*. It's so frustrating."

Sharp Tooth quashed the smirk threatening to curl his lip. "I'm sure it must be."

An itch roiled the Doyen's left hind leg. As he scratched, familiar regrets needled him, sharp as urchin spines. "If her mother had lived, then Gloss would've learned *proper* obedience." He sighed. "I made a mistake raising her like Grabber. Like an uju. I know that now."

"It was your choice to make, Doyen. No one is qualified to fault you."

Fearless fidgeted with his violet bracelet of rulership. It felt tight on his wrist.

"What's the old saying?" he asked. "Oh, yes.... 'Parents are the bones on which children sharpen their teeth.' Well, Gloss and her brothers picked my bones clean long ago. Remember that when you have pups, my friend."

"Gloss' blatant disrespect affects the other uja, Doyen," Sharp Tooth reminded. "It gives them ideas. I hear the complaints from other uju about the discord sown between them and their mates." He paused, choosing his next words with care. "Perhaps... you should discipline Gloss this time? Perhaps... make an example of her before the whole Raft."

The Lutris leader spun on his second-in-command. Lip raised in a snarl, his golden eyes narrowed, glinting with mingled displeasure and sadness.

Sharp Tooth gulped and dropped his gaze. *Maybe I went too far,* he thought, steeling himself for chastisement. He bowed in the customary submission posture.

No reprimand came. "That'll be all, Saia," Fearless growled. "Bring me my food."

Relieved, Sharp Tooth tugged his whiskers in respect. "Yes, Doyen." He crossed the kholo-threshold and exited the pryzoa chamber.

The fibrous strands fell back into place, once again sealing Fearless into his self-imposed solitude. The Lutris Eehr sighed and shook his furry head. "Disobedient children and ambitious underlings. They'll be the death of me."

Fearless pried a fiery-bright limpet from a hovering tire. He turned the hard-shelled mollusk over in his paws. Responding to his touch, the organism's light oscillated through a spectrum of perturbed reds. Fearless imagined that, to a pryzoa, all non-Garden life must feel cold, abrasive, and so very, very slow. Envoric sages suspected the touch of any creature not born in Liminal's current, and therefore of 'low light', sparked great irritation within the pryzoa's enchanted, yet simple, nervous system.

Such a lowly animal as this snail would be beneath consideration, were it not First Life. Limpets weren't food, nor dangerous. In truth, they were little more than rocks. Yet, evolution within The Garden vaulted this humblest of creatures into purest treasure — and that was before Liminal fell under the pincers of The Voracious. Now, even the tiniest individual surpassed in worth a pile of sea urchins bigger than High Split Rock.

"You're my *true* pride," Fearless confessed to the pryzoa, its biolumi-nescent fire dancing about his whiskered face. Claret light sparkled in the Alpha's covetous eyes. "You don't disappoint, you don't disobey. You just grant power, which I accept... and gladly."

He gently set the luminous gastropod back on the tire. And then, with a clawed finger, flicked the ember-like shell.

Clink.

The tiny jolt sent a ripple of distress through the other pryzoa. In succession, they flared brighter and brighter, filling the whole chamber with near incandescent light.

Fearless turned his head from the radiance, lest he injure his eyes. The kholo thicket beneath the levitating tires bloomed. Tendrils shot up, flame-like, in a magic-fueled growth spurt, soon diminishing as the shockwave of pryzoic energy dissipated through the patchwork walls and into Tanglesafe —

The Raft floated above Gwelth; all suppertime contentions forgotten.

Family units snuggled together, mates nuzzling one another. Squirming pups held in their mothers' or older sisters' arms wanted to break free and play, while bachelor males kept close, jealous eyes on the unmated females and each other. Most Lutris were content. Tonight's urchin harvest provided enough for the higher status otters to eat their fill, while the lower ranks were far from satiated. But, for now, bellies — either full or empty — were ignored. All thoughts and eyes were turned skyward to the cloud-obscured moon and what it symbolized.

Cries Often excitedly tugged his sister's arm. "Elihuul, Gloss! Elihuul comes!"

"Yes, brother." Gloss nuzzled him affectionately. "I feel it, too."

As the frenetic energy of the First Life initiated by Fearless dispersed through the kholo and into the tangles and knots of nooree, the surface of the ocean began to roil. Many pups slipped free of their parents to frolic in the choppy sea. Cries Often darted away to join them, splashing among the lapping waves heralding the miraculous event about to unfold.

Under cover of darkness and storm cloud, the water within the communal pool began moving as pryzoic energy inexplicably *pushed it away*, forming a bowl-shaped depression. Kelp and kholo walls holding back the displaced seawater defined the concavity. Though Gwelth remained submerged and unseen, the light of the forty-one pryzoa it held glimmered in the depths — like drowned, organic stars calling the faithful to worship.

And the Raft, as one, began to sing.

"*K-kk-kkk-ki-i-iii-K-kk-kkk-kr-r-rrr-K-kk-kkk-ku-u-uuu*," they sang in mimicry of Deshi-Oad's deafening sonar-clicks. "*K-kk-kkk-ku-u-uuu-K-kk-kkk-kr-r-rrr-K-kk-kkk-ki-i-iii...*"

The harmonic praise of three hundred and forty-four sea otter throats filled the cold air above Tanglesafe. The males' vocalizations hung in registers lower than the females. Pups mimicked their parents' song with squeaky fervor. Of course, the Lutris could only approximate the Divine Impetus as their anatomy proved woefully inadequate. The *true power* of Deshi-Oad's echo-locative voice caused the very sea to boil and could crush bones to meal.

The Lutris' love for their Deity sprang from a primal place, one that inspired instinctual fear in lesser animals. This love — akin to the distress Monoic creatures felt for the seamount and the waterspout, the shark bite and the eagle's talon — resided deep in their souls.

As Elihuul's hymnal reached its full-throated crescendo, the waxing moon emerged from behind a tattered curtain of heavy cloud. Gwelth broke the surface in perfect synchronization with this lunar reveal, and with it an unforgettable sound —

PHHHFFFFFFFFFFFFFTTT!

On contact with the outer atmosphere, the stale oxygen bubble trapped within the Lutris sanctum burst, the force resembling the mighty breath-spray of the Whitest Whale.

Let every drop of The Blue rejoice! Let every Envorah cower! For in that moment Gwelth — and by extension Tanglesafe and all the gathered Lutris — breathed the same air as the mighty lungs of the Divine Impetus. All were now joined intimately, inexorably, together.

Pryzoic light gushed from a hundred gaps in Gwelth's disarticulated structure, lancing the night like glowing urchin quills. The rainbow light illuminated every Lutris face and sparkled in every eye. Even squirming pups and impatient younglings couldn't look away.

A flock of Envoric seabirds, Pijper among them, landed on Gwelth's driftwood and whalebone rooftop. The birds wanted a closer look at the pryzoa, whose luminous mysteries enraptured them even more than the Lutris. Many, if given a chance, would swoop into the chamber, steal the First Life, and devour it on the wing.

But none dared to take the risk. The tips of a hundred spears would mete out swift punishment for such a theft. So, the gathered Vialae contented themselves with watching the exquisite lights and coveting them in secret.

And then, overhead — in joyous release — the rains began to fall.

CHAPTER 15

HOLT SWEET HOLT

J agged lightning slashed the horizon.

For that blinding instant, the towering crags of High Split Rock were thrown into sharp relief against the storm's furious downpour. An ancient conifer crowned the enormous monolith which stood over one hundred and fifty tails high, its eroded foundations perpetually wave lashed. High Split Rock dominated several smaller sea stacks orbiting it like meager servants. The majesty of the Lontra home stood undeniable to all who saw it.

This was *truly* the center of the wider Envoric world — yesterday, today, and every tide not yet realized. Until the very end of time.

Great Ookl be praised...

Home, Sleek thought as an ear-splitting thunderclap shook the sea. *I made it. Finally.*

As bitter storm winds punished The Blue, Sleek dove. He arrowed twenty tails below the surface towards the Holt's entrance hidden amongst a jumbled slew of crevices and boulders. An *Etcax*, a yellow mackerel with five black stripes slashing its body, dangled from the tip of his spear. A tail in length and skewered through the gills, the fish still twitched sporadically.

A fractured granite overhang, reminiscent of a reclining otter, disguised the submerged entrance to the Lontra stronghold. The Holt's most devout members swore Old Father Fathom fashioned the entryway Himself, camouflaging its length in a colorful sea anemone and coral tapestry.

Sleek swam into the snaking tunnel, mindful of the knobby ceiling above, the pitted floor beneath, and the motionless water all around. He sped through pure darkness until a smudge of blue — the Holt's entry pool — appeared up ahead.

It grew at Sleek's approach, casting its feeble light into the barnacled passage. Beneath the roughly circular opening a sunken midden of fish skeletons, crab shells, and scraps from countless other meals lay scattered. Tufts of nooree, cultivated for their specific nutritional or medicinal qualities, grew in the submerged passage, softening its jagged walls.

Sleek surfaced within the low-roofed chamber that served as High Split Rock's main egress-point into The Blue. He inhaled the familiar atmosphere of home.

A wash of pungent odors hit his nose — moldered food scraps, the sharp ammonia-tang of urine; the putrefied-fish stink of excrement, or *spraint*. Behind it all, the unique 'signature' scent of every Holt member intertwined with those ever-present smells. Sleek sniffed and sniffed:

nothing seemed out of the ordinary. Overall, the romp smelled healthy and balanced.

Sleek shook water from his dark-gray coat and began his toilette. Once, he'd been the owner of a pelt of deepest indigo, an honor proclaiming his status as Garden Aware; the nineteen tiny blue patches on his right forelimb the last faded remnant of this once resplendent coloration. Like other Aanandi otters, Sleek had eaten from within Liminal's border since kit-hood and his naturally gray fur adopted the vivid hues of his favorite pryzoic meals — the electric-blue mussels and vivid-violet rock shrimp, as plentiful in The Garden as sand grains on the beach.

Sleek didn't know why he preferred those specific pryzoa. Perhaps the flavor? Or the mouthfeel? Maybe that odd *tickle* against his tongue when he chewed them? Whatever the reason, this regular diet of First Life had shifted his pelt from bland to brilliant.

But that was when Liminal's miracles were easily harvested, and Aanandi luxuriated in eating only what their palates found pleasant. With Paradise stolen, the wondrous rainbow of pelt colors had faded — along with their cherished sapience.

Maybe I'll get some of my proper color back, Sleek thought. *Hope I don't turn red. Yurch. I would not look good in that color!*

Starting with his torso, Sleek's ten nimble fingers fluffed each individual hair, while his tongue licked away dirt and the rare clinging parasites. He wasted no movement, meticulously grooming himself down to his webbed feet and handsome tail.

Lastly, Sleek examined and cleaned the gash on his right hind leg. Though painful, it proved superficial. It would heal fast and leave behind an impressive scar, as a reminder of the consequences of carelessness.

Next time I'll get out unscathed. By Ookl's Ink, I swear it.

With spear and skewered mackerel in paw, Sleek exited the pool chamber through an adjacent fracture corridor. Cave darkness blotted out all light.

Dozens of dens and cavities connected by eroded rock arteries riddled The Holt's interior, from the waterlogged basement to the tree-crowned peak high above. Generations of Lontra paws had worn the rock floors smooth.

Humidity lessened as the corridor inclined away from sea level. Storm winds whistled from a slender wall crack, followed by a flash of lighting and subsequent thunderclap.

Eventually, Sleek arrived at the base of multiple broken stones forming a natural staircase. Beyond lay the warm heart of the Holt community — the Great Hollow.

His wounded leg smarted with each leap up the stairs, but he ignored the pain.

As Sleek neared the top, his whiskers twitched in excitement. He poked his furry head inside the chamber, and smiled —

Beyond, a ureola constellation glowed against a spiderwebbing backdrop of rainbow-hued kholo tendrils clinging to the rocky walls and vaulted ceiling. The burnished bronze and golden eyes of five generations of river otters shone in the Great Hollow — over six hundred animals.

Genders, regardless of rank or age, mixed freely. Alcq-pierced adults groomed one another, sharing gossip and laughter. Others chattered while juggling a trio of small stones, a common pastime among the Lontra that honed forelimb dexterity. Unmated females, tails elegantly decorated in fashionable, seashell-studded kelp wraps, cheered and giggled while eligible males wrestled in boisterous tests of strength. Playful kits mimicked their elder siblings and tussled in their own mock contests.

The *tap-tap-tap* of acuur cracking open shellfish supplied a harmonious, if chaotic, percussion. In the background a whole vocabulary of barks, coos, whines, growls, yelps, and other vocalizations accentuated the numerous hijna-conversations filling the Hollow.

The combined energy of so many 'voices' made for a powerful roar in Sleek's head. He'd heard the telepathic dialog all his life. Even as a blind kit at his mother's teat, The Holt's hijna invited him into its beautiful chorus.

As he surveyed the romp, guilt stung the Saia. *I shouldn't have been so greedy,* he thought. *I was thinking only about myself.*

The state of every Lontra pelt indicted Sleek for his selfishness. What had been a panoply of colors — from warm auburns and ambers through various shades of blue and indigo, down to a mosaic of yellows and even kelp-green — had faded to Monoic dullness from lack of pryzoic essence. True, unique white patterns blotched the throat of each animal, distinguishing one Lontra from another. But against coats of common brown, rust, charcoal, and black, it only emphasized the loss of their collective splendor.

Guilt soon fermented to anger. *I should've brought back enough pryzoa for the entire Holt, no matter the law! Who'd dare denounce me then? The law can drown!*

Even the two pryzoa he'd brought out of the Garden, meager as they were, held enough power to burnish the bronze-within-bronze eyes of many in the romp. Their Kleaa would be bolstered by the tiniest nibble. During Sleek's carefree youth, Liminal had given freely, and all Lontra were Aanandi. Now, less than a quarter of The Holt's population claimed that rarified status, most belonging to the oldest generations. The romp's communal sapience dwindled with each passing tide, like fresh water evaporating in a shallow pool.

Sleek considered the grim possibility that, some dark day, no further Lontra Aanandi would ever exist. The prospect struck him like a cold wave.

Could this end? Someday... maybe even in my lifetime... could it all be gone?

As the Saia watched his beloved romp, he felt, like a pearl forming around a speck of grit, a resolution solidifying in his soul. Sleek vowed he would *never* let that dark day arrive, no matter the cost. He would do whatever it took to keep his Holt speaking...and singing.

All bitter thoughts dispersed. *It feels wonderful to be back,* he thought. *Well, here goes...*

Sleek stood *uhlee* — his privilege as a Beta to walk upright on two legs and therefore dominate — and crossed over the rocky threshold. He strode into the chamber, which acted as both dining hall and communal den. Under his feet crunched a carpet of dried grasses, pine needles, and fronds of seaweed mixed with the nibbled bones and broken shells of past meals.

Hardy mosses softened the ancient stones, while a mosaic of splotchy lichens colored the long, thin cleft hewing the vaulted ceiling. This crack formed the bottom of the great, tapering gash that gave High Split Rock its name.

As Sleek maneuvered past cliques of otters towards the central food mound, where dexterous paws would fillet, portion, and distribute his mackerel, shocked silence followed in his wake. Many otters dropped *ootith* as he passed — the submissive, four-legged stance used to show respect to those of higher rank — and welcomed him with a customary whisker-tug, or a polite "*nookeelee*" welcoming. Others just gawked.

Sleek replied to the greetings, emphasizing one syllable over another of his nookeelee based on the rank of the otter he addressed. He caught the words "pryzoa," "Liminal," "trespass," and "aijeer" sparking through the blur of hijna-chatter.

None dared question him directly. Rank-etiquette prohibited such challenges.

Sleek passed a clutch of kits eagerly trying to pry open a clam with an oversized acuur. Nearby, a group of boisterous Epsilon juveniles encircled a pair of blue-shelled crabs locked in combat. They barked and hijna-cheered as the battling crustaceans tumbled on the stony floor. From the back of the group, several kits, too young for either name or rank, jockeyed for a better view of the action. Engrossed in the fun, none acknowledged the limping Beta.

Scattered among the bustling and noisy romp lounged the *Oyyan*, the 'honored injured,' those surviving Lontra belonging to the generation of Sleek's parents and grandparents. These elders, now whisker-thin and graying around the muzzle, were veterans of That Scathing Tide, the Cu-ursuurq. The healed wounds marring their pelts were the mementos of that bloody campaign, and they wore those scars with pride. Even those with paws or limbs lost in battle with The Voracious did not bemoan their misfortune.

Here, an eye was gouged out; there, an ear shorn off; and many a once-beautiful tail was now reduced to a misshapen stump. Yet, their hijnas still rang with joy in the Hollow, their laughter still infectious — their wisdom still necessary and prized.

Sleek proceeded to the food mound. A bounty of delicious keerth, some bluish-white and others mottled brown, made up the bulk of the communal banquet. A variety of meaty fish rounded out the collection. Though it held more food than the romp could eat tonight, whatever wasn't consumed would be had for breakfast. Nothing ever went to waste, and the pervasive kelp flies that swarmed the wrack zone — and befouled their locally caught 'shallows-meat' — were never present. High Split Rock existed too far from The Still for those pests to reach.

Cleaner, an Oyyan Gamma with a missing hind-paw and pelt the color of dried kelp, presided over the food mound. His team — two assistant cleaners and three apprentices — worked at gutting, scaling, and filleting the catch with their sea-glass, or shark-tooth acuurs. The paws, arms, and bellies of the six otters glittered with shed fish scales. Discarded innards, sliced off fins, and cut out bones piled nearby.

No one, except the Den Sire and the Holt's most senior members, remembered Cleaner's weaning-day name. Sleek never knew; to him, the old Lontra had always just been Cleaner. He had presided over the food mound since before Sleek's birth. Someday, when he died and joined the ancestors swimming Oussia's radiant waters, one of Cleaner's five assistants would ascend in rank and claim his name-title.

Cleaner demonstrated proper scaling technique to his youngest apprentice, a sub-adult named Spinner wearing the purple ureola of a Loyc-Epsilon. Sleek paused to watch the skilled paws of the master work on a fat perch, and to listen as he schooled the novice.

"The trick, Spinner, is to scrape *against* the scales, starting from the base of the tail towards the head," Cleaner instructed. "Against. And gently." His acuur, a razor-sharp flake of lime-green sea glass, rasped across the body of the gutted perch in his grip. "Short, quick scrapes work best. Not too deep, mind you, or you'll gouge the flesh. Now, you try." He tossed the scaled fish to one of his assistants, who snatched it from midair and began to fillet it.

Spinner nodded. "Yes, Cleaner." He plucked a small halibut from the pile. Muzzle wrinkled in concentration, he set about applying what he'd just learned and carefully scraped, scraped, scraped the scales away —

Sleek took a deep breath and stepped up to the mound. "Nookeelee, Cleaner," he said with a whisker tug, offering the mackerel dangling from his spear. "Another morsel for the pile. It's not keerth, but still...."

The acuurs of Cleaner and his crew froze. Five pairs of bronze eyes, and one gold, fastened on Sleek in stunned surprise. The Beta waited, an anxious flutter in his gut.

Finally, the old Gamma cleared his throat. "Nookeelee, Sleek," he replied, returning the whisker-tug. Spinner and the rest of the crew followed his lead. With a sharp yank, he pulled the mackerel from Sleek's lance. "Oh, that's a good-looking Etcax. Healthy and well-muscled. Maybe even some roe if we're lucky."

"Did you expect anything less?" Sleek asked, now relaxing a bit.

Cleaner passed the mackerel to Spinner, who set aside the partially scaled halibut. "I've too much work to entertain such questions." Hijna ripe with disapproval, he added, "Everyone knows you're a fine hunter of fish. No need to hunt for compliments, too."

Rusty-haired Spinner pointed at Sleek's wound. "What happened to your leg?" In stark contrast to Cleaner, the young apprentice quivered before the Saia, awestruck by him.

For an instant, Sleek considered a bold admission of his deed. After all, he glowed with fresh enhancement, plain for all to see and smell. But he decided against it. Allowing the wrongdoing to go unacknowledged might delay the inevitable punishment.

Sleek had his falsehood rehearsed and ready. "Would you believe it?" he chuckled. "I was minding my own business and was just about to take the first bite of a juicy silverside I caught, when out of nowhere a *gribn* swooped in and grabbed it. Clean off my spear! When I chased after it, I gouged my leg on a barnacle. My lucky night, right?"

"A barnacle..." Spinner blinked, confused at the notion, "...cut you?"

"Oh, yes. A sharp one," Sleek added with a firm nod and cough. "Quite jagged."

Cleaner's nose twitched, as if it smelled something sour. "Intriguing. You were lucky to escape with your life. I'm sure I don't need to tell you how deadly barnacles can..."

"Where's my father?" Sleek interrupted. "I don't see him in the Hollow."

Cleaner's eyes narrowed. He scratched the fur under his alcq. "Den Sire dined earlier and left. I think he's omen-diving with Uuvaloo. But I couldn't say for sure."

Sleek plucked a juicy squid from the food mound and nibbled on a tentacle. *Not as tasty as the pryzoa. Not even close,* he thought. "Have either of you seen my mother?"

Spinner pointed to the back of the Great Hollow. "Suckling Mother's feeding Chaser in the sick den, Great Ookl protect her." Both Cleaner and the young Epsilon reverently nibbled the tips of their tails at Spinner's invocation of Old Father Fathom's true Name.

Cleaner's bristly whiskers drooped. "He's having difficulty feeding himself now. Your mother risks her life tending him. What if his ailment is passed to her?"

"And what if it isn't?" Sleek's hijna held the slightest hint of rebuke. He took another bite of squid. "If you were in the sick den, you'd be glad of her nursing." Cleaner harrumphed, annoyed with the veiled reprimand. "I was just trying to make a point about The Holt's safety. Apparently the wrong one."

"Apparently." Sleek grabbed another squid from the mound of shallows-meat, slung the ynth over his shoulder, and strode uhlee through the crowd of staring, murmuring Lontra.

"He thinks he can scold me?" Cleaner's lip curled in anger. "After what he did?"

"He's Beta," Spinner reminded his flustered mentor. "And the bravest uju in the Holt."

Cleaner rolled his golden eyes. "Great Ookl save us from such youthful foolishness." He took a deep, calming breath, and pointed to the mackerel in Spinner's paws. "Now, let me see you clean that fish. Properly."

CHAPTER 16

SCHEMING AMONG FRIENDS

At the center of the Hollow, centuries of falling water had carved a basin into the rock. This natural pool served as the Holt's reservoir of drinking water. Thanks to the storm, raindrops now fell in a steady dribble from the ceiling cleft. The surface of the pool splashed and rippled. Dozens of Lontra competed for space at the water's edge to drink and wash.

Three handsome young males — Swims Past, Nimble, and Watches — lounged on a rock shelf above the pool and watched the goings-on below. Still wet from a long night of hunting, each wore the distinctive amber ureola of a Dyah-Delta, and a turritella shell alcq. A trio of whalebone spears, each tip serrated differently to match the owner's personality, leaned on a nearby rock.

Milk-brothers to Sleek, they'd all shared the royal teats of Suckling Mother and partook of her carryover essence — that cherished *Honeaa* — while still womb-blind kits. Though Sleek outranked them by virtue of his parentage, the four males regarded themselves as equals.

"Hey, spraint-heads," Sleek called as he approached.

The three Dyah leapt to their feet as if they'd all been stung by a jellyfish.

"Great Ookl!" gasped storm-gray Watches. "Sleek...you...you didn't."

Sleek set his ynth beside theirs. "Oh, yes. I did."

Russet-hued Nimble almost choked. "Are you crazy, you stupid *ghezzi-ghez?*"

"Probably." Sleek laid his keerth aside, filled his cupped paws with cold, refreshing rainwater, and drank.

Ebony-coated Swims Past chattered his teeth, the closest thing to a true laugh a Lontra could muster without hijna. "Crazy is right. And braver than any of us. Sleek, you're the *uju!*"

Sleek retrieved his squid and took a bite, smug and happy to bask in the praise of his three best friends.

"How fares The Garden?" Nimble asked. "Did you run into Chaac'Xib?"

Watches hissed in dismay, his ears folding back in alarm. "Don't speak its name, spraint-head! It might hear you. It's bad luck."

Swims Past rolled his eyes. "That's superstitious nonsense, and you know it." He looked back at Sleek. "Tell us everything, oyster-breath."

Sleek finished the keerth in two more bites. "Gather 'round, kits."

His milk-brothers formed a semi-circle around Sleek, who wove the story of his extraordinary adventure with all the hyperbole he could muster. The three Dyah listened in rapt attention, laughing, and gasping as the tale unfolded. Of course, Sleek omitted the most damning parts. No one, not even his closest friends, could know of the living pryzoa brought to the surface and hidden in The Gnaarl.

"What a story," Nimble exclaimed. "You're lucky you just ate one pryzoa. More than that, and the scithma-snaag'll bite you. Scramble your brains. More than they already are."

"What am I? A kit?" Sleek asked. "I'm not stupid." And then thought: *Yurch, I am not looking forward to my dreams tonight. I'm going to get bit.*

"Stupid? We won't call you that... to your face," Swims Past chided. "The next time you plan on sneaking into Liminal, at least let us know you're going. That way, we can divvy up your stuff when The Voracious eats you."

"Ookl's Ink!" Watches exclaimed. "What a terrible thing to say!"

"Stop being such an old *uja*, Watches," Swims Past retorted, using the feminine pronoun to describe his friend. "Sleek knows I'm joking. Besides, what he did was suicidal. Next time, if there *is* a next time, he might not escape with only a gashed leg."

Sleek snorted. "Next time, you all should come with me."

"Den Sire's going to chew your ears to ribbons for this," Nimble warned.

"Yes, I know," Sleek's whiskers drooped at the reminder of his impending chastisement. "But the prize is worth the pain." His whiskers snapped back up. "When was the last tide any Lontra had the stones to do what I did?"

"Careful, brothers," Nimble warned, "or you might get knocked down by our Saia's enormous head."

"Sleek's earned his bragging rights," Swims Past shot back.

Nimble grumbled but didn't deny the declaration. "While you were off pulling your selfish little stunt, Sleek, we were out hunting. We could've used your help tonight. Several fish got away from us, including a nice, fat *nyoota*."

Watches nudged his companion. "No thanks to you, not-so-Nimble. I've seen clams swim faster than you."

"Go twist your whiskers!" Nimble snapped, in no mood for jokes. A still healing wound across his tail served as a painful reminder of territorial tensions with the Lutris, and the sharp baleen spears wielded by their graehls. The damaged tail slowed Nimble during the hunt. He resented the injury, and the Lutris who inflicted it even more. "I'm getting my speed back," he muttered, "in case you haven't noticed."

"Trust me, we haven't," Swims Past sniped.

Nimble growled a profanity and self-consciously tucked his tail between his legs.

"Swims Past!" a strong female hijna called out. "I need you!"

Wincing, Swims Past muttered, "Yurch."

The four friends turned in unison to see Swims Past's tawny mate, Finest, and her three chocolate-brown graehl-sisters — Groomer, Nestled, and Curious — approaching. Amber ureolas glowed about their wrists. Unadorned tails, along with turritella-shell alcqs, underscored their hunter status. Each uja gripped a sharpened, calcified baleen ynth in her paw.

Finest and her graehl were an accomplished hunting unit, every bit a match for Sleek and his milk-brothers. Rather than fostering resentment, this truth stoked a burning competitiveness within the males, salted with grudging admiration. The rivalry honed all their predatory skills.

"Oh, *kalaayaa.*" Swims Past's joviality shriveled. His hijna-tone shaded that endearment — meaning 'beloved' and 'for you I'll submit' — decidedly to the latter. "What's the problem?"

Finest offered her spear to Groomer and marched towards him upright, her beautiful face as cold as hoarfrost. The other females hung back, raking the males with challenging looks. Swims Past wisely dropped ootith, ears folding back docilely.

"Don't you kalaayaa me," Finest snapped. Sandy blond fur and a trim, well-muscled tail made her exceptionally beautiful by Lontra standards. She clutched to one of her four teats a three-week old kit, blind and soft. It squirmed and yipped in search of a meal.

"Did I do something wro..." Swims Past began, but Finest cut him off.

"Sleeeeek! You idiot," she hissed, glaring at the Beta with eyes narrowed to furious bronze slits. "You snuck into the Garden...without telling the rest of us? How could you?"

Sleek pulled himself up a little taller. "It was a spur-of-the moment thing. I knew if I said anything, you might've tried to stop me."

"Not us. Your parents, maybe," Finest countered. "We would've insisted on coming with you." Her graehl-sisters all nodded in agreement.

"And that's *exactly* what I didn't want."

"Oh? You think you're the only one who can snatch Liminal's gifts now?"

Sleek frowned. "That's not it at all. I had to know if it could be done first. And if not, then I'd be the only one to die." He swung his gaze around the group, taking in all their faces, and mustering his most endearing smile. "You're my friends. I couldn't risk your lives."

Even as he spoke the words, Sleek berated himself for his dishonesty. *You didn't tell anyone because you wanted all the glory for yourself.*

Finest shook her head, a smile curling her elegant mouth. "Ookl as my witness, you've always been one for foolish risk-taking, Sleek. But... *yurch!* I must tip my tail to you." She shoved the mewling kit into Swims Past's arms. It wiggled impatiently. "Here. Take your son. I'm going hunting with my girls."

Swims Past had loved Finest since kit-hood, and they'd mated soon after both achieved Dyah-Delta rank — but the responsibilities of matrimony and fatherhood were more than he'd bargained for. He still hadn't quite reconciled himself to mated life.

"But, Finest, my darling..." Swims Past lowered his hijna so just his mate could hear, "....my rainbow, my dawn coral, my sweetest sea foam, I was looking forward to spending some time tonight with my milk-brothers. Besides, the storm is still blowing fierce. Maybe you can stay in the den and go hunting tomorrow?"

Finest's crisp answer left no room for debate. "Nope. Sorry. Not going to happen." She pinched the short hairs of Swims Past's chin to drive her point home. "I've been cooped up tending our kit for too many tides. Now it's *my* time to cast the Hunters Eye. End of story."

Other Lontra at the drinking pool were beginning to take notice. Some hid snickers behind raised paws, while others smirked or pointed in jest. Finest's temper, well known among the romp, could oftentimes be fiery. Sleek almost felt sorry for his friend. Almost.

Swims Past nodded, his ears folded back tight against his head. "Yes, of course, kalaayaa. Whatever you wish. Be safe."

Finest gave her mate an affectionate nose-nibble. "I'll be late, so don't wait up."

She stepped back. Groomer tossed the spear back to Finest, which she deftly caught with one paw. The four females then turned and left The Hollow on two legs, walking tall and proud.

Watches flashed a toothy grin. "Well, that was enlightening." He put his paws to his cheeks in a mocking gesture. 'Oh, my rainbow, my dawn flower, my sweetest sea foam.' You're such a pathetic *nataaq*."

The profanity, comparing the genitals of Swims Past to a dead jellyfish or pulpy bit of chewed matter, made Nimble chortle. "You can say that again. I wonder who wears the ureola in your den?" Everyone knew the answer.

Swims Past sighed, put the kit to his chest, and stroked it. It clung to the loose fur around his neck and nuzzled. "She's right, you know," he admitted. "She's been stuck watching Junior. Some hunting time in The Blue with her graehl will do her good."

Watches gnawed a tentacle off a squid, glowered at the unappetizing remainder, and tossed it away. His whiskers drooped. "Ookl's Ink. I'm *sick* of keerth and clams every night."

"Why can't you be happy with what you have?" Nimble scolded. "You're always wanting more. It's selfish. *You're* selfish."

"Am not!" Watches snapped, bristling. "Selfish? Me? You don't know what you're talking about!"

"Touchy, touchy," Sleek interjected between mouthfuls of keerth. "You need to lighten up, Watches. Nimble's just pointing out that you should be a little less... I don't know. Picky?"

Watches' stiff posture loosened as he sighed. "They're so plentiful we don't try for anything else. I want something hard-fought and fierce. It'll taste all the better for it. Like aorxa." He nodded sharply. "Yes, yes, aorxa for sure. Ten tails long and full of teeth."

Swims Past frowned and shook his head. "Moving on to another, more sensible topic: what are we going to do about Suckling Mother's weaning-day?" He patted his fussy kit on the back. It burped and kept squirming. "It's fast approaching."

Watches shrugged. "I don't know. We could make her something out of kholo. A basket, maybe? Or bribe Cixtindi with black mussels to weave her a new neck ureola?"

"A basket's boring," Sleek said. "And she already has the loveliest ureola in all The Blue. It's even better than Father's."

"We could catch her a crab?" Swims Past suggested. "Or maybe a big, juicy lobster?"

Watches nodded enthusiastically. "Hey, yeah. We could rig nooree traps. Use dinner scraps for bait. I've seen some good-sized lobsters in our territory lately."

"I like that," Nimble agreed. "Suckling Mother loves lobster."

Sleek swallowed the last of his squid, spat out the tiny beak, and then washed his paws in the communal water pool. "I know something she loves even more."

"What's that?" Watches wondered.

A mischievous smile lit Sleek's handsome face. "*Tender nacre*. I say we sneak into Abundance and fill up Den Sire's majl with it. Bring back enough for the *entire* Holt."

The three Deltas knew Sleek well enough to tell he wasn't joking. With whiskers twitching and eyes full of worry, they glanced at each other and then at their friend.

"What?" Sleek met their troubled gazes. "Have I got something on my face?"

"I know you haven't forgotten, Sleek, so I'll just give this reminder," Watches said. "Abundance is off limits. By treaty."

Sleek shrugged. "So?"

Nimble shook his head, as if trying to dislodge a pebble from his ear. "*So? Kex*-me, Sleek. You're already in deep trouble. Do you want to break yet another law?"

"I didn't break the law *entering* Liminal." Sleek's chest tightened at his duplicity.

"Technically, no." Nimble shot back, hijna crackling with frustration. "But you know how the Den Sire feels about even trying. The example it sets of those *few* who return verses those *many* who don't. It makes others want to attempt it."

"And possibly get maimed," Swims Past added.

Watches nodded. "Or even die."

"Den Sire plucked his whiskers to ratify the Treaty of Abundance with the Lutris," Nimble said. "If he hadn't, the killing would've continued until all of us, Lontra and Lutris alike, were dead trying to control it. Now, neither tribe owns Abundance's nacre. And *none* may enter. It's better that way."

Sleek shrugged again. "We weren't even in our first graehls then. We didn't know spears from uboo quills. The treaty shouldn't apply to us. It's a new generation. Tides have changed."

Watches nibbled the tip of his tail in worry. "How can you say that? Abundance is aijeer. If we're caught it means banishment. Maybe death. Ookl's Ink, maybe even war."

Sleek snorted. "Don't get ahead of yourself, bishq-for-brains. That's only *if* we get caught...which we won't. If we're successful, who knows? Maybe you'll get a bump in rank."

Nimble wasn't convinced. "That's a Diuun Dunn-sized maybe."

But Swims Past understood Sleek's devious plain. Tantalizing possibilities began to crystallize in his mind. His kit started to hiccup, and as he bounced it on his shoulder, he pondered the amber ureola around his wrist, fantasizing about how proud Finest would be if he wore a Gamma's green. The rank upgrade might win him more power within his family unit.

"Just think about it, brothers." Swims Past lowered his hijna so those outside their circle would not overhear. "Sneaking into Abundance under the stunted noses of the Lutris? Getting out with a majl bursting with nacre? The Holt would be talking about it forever." He paused, then added, "By Ookl, we'd be heroes."

"*Ptahhf!*" Watches huffed the obscenity. "Den Sire will *never* let us use it his majl. He and Cixtindi spent how many tides weaving it? A hundred? More? If he catches us taking it, we'll get our ears bit clean off and demoted to Nihl. It's the red ureola of shame for sure!"

"He won't catch us. I'll make sure of it." Sleek's hijna echoed with confidence.

"You'd better, or you won't have any ears left at all," Watches replied. "Or a tail."

"Stop." Sleek held up a steady paw. "It's just an idea, for Ookl's sake." He retrieved his ynth and gave his cohorts a parting whisker-tug. "No need to decide tonight. Just think on it."

Sleek left his friends and skirted the noisy throngs of chattering Lontra, ignoring their pointed comments as he headed towards the far wall of the Hollow. There, a feathery thicket of low-hanging kholo draped the stone, upon which were etched many sacred *Ahmijna*, or 'The Enduring Voice.' These petroglyphs, painstakingly scratched into the granite, chronicled the Lontra's history; their mythic origins in the All-Light Ocean; the arrival of the river otters to High Split Rock; the dark days of the Ulurii genocide; and, most recent, The Cruel Dweller's occupation of Liminal, and the bloodstained failure of the Cuursuurq to dislodge it.

On the floor beside the kholo-fronds rested the ancient Lineage Stone. A misshapen lump of rock also scrawled with Ahmijna-glyphs, it listed the names of every Lontra that lived, or died, in High Split Rock. Thousands of tiny name-etchings — variants of circle, dots-and-dashes, intersecting lines, and simple shapes — covered the hallowed boulder. With the steady arrival of new generations there would soon be no space left to record their names. When the day came, a new Lineage Stone would be inaugurated.

Beyond the Lineage Stone, clinging to the granite wall among the rain-bow-hued tangles of dangling kholo, the boneless personage who Sleek sought labored. With a mischievous smile, the Beta stalked his unwitting friend, and lunged —

CHAPTER 17

CIXTINDI'S WARNING

"G ot'cha!" Sleek cried while tickling the Ulura's sensitive nerve plexus at the base of his posterior siphon.

"Aaa-h-h!" Cixtindi hijna-shrieked as his boneless body seemed to unravel.

A fright-mosaic of yellow splotches and clusters of finger-like protuberances, an inheritance of his cephalopod camouflage trait, erupted across his normally smooth skin. Reflexive spasms rippled down his six tentacles. His acuur — a razor-sharp crescent of porcelain, perfect for slicing kholo —

slipped from his twenty boneless fingers and skittered across the floor. He looked like a hooked fish flopping about on the stones.

"Cixtindi, you old sea slug!" Sleek greeted, teeth chattering as he laughed. "For someone who can look ahead and behind simultaneously, you sure are easy to sneak up on."

"Don't -gloopf- do that!" the Ulura burped. From atop his snail-like head, a pair of rubbery eyestalks extended towards Sleek. "You nearly made me ink myself!" Two orbs, split with W-shaped irises, regarded the grinning Beta with annoyance. His vision, extending into realms of light hidden even to the Lontra, saw on Sleek the invisible fur pattern unique to each member of the romp.

"Now that's an unpleasant thought," Sleek replied. "Uuurgh."

Cixtindi's fright pattern faded, his skin coloration reverting to its normal paleness. Then, in a flash, crimson flowed like spilt blood from his head to the tips of his eight appendages. "You've been to the Garden," he accused. "Against your -gloopf- father's express command!"

"Please, Cix. I've had all the scolding I can take." Sleek made no effort to hide his deed. "Yes, I entered the Garden. And look," he threw his arms wide, "I got out alive! How about a 'Congratulations, Sleek, on your amazing accomplishment,' or 'Great Ookl, I'm so glad Vile Chaac'Xib didn't kill you!' I took a risk, and it paid off."

"Are you done with your childish tirade?"

The octo-snail's mild reply took Sleek by surprise. "Yes. I suppose I am."

"Good. And don't ever speak 'its' true name. Disgusting filth. It has other monikers. Use those instead. They're safer." Yellow and orange blotches bloomed on the octo-snail's flesh for an instant, then faded. "You were foolish going into Liminal Gheelindreeliah. Brave, but foolish. I'm not sure -gloopf- whether to be proud or horrified. A bit of both, I think."

Sleek let out a sigh and relaxed. He climbed atop the lineage rock and made himself comfortable, though the elation and pride in his achievement was once again souring into glum anxiety. "Father will be furious, won't he?"

"Of that you can be certain," replied Cixtindi. "I hope you're prepared."

Sleek didn't respond; instead, he changed the subject. "Seriously, Cix...you're too easy to sneak up on. If I were Majah or Xaad, you'd be my supper right now."

"I'm focused on my appointed task, thank you very much," the respected Ulura countered. His rubbery limbs unraveled as he squirmed towards the fallen acuur. "Little better than Monoah, those two. Ruled by appetite. One can barely speak and the other -*gloopf*- has nothing worth saying." A slow inhale, more akin to a watery snort than an actual breath, marred the octo-snail's speech.

"True, but you'd still be in my belly."

"Maybe." Cixtindi retrieved his porcelain tool and returned to the kholo curtain. Sleek noticed several freshly woven amber wristlets draped around one of the octo-snail's slender tentacles. "Those must be for the *Jaarjoora*," Sleek said, now aware of his own unadorned wrist. Ten seasons ago, he'd received his first ureola — woven by one of Cixtindi's ancient, and now long dead, ancestors — on his own Naming Day.

Over the intervening years Sleek had owned, and through accident or intent, lost several prized wristlets. This embarrassing facet of his reputation loomed large within the Holt.

One of many such blemishes.

"Yes. Nine youngsters are to have their coming-of-age ceremony very soon," Cixtindi replied. "Nine ureola to weave and less than twenty tides to do it. I've completed only three so far. I waited like a -*gloopf*- fool until the very last tide to start and now I'm pressed. Luckily, their parents will supply their alcqs. One less thing for me to bother with." His boneless fingers sliced away strands of gossamer kholo with the skill and patience of a fiddler-crab surgeon. "I've been experimenting with a variety of -*gloopf*-

new knot patterns, most of which I'm satisfied with. They must be tied just right. They must last, after all."

The tying and untying of knots fascinated the octo-snail. They appealed to that part of his tri-lobed mind ruled by logic. In sharp contrast, his spawn-brother Uuvaloo found solace in writing pious sand prayers to Great Ookl.

As far as anyone knew, Uuvaloo still awaited an answer.

"Well, your knots are always improving, Cix. They're beautiful."

"Thank you, Sleek. From practice comes perfection," the octo-snail intoned. "From the simple, the -gloopf- complex. From the single, the numerous. From the tiny, the vast..."

"Okay, okay," Sleek moaned. "I get it."

"On a side note, Den Sire wants all this season's weanlings' names etched onto the Lineage Stone before the next Glow. He was most insistent. Can you -gloopf- help me? You do make wonderful etchings, for someone with so few fingers."

"Thanks. I think."

"This cohort...Quick Tail has made fine choices. Strong names befitting of future graehl hunters." Cixtindi's eyestalks darkened to a contemplative shade of blue as his forty boneless fingers wiggled and squirmed, knotting the new ureola. "I should know," he added, hijna thickened with melancholy. "Knots and names -gloopf- are my specialty, after all."

Once, all Envorah knew the Ulurii tribe as *Those Who Name*. Now, few outside the Holt even remembered that octo-snails still lived. The old title had lost its meaning. Nature pronounced dire judgment upon the boneless, aquatic sages for their crime of existence.

And the verdict — extinction by predation.

With Cixtindi and Uuvaloo's passing, there would be no further *uraacheth*, or 'naming-hunts,' and with it the diminishment of the common Envoric vocabulary. Gone were the feverish spawning-orgies and new generations of squirtlings they begat. And soon a final ending to the sand-prayers and ink poems for Old Father Fathom that dissipated in the ocean currents.

All those wonders would be gone. The Blue would be forever diminished with their loss.

For a few awkward moments, neither friend spoke. Sleek considered leaving Cixtindi to his despair. But he opted to stay, hoping a change in subject would lighten his friend's mood.

"Has Uuvaloo determined when The Glow is supposed to arrive?"

Burnt-orange waves rippled across Cixtindi's skin. *Ah, that's cheered the old slug up,* Sleek thought. *Cixtindi always enjoys complaining about his spawn-brother.*

"Hrmmph. You would think our learned *tharuuspex* would have *-gloopf-* figured it out by now. Ookl's Ink, but he thinks he's so high and mighty!"

Sleek scratched behind his ear. "What Uuvaloo's attempting isn't easy, Cix. 'Simpler to sift all the salt from The Blue,' is how Father described it."

"With the number of pryzoa we possess, it should be *easier*." The octo-snail's skin flushed pink. "Clearly, it isn't for him," he added, hijna sharp with disdain. He finished knitting another ureola, then slipped it on the same tentacle beside the others. "Complete incompetence."

The entire Holt knew the Ulurii siblings were not friends. Because neither appreciated the lifestyle of the other, much friction resulted. Cixtindi believed Uuvaloo to be a zealot, while Uuvaloo considered his brother just a whisker's span shy of being an infidel.

"My pious spawn-sibling prays and *-gloopf-* spills his ink in supplication, yet Old Father Fathom remains silent on the subject of Liminal, The Glow, or Skynthuuhrnymlex... Well, on every subject of consequence, come to think of it."

"It's believed He's 'sleeping'," Sleek replied. "That seems to be all He ever does."

"Yes," Cixtindi responded with a wet snort. "For a million tides now. Convenient." The octo-snail cut another strand of iridescent kholo off the parent-growth. "You'll need a new ureola. Again. This will be the fourth I've made you."

Sleek shrugged at the plain truth. "And I appreciate it, Cix."

"Oh, do you?" Cixtindi sighed, the rubbery flesh around his eyes oscillating with many colors as he lost patience with the princeling. "Breaking rules for personal gain aren't just selfish, Sleek," he chided. "It's unbecoming of a Saia and future leader. It fosters division instead of unity. Something we -*gloopf*- Aanandi cannot afford."

The octo-snail regretted the harsh tone, but it needed to be said. Sleek was his friend. More importantly, the young Beta would be Den Sire someday. And when the day came, his neck needed to be comfortable with the weighty ureola of kingship. That comfort came with experience, and the wisdom to do the right thing by making mistakes — sometimes painful ones — and *learning* from those accumulated scars.

To Cixtindi, that last part — the learning from scars — always eluded Sleek.

"I'm pleased you made it into, and out of, The Garden Effulgent alive. Your eyes are burnished with fresh clarity. I rejoice in your enhancement. I do. But I fear this success -*gloopf*- has further emboldened you to risk your life again in the future. You are your father's only heir. Never forget that. If you should die before..."

Sleek snorted. "Then I'll be dead, and I won't care one way or the other. My time will come when it comes. Why worry about it? I plan on living life to its fullest, Cix." *And if that means breaking every law to claim true love, then so be it,* he thought as images of Gloss, nibbling his nose in thanks for the gifted pryzoa, floated across his mind's eye.

"It's easy to be flippant about loss when you've never experienced *real* loss. It's a pain unlike any other. It hollows out your Aanandi-shade.

Consider all you have to lose — all the gifts and privileges and -*gloopf*-
responsibilities, both now and into the future — when you next decide
to break the rules." The octo-snail's eyestalks swiveled back to the kholo.
"Now, if you'll excuse me, I've a good deal of knotting to do. Nookeelee."

Sleek's whiskers drooped at the tart dismissal. "Good night, Cix." He
slung his lance over a shoulder and left the Ulura alone with his tricky knots
and troubled notions.

CHAPTER 18

PIJPER'S PLEA

"**I**s it true forty-two gathered pryzoa can alter their surroundings?" Fearless asked. "To make it more like The Garden?"

Perched on a driftwood spar jutting from a high wall in Gwelth's pryzoa chamber, Pijper gazed at the Lutris Alpha reclining on a throne mound of torn rags, shredded rope, and chunks of foam rubber. Sharp Tooth, the sole Beta in attendance, crouched beside the sparkling kholo-curtained entrance, his own gaze shifting between the feathered envoy and his troubled Doyen.

The pelican nodded his long, narrow head. "Yes. It seems to be a critical threshold. Den Sire's pryzoa pool holds that number, and it's a strange and wonderful place, hrmmm."

Fearless picked the last morsels of roe clinging to the inner shell of his fourth urchin and licked them from his webbed fingers. "Is it also true that forty-two pryzoa allows one to 'see' further into the future? Both along the broad and narrow current?" Part of him feared the answer.

"The Den Sire has made claims about things that..." Pijper fell silent, reluctant to divulge Lontra secrets the sea otters might exploit.

Fearless tossed the empty urchin shell clattering to the floor, then stood upright, whiskers stiff with impatience. "Things that *what*? Tell me, bird!" The Doyen craved any advantage he could gain over his perennial enemies.

The icy-blue diplomatic ureola on his ankle, duty bound Pijper to do whatever he could to achieve a lasting peace. Needless conflict was anathema to him. *Perhaps if Fearless knows the scope of the Den Sire's predictive powers he'll be less keen to engage in bloodshed,* he thought.

"So be it," the pelican sighed. "The Den Sire has observed things in the Meta-Oorum, both with and without the use of his *ceptual* lenses, that came to pass in or near your own territory. Events you *did not* see, Doyen."

Sharp Tooth growled. "Impossible."

Addressing the hostile Saia, Pijper raised his left wing and spread the primary feathers like fingers as he counted: "The coming of the poisonous red water last winter. Did your Doyen 'see' that? No. Eleven Lutris sickened and perished before it dissipated. The beached whale discovered in your territory long after it died, hrmmm? The one where you now harvest your spears. Or the uboorl-plague that destroyed the yellow nooree forest between your territory and Diuun Dunn's rookery? There are other examples."

"Quick Tail claims he 'saw' all those things before they happened?" Sharp Tooth chopped the air with his paw. "He's lying. It can't be."

"Of course, it can!" Fearless snapped, golden eyes flaring. The sharp bitterness in his hijna caused the Beta to lower his head. "Don't you see? He has forty-two pryzoa!"

Pijper offered one final, devastating revelation to Fearless. "Your son Grabber's disappearance. Quick Tail 'saw' that before it happened as well."

Sharp Tooth's notched ears flattened. "Are you saying the Den Sire knows what became of our Doyen's second born?"

"No," Pijper clarified, sensing the growing emotional pain in the chamber, and wishing he'd had no part in bringing it about. "Just that Grabber would go missing. Not all the 'how's' or 'whys' — but enough to know it would happen. I'm sorry, Doyen."

Pijper watched as this last truth, finally revealed, cracked Fearless open like a clamshell. "...my son." A moan of loss crept up his throat as he imagined all the agonies Grabber must have suffered — agonies his mortal enemy knew and refused to share. This insult hurt most of all. "Damn you, Quick Tail...why didn't you tell me?"

Pijper tilted his head and cocked a bronze eye at the Alpha. "Would you have listened, Fearless? Sadly, I think you would have cried deception, hrmmm?"

The Doyen didn't answer. He dropped to all fours, now looking very old and tired, and lay back upon his throne-mound. He picked another uboo from the shrinking pile beside him and split it with his Great White shark-tooth acuur.

After several heartbeats of silence, Pijper dared to speak. "You must talk to the Den Sire, Fearless. I beg you. Negotiation is the best path forward. For *both* tribes."

"Talk? To *him*? After your latest revelation? You're mad."

"For *Gayathri's* sake," Pijper exclaimed. The emissary only invoked the Vialae's mythical archetype — a great bird of cloud whose outstretched wings filled the horizon — when truly annoyed. "You can't expect the Lontra to simply leave The Blue, Fearless."

"And why not?" Sharp Tooth asked.

"Because they've have been here for *generations*, that's why not. Your demands are unreasonable." The pelican couldn't ignore the headache growing behind his eyes. It smarted like a thorn in his brain, and with no oujit to blunt it. "There must be some compromise."

"My demands are just," Fearless insisted. "Any impartial eye can see that."

Feathers fluffed in frustration, Pijper gazed up at the stormy sky churning above the latticed ceiling. Hidden behind the rainclouds, Gayathri's Egg hung silver-bright, the countless stars filling the void around it the broken remnants of the prior night's shell, scattered across the firmament by the feathered divinity Itself.

If only I could wing away there and never come back. Leave The Blue and its problems behind, forever. The emissary calmed himself. He could not afford runaway emotion. "Quick Tail will never give up High Split Rock, Doyen," Pijper pointed out. "And why should he? Sooner or later, you're going to have to accept that."

Fearless paused in his urchin-splitting to glare at the pelican. "I don't have to accept anything," he snapped, punctuating each word with a jab of his acuur at Pijper's face. "I've already told you. Talk is useless. It was useless last tide, and it will be next tide."

Outside, as the deluge assaulted Gwelth's driftwood and whalebone architecture, the pryzoic field pushing back the smothering ocean prevented any raindrops from penetrating the ceiling and soaking its inhabitants. But the incessant drumming of raindrops continued.

Pity, Pijper thought. *A shower might cool overheating tempers.* "If you won't talk, then what *do* you want to do? Go to war?"

"If I have to." The Doyen gave the urchin one final whack. The shell split. He plucked a juicy bit of meat, plopped it in his mouth and chewed. "Things cannot remain as they are."

"Those are hasty words, Fearless," Pijper replied. "And you are wrong."

Sharp Tooth's whiskers bristled with indignation. "How dare you correct my Doyen so flippantly? Visiting dignitary or no, you should show more respect."

"Now, now, Sharp Tooth, I..." Pijper began, but the Beta cut him off.

"Fearless taught us that actions speak louder than words to those who choose not to hear. And blood speaks louder still. Soon *all* of The Blue will hear us."

"There you have it," Fearless said. "My Saia makes a strong point. Simple wisdom simply put."

Sharp Tooth dipped his head and tugged his whiskers in respectful acknowledgment. Pijper turned to look at the Beta, but Sharp Tooth's bravado remained undiminished.

"You have so much to learn, my brash young Lutris friend," Pijper reminded. "There's enough bloodshed already in The Blue without shedding more for foolish pride. One way or another it will be spilled, even without you longing for it. Don't ever forget that, hrmmm."

Fearless smiled as he watched his underling spar with the wise and learned pelican. But his smile faded when those burnished-bronze pelican eyes refocused on him.

"Blood also brings predators, Doyen," Pijper warned. "Your *true* enemies. Xaad. The Irounga. Quith and Quiln. Dreaded Mimnyr. If you go to war with the Lontra, they will exploit your diminished defenses, both above The Blue and within it."

Fearless dismissed the warning with a harrumph. "Predatory birds we can manage. Only craven Lontra and other weaklings fear the bite of

Xaad," he chuffed, baring his teeth. "And as for the Irounga, they care not a whit for our plight. Full bellies alone matter to them."

"They're opportunists," Pijper countered. "They've killed Lutris before."

"And we've killed them in return!" the Doyen shot back. "Don't Irounga skull and bone ghaydn line our borders? Besides, we've long since put aside our hostilities with Diuun Dunn. He values our trade more than our politics."

"Old Blubber Snout increased his reward for information on the whereabouts of the Ulurii," Sharp Tooth added. "He may even give up one of his three pryzoa to secure them."

"His hunger to devour Uuvaloo and Cixtindi is well known." Pijper ruffled his feathers. "But I doubt he'll trade one of his cherished pryzoa for an octo-snail meal, no matter how tasty it may be. Even so, I often wonder why you haven't yet told Diuun Dunn where they reside. You know the Lontra shelter them."

Fearless scratched a pesky itch under his chin with the shark-tooth acuur. "It's no secret I'd welcome the Ulurii's final demise. Meddling *ptahhf*. They help the Lontra far too much with their accursed knots and knowledge. But, if Blubber Snout thinks I'm withholding information he so craves, I have the advantage. And thus, the reward keeps going up. And the tribute offerings. He won't interfere in our business, and neither will his minions."

"Well, if not Diuun Dunn, then consider that aorxa will come if there's war," the pelican pointed out. "Many shivers of them will be drawn to the blood. Possibly, Nolurrah himself. And no graehl, no matter how strong, can fight him off."

The fur of the Doyen and his Beta instinctively bristled at mention of the Great White Maw, whose razor-sharp teeth formed the stuff of legend.

And nightmare. Lutris alleged Fearless' own shark-tooth acuur and lip-alcq came from an aorxa bitten in half by Nolurrah.

"The White Maw hasn't swum these waters for many seasons. He's either on the far side of The Blue, or else he's long dead." The notion of Nolurrah-as-corpse made Fearless feel better, even if he guessed it to be a falsehood.

"I've heard those rumors, too. And I doubt them," Pijper said.

"Either way, I will not let fear of the White Maw sway my decisions," Fearless countered. "Deshi-Oad knows I've been patient. I've stated my grievance, made my demands, *to you*, envoy, in accordance with Envoric Law... the laws *you* helped codify."

Pijper clopped his great beak with renewed annoyance. "I know the Law, thank you *very* much, Fearless."

"And what has remaining true to the Law gained me?" Fearless whinged. He stretched his aching spine, rose from the soft throne-mound, and crossed to the hovering Penuree tires occupying the center of the chamber. He plucked off an ember-like periwinkle snail. Its light — a wondrous thing of primordial beauty — bled through his clawed fingers. "Den Sire studies the Meta-Oorum, just as I do. He may read different signs or catch different scents in this game we play. But by Deshi-Oad's White Will, *this* game *I* will finish."

"This is *not* a game," Pijper protested.

"Oh, no?" Fearless cupped the periwinkle in his paws. Its hypnotizing bioluminescence danced across his retinas, glinted off his shark-tooth alcq. "Quick Tail has forty-two pryzoa. I have forty-one. I must obtain another, even if The Blue must turn red with blood to achieve it. Then I will be able to legally challenge the Den Sire to single combat. Oh, I will beat him and take all his pryzoa for myself! And *then* I'll drive him and his tribe of thieves from The Blue and reclaim the territory they stole from us. It *will* happen."

"Yes, yes!" Sharp Tooth cried, punctuating his hijna with a loud bark and a flourish of his baleen spear. "The Lontra belong in the river, and by Deshi-Oad, *we* will send them back. The ocean is *our* home!"

Fearless silenced his hotheaded Beta with a raised paw. "Quick Tail's claimed pryzoa will win me The Skynth, and once I have *that,* I'll drive The Cruel Dweller from Liminal or slay it. And I'll claim that, too. I'll wager my whiskers on it." For a heartbeat, The Doyen grew light-headed as his inflamed emotions spun out of control. He shut his eyes, took a deep calming breath, then set the glowing periwinkle back on the hovering tire. "Control of The Garden Effulgent and its contents will be mine."

The absolute certainty in the Alpha's tone chilled Pijper to his hollow bones. "Liminal belongs to all Envorah, Fearless, not just a select few."

The Eehr sneered. "I disagree."

The pelican spread his wings, glided down to the chamber floor — the icy blue ankle ureola like a falling star — and landed before the Doyen. "Fearless, I beg you, think about your proposal. War with your Lontra kin... it's insanity."

"They are not *our* kin," the Alpha growled. "They knew nothing when they found The Blue. They could not hunt or make a spear. They didn't know the acuur or the majl. Deshi-Oad's Fluke, they didn't even know how to swim properly. We Lutris taught them *all* those things. Even their shuuhl is tainted. Poison, from snout to tail. Poison and spraint."

"Words are so much better than violence, Doyen."

"The time for words is past. My spears will do the talking from now on."

"You're being unreasonable," Pijper cried. "Can't you put the memory of the Cuursuurq behind you? Both tribes lost on that dark tide. The Lontra most of all. Two-to-one in fatalities. You should be bonded by the blood thus spilt, not sundered by it."

The Eehr returned to his throne-bed but did not recline. Thoughts of That Scathing Tide still troubled and terrified him. The Lontra suffered more loss of life during that battle, but death alone wasn't the sole contention.

"The Den Sire's paw is outstretched to you even now. Help him remake the 'kinship weave' just as you did in tide's past," Pijper pleaded. "Let the *ehlmajl*-net of peace reunite you."

"Peace?" Fearless spat the word like an obscenity. "Peace means nothing changes. Peace keeps the Lutris in the tainted shadow of High Split Rock forever. Peace is humiliation." The Doyen's eyes flashed with dread light. "Peace equals death."

Pijper recoiled. The very notion insulted all his civilized sensibilities. "This is madness."

Holding himself upright, Fearless locked his imperious golden gaze with the emissary's troubled bronze ones. "Your counsel bores me, Vialae." The Doyen's tone rippled with menace. "Perhaps I should find myself a *new* envoy."

Pijper clopped his beak in disgust and anger. "And what purpose would that serve? You have no wish to listen to good sense. If I learned anything from the Penuree, it's the settling of conflicts through killing has a way of returning with even more violence and bloodshed. They will breed worse than myzee."

The Doyen settled back down onto his throne. "War is a nooree-knot that can be untied in one's favor if one knows how. Which, I do."

"The Blue is big enough for everyone, Fearless," Pijper reminded. "Even Deshi-Oad and Great Ookl can exist in the same current."

But his final desperate appeal fell on a heart as cold as stone.

"Not true." Fearless rubbed his tired eyes. "It's Their nature to fight, and we, being Their children, must follow Their example. It's the tide of things. Tell that to the Den Sire."

"I can see your mind is made up." Pijper did not bother to hide the profound sadness coloring his hijna.

The pelican felt a subtle vibration coursing through Gwelth's architecture. The time of the Submergence had arrived. But Pijper didn't notice. The Doyen's belligerent defiance of common sense blocked out most
everything else.

"Leave." Fearless waved a dismissive paw. "I'd like to digest my meal in
peace."

"Very well." Pijper nodded to the two sea otters with as much etiquette
as a failed negotiation warranted. "I will deliver your message. Nookeelee."

With several flaps of his russet-hued wings, the envoy launched himself
up through the crosshatch timbers of Gwelth's driftwood roof and into the
rainy night sky. Sharp Tooth watched as darkness swallowed the pelican,
the sparkle of his diplomatic ureola growing ever fainter until that, too,
finally winked out.

"Do you think Pijper will relay all of what you said?" Sharp Tooth
wondered.

But Fearless did not hear his Beta's question. His attentions were turned
to the cooling temperament of the forty-one cherished pryzoa. He watched
their magical emanations fade, the rippling air around them smoothing
out. In response, the frigid waters of the communal pool gurgled and
surged about the driftwood timbers, whalebones, and plastic scrap comprising Gwelth's slipshod bulk.

The Blue enclosed the pryzoa chamber, altering the acoustics. The
structure groaned under the added weight as the smothering sea returned
to normal levels.

Fearless smiled at these telltale signs, content the Lutris-home rested
once more beneath the waves. "I wish to be alone."

"Of course, Doyen. Nookeelee." The Saia tugged his whiskers and left
the chamber.

Fearless heaved a sigh and snuggled into his soft bed. He gazed at the
First Life, his golden eyes filling with pryzoic light. After a few heartbeats,

his consciousness expanded in a breathtaking rush in all directions — he once again rode the currents of Meta-Oorum.

The narrow current called, and the Doyen answered:

"First the place, then the face..."

CHAPTER 19

COUNTING THE RAINDROPS

1 1:59 PM.

Outside, a storm rampaged.

Hayley, head propped on two thin pillows and ears attuned to the downpour, reclined on her bed. Exhausted after a full day of driving, still she couldn't sleep. Nor did the caffeine burnout that normally made her drowsy work its magic. It wasn't the patter of rain on the roof or the lament of winds lashing both home and forest that kept Hayley awake — but something deeper. Something bruised and tender in her soul had denied her a proper night's sleep for thirteen months.

Three hundred and eighty-five consecutive days.

Hayley's tired eyes watched the alarm clock switch to 12:00 AM —

Now, three hundred and *eighty-six* consecutive days...

Hayley visualized gray sheets of rain punishing the world beyond the four enclosing walls. Lightening flashed through a window. Fading thunder declared the worst had passed, but the storm still had trillions of droplets awaiting dispersal.

As many as the tears I've cried, she thought and frowned. *God... what lousy sentiment.*

Hayley wasn't given to melancholy. Still, comparing her grief to a storm made her feel, somehow, both powerful — and powerless.

Powerful: because for ten years she'd filled this room with joy during summer vacations. True, a sprinkling of angry days found their way in. But, either fun or frustrating, she shared that time with her beloved Jake. Her oh-so handsome, dependable, and steadfast husband. And the love they made — a love that could move mountains and survive all domestic adversity — soaked these walls like the rain now soaking her mother-in-law's vegetable garden.

Powerless: because, thirteen months after the bleakest day she ever endured, her life felt hollow... or, more to the point... *hollowed out.* Ayana, despite her frustrations and litany of teenage grievances, still offered Hayley a place to focus her affections, and receive it back when lucky. But it remained a mercurial love. It would slip through her fingers if squeezed too hard. And yet too light a touch and it fostered resentment. The love between mother and child, for all its rewards, was a far cry from the white-hot passion shared between a husband and wife.

Those were the flames that set Hayley's soul ablaze.

Now, because of a bee-sting, grief alone nested in those cold ashes.

Staring at the overhead shadows, Hayley took stock of her emotional reserves. Tears enough to fill the oceans were shed for Jake those first days and weeks after his death, but they eventually dried. Not for lack of pain — that swelled within her like the rising waters behind a fragile dam — but for the sake of the mundane.

The stability of routine. The appearances of normalcy.

Grief, it turned out, was much like lice: once you were infested, everyone knew... and they stayed away lest they, too, got infested.

Hayley now hoarded her tears, hoping for one good gusher to set her emotional world right. A proper cry, deep and emptying, to balance her scales and temper the angry tides raging in her heart. It had taken an entire bottle of cheap chardonnay to reach that point; and her brain and belly still complained from the indulgence.

But the wine served its purpose — and the tears shed with her in-laws cracked that fragile dam just enough to vent some heartache. But it wasn't enough. The reservoir of Hayley's grief was vaster and deeper than she ever guessed, and her unshed tears could rival the raindrops if allowed to flow freely.

Maybe... just maybe... those two waters needed to mingle for true healing to begin?

Could she use the storm's energy to accomplish this goal?

Hayley heaved a sigh. The idea was little more than greeting-card sentiment. Bad poetry mixed with cheap vino. She tried to ignore her maudlin thoughts, and replace them with something, *anything*, that didn't make her want to go scream herself hoarse in the pouring rain.

But the absurd notion felt oddly — proper. Even necessary.

Abandoning her rumpled bed, she whispered, "I gotta do what I gotta do."

Hayley tip-toed downstairs and through the living room, furniture and bookcases solid shadows scattered in the darkness. The low rumble of falling rain against the roof masked all other sounds. She neared the sofa;

the atmosphere around it still held an emotional charge from her earlier tears.

She felt that prior release at ten paces. *I can do better*. Must *do better*.

Shep snored in his doggy-bed, dreaming of human food treats as Hayley crossed into the kitchen to the window over the sink. She peeled aside the linen curtains. Outside lay a nocturnal world lashed by rain and a waning gale. She could barely discern the forest beyond as it swayed drunkenly in the wind. Her objective, a hundred water-logged yards away, remained hidden in the darkness.

Though unseen, it still beckoned to her like a roaring bonfire.

Inside a cluttered hall closet Hayley found an old blue raincoat and oversized galoshes. She slipped them on over her pajamas, then grabbed a yellow umbrella off a hook. Finding a Coleman flashlight in a kitchen junk drawer, she was ready for the storm. Hayley unlocked the back door and lingered at the threshold, staring into the rain.

Chill air, heavy with moisture, swirled against her cheeks.

"...what I gotta do...".

She stepped into the downpour and clicked on the flashlight. Its beam pierced the darkness of the sprawling backyard. She descended the back steps and made for the adjacent pasture. Heavy drops pelted the raincoat — *plink-plink-plinking* her head and shoulders in a staccato patter. With breath frosting in the flashlight's glow and goloshes squishing over the wet grass, Hayley passed the vegetable garden and reached the wooden fence.

Unlatching the gate, she entered the pasture. In the furthest northern corner Hayley's goal awaited: a hundred-year-old apple tree, sprawling branches sparse with fruit. Her pace quickened. She knew all the dangers about being near a tree during a storm, but the chances of it (or her) being struck by lightning — on this of all nights — felt remote.

As she approached, the flashlight beam flitted past the adjacent wooden lawn chair and settled on a bronze grave marker nestled at the manicured base of the apple tree. A blue vase filled with soggy garden flowers stood beside it.

A baroque border etching framed the simple, loving memory:

Jacob Henry Outerbridge

Beloved Son, Husband, and Father

Rest in Power

1946 — 1983

Hayley's flashlight lingered on the words... *Jacob.*

Ache welled within her chest... *Beloved.*

Cracks spiderwebbed through the emotional dam holding back the anguish... *Rest.*

Hayley sat on the waterlogged chair, hardly aware of doing so. The flashlight grew heavy. Hot tears welled, yearning to compete with the rain peppering her back and shoulders. But she resisted. She pushed back the pain. Strained to keep it contained.

But why? Wasn't a purifying weep the reason she'd ventured out into the storm?

"Jake," Hayley whispered. The name stung her throat. She clicked off the flashlight.

Darkness.

It seemed right to mourn without light. Nothing to reveal the ugly faces she'd make, the jerking shoulders, the snot she couldn't wipe away, the ungainly hiccups. If they ever came.

"Jake."

The dam cracked a bit more. Hayley squeezed the flashlight, trying to wrench any measure of strength she could from its plastic length. But that only further restricted the dam from bursting as it demanded. The conditions were perfect. She was far from home, yet in a familiar place. Her family slept nearby, unaware. The hour was late, or early, in fact. The storm was blowing itself out in a dwindling display of raw power.

The grave of her husband lay just a few feet away. She was alone...

Now was the time. It might never come again.

Do it now, she thought; demanded. *NOW.*

The flashlight slipped from her grip, falling into to the wet grass. With nothing left to hold them at bay, a thousand memories of her spouse and lover demanded to be recognized all at once — each one salted with a corresponding sound, or smell... or feeling.

Some were sweet. A scant few, sour. But none, bitter. They all held love.

And it was the absence of this love, the *void* it left behind, that weakened the dam like thousands of bullets concentrated at the same spot — whittling and pulverizing. Hayley pressed chilled, wet hands to her face. Lips quivering, eyes aching and swelling with unshed tears, she prayed to weep. To cry. To scream.

Give it to me. Please. I need it, she thought; and then: "...Jake."

No accompanying flash of lighting or thunder crack marked that moment the barriers in her soul surrendered, and a release — pure, purging and cathartic — began. Yet the rain suddenly started falling harder. The outpouring of pent-up energy seemed to feed the storm, and in return, was coaxed by it. Hayley couldn't see through her tears. Couldn't hear through the sobs and babble mixed with her wailing.

But it didn't matter. Hayley was past caring how her body reacted to the needed release.

She slid from the lawn chair onto the soggy grass. Propped on her knees, she rocked and gestured her anguish. She slapped at the raindrops, punched the sodden earth, ripping and clawing out soupy handfuls. Every movement expunged more sorrow. The floodgates had swung open, letting the deluge of sadness flow with more freedom than a million bottles of chardonnay could ever achieve.

The minutes ticked by. Hayley's cheeks and throat and lungs ached. Her tears now fell like the rain. Yet, behind the emotional storm, a single, comforting thought began to emerge:

I'm going to sleep like a rock tonight..

CHAPTER 20

A MOTHER'S LOVE

The Holt's sick den, located in the furthest corner of the Great Hollow, lay three tails above the main floor, away from the noise and amity of the playful romp. Beyond the stone fracture forming its entrance, the dry lair boasted a low ceiling and muted acoustics. A breeze sighed through a thin wall crack, dispersing the sickly odors that so often stifled its atmosphere.

Accidents and ailments were an integral part of Holt life. Every Lontra spent time confined to the sick den. Some never emerged. All lived with the inevitability of death. The sick den allowed the afflicted a quiet, peaceful space in which to recuperate — or die — in private, isolated from the rest of The Holt yet accessible to family and friends who wished to visit.

Sleek set aside his spear and ascended the three stone steps to the den. He stepped up to the door-fracture and peered inside.

Tonight, the low-ceilinged chamber held only two occupants: Chaser, an aging, ailing male Vlis-Gamma, and his nurse, Gentle, whose name described her personality to perfection.

No ordinary caregiver, Sleek's mother wore a milky-green Spirula shell alcq from her lower lip and an opulent ureola like a glittering ribbon of violet stars about her neck. These twin adornments proclaimed her title and rank — the Suckling Mother, Eehr-Alpha, and co-equal mate of the Den Sire. She tended the sick and wounded, aided in births, and provided counsel and soft-pawed diplomacy when needed.

But her greatest function, that of Royal Surrogate Teat, played a vital part in Holt life; the kits she chose to suckle were destined for grand rank. She performed her duties with the greatest affection and diligence, and all Lontra loved her without exception.

For forty tides, Chaser had ignored the rattling cough growing in his chest, the steady loss of muscle and fat, the thinning fur. His once sharp golden eyes grew dull and rheumy. Most of his teeth had loosened, with some now missing. With little appetite remaining, and his strength all but gone, Chaser depended on Suckling Mother's care.

Gentle fondly recalled Chaser teaching her as a kit how to sharpen the acuur, stalk the keerth, the salmon, and the grouper, and how to hurl a spear like a proper hunter. As her first graehl leader, he'd protected her more than once against hungry predators. Now he needed care, and she relished the chance to give back even a small measure of what he'd given her.

"Almost done," Gentle said. As she'd done for Sleek as a weanling just learning to eat solid food, she chewed a bit of squid, pre-masticating it so her patient could swallow. "Just one more bite."

"I don't know if I can," Chaser replied, his hijna weakened by illness. "I'm so full. My stomach feels like it may burst."

"I know. But it's just a tiny keerth. Won't you try? For me?"

Chaser stirred on his mat of scavenged Penuree beach towels. "For you... I'll try..."

A cough convulsed Chaser's weakened frame. Gentle massaged his back and neck, patiently waiting for the coughing to subside.

"Easy now, Chaser. Easy. Just breathe."

The Gamma spat a gobbet of green phlegm. "I'm sorry...you have to...see me like this."

Gentle wiped Chaser's mouth with a corner of one of the towels. "There's nothing to be sorry about. I've seen worse." She offered him a final bite of keerth, which Chaser swallowed after a determined effort. "Well done."

The weary Vlis noticed Sleek lingering at the entrance, waiting to be invited in. "Your son is here, Gentle," he said; then to Sleek, "Come in, my young friend."

Bracing himself, Sleek entered, tugging his whiskers in respect to his parent and her patient. "*Kooarii*, Mother. Nookeelee, Chaser."

He waited for the shocked reaction over his transgression and scolding that would follow.

It never came.

"We're just finishing up here, son."

Sleek blinked in confusion. *Doesn't she notice?* he thought. *Can't she smell the pryzoa on my breath?*

The Saia came forward to squeeze Chaser's shoulder. "How are you feeling, old tail?" But Sleek's sensitive nose supplied the answer — the Vlis' body reeked of a devouring illness. The Holt ascribed the mystery ailment to some pernicious Penuree evil.

"Like I've been wrestling Diuun Dunn, young-whisker," Chaser quipped. The old otter always made light of things, even his own discomfort. "Sometimes I come out on top, sometimes not. But your mother's been tending me, so I'm optimistic."

Gentle tucked Chaser into the towels, making him snug and comfortable. A weak purr rumbled in his throat. "And you've been a wonderful patient. But now it's time to rest."

Chaser nodded, but then squeezed his eyes shut as another painful cough racked his weakened body. When the spasm passed, he whispered: "Sleek, are there any signs of Diver?"

"No, Chaser. Not since his wounding. I'm sorry."

"If Old Father Fathom wills that my son sojourn for a time alone in The Blue, so be it. I have faith He will return Diver to The Holt."

Gentle pushed an abalone shell-bowl filled with medicinal *oujit* to within easy reach of Chaser's snout. "I want you to drink this," she instructed. "Here. Let me help."

She put the shell to the Vlis' mouth and slowly raised it. He sipped the brew between heaving breaths, trying his best to drain the medicine.

The recipe for this universal cure-all — a glowing concoction of pulped kholo, various nooree extracts, Honeaa-rich colostrum, and rainwater — was given to the first Suckling Mother by Old Father Fathom Himself (so the story went.) Neither Lontra nor Ulurii knew how nor why oujit worked, just that it did. Yet sometimes even the greatest magic failed and, despite all efforts, sickness and injury won.

"I'll check on you at First Tide, Chaser," Gentle promised. "Sip on this oujit tonight. I'll bring fresh tomorrow."

"I'd prefer oixrd," Chaser said with a wink. "Just a little... to warm the blood."

Suckling Mother smiled and pinched Chaser's fuzzy cheek. "Maybe. Finish your oujit."

"May Ookl keep you safe in His Coils," the old otter rasped. "And you, too, Sleek. Such daring deeds in daunting places...ambitions of the young, eh?"

Sleek's heart skipped a beat. *Yurch, yurch, yurch.*

Suckling Mother caressed her old mentor's faded mahogany-furred head. "May the Bubbles of His Breath raise you up, dearest Chaser." Her gaze swiveled to Sleek, the concern in her eyes speaking silent volumes. "Escort me to my den, will you?"

"Of course, Mother."

Together they departed the sick den, leaving Chaser floating on the verge of oujit-induced slumber. Gentle paused on the top step and looked back at her wheezing patient. Though she knew his body ached, and his dreams would be strange, she prayed her old friend would find the rest he so needed.

"He's failing." Gentle sighed and shook her head. "The oujit isn't work-ing. I'm wary of increasing its kholo-dose. Too much might do more harm than good. I fear he may not live to see The Glow."

"Chaser's strong," Sleek replied. "He might surprise us."

"True. But I think only Ookl alone can heal him now."

Mother and son descended into the Great Hollow and made their way across the crowded floor towards a side passage leading to High Split Rock's eroded upper levels. Chattering groups of Lontra cleared a path for them. They dropped ootith and offered a fond "Kooarii," while tugging their whiskers in respect. Most evenings, Suckling Mother made time to mingle with the romp, offering encouraging words to those in need, or doting on the kits of worthy females.

Not tonight, Gentle thought. She wearied from tending Chaser after a full day of Eehr-related duties of young-rearing. And, as The Holt's royal surrogate teat, all four of her nipples ached from suckling so many hungry kits. The honeaa in her milk took too much energy to make, and she felt drained. All she wanted was to retire to her den for some much-needed rest. But instead, Gentle found herself faced with a new headache. *Sleek's been in Liminal. He knows better. Ookl, give me strength.*

The two royal otters reached the slanted tunnel-fracture entrance and started up the inclined stone path. A confluence of unique erosions divided High Split Rock into nine levels. The egress-pool and oixrd-fermenting crypts at the sea level basement, the Great Hollow above that. From there, the next six levels were inhabited, with the ninth and final level being off limits to all but a select few.

In some places, the ascending fissure-passages stretched wide enough for three otters to walk side-by-side; in others, only one animal could squeeze through at a time. Kholo latices clinging to the granite walls offered soft illumination. On each level, numerous cracks and scissures worn in the Holt-stone served as entrances to den-cavities. Others extended clear through the rock, forming ventilation shafts or windows that revealed the outside storm.

Smaller dens held solo individuals, while larger cavities sheltered entire families. Many were carpeted with grasses, scattered leaves and pine needles collected from the Holt's roof. Seagull feathers or shredded, scavenged Penuree fabric softened many others. These mingled odors identified each lair and its occupants. They also perfumed the fusty tunnel and softened the ammonia bite of urine, spraint, and *squiq*, the anal-sac secretions Lontra used to mark themselves as injured, in mourning, sexually receptive or violence-prone.

As mother and son ascended, Gentle glanced at Sleek. She made note of his leg wound, the slight limp in his gait. "You're lucky to have escaped with just a scratch. Old Father Fathom watched over you."

Sleek swallowed hard. The mildness of his mother's behavior bothered him more than if she'd responded with hot ire. *But anger was never her way,* he thought. *Still...*

In truth, he felt relief Gentle finally acknowledged the Diuun Dunn-sized situation between them. "It was worse earlier..." his hijna trailed off. He avoided his mother's gaze, and the desire to say more.

"I can imagine. There's nothing like a belly full of ill-gotten pryzoa to speed healing."

Sleek nodded and the two continued on their way in silence.

Disobeying Father's edict to stay out of Liminal was one thing. That, Sleek knew, Gentle could forgive. So, too, the Den Sire...given time. But discovery of his aijeer removal of pryzoa would spell disaster. The law would force the Den Sire's paw, leaving him no choice but to banish Sleek from the Holt, and thus make any possibility of claiming Gloss forever out of reach. An otter without the protection of the clan did not survive long.

At last, Gentle spoke. "There are many forces we Aanandi must contend with, both in The Blue and beyond it. We hold power...for this tide. But tides never stop."

"We're mighty. And fierce. And quick."

"It will not be enough. Envorah hate us. Not all, of course, but enough to keep us on our guard. If we show weakness, they'll strike."

Sleek frowned, wondering what sent his mother's sanguine mind to such a dark place. The worries of Alphas were not yet his to bear — but he would know them, maybe sooner than he ever thought possible.

"Thank Ookl we have enough pryzoa to maintain our ascendancy," Gentle continued. "As long as others are obliged to tug their whiskers and stand ootith, we keep a measure of safety. And comfort. But that margin is thin as a nooree blade. Others slaver at the chance to challenge us. To challenge your Father. To draw his blood. To wear his ureola. To take his life... and his place."

Sleek never heard his mother speak so harshly. It deeply unsettled him. "It sounds like you're talking about the Lutris now. Are you?"

Gentle's disposition regained its familiar warmth, even as she ignored the question. Her mouth smiled, but the smile did not show in her eyes. "I'm proud you're so brave and strong, Sleek. But...promise me you'll be more careful."

"I promise."

Gentle stroked her son's handsome head, playfully tugged on his right ear. "I'll bring you some fresh oujit later. A scar just won't do."

"I think I might like one," Sleek confessed. "I heard that uja love scars."

"Oh, you," Gentle giggled. "My kit is all grown up."

High Split Rock's namesake 'split' began above the Great Hollow. No wider than a kit's paw at the first dwelling level, its taper expanded, tail by tail by tail. Within the first three habitat levels this growing fissure was easily stepped, and then jumped over, even by the weak or young. But, by the sixth habitat level, the crack opened into a yawning crevasse, allowing air and rain to reach the lower levels of the megalith.

To negotiate the chasm, earlier generations had fashioned kelp strands, scavenged Penuree rope, and lengths of driftwood into primitive bridges. A trio of such structures spanned the top three habitat levels, each twice the length of the one below it, and all carefully built to accommodate the unique rockface to which they adhered. Though surefooted, the Lontra still practiced caution while crossing — a wayward wind gust or failing timber could send a careless animal falling to its death.

Sleek and Gentle navigated the steep switchbacks and lengthening bridges to a passage on the sixth level. The night storm rumbled its fury each time they crossed, casting its rain and wind to ruffle their pelts and whiskers. The black sea heaved and undulated below them, clouds just as dire and agitated above. The immolating waves frothed against High Split Rock's stone foundations, vibrating through the megalith, and tickling the otters' footpads.

Beyond the final bridge, hidden in the shadow of a stony overhang, an arch of thick tree roots framed the threshold to the Alpha's spacious den. Scratched into the smooth wood of the living doorway were dozens of unique glyphs — the symbol-names of every previous Den Sire and Suckling Mother, going back generations to the first occupation of High Split Rock.

As mother and son crossed the threshold, cool, rain-scented night air bathed their muzzles. In a crevice opposite the entrance, an acuur-pruned kholo-bush smoldered. Its soft illumination threw shadows across the coarse granite walls.

A burst of lightening lit the room; on its heels, thunder rumbled.

The storm was dwindling in strength, but not without protest.

Suckling Mother moved to her bed of torn life preservers, slipped the heavy ureola off her neck, and hung the sparkling torc on a tree root protruding from the wall. *Feels so much better to be rid of this silly thing*, she thought, rubbing her neck where the collar had been. "Your Father wants to see you in the pryzoa chamber, before you retire."

"Of course," Sleek replied, gritting his teeth.

Gentle cocked her head. "You didn't think you'd be able to avoid this, did you?"

"No." In truth, Sleek hoped to escape confronting his deeds for at least another day. He sighed and changed the subject. "Your weaning day will be here soon."

"I'm one season older and grayer around the muzzle. Joy."

"Do you want anything special?"

"Healthy kits and a safe Holt. That's all." Gentle paused, then added, "Ookl willing, The Glow will arrive soon. I so hope. Then we'll all have something far more important to celebrate than a single Lontra's weaning day."

"You're not just any Lontra," Sleek pointed out, offsetting his mother's self-deprecation. "You're our Suckling Mother. *The* Suckling Mother."

Gentle dismissed this fact with an impatient flick of her tail. She plucked the Spirula shell alcq from her lower lip, set it aside. "Just between us, I sometimes wish I could just be Gentle again. Nothing more, nothing less." She yawned and stretched. "I'd be happy with that. Yes. Very happy indeed."

Sleek went to the kholo bush and stared pensively at the organic gleeds within its knots of feathery leaves and chromatic cysts. The plant exuded a delicate, sweet fragrance reminiscent of pryzoa. For some reason, the perfumes stirred up memories of Gloss. "When you first met Father, what did you think of him?"

"Oh, my. That was so long ago." Gentle's golden eyes grew distant and dreamy. "And yet, sometimes, it feels like just a few seasons have passed." She nudged the foam bedding into a comfortable mound, lay down and curled into a sleep position. Scratching her chin with a hind paw, she cast her mind down the path of memory, back to the sunny tides of her youth. "I shouldn't tell you this, but I disliked your Father at first. So arrogant and daring. Why, he once pulled the snout of Diuun Dunn himself."

"*What?*" Sleek shook his head in disbelief. "This is Quick Tail we're talking about, right? *My* Father? The practical and cautious uju?"

"Oh, yes," Gentle suppressed a giggle. "He yanked that old Irounga's nose so hard it made Blubber Snout roar. I'd never heard a sound so loud. I remember how it hurt my ears."

"How did you two even get close enough, and how did you get away? And why is this the first time I'm hearing this?"

Gentle shrugged. "It's a long story involving peace envoys between Blubber Snout and Heedful, the old Den Sire, your grandfather. I didn't think you were interested in the youthful exploits of your parents."

Sleek rolled his eyes. "Ookl's Ink! Of course, I'm interested."

"Well, you've never asked me... Anyway, I had never seen anything so bold or deliberately rash, either before or since. It was so romantic. And he won my heart." Gentle accentuated her hijna with a soft purr as she reminisced about the heady days of courtship. "Your Father was quite the rouser back then. Reckless, unpredictable. Caused your grandparents many a headache. Broke more than a few rules, though never *skoraa*."

"No, of course not," Sleek agreed. Skoraa, or 'Oath Biters,' could never be trusted and so would never ascend to leadership.

"The unpredictability made him interesting. Plus, it didn't hurt that he was so easy on the eyes! His whiskers. So thick and long. And his tail. Oooh, son, don't get me started on his tail."

"Okay. Stop, please," Sleek begged. "I don't think I want to hear any more."

Gentle gazed at her son with a mother's discerning eyes. "This is about Gloss, isn't it?"

"What? No. Of course not."

Ignoring the denial, Gentle asked, "You do plan on seeing her, again, yes? It's been, hmm, about eighty tides, hasn't it?"

Sleek started with surprise. "You...know about that?"

"Foolish kit," Gentle answered with a soft, loving smile. "I'm your mother. Mothers know most things about their children, even after they're grown. You've loved Gloss since your first *shraga* harvest. When Ookl's Eye fully opens, you sneak away and take a xhooja to the Oyster Shell. Together you hunt. I even know the estuary where you two go to be alone."

Sleek's gut knotted with worry. *If she can find out all that, might she find out about the hidden pryzoa?* "Who told you?" he demanded, then regretted his sharp tone.

Gentle's golden eyes sparkled with humor. "A teeny keerth." She paused, the hint of a frown her lips. "I like Gloss. She's strong, noble, honest, and very beautiful. She'd make a superb mate..."

This time Sleek frowned. "I hear a 'but' coming."

Gentle's whiskers drooped. Her cheerful demeanor grew melancholy. "She's *Lutris*."

"So, what if she is?"

"There has never been a coupling between a Lontra and a Lutris. Ever. We don't even know if it's possible. Even if our tribes were not on the brink of war, to take a mate, knowing there might not be any kits produced..."

"Is producing kits the sole reason to mate?"

"Don't be naïve," Gentle admonished. "That's not what I meant. Of course, there are other reasons to mate, but kits are the life blood of the romp. Without them, we cease to be."

Unfamiliar emotions welled within Sleek. Never had he looked at his mother with such simultaneous anger and sadness. "I can't believe I'm hearing this from you, of all *uji*."

"Sleek, you're an adult now, and a Saia for Ookl's sake. You're strong, quick, brave, and oh-so-handsome. You can have your pick of any unmated uja within the Holt."

"I don't want any of them. I want Gloss."

"You will take your Father's place as Eehr and Den Sire one day. It's your duty to choose an uja who is fit to become the next Suckling Mother." Gentle's hijna hardened, her gaze unyielding. "You must do this. It is our way. It has always been."

For the first time in his young life, Sleek recognized the granite foundation beneath his mother's tender character. He always suspected it lurked there but had never experienced it. Still, he refused to bend. "I'm sorry. I must be true to my heart." It hurt to defy her, but defiance was his only choice. His love for Gloss demanded it.

Gentle sighed and her entire body seemed to deflate. She rose from the bed mound and took Sleek's paws in hers. Boundless affection infused her hijna and shone in her eyes. "You have the right to make your own decisions. Your Aanandi-shade knows what you want. It tells your heart, and your heart tells you. There's no mystery. No riddle to it. If you are determined to do this thing, then I won't stop you."

Sleek folded his ears back and lowered his head. "Thank you, Mother."

Gentle nibbled Sleek's cheek, the Lontra equivalent of a parental kiss. "I can't speak for your father. I just ask that you consider what I've said. For our sake. For the Holt's."

No matter how much I think about it, I won't change my mind. I'll break every rule to win Gloss if I must! "I will," Sleek said.

Gentle returned to her bed mound, stretched a final time, wrapped her tail about her hind legs, and snuggled into the soft foam. "Before your rendezvous with Gloss, visit The Cellum. Construct a healing-ghaydn for Chaser. It may draw the attention of Great Ookl. The Old Father may choose to heal the affliction yet. And make a finder-ghaydn for Diver's safe return, as well. The romp is stronger with him in it. He's been gone far too long."

"I'll see it done." Sleek tugged his whiskers in respect. "Get some rest, mother."

CHAPTER 21

Oussia's Puddle

Ten tails above the Alpha's lair, and accessible via a natural chimney, the stone shrine known as Oussia's Puddle commanded the reverence of all who entered. Within that sacred space dwelt the pulsing core of Lontra power. In their worldview, Liminal existed as the one *true* sacred place, with the chamber housing their First Life coming in a close second.

No Lontra could bear a weapon in the shrine, so Sleek set aside his spear at the base of the chimney and started climbing. Thick roots courtesy of Old Tree, the ancient conifer topping High Split Rock like an evergreen crown, snaked down the walls, allowing him to scale the conduit with relative ease. Generations of Lontra claw marks marred the knotted wood. Sleek's wounded hind leg smarted with the upward exertion.

At the summit, a kholo partition separated the sanctum proper from a small foyer. Such proximity to the pryzoa imbued the High Polyps with a luster unseen in the lower levels.

Sleek emerged from the chimney, blinked away the kholo-brightness, and stepped forward. Normally, the partition sat inert without the customary ureola to trigger it. To Sleek's surprise, however, the polyps reacted to his proximity by coiling back and inward, like the iris of a giant, sparkling eye.

The kholo must be sensing the pryzoa in my system, he thought.

The Lontra prince crossed the glowing threshold into a sizable chamber, created by the intersection of two wide fractures through High Split Rock. One fissure opened onto a windswept ledge high above the heaving sea. A path led from this uneven platform up to the grassy roof and Old Tree's domain. Gusts of cold damp air swirled into the chamber from the tunnel mouth.

In a cul-de-sac at the end of the second fracture lay the sacred pryzoa pool itself. A boulder, partly blocking the entrance, shielded the magical mollusks from view. Though hidden, their combined enchantment rippled the air like the surface of a disturbed puddle. Intense energy generated by the First Life saturated the nearby rocks, rendering them transparent as glass. Sparkling kholo filaments and runners spread like living circuitry over wall, floor, and ceiling.

A familiar static set Sleeks fur and whiskers a-tingle. He visited this sacred grotto many times since kit-hood. He knew the shape of the four hovering stones, long-since color-leached, holding the forty-two pryzoa. He had peered through the various ceptual-lenses — harvested from the eyes of aquatic animals with the keenest of vision — that magnified the pryzoic movements to the most minuscule degree. But now a torrent of new sensations whipped through the Saia's senses, and for a moment, he felt transported back into Liminal's beautiful madness.

It's truly The Garden Effulgent in miniature, Sleek thought.

"Sleek?" Quick Tail's hijna infiltrated the memory and — *pop* — it burst.

Sleek sucked in a deep breath. *Oh, yurch*, he thought.

Den Sire stood uhlee before the boulder partition, gazing at his son with eyes narrowed to gold slits. The Spirula-shell alcq instilled his profile with the aura of leadership. He held a blunted iron nail in one paw and a notched hammerstone in the other. "Son, come here."

With ears flattened against his skull and struggling to hide his limp, the young Beta approached his father. Dropping submissively to all fours, he tugged his whiskers and kept his eyes downcast, waiting. "Kooarii, Father."

For several heartbeats, the Den Sire watched his disobedient child in glowering silence. "I see you've lost *another* ureola. This has become a bad habit. And a worse example."

Sleek tugged his whiskers. "Yes, Father. It won't happen again."

"Uh-huh." The Den Sire regarded his son, pursed his lips, then returned to his task.

For many more heartbeats, nothing disturbed the stillness in the chamber save the distant howl of the storm and the *tap-tap-tap* of metal on stone. Just as the young otter thought he'd collapse beneath the strain, his father spoke.

"We missed your ynth during the keerth hunt," the patriarch said. *Tap-tap-tap* went the hammerstone. Another glyph took shape beneath the nail's blunting point, adding to the thousands of pictograms already decorating the fracture's wall. The Envoric lexeme for divination was comprised of a group of symbols — concentric circles, intersecting wavy lines, clusters of dots and dashes — all strung together into intricate patterns. Each symbol represented a premonition gleaned from pryzoic meditation, and then engraved in the rock by all the Den Sires, past and present. Generations of wisdom, and uncertainty, scrawled to overlapping on wall and ceiling.

Yet, there was more. So much more.

Winding through and among all these Ahmijna were the stylized tentacles of Great Ookl carved into the rock. Depictions going back decades, to the first generation of Lontra to inhabit High Split Rock. Old Father Fathom resided in every tail, every inch, of Oussia's Puddle.

Sleek felt the symbolic weight of Lontra's patron deity all around him, His many cephaloid eyes accusing him... but he still didn't look at his father. "I hope my absence didn't hamper the haul."

"The graehl managed to survive." Quick Tail's whiskers twitched around a soft smile. "Clearly, you had something more *important* to do."

Sleek gulped. With any luck he could steer the conversation into safer waters, without having to confess his Liminal trespass. "I didn't see you in the Hollow tonight...I caught a juicy Etcax. I would've been honored to share it with you."

"I would have enjoyed that," Den Sire stood back and scrutinized his work. "But Uuvaloo needed me. The fluidity of the Meta-Oorum worries him." The patriarch then applied a few more *tap-tap-taps* to refine the symbol, part of a quartet of fresh glyphs.

Sleek fidgeted, casually scratching his injured leg. "Yeah. I suppose it would."

More silence followed, then...

"Did you bring pryzoa to the surface, son? Did you break the law? *My* law?"

Sleek glanced at his father, straining to gauge the Alpha's mood, for his hijna-tone, frightening for its blandness, gave no clue. But the question itself hinted at the dangerous precipice yawning before him.

"No, Father." Sleek's lie made his Aanandi-shade curl into an agonized ball — but his love for Gloss demanded the speaking of it. "I did not."

The Den Sire turned from his labor, fixing the young Saia with strong, golden eyes. They probed into his son, hunting for the truth in the murky waters of possible falsehood. He smelled the devoured pryzoa on Sleek's breath, saw the injury on his hind leg, the four abraded paws. Sleek knew his father suspected him of mischief.

"I believe you." The Eehr returned to his glyph-work. The danger seemed to have passed, until Quick Tail hijna-whispered: "...scithma-sn aag."

Sleek tensed and thought: *He knows what I did. He can smell it.* But he met the Alpha's subtle accusation with a deceiver's confidence and continued to wear the false face of innocence.

Sleek watched his father's skilled paws chisel and scratch prescient wisdom into the stone. Ease returned to him with each hammerstone strike. Yet, the meaning of the symbols eluded him. The Beta wanted to inquire, both to divert the subject away from his trespass and to glean some knowledge as well. "Is it The Glow?"

"In part." Content to play along, Quick Tail pointed a clawed finger at the image he created. "These four Ahmijna summarize all I garnered from my most recent omen-dive. And these wavy lines indicate things are in flux, while this symbol," he touched two crossed lines bisecting a circle, "foretells an increase in The Blue's discordant tides flowing towards we Aanandi. And you see the lines here that look like a spear pointing downward? It indicates all currents are shifting in a negative direction for all foreseeable tides."

Sleek rose from his crouch to sidle up and touch the glyph his father had finished — three horizontal lines within two concentric circles. "I recognize this one. It means 'pryzoa', but also something more."

"Indeed, it does," the Den Sire's hijna warmed with approval. "Pryzoa are not of this world. They abide here, yes, and mimic many shapes found in The Blue, but they remain firmly connected to Oussia, from whence

The Glow emanates and all Envoric life must some tide return. *'Life by Liquid by Light,'* as the Ulurii so eloquently phrased this exchange between worlds." He pointed to a trio of ovals, each filled with an 'X' and connected by arrows. "And these glyphs symbolize the First Life, 'awakened.' Not because they're asleep, of course. Their light remains in a steady state... until The Glow is imminent. Then they react in specific and recognizable ways. Eighty-six tides into this latest warm season, with Ookl's Eye opened, the First Life awakened."

"I remember that night. The Blue felt, I don't know... agitated, some-how. Restless.

"Yes. I felt it, too. The Glow is soon upon us. And when it arrives all the hardship, and misfortune, we Aanandi must endure will be swept away. But only Ookl knows the exact tide."

"So, what do we do until then?"

The Den Sire put a firm paw on Sleek's shoulder. "We hold fast and prepare." He set down his tools. "Walk with me."

The two river otters dropped ootith and made their way down the drafty tunnel, stopping shy of the roof exit. Outside, rain pelted the ledge with dwindling, yet still considerable, force. Quick Tail stared at the curtain of dribbling water, pensive. Father and son listened to the wind whistling above and surf crashing against the foundation of High Split Rock far below.

Sleek remained silent, bracing for the expected castigation. He wished his father would just get on with the punishment. *Is he deliberately holding back to prolong this torture?*

"We are well protected here," Quick Tail said. "We can only be dislodged if we *choose* to be, or if we do not safeguard our unity and values. We Lontra are strong. We act on our principles, not just for ourselves, but for *all* Envorah. Soon, every eye, be they bronze or gold, will be turned to The Holt for guidance."

"Not everyone wants our guidance, Father. Some will resent us for even offering."

Den Sire nodded. "True. But refusing to see the light on the horizon doesn't mean it's not there. The light shines on all things, living or otherwise. It is our privilege to help those who wish to see. Those who don't —"

"Can fend for themselves and find their own way," Sleek interjected. "Or they can die. That's how the Lutris think, and they're not wrong. Lontra first, in all things, I say."

Quick Tail turned to Sleek. Two pairs of eyes stared into each other, one old and wise the other young and defiant. "Son, it's possible you will be High Eehr of *all* Envorah someday," the patriarch stated. "Such small mindedness simply won't do."

Sleek flinched at the rebuke. "But, Father, I..."

"If you can't see a flaw within yourself, you'll never be able to mend it." The Den Sire's gazed hardened like the granite foundations of High Split Rock, then softened. "There is no one clan over another, no narrow 'Lontra first' — for when the Glow comes it'll wash over us all. If we prepare, and work hard, we can ensure this next Glow brings all Envorah together to share in the bounty. And when all bellies are full, and all minds elevated, then there will be a final peace among the tribes. And peace is the ultimate answer. You have never seen war."

"I've been in battle," Sleek protested. "I have witnessed much of what..."

Den Sire held up a paw. "An isolated skirmish over prey or a border violation isn't what I mean. War, *true war* that turns The Blue red, is something I hope you never live to see. Trust me when I say we must do everything we can to keep it from happening."

Sleek lowered his head and tugged his whiskers in formal acquiescence. "If you say so." But the tone of his hijna betrayed the young otter's skepticism.

"Would it be fair to have important knowledge, and the wisdom garnered from it, and not share it with others?" Quick Tail looked askance at his son. "As Aanandi we can learn the lessons others are incapable of learning, and then teach them in ways they can understand. There is no greater duty. It's what Ookl would have us do."

Ookl's a fiction, a mass delusion, Sleek thought. "Of course, Father."

Den Sire stood in silence beside his son, staring out into the storm. Sleek kept sneaking glances at the patriarch's noble profile. As usual, he could glean nothing from the controlled visage, the noble whiskers, the proud pelt.

Finally, Quick Tail said: "My decrees are not arbitrary. They are made for the safety and well-being of the Holt. They cannot be flouted by any member, including the Alpha's child."

Sleek ground his molars in frustration. *Don't argue! Just keep your hijna quiet.*

"You will be disciplined before the romp. Each ear bitten during the Jaarjoora ceremony," Quick Tail promised. "The entire Holt must see that not even its Saia is above the law." To Sleek's surprise, the Den Sire gathered him into his strong arms and added: "You must stop taking foolish risks with your life. If you were to die, then so would I... of a broken heart. I'd prefer to live a while longer yet."

"Yes." Sleek felt like a kit again in the arms of his father and returned the embrace. "I'll try." An ear-nip in front of the romp would be painful and humiliating, but he'd survive and heal quickly, thanks to his recent pryzoic supper. *That shouldn't be so bad,* he thought.

The Den Sire sighed and released his hold. "Let's go back. This wind is chilly."

As father and son re-entered the sanctum, a mass of gray and orange tentacles — Uuvaloo, the divining tharuuspex of High Split Rock and advisor to the Den Sire — emerged from behind the boulder shielding the pryzoa chamber and squirmed towards them. He and his spawn-sibling Cixtindi shared a basic symmetry, with subtle distinctions. Uuvaloo's body, squatter and more bulbous than his brother's, boasted longer eyestalks with smaller ocular-bulbs. One of his tentacles was reduced to a misshapen stub, courtesy of Majah, the rapacious moray eel with her venomous intellect and toxic bite.

"Den Sire, Den Sire! There are things you -*mmurpt*- must see," the octo-snail called out, his urging accompanied by a flatulent exhale from a breathing siphon. "Through the ceptual-lenses I viewed pryzoa moving in strange —" He stopped, eyestalks whipping around to Sleek.

Suppressing a snicker at the octo-snail's comical reaction, Sleek tugged his whiskers. "Nookeelee, Uuvaloo."

Uuvaloo's irises quivered in rhythm to ripples of red and yellow that raced over his skin. "Chookzl!" he swore, distressed feathery camouflage-growths distending and deflating across his ruddy flesh. "You entered sacred Gheelindreeliah, didn't you? No, no, no," he muttered, almost too low for Sleek to catch. "Ookl's Ink, give me strength. It is not my place to -*mmurpt*- chastise the Den Sire's offspring... disobedient, disrespectful kit, though he may be."

Sleek pretended not to notice the tharuuspex's snippy comment.

"As I said," the octo-snail continued without returning Sleek's greeting, "First Life are moving in odd patterns. The cyr-flames bespeak of where *The Cleaving Ynth and Shuuhl of Oussia* might be found, who may do the finding, and if Penuree will be involved."

"Penuree?" the Den Sire and Sleek said simultaneously. The notion any human monster could be involved with The Glow or Skynth felt foolish, almost offensive.

Uuvaloo beckoned the Eehr with a twenty-fingered hand. "Come, Sire. I speak -*mmurpt*- the truth. Peer through the ceptuals. See for yourself."

Quick Tail turned to Sleek. "Omen-dive with me. You could use the practice. You remember the refrain for the narrow current: 'first the place, then the face'?"

"Yes, I remember. And I respectfully decline. I'd rather meet future tides like everyone else. To do otherwise feels, somehow, like cheating. Plus, omen-diving upsets my stomach."

Quick Tail recited the old Ulurii axiom: "What are Envorah to The Blue and the waves, to the tides and the currents? Nothing but foam and flotsam." He sighed, disappointed. "The more we know about what is to come the better prepared we'll be. Someday I hope you'll learn to appreciate omen-diving. Those who see further react sooner and live longer." The Den Sire's face grew stern. "We'll speak of your punishment later. You may go."

Sleek tugged his whiskers. "Kooarii, Father." He glanced at the octo-snail. "Goodnight, Uuvaloo." With that, the limping Saia departed the pryzoa sanctum.

As he watched the Lontra princeling go, the tharuuspex's 'W'-shaped irises crinkled once more in disapproval. Sleek's refusal to accept his father's invitation both perplexed and dismayed the learned octo-snail. Such a great privilege as pryzoa-gazing should never be dismissed over the fleeting discomfort it caused the belly.

Who wouldn't wish to catch a glimpse of tides not yet born? Uuvaloo thought. *For Ookl's sake, it doesn't make sense!* "Your son is -*mmurpt*- unpredictable." His eyestalks swiveled towards Quick Tail. "Unlike his father."

"Very true. But, in full confession, I was much like him at that age," the tired Eehr admitted. "No time for rules or boundaries. And death was a distant wave far from shore."

"I find that hard to believe." Uuvaloo undulated beside the Alpha. "Shall we?"

Quick Tail sighed. "Those predictions aren't going to discover themselves."

As Alpha and Ulura retired to the pryzoa sanctum, a buffeting commotion from the rain-pelted balcony caught their attention. In the darkness outside, they glimpsed the silhouette of a great bird flapping its mighty wings for a graceful landing on the water slicked ledge, an icy blue ureola adorning its right ankle.

The sharp bronze-within-bronze eyes of the pelican diplomat peered inside as rain beaded off his feathers. "Kooarii, Den Sire. I have news from *The Center of the Circle*. May I enter?"

Quick Tail motioned his friend to approach. "Welcome *Noble Seeking Wing*, Pijper. Come inside, dry off, and offer your counsel. Come."

"Thank you." Pijper waddled across the dripping threshold and into the dry tunnel. "It's a bitter night tonight. Angry clouds." He ruffled his russet feathers to shake off clinging water.

"How long were you out there circling and waiting to land?" The Den Sire asked.

"Longer than I would've wished." The pelican clopped his beak and politely dipped his head at the octo-snail. "Uuvaloo, wisest tharuuspex."

"Pijper." The rubbery eyestalks of the Ulura bent with reciprocated respect. "So, what does -*mmurpt*- Fearless have to chafe against now?"

"Anything. Everything," Pijper warned. "That Scathing Tide still gnaws his bones."

"He's as stubborn and unyielding as a barnacle," Uuvaloo said with a flatulent exhale.

"There is much we must discuss, hrmmm? And little time to act."

"Very well." Quick Tail rubbed his temples, trying to sooth the ache growing behind his eyes. The number of problems that needed solving were like a swarm of myzee on a carcass.

How did things ever get so bad? he thought. *How did close friends become dire enemies?*

Finding those answers would prove elusive.

It would be a long, long night of searching... with no guarantee of success.

Sleek climbed down the gnarled roots of Old Tree. Retrieving his ynth at the base of the stone chimney, he descended two habitat-levels, and slipped through an irregular fissure jagged through the stone — his front door — and into his den.

The snug chamber, just adequate for an unmated Lontra, held a meager bed of frayed rope and dry grasses heaped in one corner. Bits of colored sea glass, a section of chipped mirror, curious pieces of odd-shaped driftwood, and a variety of different-sized fishhooks lined a crude rock shelf jutting from the wall. Sleek set aside his spear, went to a crescent-fracture window in the far corner of the den, and peered out. He sniffed salty night air. Rain pelted the ledge outside the window, while seventy tails below waves dashed against the foundations of High Split Rock.

Sleek sensed the storm's anger waning. In a few hours, the clouds should break and move deeper into The Still. Tomorrow's air would be scrubbed clean, soil runoff washing land-locked nutrients into The Blue.

Hunting will be good for the next few tides, he thought. *This storm will call bigger prey.*

The young otter gazed at the nocturnal world — the wind, the rain, the crashing surf — without seeing any of it. His mind skipped between anxious thoughts of his impending punishment (*"...both ears bitten before the romp..."*) to sweeter ones of love — Gloss' smile, her scent, her nibble-kisses, the golden fire in her eyes.

Sleek sighed, abandoned the window, and sought his bed. He nestled into the soft mound and listened to rain patter the rocky windowsill. It had been a busy day for the Beta, perhaps the busiest of his young life (save perhaps one other), and sleep proved difficult. So much energy still lived in his limbs waiting release, so many momentous events and close calls left to ponder and critique, and a hundred different pains competed for his attention, from nose to tail.

But the biggest ache of them all lodged itself firmly in his heart — the love for Gloss. It craved acknowledgement, like some hungry kit demanding to be fed.

I wish we could be together, kalaayaa. Are you thinking about me, as I am of you?

Sleek tossed and turned as he hunted for rest. He stretched, yawned, and stretched again until the numerous tensions in his body surrendered to the darkness growing behind his drooping eyelids.

And, far below the stillness of sleep, the scithma-snaag lurked... and sharpened its claws.

PART THREE

TIDE POOLS OF MYSTERY

"The world is full of magic things, patiently waiting for our senses to grow sharper."

W.B. Yeats (1865 – 1939)

CHAPTER 22

STAY ON THE PATH

Ayana awoke to the aromas of breakfast. She shuffled downstairs in her goldfish pajamas, hair disheveled, eyes gummy from sleep, and reflexively *tap-tapping* her glue drops. Seeing the empty couch brought the images of her elders embraced and weeping. Ayana understood that the shedding of tears often proved exhausting.

In the kitchen, Grandma fried bacon and eggs at the stove in an ancient cast iron skillet. Shep sat two paces from her ankles, hungry brown eyes fixed squarely on the sizzling people-food above his head.

"Morning, Grandma." Ayana yawned. She gave the retriever a hearty scratch behind his ears. Shep whined and licked his chops, his gaze never leaving the skillet.

"Hello, sweetie." With a decisive *snap*, an equally ancient toaster on the counter near the stove disgorged four slices of golden-brown homemade bread. "Sit and I'll bring breakfast."

Ayana settled into the same chair she used last night at dinner. Moments later, the sound of creaking floorboards alerted her to Grandpa's arrival.

"Good morning, Grandpa," Ayana said as he entered the dining room.

"Hey, princess." He kissed Ayana's forehead on his way to the kitchen, where he pressed against Grandma's back and nibbled the side of her neck. "And a fine morning to you, my love."

Grandma let out a little squeal and batted at her husband's head with her free hand. "Eugene, honestly. Ayana's watching." Her words scolded but her tone was light with pleasure. "Pour some coffee and sit. Breakfast is almost ready."

Grandpa got a green mug from the cupboard and filled it from the electric percolator. "That storm was a doozy. Felt like a month's worth of rain in one go. I'll check the gutters later." Steaming coffee in hand, he came out to the dining room — the scent of Old Spice and Folgers wafting in his wake — and sat in the chair at the head of the table. A tiny dollop of shaving cream still clung to his earlobe. "So, princess, what are your plans for today?"

"Don't know yet." Ayana pushed the sugar bowl and powdered creamer to within Grandpa's reach.

"Were you planning on visiting your father? It's been a while."

Ayana chewed on her lower lip and nodded. "I will. I promise."

Grandpa sweetened his coffee and smiled warmly at his granddaughter. "It's not something you need to make a promise for, Ayana. There's no pressure. No expectations. I'll let you figure out if, or when."

"I know," Ayana said. Visiting her Father had been, not so much a duty to perform, but something she both longed for... and yet dreaded. She understood the desire but couldn't articulate the fear, not even to herself.

"What about a trip down to our beach?" Grandpa asked.

"Yeah. I could go look for sand dollars. The ones here are always so big. I wonder why?"

Grandma entered, a plate in each hand. Shep followed close at her heels. "Grandpa thinks something special is in the water." She set a plate with two fried eggs, three strips of crispy bacon, and buttered toast in front of Ayana (*yummy cholesterol heaven!*). "But I doubt it. It's just the ocean. And you should go visit your father."

Ayana and Grandpa shared a knowing smile. Seemed like remembrances were thick in the air.

"May I have some coffee, please?" Reacting to Grandma's frown, Ayana added: "I totally drink it at home all the time. Mom lets me."

"Does she now? Hmmmm. I guess." Grandma fixed a skeptical eye on Ayana, set the breakfast plate in front of her husband, and returned to the kitchen. Shep stayed behind, positioning himself beside Ayana's chair, poised to receive any potential offerings.

"Where's mom, anyway?" Grandpa took a bite of toast. "Sleeping. She had a late night."

Ayana picked up a fork and tucked into the food. Unlike her friends, she had no silly phobias about gaining weight or being skinny; a high metabolism kept her naturally lean. She ate what she wanted, whenever she wanted — she was lucky like that — but, that was where her luck began and ended. After some silent chewing, Ayana asked, "Grandpa, what do you think is so special with the water?"

Grandpa shrugged his meaty shoulders. "It's the way the sea looks sometimes...kind of ...oh, I don't know... like there's light under the waves. And, once and a while, the water has a *tickle* when you touch it. Like static, maybe?"

"It's just how sunlight reflects off the surface," Grandma insisted, returning from the kitchen with a small cup of coffee in one hand and her own breakfast in the other. She set the cup by Ayana's plate. "And as for the *tickle*, well, that's just the salt, isn't it?"

"Say what you like, honey," Grandpa muttered, with an almost knowing smirk.

"Oh, I will, dear." Grandma smiled, patted Grandpa's hand, then sat and began eating.

"When you go to the beach keep an eye peeled for the wildlife" Grandpa said. "We've all kinds on our property: deer, squirrels, raccoons, owls. Even otters. River otters on occasion, and sometimes a sea otter bobbin' about the waves. If you're lucky you might see one."

"And why don't you take Shep with you?" Grandma asked. "He needs a good walk."

At the sound of his name, Shep wagged his tail and licked his lips. Ayana looked down at the old brown mutt. "You wanna go for a walk on the beach, boy?" she asked brightly. Shep snorted and squirmed in reply.

"Stay on the path, though," Grandpa reminded. "And mind the tide pool rocks. They're slippery and Shep's not a puppy anymore."

Ayana broke off a small piece of bacon and held it over the retriever's head. "How 'bout a treat first? You want a treat?"

At the word 'treat', Shep let out an impatient bark. His body quivered in anticipation.

"Oh, stop teasing the poor thing," Grandma said. "Can't you see he's just ready to burst?"

Ayana offered the morsel. Shep devoured it so fast he probably didn't even taste it.

Grandpa guffawed. "Lucky for you, he's long since sworn off fingers."

Shep was waiting by the back door when Ayana arrived, now dressed for the cold in fresh jeans and a thick blue wool-lined jacket. "You ready, boy?"

The dog whined and snorted in response. An old yellow leash hung on a hook by the door. Ayana tried to fasten it onto Shep's collar, but the dog plunged and squirmed with such frenzy that she gave up.

"Fine. Be a spazz."

Ayana had barely opened the door when Shep barreled into the chill fog and raced across the wet grass towards the outer fence. Beyond, hidden in the mist, forest and ocean beckoned. Within seconds, Shep had completely disappeared into the murk. Ayana didn't know the mutt's exact age, in either 'human' or 'dog' years, but he could clearly run like a puppy when he chose.

"Stay on the path," Grandpa called out from the kitchen. "On the path!"

"I will!" Ayana shut the door before muttering, "Jeesh. I heard you the first dozen times."

Fog the color of thick cotton had rolled in from the Pacific, on the heels of last night's storm. Ayana could feel it when she inhaled — it made the air heavier. Past the fence, everything seemed ghostly and insubstantial. The trees and distant shoreline were completely enveloped.

Shep skidded to a brief stop at the fence, long pink tongue dangling, and glanced back at Ayana. His intelligent brown eyes seemed to ask: "Why are you moving so slow, human girl who gives me food? Why aren't you as excited as I am?"

Shep lifted a leg, marked his territory on a fence post, and vanished into the fog.

Ayana followed, the yellow leash dangling from her hand. Rain-wet grass soaked the hems of her jeans. "Go get 'em, boy!" She wasn't worried about Shep. The dog knew every inch of the woods. He couldn't get lost — and that, by extension meant she'd never get lost, either.

By the time Ayana reached the woods, the warm glow from the three kitchen windows was all that remained visible of the house, like a trio of fairy lights. Another five steps and they vanished, too. Of the trees — western red cedars, Sitka spruce, Douglas fir, bigleaf maple and western hemlock — only their long trunks, stuck like giant pins into the earth, were visible. Their twisted canopies, heavy with dangling mosses, remained obscured by thick fog. The countless emerald ferns and tangled underbrush of berry brambles carpeting the forest floor were likewise masked. Everything smelled of moisture and mildew; of trees, soil, and distant sea salt.

Ayana had never experienced her grandparent's woods like this before. The cloying fog imbued the landscape with the strangeness of an alternate dimension. She wondered if straying from the well-worn path would set her feet onto an entirely different world, one where maybe she'd have superpowers. *Probably not,* she thought.

With a wet rustling Shep reappeared from under the carpet of lush ferns. The dog sniffed inside the hollow trunk of a long fallen, moss-laden tree. He marked his territory again before trotting on down the path, his damp, feathered tail waving like a banner.

Ayana followed, gouts of steam blowing from her nostrils. The trail wound steadily downhill. Tree roots marred the path like twisting wooden snakes. Ayana watched her footing and kept to the path, just as Grandpa had repeatedly bid. The din of relentless, crashing waves grew louder the closer she drew to the beach.

Weak sunbeams filtered through the mist, highlighting tiny currents of swirling vapor. Through the thinning fog and dwindling branches, Ayana caught sight of five sea stacks protruding from the water: the first (and smallest) stood two hundred feet offshore, the last and largest a quarter mile away. Perpetually wave-lashed, their eroded granite and limestone sides rose higher than a medieval tower. The last stack, riddled with holes and dark fractures, stood over twice the size of its closest rival. A great conifer crowned its grassy roof like a bushy green top hat. This megalith, cracked down the middle as if by a giant chisel, offered a home to legions of seabirds and, as far as Ayana knew, nothing else.

The girl quickened her pace. "C'mon, Shep. Keep up," she urged the dog as he snuffled about the evergreen understory somewhere behind.

As girl and dog strode the path on its final descent, the forest gave way to carpets of salt-tolerant grasses and ice plant already in bloom with bright magenta and yellow flowers. The trail continued down a series of steep switchbacks along the contours of a tapering hill that jutted into the ocean like the prow of a mighty ship.

Steps, constructed from old, irregularly spaced railroad ties, made up the final stretch of the trail, eventually ending at a sandy cove where Ayana had spent countless leisurely hours. On her right, an earthen berm partitioned an unknown territory. Her grandparents didn't own anything beyond that ridge. A simple driftwood and barbed-wire fence — built by her grandfather a decade before Ayana's birth — bordered the trail and delineated the property line.

As Ayana drew closer, she realized a section of hillside had collapsed during last night's storm, and it had taken an entire length of the fence with it. The aroma of wet, freshly churned earth filled the air. Ayana's curiosity demanded instant gratification, so she inched towards the crumbling edge of the fall and peered over. Below, a spray of boulders protruded from the reddish-brown soil, forming a clumsy stepladder down to the shoreline.

A few driftwood timbers, linked by strands of barbed wire, were visible beyond the spill. The hitherto forbidden beach beyond lay hidden within a foggy shroud.

Ayana squatted on her haunches to think, arm draped over Shep's shaggy neck. "What should we do, boy?" she asked the dog. He whined and licked her hand.

The universe had presented her with an unexpected opportunity. Ayana's imagination swirled with prospects of what awaited down there, each idea more outlandish then the last.

Buried pirate treasure? *Perhaps.*

A mermaid's bathing pool? *Highly unlikely.*

The skeleton of a sea serpent? *Pure, wonderful nonsense.*

But what did it matter if the discoveries were magical or mundane? Ayana would soon turn fourteen — *I'm a full-fledged teenager, damn it!* — and she felt old enough to make her own decisions about where to place her feet.

Grandpa's edict returned: *Stay on the path. You hear me, princess? On. The. Path.*

After an uncertain moment, Ayana shook her head. "Sorry Grandpa. Not this time."

She'd stayed on the path long enough.

Ayana turned to Shep. "Who's gonna know? You aren't telling anyone. Right?"

She rose to her feet and hesitated, fingers subconsciously *tap-tapping* her glue drops. *Sure is steep. I can climb down those rocks, but what about Shep?*

She took a deep breath. "Okay, boy. I know you can do this. We both can. Let's go."

With her hand firmly gripping the old dog's collar, Ayana took the first step down.

CHAPTER 23

THE DEEP SEE

Ayana had scaled her share of trees and boulders over the years. She took the first steps down the earth-fall easily enough, as surefooted (...*she thought*...) as a mountain goat —

— until her foot slipped.

She squealed like a frightened kindergartner. With one hand still clutching Shep's collar, she flailed wildly with her free hand and managed to snare a protrusion of rock. That, and the dog's instinctive balance, arrested a potentially fatal fall.

Ayana's heart pounded. Her mouth dried up even as her palms moistened with sweat. Shep grunted with the strain of supporting his young human's weight. "Too close," Ayana croaked, and then, "Shit!" as horrifying thoughts of tumbling down the slope, cracking her head against each rock as she went, made her wince with phantom pain.

Shep whined and licked her face with a wet, warm tongue.

"You saved me, boy," Ayana gave the old retriever an affectionate head scratch. "Good dog. I'll never gripe about walking you ever again. You're getting a treat for sure." Shep licked Ayana's face once more, excited by that familiar 'T-dash-dash-dash-t' word. "Okay. Let's go."

Girl and canine progressed, descending the jutting stones with extra caution, every foot placement well considered before commitment. Ayana aided Shep in traversing the trickier spots, for ease of the mutt's joints. It turned out that hoisting and heaving a wet dog — well trained as Shep was — while simultaneously keeping one's balance proved quite the juggling act.

They leapt the last few feet to the forbidden beach. The old dog's tail wagged so hard Ayana thought it might fly off and get lost in the fog. She snapped the leash to Shep's leather collar, caught her breath, and looked around.

"Oh... woooow..."

The contrast between this beach and her grandparents' cove couldn't have been starker.

Her family-owned shoreline was like a clean, flat dinner plate. This place resembled a rusty crate full of pottery shards and broken glass. No sand for walking barefoot or having a leisurely picnic. No place to fly a kite or relax and watch gulls circle sea stacks.

This beach felt like an untamed landscape on a distant alien planet. One not meant for a girl on the cusp of her fourteenth year.

Yet here she stood, just the same.

Ayana and Shep ventured further along the haphazard shoreline. A multitude of small rocks, each threatening sprained ankles, and stubbed toes, were encrusted with barnacles and mussels. A profusion of jagged boulders like stone teeth trailed into deepening waters. Sodden, stinking mounds of olive-green seaweed lay scattered about as far as she could see. Ayana prodded a small heap with her foot, sending up an agitated swarm of tiny black kelp flies.

She swatted at the few threatening to buzz up her nose. "Gaah! Get away!" Shep leapt at the swarm, snapping. "Ewww, Shep. Don't eat those." Ayana frowned in disgust. "C'mon. Let's go." She tugged on the dog's leash.

Girl and mutt continued to explore. In this place life moved to the rhythm of ceaseless tides; water rushing in and washing out. And with it, the murmurations of deep time etched on every eroded rock and exposed cliff face. Surf frothed in perpetual dialogue with stone. Eons of such back-and-forth would eventually grind them to meal. Seagulls, hidden in fog, cried hungrily as they wheeled overhead looking for sustenance among the flotsam.

Wedged between two salt-crusted bounders, Ayana discovered a clear globule of trembling gelatin — a small jellyfish, stranded by the retreating tide. Grabbing a driftwood stick, she poked at the dying creature, pondering its misfortune.

At that moment — wreathed in fog, hemmed by the sea at her back and a steep cliff above her — it dawned on Ayana how *totally* alone she was.

This state of pure isolation felt blissful. Liberating. Only trustworthy Shep stood with her to share the experience. No one else would walk where they walked, hear what they heard, or do what they were doing.

She let her imagination run free, wondering what manner of creature might even now lie hidden beneath the restless waters, pondering her existence. Mermaids or selkies, perhaps? If she wished hard enough, would some fantastic being emerge from the surf to initiate a conversation?

Without warning, a memory, so sharp and clear that for a moment, Ayana couldn't tell past from present, rocked her back on her heels —

She was on a beach, not as primordial as this one, but still rocky and wild. Her father, dressed in a heavy denim jacket and navy blue knit cap pulled over his blond hair, crouched across from her, a small tide pool between them. She held a stick in her hand. She was ten.

What'cha doing, Pipsqueak? Father inquired.

She'd found a little sea jelly on that day as well. "Looking at this thing. I think it's a jellyfish."

Yeah, looks like it, Father had said. *Hey, there's some bigger tide pools further up the beach. Let's go check'em out.* He grinned and held out his hand to help Ayana to her feet.

These rocks are slippery, he cautioned. *We gotta go slow. I don't want you to fall.*

"I won't, Dad." Still embraced by the memory, Ayana spoke aloud, but as soon as the words left her mouth, her foot slipped off a rock and into a cold puddle. Icy water filled her sneaker and soaked her sock. The shock took her breath away.

She imagined her father looking at her, teeth flashing in a wide grin. *You were saying?*

"Crap," Ayana muttered. Now, she'd have to endure the discomfort of a sodden, freezing cold foot. She glanced at Shep, who stood at attention, tail wagging. "You don't mind wet feet, do you?" she asked, then, tossing the stick into the fog, she moved on. Shep followed without protest.

Ayana spent the next several minutes helping Shep negotiate an especially rugged stretch of beach. The effort left her winded, so she paused for a much-needed rest break, and to have a look around.

She and the dog now stood amidst a landscape of countless tide pools, all fed by seawater rivulets, each one sheltering a unique population of life. Hordes of hermit crabs clambered among the rocks crusted with pink Coralline algae and volcano-shaped barnacles, searching for food. Purple rock crabs, some big as a dinner plate, were wedged into crevices to escape detection. Species of delicate and colorful fish Ayana had never seen before darted from view as she bent over a pool to peer at them. White limpets, interspersed among clumps of black and blue mussels, clung to the pitted rocks like millions of hard-shelled snowflakes. In the deeper pools, a constellation of orange, yellow, and brown starfish lay scattered among groves of pale green sea anemones. And everywhere: prickly red and purple sea urchins chewed their way through the shoreline kelp.

Curious, Ayana probed an anemone and giggled with delight as its tentacled crown constricted around her fingertip. She remembered visiting the artificial tide pools at a local aquarium, during a school field trip in the sixth grade. The recycled water-filled tanks contained a sad assortment of stunted sea stars, traumatized crags, and spine-broken urchins that had no choice but to tolerate endless poking and prodding. But this coastal biome teemed with animals that had never encountered a human, nor felt the probing fingers of a curious child —

Ayana truly believed they were all the luckier for it.

Ayana didn't own a watch.

And even if she could deduce the time by the sun's position — which she couldn't — it remained hidden behind a thick fog blanket. The earlier excitement that gripped her had begun to wane, the abundance of littoral life notwithstanding. She was getting hungry. Plus, her wet feet were cold, as were her fingers, her nose, her cheeks, her ears —

"C'mon, Shep," she said. "Let's head back."

She lobbed a tiny rock into the fog. Instead of the familiar *'clank-ker-sploosh'* of stone glancing off stone and then hitting water, she heard a dull thud as the rock bounced off something unseen. It sounded like wood, but she couldn't be sure.

Just then, a soft breeze parted the fog enough to reveal a treasure...

"Wow!" Ayana exclaimed as the outline of a boat emerged from the coiling mists. She immediately forgot about leaving or the demands of her stomach.

Ayana approached the wreck, excited past caring if her already-soggy shoes got soaked anew in another cold puddle. Peeling black paint coated the hull from deck railing to midline, fire engine red from midline to keel. Near the bow, Ayana red the white block letters declaring the doomed vessel's identity.

" *'The Deep See.'* Kind of a dumb name for a ship."

But then she recalled how her father had loved puns and clever word play, and decided maybe it wasn't so dumb after all.

As a girl, Ayana had taken a ferryboat ride with her parents, to where, she couldn't remember. She didn't know what type of craft this particular boat might be — fishing trawler, crab boat, perhaps? — but it bore only a superficial resemblance to that much bigger ferry. The old vessel, its hull crusted with barnacles and scored with a multitude of scratches both shallow and deep, enthralled her — a mystery rendered in soggy wood, scored aluminum, and brittle fiberglass.

Ayana touched the hull timbers and marveled at their weather-beaten texture. She imagined Dad, standing beside her, his hand resting atop hers as her fingers made contact. "So cool," she whispered.

Marred by a crosshatch of deep gouges, the elevated bow sat wedged within a stony cleft riven in the sea cliff, as if the boat had been frozen in place while cresting a great, earthen wave. The seaweed-draped stern rested, partially submerged, on the rocky edge of a shallow cove formed by a ring of huge boulders. Ayana heard waves dashing themselves against this barrier, their fury reduced to little more than a ripple upon reaching the waterlogged wreck.

A huge gash — ten, maybe twelve feet long — breached the hull mid-ship. "That's what killed *The Deep See*, Shep," Ayana said, glancing down at the old retriever by her side. "How do you think it happened?"

Shep whined and licked his lips.

"Is that so?" Ayana replied, smiling.

The gaping laceration looked big enough for her to crawl through. But she'd have to reach it first. A nearby boulder directly below the wound offered an easy solution.

Shep watched as Ayana scaled the rock then let out a sharp bark, as if asking to join her.

"Quiet, Shep," Ayana ordered. "I'll be back in a minute." She pointed an index finger at the dog's face. "Stay. Good boy."

With a resigned grunt, Shep sat on wet haunches and began nibbling an itching spot on his front leg.

Ayana, now within arms-length of the boat's slit belly, paused to finger the splintered planks. Then, grabbing ahold of the least jagged section and straining with pure arm strength, she pulled herself up and poked her head inside.

"Anybody in here?" she called out. "Helloooooooo!"

The deadening acoustics of the musty, shadowed interior ate her words like candy.

Go on, she imagined Dad's voice encouraging her. *Don't be scared.*

"Pfft. What? I'm not scared," she proclaimed to the waiting darkness.

With a surge of strength, Ayana hoisted herself into the jagged opening and wiggled through. The fusty air, heavy with mildew, smelled like a fart in a woodshed. Damp hull timbers muted every sound, gobbling the outside noises like a hungry animal. Odors of old motor oil and spoiled fuel soured the air, the tell-tale exhale of a lifeless engine room hidden somewhere in the darkness. A layer of salt mixed with dirt, deposited from decades of exposure to surf spray, wind and rain crusted the floor around the breach.

Ayana's eyes adjusted to the gloom. Threads of light filtered through the holes from the eroded deck boards directly above, revealing the boat's empty cargo hold.

She wasn't sure if she should be here — it felt oddly like trespassing — and yet, Ayana's heart quickened with excitement. Searching the gloom, she spotted a ladder leading to the closed deck hatch. She crossed to the rungs, then climbed until the top of her head was within half an arm's-length from the hatch.

Bracing her palms against the wood, she gave the hatch a shove. The panel lifted just enough to allow a sliver of gray light to seep into the hold, but that was quickly extinguished when the heavy latch thudded back into place.

Ayana groaned. Gritting her teeth, she once again set her palms to the wood. Bracing herself, using all the leg strength she could muster, she shoved upwards. The hatch slowly lifted, rusted hinges squealing. The strain on her shoulders nearly defeated her. Just as she decided she could no longer continue, the panel rose high enough to allow Ayana to squeeze her upper body into the gap. With one final burst of effort, she wriggled through and slithered onto the deck, scraping her butt and the backs of her thighs in the process.

Pulling her feet free of the gap, she collapsed, barely noticing the sharp vibrations as the hatch thumped close. For a few moments, all Ayana could do was to lie still, panting. When at last her heart stopped pounding and her breathing slowed, she sat up.

Pretty darn impressive of me, she thought, her face flushed with both pride and exertion.

Ayana stood and scanned the sloping deck. Piles of old rope, some coiled, others frayed and entangling tumbled and rusted crab pots, lay strewn about. Tousled fishing nets and scattered, sun-faded orange buoys added to the chaotic scene.

Without conscious thought, she tapped her glue drops. "Awesome," she whispered.

Ayana habitually used that word to describe many trivial things, so much so, that it had long since lost any real impact. But here, on the deck of this newfound domain, the adjective actually felt appropriate as defined by Webster.

Picking her way through the detritus, Ayana approached the wheel-house. It occupied the front third of the boat, five of its seven grimy windows still intact. Wiping away a layer of grit, she peered inside to see an intriguing array of brass gauges, mysterious nautical instruments, and the undamaged wooden wheel.

Ayana found the door and gave the heavy panel a push. It swung reluctantly on screeching hinges. She approached the wheel, admiring its polished spokes and handles worn down from years of use. Deciding that it was still quite beautiful, she tried turning the wheel, but it only moved an inch.

Must be jammed, she thought. *Wonder if I can fix it?*

Ayana spotted a stairway heading down into dimness. She hesitated, and almost called out, but then stopped herself. Clearly, there was no one else here. This boat had been abandoned years ago. Cautiously descending the steps, she found three doors covered in cobwebs. Ayana wasn't afraid of spiders, but that didn't mean she wanted to get bitten. Pulling her jacket sleeves over her hands, she gave the first door a hard push. Heavy, but not locked, it groaned open. On the other side lay a small room furnished with a dusty mess table and three battered metal chairs. A barren kitchenette anchored the far wall. Dull gray light filtered through a porthole.

Ayana snorted. No treasure here. She moved on, hoping for something more exciting. But the other rooms held nothing but the rusted frames of stripped bunks and tiny, empty closets. The room at the end turned out to be a small shower and toilet.

Fishermen take showers? Ayana wondered. *Guess even they get tired of fish stink and want to wash it off.*

Realizing there was nothing of real interest below, Ayana made her way topside. As she exited the wheelhouse onto the open deck, she glanced about, and noticed something... strange.

Dispersed all over the sloping deck, lay hundreds upon hundreds of empty crab shells, snapped legs, and broken claws — all stacked in delicate piles and precariously balanced mounds. Some were organized into crude star and circular patterns, others in triangles, diamonds, or wavy lines. Crowns of white and gray seagull feathers adorned some displays, while tiny stones or bits of driftwood surrounded others in odd alignments. These shell accumulations did not seem like random seagull droppings from past meals or deposits of wind and wave action.

No — in her gut, Ayana knew they were deliberate arrangements.

What manner of creature, or creatures, could have done this? And more importantly, were they lurking somewhere close by, perhaps even now watching her? Was she in danger? She hoped not.

Ayana shrugged off her unease. The discovery was peculiar. A mystery for a later date. Nothing more. She skirted the shell-decorated deck and moved aft. The tides that swallowed this section of *The Deep See* twice a day made it extra slippery, and her wet shoes found little traction. Each step threatened a tumble.

On the beach below, Shep started barking. *Sounds like he wants to go home*, Ayana thought. With a final, wistful glance about the deck, Ayana gingerly made for the deck hatch. "Ok, Shep!" she yelled. "Stop being such a sp—"

The reprimand faltered as a wet sneaker skidded on the slick deck boards, sending both feet flying out from under her. Ayana fell hard on her backside. She yelped in pain and slipped towards the partially submerged stern. Time seemed to slow like cold molasses.

No no no no no don't let me fall in the water! There could be sharks!

Her flailing hands, desperate to grab something, anything, to arrest her slide, along with her wildly kicking feet, destroyed several of the delicate crab-shell mounds. Luckily, a thick coil of soggy rope saved her from spilling over the edge into the sea. The collision knocked the wind from her lungs. Heart racing, Ayana remained stock-still as terror leached from her muscles, and her breath slowly returned to normal.

"Balls," she coughed, thankful her clumsiness had gone unwitnessed.

The whole mishap felt like it had taken hours to unfold, though in reality, no more than a trio of seconds had passed. Ayana stood. A sharp sting along her calf muscle made her wince. She kneaded the painful spot; beneath her pant leg, a beautiful scratch now awaited treatment with a hydrogen peroxide and Bactine cocktail.

Wiping a dollop of seagull shit from her coat sleeve, Ayana regained her footing. Wobbly, and mindful of the slick deck boards, she inched towards the hatch. Pain stung her calf again. Reaching down to massage the hurt, she glimpsed — nestled in the very rope that had saved her from certain disaster — a crimson sparkle.

Ayana, her discomfort forgotten, knelt for a closer look...

CHAPTER 24

FINDING TREASURE

"A seashell?"

The spiraled structure belonged to a sea snail, that much she guessed.

But it looked to be cast in glass. Vivid *red* glass. *How is that possible?*

Stranger still — unless her mind was playing tricks — it seemed to glow, like the last ember of a dying campfire. Ayana blocked the muted sunlight with her hand, looked again, and still the shell gleamed with inner radiance.

Ayana reached into the rope coil, gingerly touched the red-glass shell, and quickly withdrew her hand as static electricity tickled her fingertips. She giggled and impulsively tapped her glue drops. "Too weird."

She imagined she could hear Dad's voice, cautioning her as he did when she was little and about to touch something potentially harmful. *Seashells aren't supposed to do that. Maybe you should leave it be.*

"Nope," Ayana said aloud.

She scooped up the red-glass mystery. The static softened to a mild effervescence on her palm, like how a mouthful of carbonated soda might feel on her tongue. She spied tiny air chambers suspended in the semitransparent spiral. Then, past the odors of salt, tide, and weathered timbers, Ayana caught a whiff of something... *fragrant.*

She sniffed and sniffed again, trying to pinpoint the source, and realized the odor emanated from her cupped hands.

Dubious, Ayana brought the red-glass shell to her nose —

— and got hit with an odor unlike any she had ever known.

It held a sweetness more intense than any candy store or bakery aroma, blended with a savory umami more delicious than any steak she'd ever eaten. Her mouth immediately began to water. A sharp hunger pain made her wince.

She sniffed again. The scent tickled the same area of her brain that made infants crave mother's-milk, or that drove an animal dying of thirst to seek out water. It sparked a compulsion to taste, chew, and swallow.

Ayana brought the red-glass shell to her lips, and with the tip of her tongue, she cautiously tasted it. Her body instantly felt light and airy, as if at any moment, a stray breeze could lift her into the clouds.

This must be what magic tastes like, she thought. It was pure bliss, but it was not enough. She wanted more. She put the shell to her teeth, then — she hesitated. But... *magic isn't real.*

It existed only in the realms of fantasy. And yet, something about this shell was clearly defying the rules of reality, scattering them like the delicate crab shell mounds Ayana's kicking feet had ruined.

Damn the rules! She had to discover the truth.

Ayana carefully nibbled off a salt grain-sized fleck and crunched it into powder with her front teeth. As the morsel dissolved to nothingness, her mouth filled with a flavor beyond flavor, like electric bacon wrapped in a cotton candy bowtie. She couldn't articulate all the competing sensations it stoked, but she innately understood they went beyond simply satisfying her tastebuds. The desire to nest fought the craving to explore. Aspirations to evolve beyond the need for limbs were hemmed by the urge to sprout more appendages and scuttle into the sea.

And when Ayana swallowed, something happened like nothing she'd yet experienced during her nearly fourteen years of life. The world — or more accurately, her perception of it — *expanded*, accelerating like a comet streaking out in every direction at once.

Her sharpened vision pierced the fog. From two hundred feet away, Ayana could discern individual corn kernel-sized foam bubbles bobbing and jostling on incoming swells. Her ears likewise deciphered, behind the sounds of wind and crashing wave, the distinct rap of Shep's tongue across his wet fur as he worried a fleabite. She felt every stitch of clothing tickling her skin with a million peach-fuzz fibers. Ayana sensed her hair, nails, and teeth, growing. She felt the fresh scratch on her calf, already healing a micron at a time. Both energized and agile, she believed at that moment she could run a marathon backwards or balance her body on an index finger from a top a basketball.

Her world became inexplicable, enrapturing, and yes... *magical.*

Then, in the span between two heartbeats, the overwhelming magic was gone.

Ayana's five senses withdrew, quick as a hiccup, back to their original proportions. Reality felt muted, sluggish, and slightly lopsided. She gripped the shell tight and fought to stay on her feet as another memory of a time with her father resurfaced...

They were in a playground. She stood on a spinning yellow metal merry-go-round, clutching the railing for dear life as Dad spun the platform. She laughed and laughed, so hard it made her stomach hurt. Dad spun the merry-go-round faster and faster at her urging. But she grew dizzy. A victim of centrifugal force. Her grip faltered. She tried to hold on, but her fingers were pried loose. She let go. For one crazy moment, she was flying; the next, she lay on the ground, bawling and gasping for air. Dad ran to her and scooped her into his arms, holding her tight against his chest.

Breathe, Pipsqueak. You're okay. Just breeeeeeathe.

Eyes pinched shut, Ayana clenched her jaw, filled her lungs, then slowly exhaled. Stability returned as the memory tiptoed away...

The strange euphoria that gripped her had already faded, leaving behind only a vague sense that she'd somehow been in a state of hyperawareness. Yet, she kept enough impressions of the experience to know she had chanced upon a new path of wonder. And exploration.

Eagerly, Ayana scanned the waterlogged deck, hoping to discover more mysterious shells. But she only saw the odd crab carapace mounds and clumps of seaweed splattered with bird guano. She gazed at the red glass wonder. Its weight felt minuscule in her hands. Of the billions of people on the planet, only she'd found this amazing thing. It might be the only one in existence. A singular morsel of magic. The idea both elated and disappointed her.

Why me? What did I do to deserve this? Then, with a smile: *It's one of a kind. And it's mine. All. Mine.*

She suddenly felt powerful, and very, very lucky.

Ayana considered a second taste and decided against it. Too many questions needed answering first. *Why does it glow? Where did it come from? How come it smells so sweet? Why did I glitch out after tasting it?*

Mysteries upon mysteries, swirling about like flakes in a snow globe.

Ayana pocketed the shell and cautiously scooted back towards the deck hatch.

Climbing into the wreck had proved much easier than climbing out.

Ayana wiggled through the hull gash and began her descent, mindful of jabbing splinters, testing each hand and foot hold before committing herself. Confident at last, she dropped onto the beach with impressive dexterity. Shep, dutifully waiting, bounced on his front legs, barking with joy, tail wagging furiously.

Ayana scratched the dog behind the ears. "Let's go home, boy. Lunch time."

With a last glance at *The Deep See*, its enigmatic silhouette wreathed in coastal fog, Ayana started back down the primordial beach towards the distant rockslide, mindful of each step. Shep padded alongside, tongue lolling.

The girl knew that one false move, either because of lingering euphoria or clumsiness, could spell disaster. She didn't fancy the idea of trekking all the way back to her grandparents' home on a sprained, or worse, broken ankle.

Girl and dog reached the rockslide and Ayana helped Shep scale the tumbled stones up to the trail. The trek back through the forest seemed effortless. Ayana's floating stride, fueled by the anticipation of food and warmth, sped her without a second look past the old apple tree shading her father's grave.

The energy spent grieving for thirteen months had now been set to a singular focus: decode the magic. And the new purpose felt wonderful.

By the time Ayana slipped through the wooden gate into her grandparents' backyard, she was over an hour late for lunch. She hurried across the damp, uneven lawn towards the house, Shep trotting on her heels.

A voice from the nearby vegetable garden hailed her.

"Heavens, Ayana, where have you been? We were getting worried." Grandma rested on her knees in the dark soil, sunhat shading her frowning face. A broad-leafed weed trailing a long taproot dangled from one work-gloved hand. "You've been gone hours."

Ayana winced. *Grandma would have to be here now!* If she spoke the truth about leaving the path, and all the ensuring discoveries, she'd be sentenced to a month of lawn mowing or, even worse — bean picking and garden weeding. *Better not risk it.*

"I took Shep for a walk. Just like Grandpa asked me to."

"Why are you and Shep so dirty?"

"We were playing. In the sand. Digging holes. Time got away from me. It won't happen again. Sorry." Ayana looked towards the carport. Grandpa's 1965 holly green Ford pick-up truck was gone. Only an oil stain on the concrete remained to mark its presence. "Where's Grandpa?"

"He went into town. Things needed doing. Don't be surprised, though, if he tells you to give Shep a bath when he gets back."

At the sound of the word 'bath', the old dog scurried off, head lowered as if scolded.

Grandma gave Ayana a dubious glance, then resumed her labor. She tossed the weed aside and plucked another. "Clean up. And take off those dirty shoes before you go inside. Your lunch is in the refrigerator."

Ayana bounded up the porch steps, slipped off her wet sneakers beside the door, and entered the kitchen. She washed her hands in the sink with a bar of coarse homemade soap that smelled of lavender and milk. In the fridge, she found a cellophane-wrapped bologna and cheese sandwich.

Lunch in hand, Ayana rushed to the stairs. Shep, dirty from head to toe, collapsed onto his doggy-bed; a feeble tail thump was all he could muster as Ayana passed. Not even the promise of people food could rouse him off the cushion.

Ayana hurried up to her room and set the sandwich on the bed, then peeled off her wet socks. She reached into a pocket and withdrew her strange treasure. In the muted light its inner glow appeared even more prominent, casting a red luster against her cheeks. Ayana's heart raced in reaction.

I need a book about seashells... Oh, wait! An image flashed in her mind.

On bare feet Ayana sped down to the living room. On the bottom shelf of the large bookcase next to the TV, she found it: *Compendium of Seashells, by R. Tucker Abbot and S. Peter Dance.* She slid the heavy, glossy-covered tome from its place, tucked it under her arm and hustled back up to her room. She closed and locked the door, sat cross-legged on the bed, and opened the cover.

Ayana had no intention of actually reading the book. Glancing at pictures would suffice. She took a bite of sandwich and began flipping through the pages: the mystery shell lay on top of the blanket next to her where she could see it. It was already scenting the room like some whimsical incense cone. She gave only cursory attention to the diagrams, size comparison charts, and hand-drawn cutaway illustrations. What she needed lay at the center of the volume — the color photographic plates.

Ayana examined each image, dismissing those specimens that were too big, small, or flat; to spiky, coiled, or tubular. There were hundreds of reference species, thousands of sub-varieties. Only one entry — '*Calliostoma annulatum'*, the jeweled topsnail — came closest to matching her shell. But the book said nothing about a translucent, ruby-glassed variant. And absolutely *no* mention of any otherworldly smell or taste.

Ayana flipped past the last photo without finding an exact match. Defeated, she tossed the heavy book aside. She tapped her glue drops without thought. Picking up the shell, she pondered its origins. *Is it from another planet? Another dimension, maybe?*

Ayana sniffed the shell again. Its mystery, like a pesky splinter lodged under a fingernail, rankled. She had no patience for such things. Immediate satisfaction was more to her liking. Still, she was determined to uncover the answer to this riddle, no matter if it took her all summer.

Ayana held the crimson jewel up to her eyes. *What was it dad always used to say?* she thought. *Oh, yeah...*

"Patience is a virtue."

CHAPTER 25

A GLIMPSE OF THE GARDEN

E vening settled over the Outerbridge home like a soft purple quilt, night trailing as blackest trim. Coastal winds coaxed the forest canopy to sway below tussled clouds.

Inside, Grandma decreed her husband, daughter-in-law, and granddaughter sit for dinner: whole-wheat spaghetti and homemade vegetarian marinara sauce. Shep, still dirty from forbidden beach exploration, orbited the table on his hunt for scraps.

Haley sat across from Ayana, a sleepy-yet-contented look on her face. That cry in the storm — thirteen frustrating months of rage and grief finally expelled — hollowed her out in a blissful way. Gentle exhaustion, a healing blend of tears and joy, mixed with the tell-tale red eyes of weeping. Hayley spent the day reveling in her newfound emotional emancipation, mostly in her room where privacy allowed the shedding of smaller tears. Evening closure would be similar: cry, laugh, rest, cry some more. Her in-laws didn't push for particulars, they knew all too well how she felt. Leaving Hayley alone with her revival allowed them to do likewise.

Tomorrow would be a fresh day in a world bathed in clean, new light. For *all* of them.

Ayana stared blankly at her plate, pushing noodles around with her fork. She couldn't summon an appetite. Crucial things occupied her attention: a proper name for her newfound ship, the equipment it needed, the crab shell-piles scattered across the deck — but, most of all — that dam perplexing jeweled topsnail. It abided snug in her front pocket, demanding attention.

"Stop playing with your food," Grandpa ordered. "Eat up. *Mangia.*"

Ayana took a reluctant bite. Chunks of onion and green peppers from Grandma's vegetable garden floated in a runny tomato sauce. And was that... a piece of zucchini? Ayana frowned at the notion. *Uurgh. So nasty.*

"What's wrong, Ayana?" Grandma asked. "I thought you liked my vegetarian spaghetti."

"No. It's fine. It's just... I'm still full," Ayana lied. "...from lunch."

"That was hours ago," Hayley replied. "You need to eat. So, eat."

Ayana rolled her eyes and sighed. "Fine."

Hayley prodded her daughter's shin with a foot. "Don't disrespect," she warned.

Ayana smiled wanly, took a bite of pasta a chewed. "Mmmm." She washed it down with a swallow of weak iced tea. "Yummy."

"What did you do today?" Grandpa asked. "Besides walk poor 'ol Shep into the ground?" The elderly retriever thumped his tail upon hearing his name.

"Went to the beach. Looked for sand dollars. Dug holes. Nothing special."

"Did you stay on the path like I said?"

"Yup. Sure did. The whole time," Ayana lied again. *Twice in one night. Not good.*

Ayana hated lying, but it couldn't be helped. The adults could never know about the new beach, *The Deep See*, or, most importantly, the secret stashed in her front pocket. Adults supervised and micromanaged so much of her life — and were allowed to keep their own secrets.

So why can't I have some? she thought. Fair is fair.

As Grandpa dabbed his marinara with a slice of garlic bread, he paused and sniffed. "You smell that?" His brows furrowed as he tried pinpointing the source of the odor.

Grandma shook her head. "Eugene. Enough of your games. Stop passing gas over there."

"No, no." Grandpa protested and sniffed again. "It's... I can't place it."

"What?" Grandma sniffed in kind. "Did something burn?"

Everyone stopped eating. Perplexed eyes darted about the room as each adult tried to identify the mysterious, yet pleasant, fragrance.

"Sweet pipe tobacco?" Hayley suggested.

"Hmmm." Grandpa pursed his lips, pondering. "Brown sugar bacon, maybe?"

"I smell..." Grandma began, then smiled. "...fresh zucchini bread. But I haven't baked any in months."

Ayana knew the answer, felt it in her pocket, tingling with a vivacity that made her grin. "I don't smell anything," she said, took a bite of veggie-pasta, and presented a false smile.

She didn't realize Shep had also detected the odor — and the hidden seashell — until he'd circled the table and thrust his wet nose into Ayana's right front pocket, snuffling. Ayana jerked, scraping her plate with her fork.

The grating sound drew everyone's attention to her. Fighting a rising panic, Ayana knew she had to hide the shell in her room as quickly as possible.

"Can I be excused? I'm not hungry." Under the table she pushed Shep's head aside.

"We don't waste food in this house," Grandma reminded. "What you don't finish tonight you'll have to eat tomorrow."

"Fine." Ayana stood, pushed in her chair, and headed for the kitchen with her plate.

Grandpa cleared his throat. "Now that you're done, why don't you give Shep a bath? He could use it." His suggestive tone didn't disguise the command for what it was.

Shep fled for the safety of his doggy bed upon hearing the dreaded 'B'-word.

Ayana winced. If she must pay this price to keep her secret, then so be it. "Fine."

"Wrap your plate in cellophane," Grandma said. "Put it in the fridge."

Ayana entered the kitchen, opened a drawer next to the sink, and used the plastic wrap within to cover her meal. Sneaking out a zip-lock sandwich bag, she dropped her seashell inside and closed the seal.

The magic — and the beguiling odor it exuded — were both now luck up airtight.

Relieved, Ayana called to the dog. "C'mon, Shep. Let's get this over with."

Years ago, Grandpa built a washroom in the service porch behind the kitchen. For reasons he no longer remembered, he'd installed a big, white-enameled claw-foot bathtub, rather than a shower. Grandma used it for washing vegetables and soaking Grandpa's dirty work coveralls.

It also made the perfect place for bathing a gray-muzzled Labrador.

Ayana stepped into the tub, gently tugging Shep's collar until he finally clambered inside.

After he'd been scrubbed from nose to tail with flea shampoo and rinsed clean of soap and grime, Shep leapt from the tub before Ayana could halt his escape. As he vigorously shook himself, sending a spray of water across her face and body, Ayana reflexively turned away.

"Damn it, Shep! Now I smell like wet dog." She grabbed an old green towel off the floor and, after first dabbing the water from her face, began drying the dog's fur. He licked her hands and cheeks as she worked, eliciting giggles. "Ah, how can I stay mad at you? Apology accepted," Ayana said.

Shep wagged his tail and whined, gazing up at her with soft, golden-brown eyes.

"You want to know a secret?" The dog grunted as if in reply.

Ayana dried her hands on the towel, then pulled the zip-locked shell from her pocket. She held it up to the dog's face. "Look what I found on *The Deep See*. Treasure." She opened the bag, and the dog eagerly pushed his nose inside, sniffing.

Ayana's eyes widened in surprise as Shep froze, tail stiff as a branch. The fur along his spine rose and a soft groan sighed from his throat. Alarmed, Ayana stroked the dog's head. "Are you okay, boy?" She tried to withdraw the bag, but the retriever shoved his twitching nose in deeper. His tail relaxed and began furiously wagging, slapping the side of the tub with such force, Ayana worried he might injure himself.

She seized the flailing appendage, then yelped in dismay as Shep tried to swallow the shell. "No, Shep! *Not* a treat," she scolded, snatching the shell out of the dog's reach. "You really think I'm going to let you eat this?" She re-sealed the bag and returned it to her pocket. Clearly, the magic that had smelled so sweet to Ayana was downright irresistible to the dog.

Crouching down, she threw her arms around the retriever's neck. "Tomorrow, I'm going back to *The Deep See*," she whispered into his damp ear. "It'll be our secret. Okay?"

Shep sneezed in reply, then licked her ear.

All is darkness. Quiet.

Bottom of the ocean black. Depths of a cave silent.

And then — light.

At first, only a smear, like a campfire seen at night through half-closed eyes.

Yet the light persists. Grows brighter and brighter still. At the edges of dream, Ayana perceives a rainbow of colors. Some bright as beacons. Others flicker like bashful stars — any direct glance and they vanish into shadows.

Simple shapes manifest next: inchoate circles, blobs, lumps of matter. Then, fiery ovals appear; first one, then clusters, and then colonies teaming in all directions. Tattered, glassy-hued filaments flutter in waxing radiance. Elaborate fans, like splatters of liquid gold, wave and sift the air. Countless slender silvery tubes rise like columns supporting an invisible roof, each crowned with a tangle of deep-crimson whiskers.

What is this? *Ayana wonders.*

Usually, her dreams are mental gibberish, a tussled picture of the day's events filled with symbols and nonsense. This dream isn't behaving like anything her mind would know how to create. An alien calculus governs this world: wherever and whatever it is.

Then, from the light and color — slow movement follows. Unbearably slow.

Somehow, Ayana knows the necessity for speed doesn't exist here. There is only the perpetual journey towards a light that never gets any closer. The languid pace allows her to feel the contours of the rocks upon which she moves — every nook, bump, and jagged millimeter.

Suddenly it dawns on Ayana: Wait... What? I'm a... snail? Hah! Snail-Ayana?

She realizes the oval shaped crowded about are other snails. Panoplies of blown-glass mollusks and gem-like bivalves cling to the stones, in teaming multitudes and electric colors. Strange pillars and cones rising like otherworldly trees are a forest of rainbow seaweeds. Trellises of prismatic corals, like frozen lightening, disperse at jagged angles, amid thickets of platinum tubeworms veined with light.

Straining the limits of vision, Snail-Ayana perceives, beyond all this beauty, other forms of life to fantastic to conceptualize, let alone categorize. They shoot and surge from every free space. Snail-Ayana, at that moment, realizes she's crawling through a garden...

— A Garden of All Things.

But this crush of life is proving too much to handle. The intricacy of competing colors and forms doubles with each passing glance. Snail-Ayana realizes her limited view is a blessing: if she saw this Garden in its unfiltered entirety, she'd be overwhelmed.

She relaxes, lets the living kaleidoscope flow around her, and crawls along with it.

Until...

A shadow scuttles into view. It is massive, like a storm cloud across the sun.

It is vile, evil — implacable.

Snail-Ayana recoils. She instinctually knows it represents the antithesis of the peace and unity the light offers. The shadow swells, growing vast, darker; working to eclipse the light.

To smother it. To gorge upon it. To devour it, utterly...

Fear hits Snail-Ayana like a fist. As a snail, she can never hope to get away.

The shadow is all gluttonous appetite. Unfettered craving. It chews a swath through the delicate shapes with pincers that snip-and-snap and snip some more. Lava-hot innards coil and knot like a mass of wrestling snakes behind a transparent, armored shell.

And the stalked eyes — no emotion there; no pity, no compromise.

Just two remorseless black orbs that see everything as food. Snail-Ayana can't let those eyes find her, or the scissoring blades will dissect her as surely as they have the other mollusks and deliver the pieces to the horrible, grinding mouth. And then: the final horrors of digestion.

What is it? Snail-Ayana's terrified mind tries to produce a word to name the monster.

Then it comes to her. Crab? Oh, my God — it's a crab!

A behemoth, conceived by nightmare.

Snail-Ayana struggles to awaken, but the dream refuses to relent. Wake up! Wake up!

Luckily, the abhorrent presence does not sense her. It trundles past, pylon-like legs juddering the earth with its weight as it vanishes into shadows beyond the reach of the perpetual light. Calm returns to the Garden. The dream becomes peaceful again.

Whew. I'm glad that's over. Nothing more to be afraid —

Snail-Ayana barely forms this thought when she feels two groping and prying paws. Webbed with four digits, an opposable thumb, and long nails that tickle and prick. They are dexterous, curious; tool making.

But they aren't human.

A face with golden eyes peers down at Snail-Ayana. It's round, furred, with an arrowhead nose fringed with... whiskers? Could this be the owner of the paws? Are her snail-senses playing tricks?

Pop! The webbed hands pluck her from the rock —

Ayana awakened with a start, heart thudding in her chest. The shell falls from her clutched hand. It clinked on the floor, pulsing like a dying ember.

"What the hell?" Ayana croaked past the yelp lodged in her throat. She fought an urge to cough, failed, and began hacking furiously until, wiping away tears, she at last got the fit under control.

That was, hands down, the scariest dream I ever had.

Ayana climbed out of bed and cracked open the bedroom window. Outside, the approaching dawn softened the night. Distant sounds of crashing surf backdropped closer noises from the dark woods beyond the fence line: the twittering of early-rising birds, trilling crickets, the hoot of a hunting owl. Soft winds sighed through evergreen branches.

Ayana took a deep breath of the fragrant air. Night terror fading, she returned to bed. The lumpy mattress, pillow and thin blanket felt welcoming. Even the pervasive dog smell offered familiar comfort.

The scrape on her leg began to itch. She scratched it with the opposite heel. Yawning, she casually reached for the shell —

"Where is it?" Ayana groped around the blanket but found nothing. Panicked, she tossed away her pillow and threw back the sheets. Still nothing.

"Oh, no, no!" Eyes darting around the room, she spotted the softly glowing shell on the floor next to the bed. Dizzy with relief, she snatched it up, enclosing it within her fist. Claret light bled out from between her fingers.

Ayana lay back down and pulled the blanket around her body. She sighed and closed her eyes. She needed rest. Tomorrow would be a busy, busy day...

Happy memories of how father would come to her bedside, kiss her forehead, and say *Goodnight, Pipsqueak* eased her towards sleep.

"G'night, Dad," she whispered just before drifting off.

CHAPTER 26

OBSTACLES

Ayana awoke with a shaft of light from the newly risen sun stabbing her eyes.

She had no choice but to vacate the cozy bed. She would never willingly get up so early, but it was impossible to go back to sleep. Her full bladder demanded emptying. But, more important, the clandestine beach beckoned.

Ayana now had a place to think, to daydream — and just *be*. Alone.

The novelty of this newfound freedom filled her with quiet excitement.

She tiptoed to the bathroom, addressed her necessaries, and returned to her room. She dressed quickly, last night's nightmare already fading from memory. *Why couldn't I have been a superhero instead of a snail?* she wondered. *Flying instead of crawling? Oh, well.*

Ayana reached for her Keds, reconsidered, then grabbed her old, scuffed hiking boots instead. There'd be no cold, soaked socks today. Zip-locked mystery shell tucked snug into a front pocket, Ayana hoisted her backpack, and with boots in hand, she tiptoed down the stairs and into the dark kitchen on stockinged feet.

Ayana flicked on the light. In the walls the water pipes groaned — Grandma's morning shower. She always awoke first to make coffee and organize the day. And that meant that Grandpa still slept, as did Mom.

Ayana still had time to prepare for her grand adventure. But not much. *Better hurry...*

Ayana made two peanut butter and jelly sandwiches with English muffins instead of bread. Grandma had yet to bake a fresh loaf, so she was forced to improvise. A half-ripe banana, two cans of root beer, and a bag of ancient, miscellaneous candy discovered stashed in the back of a drawer rounded out the hasty rations. She wrapped everything in a plastic grocery bag and shoved the bundle into the backpack.

Ayana opened the patio door, paused a moment, then returned to a kitchen drawer. With the pen and paper within, she scribbled a quick note:

'Going to the beach. Back later. Will stay on the path. Promise. Ayana.'

Satisfied, Ayana stuck the note to the refrigerator with a turkey-shaped magnet then hastened out the back door. She sat on the top porch step to lace her boots, then jumped up and raced across the wet grass towards the garage. Damp morning air chilled her lungs, hands, and nose. The silent world smelled of tall woods and distant ocean.

The garage stood a dozen yards from the barn where Gingerbread and Cinnamon dreamt their equine-dreams. A hedge of overgrown juniper bushes surrounded the structure on three sides. The main door, a row of dingy windows running along the top, proved far too heavy to lift, but Ayana knew the side door always remained unlocked.

She entered the dark interior and sniffed. Aromas of oil, solvents, grass clippings, and old rubber mingled to create the distinctive odor she always identified with Grandpa. It was the smell of labor, generosity, calloused hands and a loving, tolerant heart.

Ayana flicked the light switch. The overhead bult sputtered and brightened with an electric hum. Grandma's 1972 4-door Buick and Grandpa's Ford truck were both parked under the carport beside the house; instead of actual cars, what greeted Ayana's eyes was pure...

"Chaos."

Metal and wooden shelves laden with scrap automobile parts filled one wall. A rack burdened with dozens of wrenches, pliers, and screwdrivers occupied another. A tool-cluttered workbench rested against a third. A legion of gardening clippers, hedgers, rakes, hoses, and mowers reinforced the mayhem. Boxes of out-of-fashion clothes, kitchen appliances, old Christmas decorations, and disassembled bicycles packed yet more shelves. Several discarded fishing-pole and tackle-boxes filled a dusty apple barrel.

In the eye of this cluttered maelstrom, a partially stripped, twelve-cylinder engine rested on wooden blocks. Beneath it, a yellow plastic bucket collected waste oil.

Ayana had made a mental checklist of the items she thought she'd need. Looking around, she huffed in dismay, wondering how she'd find any of it. "Crud," she muttered.

As she mulled over her plan to glean provisions, something caught her eye: a coil of blue nylon rope on a bottom shelf beside an old green Army-issued sleeping bag. Retrieving it, she thought, *This'll do...for a start.* Reassured, she got busy.

Ten minutes later, Ayana was bounding down the forest path, the backpack heavy with supplies, weighing down her shoulders. Her feet nimbly skipped over the tangles of tree roots.

Dim morning light tessellated through the canopy as the trail descended. The noise of crashing surf grew louder, the air, colder. When she reached Grandpa's driftwood fence, she leaned over and peered at the rocky bedlam below. She trusted her climbing abilities, but knowing she'd have to manage the heavy pack while simultaneously navigating the perilous cliff pushed the limits of her confidence.

One false move... and splat, she thought.

Ayana slipped off the pack and fished out the blue nylon rope. She threaded one end through the straps, secured it with a crude knot, then lowered the pack to the beach, forearms straining with the weight. Once the pack reached the sand, she tied the other rope end to her belt loop and began her descent.

With yesterday's climbing ordeal still fresh in her memory, Ayana was far more mindful about how and where she placed both boots and hands. And with no Shep to worry about, she made short work of the cliff.

With both feet firmly on the beach, Ayana coiled the rope, stowed it in the backpack, and headed down the primeval shoreline towards *The Deep See*. She leapt from jagged stone to driftwood-log to barnacled boulder, her eager mind and keen eye already plotting the easiest route over the coastal gauntlet for her next trip.

This game of littoral hopscotch, though treacherous, filled Ayana with a curious euphoria. Today wasn't a day of exploration. Ayana knew what awaited at the far end of the beach. No, today was one of deliberate freedom: a secret vacation *within* a vacation.

With the shoreline free of obscuring fog, Ayana's senses could more fully absorb the spectacle. "Beautiful..." she whispered.

On her left: a volatile Pacific crashed and heaved, its rage feeding countless tide pools.

On her right: eroded rock strata, like an earthen layer cake, revealed millions of years of Deep Time. Dangling tree roots festooned the cliff tops, hinting at a forest Ayana couldn't glimpse from her vantage. The ridge line, split at irregular intervals by deep crevices, reminded her of a row of ships with prows pointing at the sea. She stopped to peer into one.

Within lay nothing of real interest: dried seaweed, driftwood, a scrap of sunbaked trash. A rusted crab cage, a tangle of leathery kelp its sole catch, lay in shadow. Ayana pressed onward.

Half-an-hour later she stumbled to a halt and stared in disbelief — yesterday's route now lay totally submerged beneath roiling green water. She could go no further.

"You're KIDDING me!" she hollered, her outburst echoing off the cliff face. "Damn it!" She had forgotten all about the tides: two high and two low — twice a day, every day.

I shouldn't have been so careless, she thought. *Dumb, dumb.*

Ahead, Ayana spied a jumble of boulders haphazardly stacked at the cliff base, some kissing the high-tide waterline. Remnants of a prior landslide, the huge stones looked so precariously balanced that any false move could dislodge them, even a stiff breeze, though Ayana recognized this to be an unlikely occurrence. Still, the thought gave her pause.

She fretfully tapped her glue drops and weighed her options. None seemed especially appealing: try the boulders and risk a potential disastrous fall, wait hours for the tide to retreat, or return home and try again later. She needed clarity.

Ayana removed the sandwich bag from her pocket. Even through the plastic, she felt the shells strange effervescence tingling along her fingertips. The sensation was somehow reassuring. Opening the pouch, she sniffed its contents. The aroma quickened her mind and boosted her confidence. Within the span of three heartbeats, she'd pondered the threat presented by the boulders and reduced it to a bothersome yet easily surmounted obstacle.

Her choice was now clear. *Okay. The rocks it is. Let's do this...*

Ayana pocketed the shell, mustered her resolve, and made for the boulders. She had already conquered this hurdle in her mind. Now she simply needed to do the same thing for real.

Picking her way across the rockslide took all her concentration just to keep balanced. Each foot placement required careful consideration before commitment. All her senses were heightened by the danger. Just past the point of no return, a splash of cold seawater reminded Ayana that the ocean swirled and churned between the boulders beneath her feet. If she fell, she'd be sucked under and pulverized.

But she didn't fall, and the water didn't sweep her away.

Ayana had conquered the obstacle, just like in her mind's-eye, with only some scrapes on her palms from scaling the rocks. She scrambled down the damp pebbles feeling invigorated, confident, and thirsty.

Shrugging off the backpack, Ayana fished out a root beer, popped open the can, and drank. Her mouth filled with sweet bubbles, and the belch that followed — loud and proud — set her at ease. The soda lost its refrigerator chill but was still cool enough to satisfy her thirst. She finished most of it in a few swallows, then poured the rest on the rocks. She stowed the empty can in her backpack and swung it onto her shoulders. In high spirits, Ayana hurried for *The Deep See*, her hiking boots crunching stones underfoot.

"Oh, gross. What's that stink?"

It struck Ayana's nose like a fist punch. Her eyes watered. She spit to clear the horrid taste from her mouth.

Ten steps later and she discovered the cause: an animal carcass splayed among the rocks, crawling with a thousand hungry sea flies. It looked like the pitiful creature had been diagonally snipped in half by a giant pair of scissors, from its left shoulder down to its right hip. A pile of spilled innards, dried and withered by the sun, lay outside the body cavity.

Ayana grimaced in revulsion. *What* is *that? It smells like hot vomit and dumpster juice!*

Feeling a heady mix of intrigue and revulsion, Ayana inched closer to examine the carcass. She pictured her father standing beside her, thoughtfully scratching his chin. The two of them had often watched nature programs on TV together. One of her favorites had been about...

"Sea otters," she said aloud.

Could this dead thing be a sea otter? Or what was left of one? She, herself, had never seen one of the plush-furred marine mammals in the flesh; these miserable remains resembled the living otters she'd seen on TV in only the most rudimentary way. Clearly, this animal had been dead for a while, its corpse deposited among the rocks by the tide.

The eyes looked like shriveled golden raisins. Tufts of faded mahogany fur covered what remained of its leathery hide. The flesh around the mouth, drawn back in a rictus gash, exposed black gums and sharp white teeth. From its lower lip a shark tooth, about the size of Ayana's thumb, protruded. She resisted the temptation to pluck it free as a grim souvenir.

Maybe it was attacked by a shark? she thought.

The stench forced Ayana to breathe through her mouth. She found a thin stick and poked a piece of exposed bone, then prodded a sundried organ. The flies took wing, a black swarm, the visible depiction of the death-stench. Ayana spied a thin woven band encircling the right wrist of the otter. It glinted under the morning sun.

It wasn't kelp, fishing line, or discarded plastic. It almost appeared to be —

"A bracelet?" she murmured. But sea otters didn't wear bracelets. *Weird. I wonder if...*

An odd, coughing sound, "*Hruh-eeech*," broke her train of thought.

She glimpsed movement and froze.

A few seconds later, a shape rounded a boulder on four janky legs. Ayana sank into a crouch. She didn't want to startle the creature into an attack, but it didn't seem to notice as it shuffled towards the otter carcass.

As the animal drew closer, Ayana recognized it — an opossum. A nasty collection of infected and partially healed wounds covered its undernourished body. The remaining fur stood out in filthy tufts across scabby skin. Its tail looked as if it had been broken, then healed at a strange angle. It had to be the ugliest damn animal Ayana had ever seen.

"Poor possum," she whispered, then corrected herself. "*O*-possum."

The opossum wobbled over to the otter carcass and sniffed. It scarred pink nose twitched while its little hand-like paws felt the wound, face, and the shrunken eyes. The tiny marsupial then began nibbling on the otter's sundried lips, pulling the flesh away like strips of beef jerky.

Ayana's sympathy for the creature evaporated. Hadn't the sea otter been through enough?

To watch it become supper for this mangy critter was the final insult...

"Hey!" Ayana grabbed a baseball-sized rock and stood. "Get away from there! Scoot!"

The opossum looked up to regard the child with odd, bronze-flecked beady eyes. "*Hru-eeech*," it wheezed and returned to its desiccated meal.

"Yaaaah!" Ayana yelled and threw the rock.

The shot flew wide — but the projectile ricocheted off a nearby boulder and landed with a clatter, causing the now frightened opossum to leap back. Ayana picked up a second rock and hurled it. A near miss, this time, it was enough to put the opossum into flight, its rear legs kicking out as it ran. "*Hruh-eeech*," it hacked and vanished behind a boulder-mound.

"And don't come back!" Ayana hollered. She tossed the stick. Time was wasting, and she still had a boat to reach.

CHAPTER 27

CAPTAIN AYANA'S FIRST COMMAND

There it is!

Far ahead, like a toy boat grounded by wave and tide, lay Ayana's red and black sanctuary: *The Deep See.*

It rested exactly where she'd left it — just as beautiful, and mysterious, as yesterday.

Backpack bouncing as her pace quickened, Ayana covered the last hundred tide-pool and kelp-wrack strewn yards with surefooted speed. Joy swelled her thudding heart as she drew closer to her prize.

Excited thoughts pelted the inside of her skull like eager honeybees: *I'll spend all summer exploring... I need to rename my ship... I've finally found my own place...*

But, when she rounded one last boulder, reality crashed into her like a frigid wave.

"— Crap!" Ayana shouted.

High tide has submerged the keel gash.

Ayana stumbled to a halt within the vessel's cold shadow. She searched for any easy answer to this dilemma, but nothing simple came to mind. The boulder she'd climbed yesterday to access the hull was likewise underwater. The elevated prow of *The Deep See*, her only remaining choice, loomed high above her head, wedged into the cliff, daunting and inaccessible.

Her hopes popped like a soap bubble. *What the heck am I supposed to do now?*

For several forlorn moments, she remained paralyzed with indecision; then an image of her father clarified into her mind. He smiled and she could hear his voice as clearly as if he stood before her, warm and alive.

Maybe climb?

It was then she saw a length of old rope dangling off the side of the boat.

"I don't have much choice, do I?" she muttered aloud. Looking around, she spotted a driftwood branch and retrieved it.

With both hands, she swatted at the dangling line, trying to nudge it closer. After several flailing attempts, she finally snagged the rope. Gripping it tightly, she gave it a strong tug and sighed with relief as it held fast. She'd been good at rope climbing in P.E. class, but Ayana knew she lacked the upper-body strength to climb while also wearing the full backpack.

Shrugging it off, she dug out the nylon rope, then tied one end to the pack's shoulder straps. Next, she uncoiled the line and secured the free end to her belt buckle. Now, with the means to haul the pack up after she'd reach the deck, Ayana gave the hanging rope a second test tug. Reassured that it would hold, she whispered, "Here goes nothing," and began to climb.

Hand-over-hand, with gritted teeth, arms and legs burning from strain, Ayana hauled herself upward, struggling yet determined. She'd nearly made the railing — her right arm outstretched and reaching — when the rope gave way. She didn't have time to scream as she plunged five feet, and then fetched up hard when the line caught.

It pulled taut once more and held. The force nearly broke Ayana's grip. For several, heart-pounding moments, she concentrated on breathing and keeping her hold on the rope as she dangled sixteen feet above the water.

Then, with a surge of adrenaline, she hauled herself up the last few feet and onto the slanted deck. She sank to her knees, arms on fire. Her palms were red and chafed from climbing. But the pride in her accomplishment made the pain bearable.

"The captain is... now on... board," she panted. "A-ten-SHON!"

Ayana's stomach gurgled in response. *Time for breakfast.*

Standing, she hauled up the backpack, opened it, and rummaged inside for the PB&J and second can of root beer. She took a bite and washed it down with a swig of lukewarm soda.

As Ayana ate, she surveyed the ship with an appraising eye. A third of the sloping deck lay submerged, tiny waves hungrily licking at the strewn buoys, rope coils, and rusted crab pots. But it was the scattering of elaborate shell mounds that drew her attention. More numerous than her last visit, many looked freshly made, their cavities still moist with crab-innards. One such tower, rickety stacked eight shells high, sat in the hollow of an old life preserver. Crab pincers and seagull feathers, skillfully lodged in the vertical nooks, were offset by an array of squid tentacles and smooth stones ringing its base.

To Ayana, the whole structure felt like a piece of alien artwork — precariously balanced, yet oddly beautiful — and with the slightest touch, it would topple.

That was not here yesterday, she thought.

Ayana tapped her glue drops as she pondered the implications of the seemingly intelligent design behind this mound. She knelt and gently touched the structure. Not fragile at all, it held firm. This was no accident derived by wave or wind. During her absence some*one* or some*thing* had visited, without permission, *The Deep See. Her* vessel.

This could not, would not, be tolerated.

"This is my ship," Ayana declared to the wind, waves, and circling gulls. She stood and scattered the crab-tower with a stiff kick. "You hear me? Mine!"

Many cleansing kicks and shell-crushing foot-stomps followed, and soon the deck was cleared of all the crustacean bric-a-brac. Satisfied, Ayana searched the ropes and other debris for another glowing shell. But the only one *The Deep See* offered thus far rested snug in her front pocket. She vowed to scour every inch of the submerged stern once low tide exposed it in a few hours; and later, the numerous rocks and tidepools upon which *The Deep See* rested.

Ayana wolfed down the last bites of her lunch. Hunger sated, she emptied the backpack's contents on the deck: an old can of blue spray paint, Grandpa's vintage Army compass, a sheathed hunting knife, a box of wooden matches, a set of pliers, an old hacksaw blade, a pair of old leather gardening gloves, and one of Grandma's magnifying glasses. Next, Ayana withdrew a slingshot she'd made with her father's help three summers earlier. The simple weapon consisted of a wooden handle and length of rubber medical tubing fitted with a leather patch. She'd rediscovered it while rummaging through a box in the garage marked 'Odds-n-Ends.'

Ayana recalled the hours of practice honing her accuracy, well on her way to becoming a crack shot. Dad said she was turning into a real Annie, or rather *Ayana,* Oakley. But then one day, while trying to perfect a ricochet off a fencepost, she'd accidentally put a hole through the living room window. Dad revoked the slingshot, then and there. Maybe now she could sharpen her skills uninterrupted and finally become the crack shot she was meant to be.

Ayana laid the slingshot beside the other gear, then pulled the last items from the pack — three intact bottle rockets discovered inside a tool chest. At least a decade old, their fuses were long and dry. The wicked racket they'd make quickened her excitement.

Ayana retrieved the can of blue spray paint. *So, what name should I pick?* she wondered. *'The Sea O-Possum'? 'The Stinky Dead Otter'?*

No. None of those seemed right. Dad would have suggested she pick something clever. Symbolic, even. The naming of a ship — not just any ship, but *her* ship — shouldn't be taken lightly. She knew in her heart, in her very bones, she'd never again be so lucky.

The name had to be... poetic.

What is The Deep See, really? Ayana wondered. She peered into the azure sky, watching puffy white clouds drift, collide, deform, and shred on the winds. *It's not just a boat. It's more. But what? What purpose does it serve? What does it offer? What'll it allow me to do?*

The answer she sought didn't reside in the sky. It dallied closer to earth.

Ayana took the shell from her pocket, studied it through the sandwich bag. She knew the boats elusive name lingered there, trapped within its translucent whorls. The magic of the shell, and the inspiring magic of the ship, were somehow... intertwined.

Ayana didn't have to wait long for an answer. Like a lance of sunlight through the clouds, it revealed itself. Ayana smiled and shook the paint can. The pellet within clinked and clanked. With a proud voice, she declared

to all the littoral creatures within earshot: "I hereby name this boat —"
she dribbled some root beer onto the deck, " — the *'Fantasy.'* Or is it
Fanta-s-e-a?"

She decided she like the second spelling, with its double meaning, better.

She imagined Dad nodding in agreement.

Ayana tucked the glassy shell into her pocket. She poured out another
splash of soda. "I christen this boat... again... as the *Fantasea*, with an
's-e-a'."

Ayana crossed to the section of the bow adorned with the ship's name
and peered over the side. Her plan to overwrite the old name with the new
one withered on the vine as she realized she had no way to accomplish the
task without a rope harness or a platform to suspend herself alongside the
bow. And she couldn't write upside-down to save her life.

"Damn," she muttered. *Oh, well. So much for that.* In a fit of frustration,
she kicked over an overlooked tower of crab carapaces. They scattered into
the water in a series of splashes.

She took a deep breath to calm herself. A mischievous grin lit up her face.

It's bottle rocket time!

Ayana struck a match.

"Ready...!"

She held her breath and set a tiny flame to the dry fuse.

"...aim!"

The fuse hissed as fire consumed it.

"FIRE!"

The bottle rocket flared, launched off the deck with a "*vruuush*!" and vanished into the soft fog. It exploded two seconds later with a '*flash-pop*' of igniting black powder. A halo of fat sparks drifted to earth and were extinguished.

"Not bad." Ayana was surprised they still worked.

The Fourth of July had always been Dad's favorite. His fireworks show grew to become the biggest in the neighborhood. Eventually, no other family even bothered. Everyone just came over and set up their folding chairs and blankets on the Outerbridge lawn to watch Jake's extravaganza. Ayana's three bottle rockets paled in comparison, but at least she was trying.

She grinned and struck a match to the second bottle rocket. "Fire!"

Smoke trailed its gentle arc through the air. It detonated with a disappointing '*shhhpop*,' but still produced an adequate shower of sparks.

"Hmmm." She crinkled her nose. *That one was half a dud.*

One more for good measure. Ayana stuck a final match. "Ready, aim..."

As she prepared to ignite the last rocket, her feet skidded on the wet deck. Ayana wobbled, hands flailing. The matchbox slipped from her fingers and tumbled into a puddle.

"Crap," Ayana groaned, disappointed she'd slipped twice on her boat in two days. She scooted to her feet and retrieved the soggy matchbox. The matches were soaked. "Damn it. I need to snag a lighter." She tossed the soggy matchbox aside and put the bottle rocket back in her pack. "I'll save you for later."

Ayana stood. She tapped the glue spots on her arm and scanned the deck. *What to do next,* she thought; then, *Yes. I'll clean.*

Donning the gardening gloves, Ayana spent the next hour arranging crab cages into organized piles like rusted building blocks. She coiled ropes, stacked buoys, moved aside toppled equipment. While she worked, the tide slowly retreated, liberating the stern of the *Fantasea* from the lapping waves. As the last traces of fog burned away, the sun began to beat down in earnest, forcing Ayana to shed her coat and sweater. She realized that not packing a hat and sunscreen had been a big mistake. Likewise, her failure of bringing just soda instead of water.

As Ayana wiped her sweaty forehead, a harsh sound from the beach — a half hack, half wheeze — caught her attention. She froze and listened. *What is that?*

She heard it again... and then the sound of clacking stones. Something on the shore was scurrying around the ship.

Ayana snatched up the slingshot, along with two small rocks she found inside a coil of rope and leaned over the starboard railing. She scanned the stony beach below.

Nothing.

Ayana rushed to the port side. The same disheveled, scab-covered opossum she'd seen earlier was sniffing around the barnacled rocks in its search for food. "I told you not to come around here," Ayana yelled. "But you didn't listen."

The gaunt creature looked about as if searching for the source of the noise.

Ayana loaded her slingshot and took aim.

"*Hruh-eeech,*" the opossum wheezed-coughed, then resumed its business.

"Don't take that tone with me!" Ayana pulled back on the rubber tubing. "Now you'll have to pay the price." With a squinted eye she finessed her aim, sneered — and released.

Whack.

The rock struck the opossum in the middle of its ribcage. It squeaked in pain and somersaulted onto its back, where it lay twitching and kicking its legs.

One more should do it. Ayana loaded the second stone, aimed for the animal's head, and prepared to fire.

The opossum gasped and coughed, struggling to right itself. Witnessing its anguished attempts caused Ayana to falter. That first shot might have broken one of its ribs. She thought she saw blood.

A clear image of her father's face sprang into her mind. He looked... profoundly sad.

Did that make you happy? he seemed to ask.

Ayana lowered the slingshot, cheeks burning with shame. Bitter bile stung the back of her throat. *Why did I do that?* she thought. *That opossum did nothing to me.*

Hurting animals, no matter how ugly, did not reflect the person Ayana strove to be. Wasn't there enough suffering in the world without her inflicting the pain of her own petty grievances upon it? *It probably hates me now,* she thought. *And I wouldn't blame it.*

"*Hruh-eeech,*" the opossum hacked, blood dribbling from its mandible. Footing regained, it crawled beneath the *Fantasea's* keel and out of sight.

"I'm sorry I hurt you, little opossum," Ayana murmured. Her voice trembled, tears building in her eyes. "I know what I did was bad. I know I messed —"

A wave of queasiness hit Ayana, crumpling her to the weather-beaten deck. Images of her cruel act ricocheted inside her skull, tormenting her. Ayana rested her head on her knees, hot tears wetting her denim. She tossed the slingshot away in disgust. The nausea passed, but the guilt only sharpened.

Her father would've never deliberately hurt an animal: he'd always taught her to be likewise kind. She'd let him down.

Ayana thumped the nineteen glue drops on her arms, racking her brain for a means of atonement. Anything to assuage the absolute misery in her heart. She'd heard an explanation once of the concept of karma. If, in fact it existed, and Ayana had upset its scales, then she had to find a way to restore the balance. It made sense therefore, that a pain inflected on another could be cancelled out with an equal pain inflicted upon oneself.

Ayana couldn't shoot her own ribs with the slingshot, but there were other agonies she could employ. She reached into the backpack and withdrew the magnifying glass. She trained the lens over her hand, turning the sunlight into a searing point behind the first and second knuckle. At the first bite of heat, she began counting.

"One-Mississippi, two-Mississippi, three-Mississippi, four-Mississippi —"

At "five-Mississippi," Ayana jerked the lens away, yelping in pain, yet pleased with herself. She probed the throbbing injury, smiling at the ripe blister already forming. With any luck, it could grow to the size of a dime. A decent enough reparation for the hurt she'd caused the opossum.

Satisfied with her penance, Ayana turned the lens-light onto the deck board. She focused the beam into a white-hot pinpoint. The wood darkened and started smoking.

Armed with this makeshift laser, she began to draw an opossum.

CHAPTER 28

GETTING BACK ON THAT HORSE

H ayley soared through air swirling with watercolor possibilities. Clouds of musical confetti floated above her head. The world below teemed with indescribable shapes of joy like abstract balloon-animals filled with laughing gas...

...and she awoke to the sound of her own laughter.

Soft morning light filtered past the old lace curtains, banishing the bedroom shadows. The young widow stirred, then kicked aside the thin blankets. She stretched, luxuriating in the sensation of her limbs and back. Her cheeks ached, as if she'd been smiling all night.

Hayley couldn't remember the last time she'd laughed inside of a dream. It had been years, decades, even. Perhaps the long-overdue emotional release of two nights prior — exhausting for both her body and soul — had finally freed her spirit from the nightmares which had kept it grounded, like so many lead weights, since Jake's death.

She fervently hoped so. She was so very tired of being sad.

Rising with a yawn, Hayley crossed to the window and peered out. The details of the dream, so fresh in her mind just seconds earlier, had begun to fade. Only impressions lingered...and those, too, were evaporating fast. But her smile remained.

Past the dusty glass, outside the pasture, beyond Jakes grave under the apple tree, the evergreen woods struggled to reveal themselves in thinning fog. *I know the feeling*, Hayley thought. *I'm trying to reveal myself, too. Little by little.*

Hayley filled her lungs with the first deep breath of the day — and the alluring aroma of hot pancakes teased her nostrils. Her stomach immediately growled with hunger. Throwing on a well-worn blue terrycloth robe she left the bedroom.

Hayley headed down the hall, pausing to knock on Ayana's door. "Wake up, honey," she called softly. "It's almost nine. Come down for breakfast."

No response.

Hayley considered entering the room but decided against it. *Let her sleep,* she thought and descended the stairs. *You're allowed to be lazy during summer vacations.*

Martha offered a cheery greeting from the kitchen as Hayley entered the dining room.

"Good morning," Hayley called out to her mother-in-law. "Are those pancakes I smell?"

"Yup," Martha said over the sound of sizzling batter. "They'll be ready soon."

Hayley sat at the dining table, her stomach rumbling. Her mother-in-law might not be especially talented when it came to cooking suppers, but her breakfasts were wonderful. Martha's special pancake recipe had always been a favorite of her family's.

"Where's Eugene?" Hayley asked. She filled a glass from the juice pitcher on the table.

"Outside. Doing chores. He wanted to get an early start on the day."

Hayley sipped the tart refreshing juice. "I had the most incredible dream," she said. "I think I was riding a horse faster than the wind. Maybe a horse. I can't remember now. But it felt like... flying. *Really* flying."

Martha plated two fluffy pancakes, then brought them to the table, along with a cup of coffee. "Flying dreams are extra special. It means there's light in your soul."

Hayley smeared a dollop of butter on the hotcakes. "I actually woke up laughing." She drowned her breakfast with real maple syrup as thick as tree sap. "It's been... God — forever since I've done that."

"Not so much syrup," Martha gently chided. "I want you to actually taste my pancakes."

"Sorry." Hayley took a bite, savored it. Martha's pancakes were like eating dessert for breakfast, minus most of the guilt. "Mm-m-m-m. God, these are the best."

Martha fetched herself a mug of coffee from the kitchen, then joined her daughter-in-law at the dining table. She sipped and smiled. "Thank you, dear. The secret is real buttermilk. And just a pinch of cinnamon."

"Best I can manage these days are frozen waffles." Hayley sighed, a twinge of guilt pricking her heart. "And then... only if they're on sale."

Martha sensed Hayley's ache and patted her hand. "You're a wonderful mother, Hayley. Don't you ever feel otherwise. Times may be tough now, but, just like your dream, you'll soon be flying."

Hayley's breath caught in her throat. She looked at her mother-in-law with moist, stinging eyes. She'd believed herself to be all cried out — apparently, there were still a few tears left in reserve. "Thank you, Martha. I'm trying. Really trying."

"You're succeeding. Now, finish your breakfast. Afterwards, you should go for a ride. Fresh air, sunshine, quiet trails. It'll do you wonders."

Hayley wiped the tears pooling in the corner of her eyes. "That sounds wonderful."

"And Heaven knows those two old nags don't get much exercise these days."

"Make that three," Hayley said.

Martha gave her a wink and a smile. "More like four."

The promise of a horse ride instantly made Hayley feel better, the dark clouds of recent events parting to let in a blessed ray of sunlight. She'd learned to ride as a child while visiting her own grandparents' farm in Illinois. But the last time she'd ridden had been the summer before Jake's death. They'd taken Cinnamon and Gingerbread on the trails threading the thick coastal woods surrounding the property. Jake would be dead two months later.

That summer had been the last time Hayley could remember being *truly* happy.

"Ayana never cared for horses. Or dolls. Or bikes... honestly, I really don't know what she likes, outside of her music and teen magazines." Hayley took another bite of pancake. "I'll try my luck and see if she'd like to ride later. I'll let her sleep in for now."

"Sleep? Ayana's down at the beach. She was gone before I started coffee."

"She did *what* now?" Hayley asked. That didn't sound at all like her doleful daughter.

Martha slid over a piece of paper. "She left this."

Hayley read the scribbled note aloud: "*Going to the beach. Back later. Will stay on the path. Promise. Ayana.*" She pushed the note aside. "That's twice in two days. She actually likes the beach this summer. Guess I was wrong."

"Good." Grandma nodded. "She's found something to occupy herself besides television. Nothing wrong with being outside in the fresh air. Sunshine is good for the soul."

Hayley picked at her breakfast, heaved a sigh. "Martha, I'm worried about her. Something's not right."

"Why do you say that?"

"It's...well..." Hayley fell silent, eyes welling with tears once more. *If I'm not careful, I'll spend this entire summer crying like an infant*, she thought.

Grandma scooted closer. "Honey, what is it? Is she sick?"

Hayley shook her head. "Not physically, no. But..."

"Then what's wrong, dear?"

Hayley stared at her hands, now clasped tightly around her coffee cup. "After Jake... passed, Ayana changed. She isn't the person she was. Her grades have fallen off a cliff. She's walked away from all her friends. She spends most of her time alone in her room, and when I try to interact... all we do is fight. And I get it. She misses her dad. But..." Hayley met her mother-in-law's worried gaze. "She talks... to her *father.*"

"Is that all?" Grandma's fright evaporated. "Ayana's still grieving. It seems only natural to me that she'd talk to her father."

"No. You don't understand. She really *talks* to him. And she *listens*, and then answers back. It's like... I don't know... she *sees* him. Like Jake's standing right there in front of her."

Martha wrapped her arms around Hayley, drawing her into an embrace. "Don't worry,. Ayana is just talking to the memory of her father. That's all. My granddaughter is a strong one. Like her father... and her mother. It'll take time. And patience. And love. Lots and lots of love. You have, *we* have, the whole summer to bring her around. She'll be fine. You'll see."

Hayley sighed and reluctantly nodded in agreement. "I'm sure you're right."

Grandma kissed Hayley on the forehead. "Of course, I am. Didn't you know? Grandmothers are always right."

After a quick shower, Hayley changed into sturdy jeans, long-sleeved sweater, and a thick, fleecy jacket. She tied her hair back into a short pony-tail and covered it with a red scarf. A pair of beat-up old cowboy boots completed her riding attire.

Making her way through the cool morning air and out towards the barn, Hayley felt a carefree excitement she hadn't known in quite some time. When she entered the faded white and brown-painted barn, the rich aromas of hay, sawdust, and horse manure rekindled in her mind the thrill of the galloping dream.

For one delicious, exuberant moment, she felt almost... airborne.

"Good morning, Cinnamon. Good morning, Gingerbread."

Both horses came to the fronts of their stalls to regard Hayley with liquid brown eyes. Hayley reached into her jacket pocket and produced two garden-grown carrots. She fed one to each horse. Their hungry mouths tickled her palms as they crunched the treats.

Hayley stood back, hands on her hips. "So? Which one of you wants out more than the other?" Cinnamon snorted and tossed her head. Hayley smiled. "I guess you're the lucky girl."

She fetched a halter from a peg on the wall dividing the two stalls, slipped it over the sorrel mare's head, and led her outside into the morning sunshine. After securing the lead rope to a hitching rail, she reentered the barn for a currycomb, dandy-brush, and hoof pick.

Hayley had always enjoyed grooming horses. She found the soft sound the brush made as it whisked across the animal's coat to be deeply relaxing. Switching to the comb, she ran it through the mare's soft mane, admiring the sturdiness of her limbs, imagining what thoughts moved through the beast's head. Maybe just static?

"It must be easy being a horse." Hayley resumed brushing the mare's muscular flanks. "No worries besides eating, sleeping, and pooping. Do you want to run free, girl? I know I do."

Cinnamon whickered softly and lipped Hayley's sleeve as she gave the horse a final swipe of the brush. Stowing the grooming tools in the barn, she returned with a saddle and bridle where Cinnamon waited, hip-shot and lop-eared, clearly enjoying the fresh air and sunshine.

Hayley had learned the proper way to tack up a horse from her own grandfather: pad on first, then saddle, then bridle. Don't knock the animal in the teeth when inserting the bit; always check the girth a final time before mounting, since horses were wily creatures and often held their breaths during the first tightening. A novice rider might find herself pitched to the ground when the saddle unexpectedly came loose — a lesson she'd never forgotten.

Satisfied, Hayley removed the halter, leaving it dangling by the lead rope from the hitching rail. Taking the reins, she led Cinnamon over to the old tree stump that served as a mounting block. She slipped her foot into the stirrup, then hesitated —

"Jake," she whispered.

Never before had she ridden her in-laws' horses alone. Jake had always been by her side. They'd made it a special tradition, a couples-only activity to be shared each and every summer.

Yet now, here she was, going out by herself with barely a thought about her dead husband. A twinge of guilt nibbled at her heart. Where was the remorse she should feel for getting on with her life, and for leaving the ghosts of her past behind, like a plodding dairy truck in the rearview mirror?

I've had my fill of remorse! Jake would want me to move on!

Cinnamon turned to regard her with placid equine curiosity. "What are you waiting for? Is that what you're trying to say?" Hayley chuckled.

Heaving herself into the saddle she goaded Cinnamon towards the woods with a solid tap of her booted heels.

Time ticked by to the gentle cadence of clopping hooves. Hayley lost herself in the pleasures of a beloved, yet nearly forgotten, pastime. Though a tad stiff with age, Cinnamon proved a game mount, and carried her rider with a sure-footed pace along the woodland trails. Sunlight broke through the evergreen canopy, casting a mosaic of leafy patterns on the forest floor. Familiar trees, both towering and toppled, wore thick coats of green lichen, and studded with fungi of cream, brown and orange. Hidden insects trilled in dense thickets. Lush aromas of fiddlehead fern, stinging nettle, and blackberry bramble mingled with the heady perfumes of pine and soil, mud and mildew, and the salty fragrance of the Pacific.

In a patch of sunlight hemmed by evergreen shadows, Hayley pulled cinnamon to a halt to watch a swarm of honeybees competing for nectar amongst the petals of a red-flowering currant shrub. Whizzing hither and thither, they lingered just long enough to drink the sugary offering of one bloom before darting off to another, their hind legs heavy with collected pollen.

The peaceful sight sent Hayley's mind along memory's path back to a final time she and Jake had ridden together. They had laughed at life's challenges then, feeling invincible, untouchable —

Immortal.

Until that fateful day when an insignificant honeybee taught them otherwise.

The message of that soul-searing moment remained etched indelibly in her mind.

...All things must end...

Hayley gave Cinnamon a firm tap with her heels. The mare snorted and, with a lively step, started along the trail. Horse and woman left the bees to their labors.

Hayley glanced at her wristwatch. She'd been out riding, lost in memories, for two hours.

Better head back, she thought. *Cinnamon must be tired, and I really need to pee.*

She turned the mare's head towards home and urged her into a slow, rolling canter. Cinnamon was eager to comply. Thirty minutes later, horse and rider trotted back into the yard. The young widow guided the horse to the hitching rail and pulled her to a halt, just as Grandpa exited the barn pushing a wheelbarrow laden with dirty straw and manure.

"Oh, hi, honey," he called out. "Martha wants to put lunch on the table, and she needs you to fetch Ayana from the beach."

"She's not back yet?" Hayley swung from the saddle and lifted the reins over Cinnamon's head, letting the ends drop to the ground. The mare stood rooted in place, trained to not move when her reins touched the dirt.

"Nope," Grandpa replied. "Guess she's having too much fun."

"As soon as I get Cinnamon settled, and use the bathroom, I'll go find her."

"Sounds good." Grandpa pushed the wheelbarrow around the side of the barn towards the rubbish heap. "And don't forget to stay on the path."

I'll tell Ayana she's to help her grandfather with yard chores, Hayley thought as she haltered the mare and led her back into the barn. *I'll help, too.* She rubbed Cinnamon's nose. "Thanks for the ride, girl. I really needed that."

Cinnamon snorted and bobbed her head in response to the caress.

Clearly, it was good for both of us.

PART FOUR

MARE MUSTELIDAE

"Thus, life by life and love by love
We passed through the cycles strange,
And breath by breath and death by death
We followed the chain of change."
Langdon Smith (1858 – 1908)
Evolution, 1895

CHAPTER 29

DREAMS OF DISTANT TIDES

*S*leek's dreams arrived like a flock of hungry cormorants.

They dive-bombed his subconscious, sending nonsensical images rippling across his mind's eye. Fragments of the day's events, both in The Blue and below the earth, collided and overlapped. But the residual pryzoic energy still firing Sleek's neurons began to heighten his dream-state, lifting and clarifying, honing it like a spear tip — sharper and sharper, still.

This forewarned scithma-snaag roiled the precious memories within Sleek's mind, presenting them as a lesson to be mined for any gems of wisdom hiding within.

The young otter no longer dreamed.

In vivid detail, he began to relive the most important day of his life from six winters earlier...

Sleek swam just below the surface. Morning sunlight warmed his flexible back. Upswelling currents chilled his taut belly.

His limb strong parents, newly ascended to their exalted Alpha status, kept a watchful eye on their rambunctious adolescent. The trio formed the tip of a hunting band boasting over a hundred adult Lontra, plus half-as-many juveniles on the cusp of full maturity. The eyes of every river otter shone brilliant gold-within-gold. Not a single Envoric bronze could be found. Ureolas, like a galaxy of colorful stars, sparkled all about. Their brightness rivaled the sunbeams diffusing into the murky ocean depths.

Though still considered a juvenile, Sleek — who'd only recently participated in the Jaarjoora where he received his proper weening-day name and the blue ureola of a Beta — had finally been deemed old enough to carry a hunters ynth on this, his first *official* hunt. The Den Sire had fashioned the spear himself. Sleek was eager to use it, to prove his growing skill and worth to himself and his romp. His indigo pelt bristled with anticipation.

The graehl traveled on the surface for ease of breathing. Excited hijna-chatter buzzed through the musteline collective on the banquet to come. Today would be remembered fondly, both in the mind and in the belly.

All river otter hunters carried a calcified baleen spear in dexterous paws, their serrated tips as varied as the personalities of the animal wielding it.

They swam using the 'three limbs and tail swishing' hunters-stroke. Other otters clutched sections of furled majl-netting. The remaining few hauled lengths of whalebone, the purpose of which Sleek did not yet understand.

The young Beta spotted his milk-brothers Swims Past, Nimble, and Follows amongst the Anandic multitude. The trio swam beside their parents, gripping newly hewn baleen spears, their wrists adorned with the amber ureolas of Loyc-Epsilon. Below, his dear friend Diver arrowed through the water beside his proud father, Chaser — hale, and in his prime.

The Lontra legion sped through the sea. Multiple of otter shadows flitted over the kelp groves swaying far below. The collective-shuuhl of the swimming romp shed a deluge of silvery bubbles rising to the surface. All creatures fled before the massive graehl. Even a hungry shiver of prowling aorxa blue sharks retreated rather than risk a lance in the gills.

Lucky for them, on this day, the Lontra were not after just *any* prey.

Hijna calls rang out from the forefront and passed through the graehl, signaling the groups arrival at its initial destination. Individual animals began backpedaling in unison until the entire graehl floated to a stop.

A thick granite column known as Deshi-Oad's Rib loomed before the romp. Robed in emerald nooree tufts, and a rainbow of feather-corals and sea anemones below the waterline, it jutted from the depths like a colossal urchin spike thrust into the seabed. Above the waves, many tides of seagull guano coated twenty tails of the pillar, turning it white like some monstrous, sun-bleached bone.

Sleek tightened the grip on his ynth. His keen eyes scanned the empty ocean. Anxiety quickened his pulse, tickled his stomach. He had no reason to be afraid — nothing in The Blue could harm him with the full strength of the romp at his back.

And yet he could not shake the prickle of The Scare's fight-or-flight impulse.

Beside him, Sleek sensed his father tense. "They're here," the Den Sire cautioned.

The glow of an Alpha's violet wristlet materialized from the murky Oorum, followed by a Beta's blue. More and more wristlets followed — greens, yellows, ambers — until, before Sleek's astonished eyes, the Lutris Raft, numbering as many, if not more than the Lontra, emerged. Their combined ureolas glowed like a rainbow constellation in the aquamarine.

Each sea otter clutched either a spear or coil of similar majl-netting. Their alcq-pierced faces appeared just as anxious as Sleek felt, their gold-within-gold eyes sizing up the romp. He saw great strength in those faces, and an ancient pride not to be trifled with.

And, for the younger generations, a distrust of strangers.

At the head of this opposing force swam a large male — none other than its leader, Fearless. He held the Eehrynth, the Alpha's Lance, in his webbed paws. A prominent, three-inch long blue turritella alcq pierced his lower lip. To Sleek's young eyes the Doyen appeared poised and formidable. The sight of his legendary weapon sent a thrill of terror down the princeling's spine. Fearless matched the regal appearance of Quick Tail in all ways but one — the Den Sire wore the ornate kholo torc signifying command of *all* Envorah.

Even the Lutris Eehr must swim in the shadow of a greater power.

Sleek had never seen more than a pawfull of Lutris before now, only the occasional diplomatic mission from Gwelth visiting High Split Rock. He never imagined that their Raft held such numbers. His callow mind conjured scenes of unprovoked violence that heightened his fear. If war began, who would win?

Struggling to hide his trembling, the young Beta trailed his parents as they swam forward to meet the sea otter king. As they drew closer, Sleek noticed two smaller Lutris accompanied the Doyen, one beside him, the other in tow.

The Alphas stopped, a spear's toss between them, and for several tense moments, each Eehr observed the other. At their backs, an anxious host of golden eyes watched, ready for whatever would happen next.

Finally...

"Nookeelee, Fearless, Lontra-friend and Lutris Doyen." The Den Sire's hijna projected clear and amiable, his smile genuine.

Fearless tugged his thick whiskers and pointed the Eehrynth's tip to the seafloor, a symbolically submissive gesture. "Kooarii, Den Sire, High Eehr of *all* Envorah. And dearest Suckling Mother, loved and cherished." Though gruff and unsmiling, the Doyen exuded as genial an air as his counterpart. "It is grand to see you again. It's been too many tides."

Gentle nodded. "Indeed, it has, Fearless. You are looking fit and well fed."

"Our many uboo fields are bountiful." Fearless' intense gaze fastened onto bashful Sleek. "And who is this handsome young uju?"

"Our son, Sleek," Gentle replied proudly. She took Sleek's paw and pulled him forward.

"Ah-h-h, yes. Of course." A tiny smile heightened The Doyen's dour countenance. "You were just a blind kit when I last saw you — the very night of the last Glow when your sneaky father won *The Hasten* and became High Eehr. Lucky nataaq."

An exasperated Quick Tail rubbed his eyes. "Ookl's Ink, not this old gripe again."

"Oh, Fearless." Gentle playfully pinched the Doyen's forearm. "That rush through The Winnow is so dangerous. You were the only ones to complete the contest, and you both nearly died bringing your pryzoa out. It was nose-to-nose at the end. It could have gone either way."

Fearless gave Gentle a knowing grin. "As you say, Suckling Mother. Still, it makes me grind my teeth. A full belly slowed me, and I had an injured foot. Otherwise, I'd be High Eehr now. Yurch. One *kexxing* whisker-length."

Sleek smiled at hearing the Lutris Alpha, known for being so grim and serious, use the same profanities he and his milk-brothers so often enjoyed. He never heard his father swear.

Quick Tail fixed his rival with a bemused eye. "I'm not called 'quick' for nothing."

"Deshi-Oad's Stone Teeth, that's true enough." The Doyen smiled and turned his gaze back to Sleek. He appraised the young Lontra, nodding. "You have your parent's bearing, Sleek. That's a fine start for a future Eehr. If you can hold onto it. You never know where the next challenge will come from."

The young Saia tugged his whiskers. "Thank you, Doyen," he returned politely, the thrill of being recognized by an Alpha partly dispelling the fright lodged in his belly.

Fearless gestured at the two smaller Lutris, both of whom had remained behind the Doyen during the greetings. The larger of the two — a young male with a prominent Turritella alcq and wielding a serrated keratin spear in his paws — swam up to float beside the Doyen, while the smaller female lingered a tail-length in the background.

"Grabber," Fearless announced for all to hear. He pointed the Eehrynth at the young male, his hijna ringing with pride. "*My* son."

Grabber offered a bold, intelligent gaze and a respectful nod. "Kooarii to you all." Larger and heavier than Sleek, and a full season older, he resembled a diminutive version of his father.

He and Sleek locked golden eyes. Before the young Lontra looked away he saw, not quite hostility, but a studied reserve in the other's glance. Within their wordless exchange, questions were asked, boasts proclaimed, and challenges thrown.

During this tide, the long contest between Betas would formally begin. Their relationship could be a contentious one if naked ambitions alone guided it.

Fearless turned and nodded to the smaller Lutris, who swam to his other side. "My daughter, Gloss."

Sleek stared, mouth agape. His heart began pounding against his breast-bone. He had never seen *anything* so beautiful.

The young sea otter tugged demurely at her stylishly curled whiskers. In an etiquette display demanded of all juvenile and unmated female Lutris when greeting those of higher rank, she folded her tail over her crossed hind legs, its upturned tip touching her belly. "Kooarii, Den Sire, Suckling Mother..." Gloss fixed Sleek with a golden gaze as bold as her brothers. "Nookeelee, Sleek."

Gloss. Her name is Gloss! And she just said my name!

Gentle gave Sleek a nudge. "Yes, she is exquisite, isn't she?" her hijna directed at him. "Close your mouth, son. Remember your manners."

Mortified, Sleek did as his mother commanded. He gulped. "Nookeelee, Grabber... and...G-Gloss."

A smile flitted across the young female Lutris' face — amused yet lacking the barbed sarcasm so many uja of his own peer group would've offered in response to Sleek's obvious discomfort. Holt females were a mischievous and bewildering lot, encouraged to challenge males at every turn. To the young Saia, they stood as competition.

But *this* uja...

With her probing golden eyes, feathery whiskers, silver fur, and impec-cably groomed tail adorned with a colorful kelp and seashell band, she'd kindled a fire in his adolescent heart he didn't think any Lontra female could ever quench. Sleek never wanted her to leave his sight.

"Your daughter is stunning, Fearless," Gentle said. "And such a fashion-ably wrapped tail, my dear." She swam forward to take Gloss' forepaws in hers. "Your beauty does your father and your Raft proud."

"Thank you." Gloss offered a whisker-tug genuflection. "That is kind, Suckling Mother."

"Please, call me Gentle."

Gloss tugged her whiskers again and smiled. "Thank you, Gentle."

Quick Tail's brow furrowed. "Forgive me, but I thought you had three children?"

The Doyen's thick whiskers twitched as if he'd just devoured something bitter. "My other...is sick," he replied in clipped tones. "He remains be-hind."

The Den Sire recognized the tension behind Fearless' words and wisely changed the subject. "Come, let Raft and Holt rest a while before we swim on for the harvest."

Fearless nodded. With a symbolic tail-flick, he released the Raft to their leisure. Den Sire did likewise. Adult otters from both tribes mingled, of-fering polite whisker tugs to one another. Some had shared graehl-duties together in the past. For them, this comingling came easily. Prior friend-ships were rekindled. Hunting stories exchanged. Weapons displayed and admired. Scars of old wounds regaled, hijna-laughter ensuing on how and why new injures were acquired.

For youngsters, this socializing proved awkward. Embarrassed, many hung back in gossiping cliques as the waters of sociability warmed between them. First one advanced, then a few more, and then all the adolescent Lontra and Lutris swam to receive each other. The casual nookeelees of home, shared between acquainted otters, were not given. Instead, they offered the formal, "*Yaeeeli*," — an abridged version of the elaborate Ulurii greeting, "I am me-you are you-we are equal" — used between unfamiliar Envorah. This respect for strangers neither incited or pacified, but instead acknowledged equal status between animals, regardless of rank other than Eehr — everyone tugged the whisker and gave a deferential "Kooarii" to an Alpha.

As the sun angled towards noon, a sense of camaraderie settled on both tribes. Each hunter itched to test their mettle and discover who surpassed whom with spear and net, tooth, and claw. The tide for individual distinction would arrive soon enough. For now, all needed to curb their impatience. Greater tasks awaited their energies.

Meanwhile, the Alphas, along with their ranking Betas and Gammas, convened amongst the barnacled alcoves of Deshi-Oad's granite column to discuss the coming hunt. Sleek's rank earned him a place, but not a voice. His youth and inexperience precluded that. For now, his job was to listen. And learn.

The Lutris — males, all — kept casting surreptitious frowns at the spear-toting Lontra females in attendance. Clearly, the presence of armed uja bothered them. Puzzled by this gender-based enmity, Sleek resolved to ask his father about it later.

Quick Tail and Fearless climbed from the sea onto a small stone ledge. Shaking excess water from their fur, they crouched side by side and addressed the floating hunters.

"We've received news from our Vialae messengers earlier," the Doyen began. "They confirm Irounga are trailing the quarry at Oorum-distance and await our arrival. They also say the school is the largest ever seen. Their numbers are like the grains of sand on the beach."

Excited, and hungry, murmurs rippled through the blended graehl.

"The Irounga are valuable allies," Quick Tail added. "Without their help, this hunt would be much more difficult."

A large Lutris Gamma growled and shook his head. "Their help is expensive, given what they contribute. I don't like it, or them, one bit."

"But, that trick with the bubbles..." another Vlis, a Lontra this time, began, but Sleek's mind tuned out the hunters' debate.

He scanned the gentle swells, searching for Gloss.

He found her amongst the socializing otters, gathered with a bevy of females conversing with the Suckling Mother. Many were beautiful, but for Sleek, none matched Gloss. He wondered what a nibble-kiss from her would feel like, or the touch of her paws upon his cheek. His heart fluttered in giddy speculation.

"Son." A deep growl from the Den Sire drew Sleek's attention back to the convocation.

"Old Blubber Snout demands more and more compensation for sending his Bitten," Fearless huffed. He fingered the tip of the Eehrynth, admiring its lethal point. "His gluttony grows with each passing tide. It's disgraceful."

"But we can't do it without them," a female Dyah-Delta Lontra replied, her equal-ranked graehl-sisters nodding in agreement. "Without the Bitten, the hunt is over before it begins."

The Lutris ruler snorted. "So, you say, uja."

The Dyah glared at Fearless, but Quick Tail's upraised paw stayed her angry retort. "Yes, it's true about Diuun Dunn's greed, but even his legendary appetite will be satisfied. Don't let it bother you. There will be enough to fill every belly many times over."

"*This* time," Fearless grunted. His Lutris hunters sneered in agreement.

The conversation continued, but Sleek heard none of it. He should have been listening to his elders and learning what he could, for someday he would be Alpha. But his Aanandi-shade swam far afield, considering all else meaningless except for Gloss.

As if sensing his longing, Gloss turned away from her own companions, searching, until her bright golden eyes found and settled on Sleek. She smiled. Bashfully, he smiled back.

The Saia felt a surge of confidence under that lovely gaze. His heart hammered in his chest. A newfound strength seemed to follow from Gloss' beauty directly into Sleek, and with it the sense no obstacle proved so insurmountable he could not overcome it...

To the young Beta, at that moment, it felt like all things were possible.

The hunters' council concluded just before midday.

Den Sire gave the signal, and the three-hundred-strong otter armada left Deshi-Oad's Rib and headed for deeper waters. A great flock of hungry seabirds kept pace with the united graehl. Shrill caws and flapping wings filled the sky, supplying a chorus of anticipation for the upcoming feast. Many Envoric birds accompanied this flock. Vialae didn't socialize with such rabble. But for a free meal even they would tolerate the bothersome squawks of their dimwitted cousins.

A short distance from Deshi-Oad's Rib lurked the next objective: an enormous xhooja. Persisting tide after tide, season after season, this perennial quicker-water flow was well known. Vast in comparison to coastal conduits, and sometimes used for those rare deep-sea hunts, this xhooja would cast the mixed Lontra-Lutris graehl far from the coastal currents they knew at speeds they could never achieve on their own.

Sleek inhaled and dove, shadowing his parents, the Doyen and his two children. Twenty tails below the surface, tell-tale deformations in the swaying kelp groves heralded the xhooja's proximity. Sleek soon spied the agitated water within the swift flow. It snaked and coiled through the aquamarine like some elemental eel, the bubbles it contained zipping faster than a dive-bombing cormorant.

Sleek watched the three Alphas pierce the silvery slipstream and get whisked away into the Oorum. He quickly followed... and felt his body catapulted forward with breathtaking speed. In the past, Sleek used shallower, slower xhooja while swimming with his father and friends in the waters around High Split Rock. But, as of this moment, he'd never moved so fast in his life.

The acceleration almost made the Beta drop his spear.

This is what flying must feel like, Sleek mused. He couldn't help but smile at the notion.

He glanced over at Gloss and Grabber. Paw-in-paw, the siblings beamed with joy. Sleek looked further behind him. Every otter he spied wore the same euphoric grin that only the hurtling power of a xhooja could induce.

The blended graehl rode the quicker-water as it wound and twisted through The Blue. Joyously swept along, youngsters and adults alike relaxed and gave themselves over to the power of the conduit. The energy they saved moving in this fashion would be much needed for the labors to come.

As the xhooja hurled the tribes further into pelagic waters, Sleek realized he had never been so far from home. The sea floor, visible in the littoral shallows around High Split Rock, vanished below into a midnight Oorum, unseen and menacing.

Sleek decided he didn't like it much out here. Too cold and dark and scary.

After a while, the Den Sire and Doyen signaled to the graehl the time to leave the xhooja had arrived. With powerful thrusts of their tails, the Alphas exited the slipstream. The comingled graehl followed their leaders, departing the quicker-water with impressive coordination.

Sleek broke the surface, snatched a quick breath, then submerged. Ten tails below, his parents and the Doyen floated, motionless. They watched the murky Oorum, bodies tensed.

Sleek swam beside the prone Alpha's and halted. "What's going on?"

"They're almost here," the Doyen replied. He placed a firm paw on Sleek's shoulder. "Follow the lead of my son. And be ready."

Grabber brandished his spear in a dramatic fashion, knowing that his rival now watched. But the eyes of the young Saia were turned towards Gloss, who floated behind her father's strong back. There was no fear in her gaze, only... curiosity.

Sleek shivered with a mingled sense of dread and excitement. He tightened his grip on his own ynth. *The Irounga! The Irounga are coming!*

The otters waited...

Just as the young Beta thought he would explode, a phalanx of shadows emerged from the gloom. It drew closer and Sleek counted twenty black sea lions clustered together under the watchful eyes of four larger Northern elephant seals. In elegant unison, they altered course and swam to meet the waiting graehl, the quartet of elephant seals in the lead.

The smallest sea lion doubled the length of the largest otter, while at nine tails long and individually heavier than the combined weight of seventy adult Lutris, each Northern elephant seal looked like a streamlined gray-pink torpedo of blubber and muscle. Their rudimentary hind feet, each with five webbed toes that alternately fanned and flexed, propelled them gracefully through the water despite their vast bulk. Large pectoral fins dangled at their sides. But it was the fatty proboscis hanging off their faces that captured Sleek's attention most keenly. The appendages gave the massive creatures both a funny and terrifying appearance.

The vanguard of otters raised their barbed spears, poised and aiming at the vulnerable eyes, snouts, and throats of the bulls; thick layers of fat protected all other targets. The Den Sire and Doyen swam forward to meet the four seals, their flanking guards armed and watchful. Sleek and Grabber accompanied their fathers, though they remained a half-tail behind.

The quartet floated to a stop before the two Alphas. Peering past his father's shoulder, Sleek gazed in awe at the four bulls. He'd never seen Envoric animals so large, so imposing. Though massive, compared to the legendary girth and grandeur of their mighty Southern elephant seal liege — Diuun Dunn, also known as His Grand Corpulence, or more commonly, 'Blubber Snout' — these four bulls were little more than children.

Sleek couldn't envision a creature of such size. It boggled his mind.

The Irounga glowered at the otters, eyes like dollops of molten bronze. They projected a humorless intelligence with no patience for banter or pleasantries.

Those eyes made Sleek nervous.

Quick Tail drifted closer to the quartet, lowered his spear, and tugged his whiskers. "Nookeelee, Irounga friends. It's good to see you."

The largest bull, his face a brutal mosaic of scars both healed and fresh, including one where his left eyeball used to be, wrinkled his flabby trunk. A growl accentuated his terse hijna. "Kooarii. Blubber Snout sends us, his trusted Bitten, to assist this harvest."

Sleek had heard the story of how all servants of His Grand Corpulence boasted a bite scar ritualistically placed somewhere on their bodies by a member of his pampered harem. But only Diuun Dunn's most trusted, elite minions — the Bitten — had those crescent wounds notched into their heavily calloused necks by Blubber Snout himself — an esteemed, if painful, honor.

That ceremonial injury carried deep lineage of agony itself. Long ago, Diuun Dunn had nearly met his death in the jaws of the White Maw, Nolurrah, who likewise had been incised by the stone teeth of the Whitest Whale, Deshi-Oad, the Devine Impetus.

For this single tide, all disparate species were allies for a common bounty; still, the otters knew they must handle these particular seals with extra caution. The allegiance of the Bitten to Blubber Snout bordered on fanatical, their temperament boiling with the same volatility as their mighty liege.

The one-eyed bull continued. "For our bubbles, His Grand Corpulence demands eight of your majl to fill his belly. Do you accept these conditions?"

"Eight?" Fearless snapped, brow furrowing with anger. "Chookzl. That's too much for so little help."

"That is the final price," the Irounga stated bluntly. "There will be no negotiation. And you will provide it with no expectation of your majl's return."

"I should take this heaping pile of spraint's other eye," Sleek heard Fearless whisper to his father. "Offer two majl and tell him to consider themselves lucky."

The Den Sire nodded as he pondered his options. "Perhaps."

Sleek's gaze swept between Quick Tail, the impatient Bitten, Fearless, his son Grabber, and then back to his own father. Behind him, intermingled Raft and Holt awaited the Alphas' decision. Sleek spotted Gloss among the expectant throng, watching — *him*.

To be the subject of such alluring scrutiny! The young Beta shivered with delight.

"What's your answer, *tiny* Aanandi?" One-Eye demanded, the contempt in his hijna as plain as the calloused blubber swaddling his ruined face.

"Don't talk to my father like that!" Sleek shouted.

Almost as soon as he uttered the words, he realized he'd made a grave mistake.

A collective hijna-gasp of shock rippled through the otter ranks. Quick Tail and Fearless spun in unison to pin the young Saia with furious looks.

The lead Bitten's single eye narrowed to a bronze slit, his pinniped comrades growling in insult.

Sleek's mother hissed his name, but he paid no heed. It was far too late to back down. Besides, knowing Gloss watched him further emboldened the young Beta.

Confident in his bravery, Sleek swam forward and brandished his ynth at the elephant seal's droopy proboscis. "He's the Den Sire, High Eehr of all Envorah, including *your* master Blubber Snout! Show respect or I'll...I'll... take your other eye!"

One-Eye lifted flabby lips to expose massive teeth. A watery snort underscored his reply. "You may *try*, Lontra brat."

"Sleek! That's enough! Get back behind me!" Quick Tail's hijna crackled with anger.

"But father, he insulted you in front of..."

"*Now!*"

Sleek beat a quick retreat, dizzy from a mix of terror, exhilaration, and disbelief at his own audacity. *Did I just face down a Bitten?* he thought. *Ookl's Ink! What'll Gloss think of me now?*

When he reached his mother's side, Sleek glanced at Gloss, but he could not read her expression. The Saia decided that, for now, he'd be wise to keep silent.

With his son's unexpected outburst ended, Quick Tail swam towards the Bitten quartet. Tiny in comparison, his noble demeanor and glowing ureola-torc more than compensated for their greater bulk and collective haughtiness. "You master drives a hard bargain. Eight majl is a steep price, don't you think?"

"I do not question. I serve," One-Eye growled. "Do you agree to the terms?"

Quick Tail rested his lance on one shoulder and cocked his head. "If I say 'yes,' then both Raft and Holt will feast for days, and Blubber Snout fills his belly." He tapped his chin with a clawed finger. "If I say 'no' as my allies advise, then we would attempt the harvest anyway, but without your help." He paused to glance at Fearless before continuing. "If we fail, then everyone returns home empty-pawed and hungry. Unfortunate, but such is life in The Blue. But...if we're successful, well... we would *never* need the Irounga again. Either way, it wouldn't go well for *you* at all."

All four Bitten spluttered in unison. "What are you saying?" their cycloptic leader demanded, a hint of anxiety creeping into his hijna.

"I'm saying...I know of Blubber Snout's temper," Quick Tail replied. "I've seen the carcasses of those who disappoint him. And to give false information using his name? Ookl's Ink! Can you imagine his rage?"

"Are you calling us liars?" One-Eye bellowed. "I should bite you in half for that, little *Den Sire*!" The massive creature and his fellows poised themselves to lunge.

In the space between two heartbeats, a protective picket of deadly-sharp spears surrounded the Den Sire. Sleek raised his own ynth, heart hammering in his furry chest.

Will there be bloodshed after all? he wondered.

Quick Tail whirled to face the graehl, paws raised. "Hold! Everyone...spears down!"

For an instant, it seemed like all motion in the Blue stopped. Then, like a bubble bursting, the threat of violence dissipated as the Bitten relaxed and the otters lowered their weapons.

Quick Tail turned back to address One-Eye, his hijna mild and amiable. "Liars? Oh, no, no. I'm saying nothing of the sort, friends. I have it on trusted authority that Diuun Dunn only wanted *four* majl, not eight. Could you have misheard your liege? Or his instructions weren't clear to you?" He shrugged, then added, "But, if you say eight is the final price, then I feel it prudent we send a Vialae to the rookery to clarify the matter."

Fearless caught on to Den Sire's clever feint. "Quick Tail...are you suggesting we insult Blubber Snout by having him *repeat* himself? Wouldn't he be enraged?"

"I'm afraid so," Quick Tail replied. "But what else can we do? We need an answer."

One-Eye's smug hostility faltered. Diuun Dunn's violent temper echoed across the Envoric world, and blood often followed. The three Irounga floating behind him exchanged worried glances. Their lives were now in serious peril.

"Can you envision the pain he'd inflict on those who'd jeopardize his meal?" Fearless chimed in with relish. "Deshi-Oad's Fluke, he'd crush their skulls, or tear out their throats. Perhaps he'd only castrate them before his laughing harem. Maybe even kill the pups they sired. I've heard he eats pups from time to time."

"It must be risked in order to settle this misunderstanding." With a resigned shake of his head, Den Sire turned to Sleek. "Son, find the fastest Vialae messenger you can. I'll meet them at the surface with instructions." He looked back at the Bitten and tugged his whiskers. "My apologies, dear friends. But I'm afraid we'll have to postpone this harvest. Let's reconvene at Second Tide tomorrow."

"We cannot!" One-Eye argued, his remaining eye blinking rapidly. "Blubber Snout demands we return today with his meal."

"We don't answer to Blubber Snout," Fearless growled. "Come back tomorrow."

The Alphas and their retinue spun and headed back towards the waiting graehl.

"Wait! Wait!" One-Eye cried, his hijna ringing with desperation. "Please don't leave! This has been a misunderstanding!"

The otters turned to face the Bitten. Their arrogant demeanors had deflated to quivering, cold fear. Quick Tail and Fearless exchanged knowing glances.

"Misunderstanding?" Quick Tail cocked his head. "How so? You presented your master's offer. We declined. Where's the confusion?"

"On *our* part," the cyclopean bull confessed. "*Our* error." His fellow elephant seals nodded their massive heads in frenzied agreement. "*We* confused the demands. Eight majl is an obvious mistake. Four is correct."

"I see." The Den Sire stroked his chin and then turned to Sleek. "What do you think, son? Should we send for clarification or put this behind us and resume the harvest?"

Startled to be consulted given his earlier misconduct, Sleek stared wordlessly at his father, but recovered. "It was an honest mistake. Let's forgive and forget. Four majl is fair."

Quick Tail smiled, pleased his son had absorbed the core of his lesson.

"Well said, young one. Yes, yes, well said, indeed." One-Eye's obsequious praise made Sleek frown. Again, the other Bitten enthusiastically nodded, gelatinous snouts wobbling. "There's no need to bring this to the attention of His Grand Corpulence."

The Den Sire smiled. "No, friends. Not a word of this shall be spoken of to your master."

"Good, good," replied One-Eye. "Then, with your approval, we'll begin."

The Den Sire nodded firmly. "You may."

Dismissed, the Bitten quartet swam off to collect their sea lion minions and issue brusque orders to move out. Laggards received bites to their flippers to spur them forward.

Sleek watched the Irounga vanish into the Oorum, wishing he could punish the Bitten for their insults to his father and himself. He wanted to hurt them for their arrogance, and in doing so prove a larger size did not guarantee superiority.

But wait. Hadn't the Den Sire's cunning shown that power did not have to come at spearpoint to be wielded successfully? Many forms of leverage could be found if one knew where to look, exercised patience, and kept a cool head.

With this lesson relearned, the memory-dream continued.

CHAPTER 30

CASTING THE HUNTER'S EYE

"Look there, Sleek." Gentle pointed into the distance. "The *shraga* come."

The otter graehl and their Irounga allies hung motionless at Oorum-distance — several dozen tails away — from a vast school of fish that filled The Blue with the twinkle of countless scales, like some submerged pearlescent storm cloud. Bright teal fins and sunset-red striations adorned the bellies of the mackerel-shaped fish, heightening their beauty as they arrowed and oscillated through the water. The quicksilver shoal glinted like innumerable stars.

The young Saia stared at the riot of color and motion, entranced. "Th ey're... amazing."

"And delicious." A purr of hunger-soon-satisfied warmed Suckling Mother's hijna.

The shraga — also called *sunset fish* for the color of their crimson belly stripes — emerged from the benthic darkness once every four seasons, milky-white, nearly blind, laden with roe and famished. Only reaching the upper, sunlit waters did their eyesight return and the glorious colors of their skin ignite.

"Many believe they nibble the skin off the wounds Deshi-Oad inflicted by Old Father Fathom," Gentle added. "The Ulurii say that's what makes them so special. They're a sacrament between Great Ookl and us."

"Sacrament? Is that *really* true?" Sleek asked.

"Well, if you ask The Doyen, he'll tell you shraga pick the wounds of The Whitest Whale, injuries visited by our Old Father, Himself."

Sleek's handsome snout scrunched at the absurd notion. "But that's the *exact* opposite."

Gentle winked and playfully tugged her son's whiskers. "Blindly believing in something with insufficient evidence is unwise. See it with your own eyes first — and you will be wise."

Sleek nodded. "I will, mother. But... don't you believe in Great Ookl? Have you ever seen Him?"

"Let's talk about that later." Gentle smiled, caught on the logic-spear of her son — the same reasoning ynth she just sharpened for him. "It's time for the Irounga to earn their four majl. Let's get closer."

Sleek peeled his gaze from the horde of dazzling shraga and watched as the Bitten and their pinniped minions went to work. In unison, the quartet of elephant seals and twenty sea lions surfaced, inhaled, then dove for predetermined positions around the multicolored shoal. The Bitten hijna-barked commands, and with well-practiced coordination, all the Iroun-ga exhaled streams of silvery bubbles.

The chromatic shraga school immediately recoiled. It did not dare cross the boiling curtain, nor could it veer in any other direction for rising bubbles now hemmed it on all sides. Alarm rippled through the shoal. Fish at the outer edges of the mass rushed for the center, each speeding to occupy the nucleus of an ever-shrinking sphere. This forced outward fish previously at the center, which then panicked at the sight of the bubbles and fled back towards the middle.

Quick Tail swam up to join his mate and son. "This is why we employ the Irounga. Their bubbles cause the shraga to panic. They instinctually contract into the *khooradn*."

"Koo-ray...den?" Sleek asked.

"The 'many moving as one'," Quick Tail clarified. "Those countless shraga now behave like a *single* fish. And our 'kinship weave' is how we catch them."

The bait-ball rapidly shifted direction, speed, and orientation. Sleek found the vacillations of color and motion hypnotizing — the khooradn seemed to behave as both a solid and a liquid. Such splendor felt like a promise of the bounteous harvest to come. Sleek could almost taste the shraga feast.

"The time for watching is over," the Den Sire ordered. "There's much work for us to do."

As the Irounga continued blowing bubbles, the otters unfurled the individual sections of net. Dexterous fingers joined them into a single, colossal, fish-catching lattice — the *ehlmajl*-net. Half the sections of this 'kinship weave' — regarded as a symbol of unity between the two otter species — had bent Penuree nails and lengths of curved bone woven into the edges. Crude eyeholes punctured the other half, allowing for quick, easy assembly.

Once they finished construction, ehlmajl teams — many dozens of Lutris and Lontra now cooperating side-by-side — pulled the cross-hatch-net taut. Irounga employed their bubbles to maneuver the khooradn above the net, coaxing and cajoling it closer with each strategic exhale.

All was in readiness.

The Den Sire touched his lance to the Doyen's, conferring authority to the lesser Alpha to start the harvest. With a sharp, acknowledging nod, Fearless darted between the swirling khooradn and the patchwork net. Hundreds of golden eyes watched, captivated, as the Lutris Eehr reached out a paw and the bait-ball shrank from his webbed fingers in a smooth, fluid-like deformation. Not even the surly Bitten could hide their fascination.

Fearless raised the Eehrynth and with a powerful hijna shouted, "MAJH-EE-E!" — the cry for singular, urgent action.

Together, the otter teams launched upward, pulling the lattice towards the surface. As the net rose, the khooradn, unable to escape, rose along with it. The shraga circled in growing frenzy. Fins and tails scraped their neighbors, dislodging scales that drifted through the currents like opalescent snow. Fearless swam out of the way and joined his son among the cadre of spear-toting hunters encircling the ehlmajl.

Sleek trembled with excitement. He yearned to join the hauling effort, but the time for his contribution had not yet arrived. For now, he contented himself with swimming beside his father within the protective ring of hunters.

Thud-plop-splash!

The sounds drew Sleek's attention towards the surface. He growled in dismay.

Like tossed spears trailing clouds of bubbles, dozens of hungry seabirds were plunging head-first into the water, attacking the rising khooradn.

Their wings acted like fins, allowing the birds to swim down, snatch a shraga in their beaks, and return to the surface to eat.

"Father!" the young Beta cried. "Those birds are stealing our catch!"

"No, son," Quick Tail replied. "The Vialae are our invited guests. As for their dim-witted Luuhni cousins... well, there's no easy way to stop them, is there? All we can do is try to fend them off once the net breaks the surface."

Reassured, Sleek smiled at the absurdity of the sight. *Birds that swim like fish!* he thought. *Now I've seen everything.*

The otters did not let the diving birds distract them as they lugged the net towards the surface. They heaved and pulled, legs kicking and tails swishing. The edges of the kelp-and-twine mesh came together to trap the frightened shraga within. Laughter and encouraging hijna-shouts lightened the otters' toil, as did the promise of the pending feast.

Upon orders from the Bitten, the sea lion crew abandoned their bubble-work to lend their powerful flippers to the hauling effort. Each Irounga took a mouthful of netting and pulled with all their strength. The net soon reached the surface with a gurgling splash.

Sleek emerged with it. He sucked in a needed breath, then stared in wondrous delight at the sight before him — tens of thousands of shraga, hundreds maybe, roiled the water within the net, splashing and leaping in a desperate bid to escape. It reminded the young Beta of raindrops striking the surface of the Great Hollow's drinking pool.

Otters and seals ringed the seething cauldron, their heads bobbing on the surface swells. Each yelped excitedly to the other in congratulations on a job well done. Hunters patrolled the perimeter, spears protruding from the water like urchin quills, ready to fend off the hordes of hungry Luuhni filling the air. Their incessant caws and squawks added to the mayhem.

Quick Tail surfaced beside Sleek, followed a heartbeat later by Gentle. The Den Sire pointed his regal ynth at a smudge on the horizon.

"That's our goal," he said. "The Oyster Shell. That's where we dine."

Sleek could just make out a small skerry rising from The Blue — their third and final destination. One thousand tails distant, a crescent-shaped island — an unremarkable lump of flat stone — would provide a fine banquet site.

"That's not so far away," the eager Saia commented.

"It is when every hungry mouth in The Blue wants to steal our catch," the Den Sire cautioned. "We'd best get on with it." He waved his spear overhead. "Shut the ehlmajl! All paws, quickly now!"

The graehl leapt to obey, bringing the edges of the net together like some great closing mouth. Content to exercise patience, Vialae circled above. They knew it would reward them in the end. Their Monoic cousins, however, lacked all restraint. They bombarded the khooradn as if the net didn't exist, becoming trapped underwater as the mesh closed over their heads. Many Luuhni drowned, their limp bodies buffeted by the frenzied shraga.

Once the edges had come together, lengths of whalebone were threaded through the joined seams, securing them tight. Over three hundred otters, twenty sea lions, and four elephant seals combined their strengths to pull in unison against the current. The bulging net crept towards the crescent Oyster Shell. Still the Luuhni refused to relent. They landed on the mesh and stabbed at the catch, their beaks threatening to tear through and reach the fish.

"Protect the ehlmajl!" the Doyen shouted. "*Majhee!*"

Besides those drowned, many more foolhardy birds met their deaths upon the piercing tips of baleen and whalebone spears. Circling Vialae cackled in cruel amusement at the absurd behavior of their half-witted Monoic kin.

Eager to lend his ynth to the effort, Sleek started forward but a tug on his tail stopped him. "Let others deal with the birds," the Den Sire ordered. "Our challenge lies below."

Sleek and Quick Tail dove to where nearly a hundred hunters floated in a close orbit about the net. Each otter surveyed the sea, barbed lances at the ready. Sleek felt cold whiskers of dread tickle his stomach — they clearly knew something he didn't.

Father and son took their places among the gathered net guardians. "What now?"

"We wait," Quick Tail replied. "Keep your eyes open and your spear ready."

Sleek's pulse quickened with nascent pride at his inclusion in the ranks of the hunters. But that emotion soon passed as the water transmitted the shraga's panic to hairs along his spine, stoking his anxiety.

"Relax, Sleek. There's nothing to fear. Trust in your courage and your kin. Find and center your Hunter's Eye. This is what it means to be in a graehl."

"Yes, father." But the fear didn't flee.

The hunters floated along with the net, every nerve stretched taut, senses on the highest alert. Their collective tension set up a dull ache at the back of Sleek's skull. *What are we waiting for?* he wondered. If something didn't happen soon...

"Inky *chlooq*!" Chaser swore. "*Dhanda*! Dhanda! The dhanda are coming!"

Diver pointed his ynth at a group of shapes fast-approaching out of the Oorum. "The 'ever hungry' are here! Get ready!"

Like a volley of great cerulean arrowheads, a gang of Pacific blue-fin tuna sped into view. Between four and five tails in length, the heavily muscled, warm-blooded dhanda were opportunistic hunters, and fast enough to catch any prey they chose. The slow-moving net made for an irresistible target.

Sleek only knew tuna flayed and portioned into bright red chunks for the evening meal. Now, a whole gang of them challenged the graehl, alive, majestic — and determined.

The dhanda mob circled the khooradn just beyond the reach of the otters' spears, zipping through the snow of dislodged shraga scales like hungry blue wraiths. Unopposed, the tuna would attack in unison, tear the nets to shreds, and scatter or devour every shraga within.

Only ynth and courage could protect the hard-won harvest now.

Sleek watched a tuna speed towards Grabber's position in the protective phalanx. The Doyen's son intercepted the marauding fish with a sharp jab of his lance and a potent hijna-roar. The dhanda veered off, its muscular tail propelling it away in a flash.

Shouts of praise rang out. Grabber basked in the moment, his whiskers bristling proudly. He shot Sleek a smug, haughty glance, as if throwing down an unspoken challenge.

Feelings of competitiveness, far more intense than he'd ever experienced with any of his romp-mates, twisted in Sleek's breast. He yearned for the chance to prove his mettle, to take the fight to the dhanda — and by extension, to his rival Grabber.

"Don't worry about tail-chasing others," Quick Tail said, as if reading his son's mind. "There'll be plenty of challenges during this hunt for both you and Grabber. Focus on protecting the net. Let Ookl decide whom to honor."

How does he do that? Sleek thought. "Yes, father."

Moments later, another tuna, a full tail larger than the one Grabber repelled, launched itself at the net — and only Sleek floated in its way. The Beta's grip tightened on his new spear, yet the weapon's heft still felt unfamiliar in his paws. As the dhanda sped towards Sleek, the truth of his inexperience clouded his confidence.

Sleek imagined Grabber's eyes upon him, watching and appraising. He dared not waver.

"This one's for you, son! You can do it!"

Sleek braced himself, clenched his teeth, and jabbed. The spear found its mark in the barreling tuna, piercing the flesh below the right pectoral fin. The force of the collision knocked Sleek back. The ynth almost spun out of his paws. He managed to hang on, and with great exertion, drove the flattened fishhook tip deeper. The lance bowed with the force of his thrust.

"Get out of here!" Sleek shouted. "This is *our* food!"

"That's it!" Quick Tail said. "Show that dhanda what a Lontra hunter can do!"

The dhanda thrashed once, twice, and finally pulled free in a gush of scarlet. With a pump of its tail, it fled back into the Oorum, leaving blood in its wake.

By now, the task at paw riveted every hunter's attention. With grim concentration, they defended the catch against the relentless onslaught of tuna. None offered any cheers or praise for Sleek, as they'd done for Grabber. But that didn't matter to the young Saia. The glint of paternal pride in his father's eyes and Grabber's unexpected nod of acknowledgement was enough.

For the first time in his life, Sleek knew the joy and privilege of the hunter's bond. As he faced the gathering storm of hungry tuna, graehl-mates struggling by his side, he realized he never wanted to be anywhere else.

The scent of frightened shraga filled The Blue. The tuna horde swelled — fifty became one hundred, then two, and then five. Then more than Sleek could count. Individual tuna kept breaking from the ravenous shoal to strafe the net, attempting to find a weakness. Sharks joined the frenzy, as did myriad species of larger prey-fish, all eager to capitalize on whatever shraga slipped past the legions of relentless dhanda.

Lutris and Lontra guards repelled nearly every attack. They reveled in the martial toil and attendant glory that defending the ehlmajl bestowed.

As they labored, they hurled bold challenges at the relentless enemy.

"You can't get past me!" a Lontra female Dyah-Delta cried.

"Do your worst! You'll never breech this net!" This from a Lutris Gamma.

Someone shouted, "Kex to all you stupid dhanda! *Ghezzi-ghez!*"

Another hunter took up the vulgarity, then another. "*Ghezzi-ghez! Ghezzi-ghez!*"

Soon, the entire guard detail joined in the profane chant, including — much to Sleek's surprise and delight — his customarily sober father.

As the lewd revelry continued, the otters at the surface pulled the net towards the Oyster Shell. Inch by laborious inch they struggled, beleaguered all the while by Monoic seabirds above and an opposing current all around.

Midway to the final goal, the tuna shifted tactics and began attacking *en masse*. Each otter now had to fend off four or five dhanda instead of just one.

There's too many coming in too quick! Sleek thought as he jabbed at the face of an approaching tuna, forcing it to collide with a second. The Saia's lungs burned for a fresh breath, but he didn't dare stop fighting.

"That's it! Stay focused!" Quick Tail cried. "Ookl's Ink, this could be the largest haul we've *ever* had!"

"We don't have it yet!" Sleek responded.

The Den Sire's eyes flared with fierce golden light as he thrust his lance at an inbound dhanda. "Just keep your back to the net and your ynth in their faces! Focus your Hunter's Eye!"

The tuna horde pressed ever forward, colliding, and crashing into each other pell-mell in their attempts to feed. Powerful mouths tore into the net before prodding spears could drive them off. The khooradn's desperate bid for escape further weakened the weave until a dozen rents opened, leaking a steady stream of escaping shraga. Some flittered past Sleek's nose and swam for freedom — only to be devoured by the opportunistic dhanda.

"Ehlmajl menders!" Fearless shouted. "Below, NOW!"

A squad of female otters abandoned their pulling duties and dove. Each clutched a plijet-varient spindle wrapped in glowing kholo thread tipped with an urchin spine. They fanned out, encircled the net, and found each tear. Then, with practiced efficiency, they threaded the High Polyp lengths into the broken weave and cinched the hole closed, biting off and tying the strand to finish the repair. Each mend took a few, precious seconds.

Sleek spied Gloss from the corner of his eye. Part of the net-patching crew, she had moments earlier, been sewing shut a tear behind him. But no longer. Gloss spun to face him, the kholo-spindle loose at her side. A sassy smile lit her exquisite face.

"Nookeelee, Sleek." Gloss' presence warmed the chilly water like the noonday sun.

All thoughts of shraga, dhanda, or protecting the net vanished from Sleek's mind. The fire in Gloss' golden eyes seared away all else. "Uh-h...u h-m... n-n-nookeelee," he stammered.

Gloss smiled, amused by Sleek's discomfort. Suddenly, she cried "Look out!"

Sleek turned and saw three dhanda arrowing right towards the bulging net. Their line of attack took them straight through his love-lowered defense. "Oh, yurch."

Almost too late to react, Sleek shook off Gloss' spell and jabbed erratically with his ynth. The trio of hungry tuna veered off and sped away — luck had prevailed. This time...

Gloss' gaze settled on the weapon in Sleek's paws. The longing within her eyes to wield the spear struck him and demanded action. What harm would it cause?

Sleek offered Gloss his spear. "Here. Take it."

Gloss kicked away from the lance — yet her eyes remained fixed upon it. "I'm not allowed. Father says."

"I won't tell if you won't. Hurry! The dhanda are coming!"

Still hesitant, Gloss looked about. Her father, brother, and their trusted subordinates were busy defending the net. All eyes were turned elsewhere in their duty — all but Sleek's. None would notice if she dared to accept his offer.

Abruptly, her fear fell away. Her moment had come...

Gloss proffered the plijet-spindle to Sleek. He took it and placed the lance in her paws. His heart fluttered when their fingers touched. The spear looked so natural, so integral to Gloss' being, like the lovely whiskers adorning her face... a face now adorned with a fierce, joyful grin.

Dhanda swarmed all around the two young otters. Opponents enough to spare —

Gloss cried, "Yaaargh!" and flung herself into the fray.

She jabbed at the cheek of one tuna, whacked a second on the snout with the butt of the ynth, and slapped a third across the eye with the tip of her tail. The fish scattered, leaving the two otters drifting amidst a temporary lull in the attack.

Gloss swam over to Sleek and offered back his weapon. "Thanks. That was fun."

Dumbfounded, Sleek could only nod and retrieve the spear. The skills this adolescent Lutris female had just displayed rivaled those of any seasoned hunter. Sleek knew he was outclassed.

"Gloss! What are you doing? There are tears to mend," called an impatient Gamma Lutris female. "Stop playing with that silly uju and get to work!"

Gloss' ecstatic grin faded. A flash of helpless anger darkened her pretty features, then morphed into resignation. "I'm coming, uja!" she hollered back. "Sorry-sorry."

She reclaimed the kholo-spindle from Sleek. Their paws touched a second time, and an electric jolt rippled down the entire length of the young Beta's body.

"I'll see you at the Oyster Shell. 'Bye, Sleek." As she swam to rejoin the other net menders, Gloss' tail caressed the back of Sleek's neck in passing, sending another shiver of excitement cavorting down his spine.

"Bye." All the stunned Saia could do was float, dreamily clutching his spear to his chest amidst the falling snow of dislodged shraga scales — until the wake of a passing dhanda jarred him back to reality.

Composure regained, Sleek reclaimed his spot before the net and rejoined its defense. He shot a glance over at his father, who looked his way, a troubled expression etched on his regal countenance. Unsure of the reason for Quick Tail's frown, Sleek turned his attention back to the swarm of marauding tuna and other prestige prey-fish, steadied his grip, slowed his pulse, and jabbed.

CHAPTER 31

THE LAST SHRAGA FEAST

S leek surfaced for breath — between incoming dhanda attacks.

From twenty tails offshore, he watched the hauling teams of co-operative Lutris and Lontra slip from the sea — lovely Gloss among them — their multi-colored pelts glistening with water, their paws clutching the weft of the great ehlmajl-net. With common cadence they cried, "Maj-he-ee! Maj-he-ee! Maj-he-ee!" and, inch by inch, heaved the bulging net from the sea and into the crescent-shaped granite enclosure that formed the Oyster Shell.

A series of low, smooth steps led from the water into the spacious tide pool at its center. Countless protrusions and niches scalloped the surrounding walls of the skerry, forming individual dining areas for those animals wishing to eat their meal in peace, above the raucous mob. Patient and watching, Vialae occupied the highest, most inaccessible reaches of the coarse and guano-stained Oyster Shell. Their restraint would soon be rewarded with full bellies.

Otter teams stopped short of dragging the net completely out of the water, lest the enormous weight of the struggling khooradn sunder it. Halfway up, they released the ties and emptied half the contents of the swollen net. In a squirming, flashing quicksilver-wave, innumerable rainbow fish poured onto the wet steps. They flipped and flopped in gasping frenzy, scales reflecting sunlight like thousands of tiny, summersaulting mirrors.

Otter teams busied themselves separating the dying shraga into piles based on size, color, and overall desirability. Armed graehls fought off the persistent flocks of Luuhni overhead and prowling shoals of dhanda below.

As the shraga were plucked and pulled from the majl, each constituent-segment was detached, rolled, and reclaimed by its maker. Tiny shells incorporated into the weave formed unique signatures so their owners could be identified. With the nets sorted and stowed, the feast began. For a tide-cycle — six full hours — the hollow of the Oyster Shell reverberated with a mighty rumpus. The barks, yelps, and playful growls of the otters mingled with a chorus of caws and squawks of the many birds vying for scraps. The cacophony exhilarated all attendees.

So many shraga had been harvested that even those with the hardiest appetites could eat their fill and still an enormous surplus remained. These leftovers would return to Holt and Raft, so that those animals who, by necessity, had remained behind — the very young, the elderly, pregnant and nursing females, the sick and infirm — would receive their share.

Both tribes would dine well for many days, increasing in size and weight; and the Vialae would enjoy a hundred tides of plucking the abundance of shraga scraps from the Oyster Shell's countless nooks and crevices.

With such bounty available, the otters could afford to be selective. Only the choicest portions were eaten, and the scraps tossed onto the rocks to be fought over by the birds. Dhanda and hundreds of smaller scavenger fish picked clean any leftovers that spilled into the sea. Many otters dined in family units, while others mingled and chatted freely between species while they ate. Squads of skilled cleaners worked the massive pile. Razor-sharp accurs dispatched, filleted, and portioned the catch. Many otters enjoyed indulging their primitive impulses and chose to eat the shraga *old style* — alive, wiggling, and headfirst. They claimed it made the fish tastier.

And who ever needed a better reason than that?

Sleek sat beside his mother and father on a flat ledge of sun-warmed rock. Nearby, the Lutris Doyen and his children lounged on their own rocky sill, while two-dozen armed hunters of both species mingled and dined peacefully below. The quartet of Bitten waited beyond the periphery of spears, their sea lion lackeys huddled behind their massive bulks, hungry and awaiting instructions.

The normally belligerent elephant seals were visibly humbled. They kept their bronze eyes lowered, and their heads close to the wet stones. The time for payment had arrived, and the success of their errand, not to mention their lives, now rested in the Den Sire's paws. If the Aanandi High Eehr reneged on his word, which, after the Bitten's earlier behavior, could be argued as justified, then at the very least the Irounga faced banishment; or, at worst, death in the jaws of their colossal liege.

Their one-eyed leader quivered with anxiety. Sleek could tell by the look on the bull's face that he deeply regretted his earlier, ill-considered strategy of insults and lies.

The Den Sire finished his meal, then stood on two legs at the lip of the ledge, his wise golden eyes settling on each seal. "Well, friends, the time has come for us to part ways."

"Yes, Den Sire," the one-eyed Bitten replied, his hijna resonant with humility.

"It's been a wonderful haul. Your master will feast well."

"Most assuredly, Den Sire."

Quick Tail pointed with his Alpha's lance at four nets lying on the wet stones, each crammed to bursting with shraga. It took an eight-otter team to drag the heavy nets to the pinniped assemblage. Sewn closed for the long trip to Blubber Snout's distant island rookery, they were fitted with a special harness of woven kelp designed to fit around the necks of the sea lions. The famished Irounga eyed the nets longingly but a contingent of ynth-wielding otter guards prevented the seals from touching them.

"As agreed, four full majl. I'd consider it a personal favor if they were returned to me. Intact, if you please."

One-Eye nodded and nervously chewed his lip. "We'll do our best, Den Sire."

"See you do." Fearless stood beside Quick Tail. His gold eyes projected a coldness that countered the Den Sire's warmth. The Eehrynth hung loose in his grip, its lethal, stone-sharpened tip aimed directly at the elephant seal's remaining eye. "I hope you've learned a thing or two about the futility of attempting to double-cross us. We are smarter than you and not to be trifled with. And remember that our spears *always* find their mark."

The Bitten lowered their heads until their fatty snouts touched the wet rocks. Their soft growls betrayed how difficult this prostration was for them.

"Raise your heads," Quick Tail commanded. "All the Irounga tribes are our friends. We all share The Blue, swim with joy, and hunt with pride. Our allegiances may differ, but our hearts pump the same red."

"True, Den Sire, true." One-Eye chanced an upward glance and found Quick Tail smiling. The dread shivering through his blubber began to ease.

"To show my appreciation of all your hard work, and to dismiss any misunderstandings we may have had earlier, I present you with a gift."

All heads turned as another eight-otter team dragged up a fifth majl-net filled with sunset fish and deposited it before the Irounga. With a sharp tug on its holding straps, the hauling team opened the net, spilling a generous mound of shraga onto the water-slicked granite.

The seals eyed the food, whiskers twitching as they sniffed the delicious aroma. Sleek heard their empty stomachs grumbling from ten tails away.

Fearless turned to his fellow Alpha, aghast. His whiskers bristled. "Are you mad? That's *our* shraga you're giving away!"

Quick Tail ignored the Doyen's impolite outburst. "You've all worked hard. If not for your bubbles, this harvest wouldn't have been successful. Diuun Dunn needn't be the only Irounga who eats today."

"Thank you, Den Sire." One-Eye said. The other Bitten agreed with exuberant nods.

The four famished elephant seals waddled towards the glistening pile of shraga. Their mouths got within a whisker-length from taking a first bite.

"Wait," Quick Tail snapped.

In one lethal motion, a row of ynth-toting hunters leveled their barbed weapons at the Bitten's heads. The pinnipeds halted, bewildered, strings of saliva coiling from their mouths.

Quick Tail shrugged. His royal mouth twisted in a mischievous sneer. "I'm sorry, friends. I should have been clearer. You may eat, but only *after* your subordinates do."

The one-eyed Bitten and his cohorts gasped. Their jowls and snouts jiggled as they searched the Den Sire's face for any clue showing they should be laughing at this tasteless joke. They found none.

"What?" One-Eye barked. "That...that's... unacceptable!"

"Nevertheless," Quick Tail replied. "I watched you closely. Your underlings did most of the work. And, for their efforts, they shall eat first."

From the relative safety of his elevated ledge, Sleek observed the Bitten's dismay with amusement. With a few simple words, his father upended their entire size-dominant hierarchy. Now, the massive creatures sputtered and moaned as if afflicted by blood-sucking lampreys.

The sea lions — tired from hours of labor with nothing to show but empty bellies, and with a few still bleeding from disciplinary bite wounds — looked at each other quizzically, unsure whether to accept this generosity. All hesitated. A few even backed away.

"Please, friends, this is *your* gift," the Den Sire coaxed. "We will not sit by and have those who toiled to fill the bellies of our kin go without."

Fearless' furrowed brow underscored the distaste he felt over the High Eehr's decision.

"So, come," Quick Tail urged. "Don't be afraid. Eat your fill. There is enough for all of you. And, when you've finished, your Bitten."

The elephant seals *harrumphed* and bellowed in protest. But the sharp spears of the otter hunters persuaded them to shuffle aside and let their minions come forward. The sea lions reluctantly waddled towards the shraga heap and began gulping down fish after fish without chewing. Their previously cowed psyches lightened with each swallow as their empty bellies filled. Their palpable joy countered the Bitten's ire.

At the island rookery where old Blubber Snout reigned supreme, size and strength decided everything for those who dwelt within his shadow. But here — for this one fleeting meal, in this one passing tide — the last were first, and those accustomed to being first due to their size, had to wait their turn.

Sleek nibbled on his sixth and final shraga, a scattering of bones and other inedible scraps littering his dining ledge. Blissfully full, he wished for an elephant seal's roomier stomach so he could keep gorging.

On an adjacent shelf reserved for the Alphas, his parents lounged, chatting with Fearless about the nuances of inter-species trade, kelp forest upkeep, graehl compositions to offset skill shortfalls, rank advancement views, and other topics only rulers found interesting. Below, on another ledge, Gloss and Grabber, having eaten their fill, napped side-by-side in the warm sun.

Sleek had been watching Gloss all day, sometimes secretly, but oftentimes openly. He didn't mean to be rude, or to make her uncomfortable, but he felt compelled. Sleek knew Lutris females weren't allowed to hunt. He found this custom absurd, yet he witnessed her skill with his own eyes, a skill that she should not have possessed.

But she did. The mystery of how Gloss acquired that skill — she'd learned to handle a spear some*how*, from some*one* — baffled and intrigued him.

As the young Beta pondered this, Eager, a female Lontra hunter holding the rank of Vlis, stepped onto the Alpha's ledge. With ynth in paw, she bowed her head in respect and awaited recognition.

"What is it, Eager?" Quick Tail asked.

The Gamma tugged her whiskers in deference. "Kooarii, Den Sire, Suckling Mother, Doyen...I'm sorry to interrupt your meal, but sentries have reported that *they* have arrived."

Interest piqued, Sleek set aside his meal for a closer listen. *They? They who?*

The Den Sire nodded. "They're earlier than expected, but that's their prerogative. See the waters are cleared of predators. Take as many hunters as needed. Quickly, now."

Eager tugged her whiskers in acknowledgment and dropped off the ledge into the throng of feasting otters below. A team of lesser-ranked Lontra fell into step behind the Vlis-Gamma as she barked orders. One by one, they slipped into the sea to execute her directives by spear-point.

"Fearless, I need your best graehl positioned at the arrival pool and watching the sky."

"Done." The Doyen leaned over the edge of the shelf and touched the shoulder of a Beta with the shaft of the Eehrynth. "Make it happen, Bravest."

"Yes, Doyen." As Fearless' second and close friend, the Saia named Bravest needed no further instruction. The Beta tugged his whiskers, grabbed his spear, and rushed off to fulfill his Alpha's command. "Follow me, son," he said to a young Loyc-Epsilon with an oversized canine tooth protruding from his mouth. "We've work to do."

"Yes, father." Sharp Tooth tore his infatuated gaze from Gloss as she slept, fetched a baleen spear, and followed his father into the water.

Quick Tail took a final bite of his meal, then set the remainder aside. He glanced at his son. "Come with us, Sleek. You'll want to see this."

"What is it?" the young Lontra asked.

"The Ulurii are here," Gentle answered.

Ulurii! That exotic, tantalizing word set Sleek's heart to racing. Respected by most as the sages of the sea, octo-snails were the only denizens in all The Blue believed to converse with Old Father Fathom. They had even constructed the language that formed the backbone of the Envoric culture... or so the rumor went.

Sleek shadowed the Alphas to a shallow, water-filled depression bordering the Oyster Shell's sloping, granite lip. An eroded curtain of stone, heavy with barnacles and clinging mussels, partitioned much of the pool from view of the feasting otters. Sentry Lutris mounted many of the scalloped ledges of this curtain, their barbed lances aimed skyward to ward off any bird bold or foolish enough to chance an attack.

The Alpha trio, a paw-full of Betas, and thrice as many honored Gammas and Deltas, arrayed themselves on the rocks above the lapping waters. A closed kelp-net filled with shraga lay between the Den Sire and Doyen, each Alpha gripping its kelp and twine crosshatch. None of the otter delegates bore weapons of any kind. Not even the Eehrs were exempt. Ancient etiquette decreed that no tool capable of spilling blood or ink be allowed in the august presence of the soft-bodied octo-snails. And no otter assembled would ever break that sacred custom.

Sleek's eyes scanned the sparkling waves, searching for any hint of the mysterious visitors. After a few moments, several dark shapes, their spheroidal profiles distorted by the rippling water, appeared at the lip of the protective pool. They moved slowly, cautiously, as if hesitant to expose themselves to the open air — or the scrutiny of others.

Excitement thudded in Sleek's breast, colored with an anxiety he couldn't dismiss or explain. For some reason he felt once more like a tiny kit awaiting a disciplinary ear-bite by his parents. *But why?* he thought. *Ulurii are just like any other Envoric creature... aren't they?*

As the Beta watched, a set of ocular orbs mounted on slender, rubbery stalks broke the surface. The lidless eyes fixed the assembled otters in a penetrating gaze, only to vanish under the waves once more.

"Do not move..." Gentle cautioned her son. "...or show fear."

Sleek obeyed his mother and remained frozen.

But his heart still thudded.

CHAPTER 32

A BONELESS DELEGATION

The first pair of eyestalks reappeared, followed by several more of varying color, girth, and length. Ocular orbs, shining with unmistakable intelligence, scrutinized the scene, W-shaped irises quivering. One set however, stood out. Unlike the others, its orbs were opaque and white as a fair-weather cloud.

The otters waited in respectful silence as the Ulurii decided on how to proceed.

At last, seven large shells emerged from the chilled water, each propelled on a squirming mass of eight pink, green, blue, or gray tentacles. The shells and their boneless occupants presented a rainbow of color, texture, and writhing anatomy. The shells ranged from spiraled trumpet to the pearlescent whelk, from the spiked conch to majestic nautili. Strings of Ahmijna characters were scrawled over each shell — symbols of faith and devotion to Great Ookl — etched there by ancient acuurs held in rubbery hands.

Most Envorah knew that octo-snails possessed tri-lobed brains quite unlike the dual hemispheres possessed by other animals. Lontra elders guessed this unique anatomy endowed them with their peculiar nature, and the ability to create language.

With their gorgeous shells aglow in the late afternoon sunlight, the seven Ulurii made an imposing, bizarre, and oddly majestic sight. Spectacles like this occurred seldom upon the surface of The Blue. Sleek watched as the enigmatic cephalopods undulated closer to his father and the net of sunset fish, their muscular tentacles flexing and pulling. The excitement he'd felt prior to their arrival morphed into a deep reverence and — though he'd never admit it — a touch of fear. Only once before did he encounter the Ulurii, back when he'd been an untried adolescent two seasons prior.

Sleek remembered that day well. After much preparation by the Lontra, an octo-snail delegation had paid an official visit to High Split Rock, arriving up through the moon pool to a scene of boisterous celebration. Sleek couldn't be certain, but he thought many of the same individuals forming this delegation were the same as those from before.

He did recognize one octo-snail, however. She was quite unmistakable.

Umthoothee — the aged, blind matriarch of the Ulurii ruling quorum, the *Oumuo* — wiggled towards the Den Sire and Doyen. Larger by half than the others of her kin, and glistening with a thin layer of pearlescent mucous, she boasted an emerald-hued nautilus shell whose weight caused it to tilt on her boneless body. Tiny periwinkle and topsnail shells, fashionable and elegant, adorned her tentacle-arms and secondary eyestalks.

Undeniably ancient, no one knew Umthoothee's actual age. Even she had forgotten.

"Venerable Umthoothee, we're honored to host the Oumuo," Quick Tail stated.

The Doyen nodded and tugged his whiskers. "Please share in our harvest."

Like all female octo-snails, Umthoothee sported colorful feathery growths that sprouted in twin vertical rows below her secondary set of eyestalks. They twitched and fluttered as she spoke, as if engaged in ghostly respiration. "Thank you and may Great Ookl -shlrrp- keep you safe in His coils."

The Den Sire tugged his whiskers. "And you as well."

With greeting pleasantries concluded, the matriarch raised her two primary arm-tendrils. Forty noodle-like fingers touched the snout and whiskers of first Quick Tail and then Fearless. The facial caress told Umthoothee much.

"Quick Tail, you feel stouter than the last time we met," the octo-snail matriarch commented with a hint of snark. "Eating well, I gather."

"Stout?" The Den Sire bristled. "Well, I, uh, I do dine when the mood takes..."

"And Fearless, I notice you've still got that mole on your cheek. You should let a crab snip it off for you."

"Nice to see you, too, Matriarch." The Doyen snorted at the good-natured jibe. "And it's a scar, not a mole."

"Of course, it is. You know, at first, I didn't recognize your hijna. Chookzl, I must be -shlrrp- getting old and shriveled."

Quick Tail smiled. "No, Umthoothee. Not old. Venerable, with all respect."

"Ookl's Ink, it's the same thing. Just a kinder word, is all. But then, you always were a flatterer, Quick Tail of the Lontra." The matriarch made the Ulurii version of a chuckle, a rapid clicking of the powerful beak hidden in the center of her tentacles, followed by a series of rasping sounds accompanied by the hijna command: "Prepare the shraga."

A group of subordinate males, smaller and less ornamented, obediently crawled from the sloshing water and converged on the shraga-filled net. They entwined their muscular tentacles through the mesh and hauled the bounty back into the sea's frigid embrace.

"What do they do with the shraga?" Sleek whispered to Gentle. As far as he knew, cephalopods didn't eat fish, just crab and other hard-shelled prey.

Gentle leaned in close, keeping her hijna discreet. "Just like we use pryzoa to omen-dive, Ulura use shraga to predict future tides. It's a sacred ritual dedicated to Great Ookl."

"But how?" Sleek asked, far more forceful than he'd meant to.

"Eh?" Umthoothee's blind eyes snapped towards the young Beta. "How's that?"

Embarrassment cut through Sleek, like a spear through fish. He'd inadvertently inserted his hijna into a conversation reserved for adults, and now paid the price of unwanted attention as all eyes fastened on him. "Oh, uhm, I was wondering... how... uhm... how..."

"Yes?" Umthoothee's primary eyestalks elongated. Her cataract-clouded orbs pointed uncannily at the Saia's face, as if she could see him. "How's -shlrrp- what? Spit it out."

Sleek's parents and the Doyen looked at him expectantly. The young Lontra fidgeted with his paws, hesitant to speak and half-tempted to bolt into the sea — until he caught a glimpse of Gloss peering at him from behind her father's broad shoulders. Her encouraging smile warmed Sleek like sunlight, stirring the tender sprig of his chilled confidence back to life.

The young Beta tugged his whiskers and lowered his head in respect. "I was wondering, venerable Umthoothee..."

"There's that lousy word again," the octo-snail matriarch groused. "I *hate* that word."

Sleek swallowed hard. "...how shraga are used to predict future tides? With all respect."

"I like *-shlrrp-* the manners on this one," the aged Ulura said around a wet inhalation. "He's slow to get going, but curious and respectful. And such a clear, sharp hijna. Come closer youngling, so I may 'see' your face."

Sleek inched towards the octo-snail matriarch, reluctant to draw any closer. Not out of fear or revulsion, but from an acute sense of mystery. Something unseen charged the very air around the Ulurii, bristling the hairs on his neck and spine. Sleek's ears, nose and whiskers couldn't sense it, but his Aanandi-shade certainly did.

"Ah-h-h," Umthoothee wheezed, her fingers wiggling over the contours of Sleek's face. They felt like cold, rubbery worms. "Oh, you're a handsome Lontra, aren't you? You must stir the hearts of all uja in the Holt."

Sleek blushed. "I don't know about that."

"Don't be modest. Of course, you do. I can 'see' your *-shlrrp-* parents are, hm-m-m... Quick Tail and... Gentle?"

"Yes."

"My fingers still got the touch. What's your name, young uju?"

"Sleek."

"Now that's a strong name. It's a name that will challenge The Blue." Umthoothee removed her rubbery hands from his face, down to the kholo-bracelet on his right wrist. "And I do believe I wove your ureola. Yes, yes, you'll have a vital future, Ookl Willing."

"Thank you." Sleek nodded in polite agreement, unsure what Umthoothee meant by 'a vital future.' But he didn't wish to question her any further.

"So, handsome Sleek, shall I show you *-shlrrp-* how the shraga of Old Father Fathom reveal tides not yet known, waves not yet born?"

Sleek glanced at his parents, who nodded. "Yes, please," he replied. "If it's no trouble."

Umthoothee's eyestalks recoiled. "Trouble? I offered to show you, didn't I?"

"I'm sorry—"

"That doesn't require an answer." Umthoothee's clouded eyes swiveled on their stalks, blindly searching the quorum. "Cixtindi... Uuvaloo?" she called. "Where are you? Doesn't matter. Front and center. And bring a shraga with you."

The two smallest octo-snails obediently crept towards their matriarch. Youngest of the Oumuo, yet by seasons lived twice as old as Quick Tail, they still bore vestiges of their squirtling respiratory mantle-combs. Naked of shell, they displayed the ruddy hue of Ulurii humility.

"We obey, Umthoothee," they replied with one hijna.

Sleek wondered at their lack of shells. To him, it seemed like certain death since every predator in The Blue considered octo-snails a delicacy. Umthoothee wrapped her tentacle-like arms around both the young males and gripped their primary eyestalks.

The two unshelled Ulurii looked so vulnerable compared to the undeniable majesty of their matriarch. Their eyes were clear and keen, the W-shaped irises filled with curiosity and boundless optimism.

If given the chance, here were beings Sleek could befriend.

"Let me introduce you to our -*shlrrp*- newest tharuuspex acolytes: spawn-brothers Cixtindi and Uuvaloo." Cixtindi, the slenderer of the two siblings, possessed longer primary eyestalks and a complexion much less crimson than his brother. "They also happen to be my great-great-great-great-great-*great* grandsquirts," Umthoothee continued. "Still inexperienced acolytes, mind you, and their ink isn't as dark as it could be. But they're showing promise, and -*shlrrp*- will soon undergo the *heeqoo* to find a proper shell. But for now, they're naked *shisslaaq*. Isn't that right, squirtlings?"

"Yes, Umthoothee," Uuvaloo and Cixtindi replied. Their flesh oscillated in the standard red and blue deference-patterns young octo-snail used when addressing an elder.

Sleek found the pigment displays fascinating, as well as the words. What did 'heeqoo' and 'shisslaaq' mean? One suggested an action, the other a slight. Or maybe the reverse? Or something else entirely?

Aside from the vernacular common to all Envorah, much of the Ulurii language remained undecipherable. Octo-snails loved to invent words for ideas and concepts no other animal bothered to ponder, like a blemish on a stone, the elasticity of a kelp frond, the smell of the clouds, or the texture of a shadow. Poetic souls, through and through.

"Kooarii," Cixtindi and Uuvaloo said in unison to the Alpha trio. Their eyestalks swiveled to Sleek and, with one hijna, offered the common greeting of their species: *"Ucaay-yaeeeli-uraari-omaweera."*

The Ulurii splayed their tentacles with perfect manners, their chromatophores blotting their skin green and blue in respect. Slurping breaths accentuated their friendly hijna-voices.

Sleek, along with his parents and other gathered otters, gave a polite whisker-tug and replied in kind: "I am me-you are you-we are equal-I am you-you are me-equal are we."

"Good. With that formality cleared up, and you're all properly introduced, which of you will instruct my son on your esoterica?" the Den Sire asked.

The juvenile octo-snails each raised a slender tentacle to volunteer.

The Den Sire smiled. "Let the lesson proceed."

Cixtindi's eyestalks bent in the octo-snail equivalent of a nod. "Old Father Fathom, blessed be His Ink, sends shraga from the -*gloopf*- depths" he began. "They nibble the wounds inflicted by the stone teeth of His eternal counterpart, The Divine Impetus."

"We are forbidden at this stage of our -*mmurpt*- development to utter the accursed *true* name of The Divine Impetus. Only Its title," Uuvaloo interjected. Black fractal patterns rippled across his body. His forty noodle-fingers bent and twisted into warding and banishment symbols only Ulurii understood. "It is a name most foul. Most unclean."

Every Lutris within hijna-range tensed in affront. Even Gloss' golden eyes looked hot enough to burn holes through the rude acolyte's rubbery flesh.

The Lontra all waited, alert and uneasy — Den Sire included — for the Doyen to react.

"Wretched *ptahhf*," Fearless growled, holding onto his anger by a slender claw. "Almighty Deshi-Oad doesn't give a greasy dolphin turd if you speak His name or not. And, in fact, the shraga clean *His* wounds, not Ookl's. Add that to your lesson."

"Uhm-m-m..." Uuvaloo's skin bleached bone-white, then orange with chagrin and alarm. "I meant -*mmurpt*- no disrespect, Doyen." He glanced at Umthoothee for guidance.

"Old Father give me strength," the elderly matriarch burped, her eyestalks contracting in exasperation as clashing amber and blue colors flashed across her rubbery skin. "Apologies, Doyen. Uuvaloo is still in -*shlrrp*- training and struggling in his lessons."

"Apology accepted." Fearless nodded curtly at the Ulurii matriarch, his agitation blunted.

Uuvaloo shrank back in shame. Cixtindi — realizing the lesson must continue, even under angry eyes — produced a razor-sharp crescent shaped acuur of pearlescent abalone shell from within with his writhing tentacles.

"At H-His com-m-and..." he stuttered, nervous under all the attention. He quickly regained composure. "...schools of shraga are dispersed into The Blue to spread His inky wisdom." He reverently laid the tool across the shraga's upturned throat and pushed. The tender flesh split with a clean cut. "First, you open the sunset fish from throat to tail. Your acuur must *-gloopf-* be sharp, for Ookl demands the incision be one, clean motion, like the wave birthed at sea moving, uninterrupted, only to die upon the shore."

"May I try?" Sleek asked.

Cixtindi's large, emotive eyes swiveled towards the young Beta. "Of course."

Sleek tugged an acuur from his ureola. He set it to the incision begun by his cephalopod teacher and began to cut. But the green sea glass of his multi-tool was dull from many tides of use. "Yurch," he muttered, clumsily sawing the fish's belly. "Mine needs sharpening."

The octo-snail offered Sleek his keener blade. "Try mine."

"Thank you... Uuvaloo?"

"No, no. I'm *-gloopf-* Cixtindi."

Sleek tugged his whiskers. "My mistake. Sorry."

"No need for apologies. It's difficult for us to tell Lontra and Lutris apart as well," Cixtindi confessed. "Many of you look identical." Sleek didn't know whether to laugh or take offense. The Ulura continued his instruction, so the young Beta let the comment slide. Cixtindi pointed at the splayed shraga in Sleek's paws. "Now, once the fish is opened, you'll notice how the... oh, chookzl!"

A great commotion of flapping wings and angry shouts caused the octo-snail to curse in alarm. His muscular body instinctually contracted,

tentacles and eyestalks withdrawing into a defensive ball. Sleek looked up
to see three Luuhni cormorants brazenly attempting to get past the spears
of the sentries, intent on making meals of the unshelled spawn-brothers.
In their zeal to reach their intended prey, their wings buffeted each other as
well as the otter defenders.

All Oumuo ducked into their shells — all except defiant Umthoothee.
She remained, unmoved and even looked a bit bored. Predation attempts,
both from above and below, were just a part of her centuries-long life.
Cixtindi and Uuvaloo slithered towards the protection of their ancient
grandmother's outstretched tentacles. The spawn-brothers squirted ink
and wailed in terror with flatulent exhalations and rapid beak clicks. Ridges
and blebs of alarm rippled across their blanching skin.

Sleek recoiled in disgust as a splatter of dark purple liquid wet his leg.
"Yurch!" he hollered, dropping the shraga. Slashing at the marauders with
his acuur, he cried, "Get away, you kexxing birds!"

All the spears jabbing at their undersides evaporated the cormorant's
confidence. Cawing in frustration, the Luuhni broke off their attack and
scattered in a cloud of coal-black feathers. The entire episode unfolded
within the space of a few heartbeats.

"It's over," the Den Sire said. "Everyone can relax."

Fearless glowered at the retreating birds. One by one, the octo-snails
reemerged from their shells with awkward attempts at dignity, their rubbery skin a palette of alarmed pigments.

"Well, that sure stirred things up," Umthoothee stated tartly as she
unraveled herself from her grandsquirts' tentacles. "Dangers of being a
delicious -shlrrp- Ulura, sad to say."

Sleek offered his paw to Cixtindi for support as the young octo-snail
relaxed his multiple limbs and righted himself. "Are you alright?"

"Oh, yes. I'm -gloopf- a tad ashamed," the octo-snail confessed, "but
otherwise fine." The frantic pulses of color lacing his skin softened as

his composure returned. "Squirting ink in public like that is, well...it's unseemly. I'm sorry I splashed you."

Sleek sniffed the ink fouling his leg. He wrinkled his nose in subtle distaste at the pungent smell — a mixture of rotten fish and sun-heated kelp.

Cixtindi flinched green with embarrassment. "Oh, dear, oh, dear..."

"Don't worry about it. It's nothing The Blue won't wash off," Sleek reassured. "Continue with the lesson."

Cixtindi retrieved the opened shraga from the wet rocks at Sleek's feet and handed it back to him. "Now, peel back the flesh to reveal the innards. See how they are arrayed? Notice their -gloopf- beautiful color and shape? What is the quality of their scent? Touch them to discern firmness. And don't worry that you don't know the Ulurii names for each organ, nor our wisdom behind their function," the octo-snail added, as if tutoring a fresh-hatched squirtling.

Sleek did as instructed, but the splayed viscera seemed unremarkable. "I don't know what I'm looking for," he said with mild impatience. "How does this tell me the future?"

Cixtindi extended a boneless hand, and Sleek placed the shraga into it. The twenty fingers enclosed it like a clump of writhing worms. "It is difficult to explain while on land. Only in The Blue do the -gloopf- true glimpses beyond the Oorum appear. Suffice it to say, when cast to the currents, the drifting organs tell us many useful things."

Sleek's handsome nose twitched in confusion. "Like what?"

"Well, Old Father's moods, for one. Or, which foods He'll bring, or lives He'll take. The waves He'll stir, the stars He'll -gloopf- make. Many, many things." The octo-snail held the pearlescent sunset fish with deep reverence. "Even where He's hidden our promised *Skynthuuhrnymlex* — and who may discover it."

"You can tell all that from fish innards?" Sleek asked.

"Oh, yes," Cixtindi's cold flesh danced with the pulsed colors of his devotion. He seemed oblivious to Sleek's implied skepticism. "Unlike pry-zoa, which offer just mundane glimpses, the -*gloopf*- bellies of shraga hold hidden messages directly from Great Ookl. They nibble His flesh, you see. And when you from eat *them*, you eat from *Him*."

"Eat? Him?" Sleek found the idea of devouring a deity, imaginary or not, disquieting. "And that's important *how*?"

"It...it just *is*," the octo-snail replied. "How can you compare the triviality of surface conditions to the -*gloopf*- unknowable depths where He dreams? All truth lies deep where darkness reigns and the Oorum vanishes entirely. Surface light does nothing but shine on illusion and confusion. Truth lives in the abyss, unseen and everywhere."

"How can you know for sure what you said is *true*?"

"Well...I...oh, that's just -*gloopf*- silly talk. Of course, it's true," Cixtindi replied with recited, if not very believable, conviction. "Great Ookl says so."

Sleek remembered the earlier logic-lesson of his mother. "But have you ever *seen* him?"

Cixtindi sputtered, "I... well..." He looked at his spawn-sibling, his matriarch, and then the other Ulurii for guidance. The simplicity of Sleek's questions appeared to have cut his faith surely as a cormorant's beak would his tender flesh.

"No one's seen Him for countless -*mmurpt*- tides," Uuvaloo interjected on his fellow acolyte's behalf. He defiantly shook his rubbery head, eye-orbs fixed on Sleek. "Not even Umthoothee has seen Him. But we don't need to see. We *believe*. That's enough."

Sleek turned to his parents, and then Gloss, with eyes silently screaming frustration. "I believe in fish because I've hunted them." He fixed his gaze back on Cixtindi. "I believe in pryzoa because I've tasted them. I believe in clouds because I see them. How can you believe in something you've never witnessed?"

Cixtindi seemed poised in thought. His features were too strange for Sleek to read.

Uuvaloo squirmed closer to the young Lontra and raised a tentacle. "First, Old Father Fathom deliberately remains hidden to -*mmurpt*- test His Chosen Coil." He raised another tentacle. "Second, by hiding He reveals to us the Blue's unseen truth." He lifted a third appendage. "And lastly, you must accept His word with a humility —"

Sleek snorted. "No offense, Uuvaloo, but that makes no sense."

An unpleasant rasping sound issued from the thickset Ulura's hidden beak. His entire body turned black with insult. He reared up, tentacles waving. "You...you ...how *dare*..."

"Oh, dear me, my -*shlrrp*- skin sure is getting dry." Umthoothee wiggled between Sleek and her irate great-great-great-great grandsquirt, her urgent movement and violet skin flashes a sharp contrast to her bland words. "At my age I can't afford any more wrinkles. And before you say anything snarky, Fearless, it's not vanity. Ookl wouldn't approve."

Sleek wanted to keep arguing. Riling the sanctimonious Uuvaloo thrilled him in a way he couldn't fully explain. It seemed as if the Ulurii's fatuous ideas were prey, to be skewered on the spearpoint of Sleek's self-obvious reason. He had his mother to thank for that.

But he also remembered what nocturnal hunting taught him: not all things are readily visible, and both prey and predator can hide themselves — and switch places once disguised.

Perhaps I pushed too far, too fast? The young Lontra offered the octo-snail siblings a polite whisker-tug. "Thanks for the lesson. There is much I don't yet understand. I appreciate your patience in teaching me."

Umthoothee's skin color warmed to pink at Sleek's gracious concession. "Oh, yes. I do like this one. Like I said, such -*shlrrp*- splendid manners.

Many questions live in you, Sleek. Some more relevant than others. Your parents must be proud. Until next time, young uju."

A sequence of muffled *click-snaps* issued from the beak deep in the matriarch's abdomen, signaling the time arrived for the Ulurii to depart. They obeyed without hesitation or goodbye, undulating for the lapping waves on coiled, glistening tentacles. One-by-one they left the skerry and submerged from view.

Cixtindi lingered last. He took Sleek's forepaw in a strong tendril and drew him close. "I thought your questions were *-gloopf-* quite astute. They raised ideas I'd never considered. You've given me much to ponder. Friend."

Sleek smiled. "Friend."

Cixtindi turned and crawled into the water, his entire being afire with a new, restless drive. That energy, kindled by Sleek's innocent confusion, would shed much-needed light onto the doctrinal darkness holding the Ulurii species captive.

Only Great Ookl knew for sure if that light would set them free.

CHAPTER 33

HEARTS ADRIFT TOGETHER

The shraga feast was winding down.

Though a pawful of otters still dined, most digested while lounging on the sun-warmed rocks or floating upon gentle waves. Still others made for the designated area at the skerry's northern corner to relieve themselves on rocks close to the water, so the sea might wash away their spraint.

Sleek felt as bloated as a swollen sea slug. He gorged himself nearly to bursting, and now his every bite of shraga demanded release.

Unlike most Lontra, Sleek never felt comfortable answering nature's call while others watched or listened. Especially now if those eyes and ears belonged to beautiful Gloss. He acknowledged the irrationality of his shyness, even as he grabbed his spear and scurried across the Oyster Shell, the pressure building in his abdomen.

With growing urgency, Sleek bypassed the crowded lavatories and slipped into The Blue. He sped through the water, the mercurial shuuhl clinging to his pelt leaving a trail of bubbles.

After swimming a discreet distance from the Oyster Shell, he scanned the Oorum for movement — otter, or otherwise. Certain of his privacy, he found the perfect spot hidden amongst a rainbow of feather-corrals and sea grass.

Utmost relief followed.

Afterwards, Sleek felt light, unencumbered, and brimming with energy. But the idea of returning to the skerry held no appeal. He wanted to revel in this solitary moment.

I'll go on a tsullee-hunt, he thought, and swam in search of suitable quarry.

For otter hunters, the tsullee, or 'blunt spear touch,' had nothing to do with procuring food; rather, they used it to hone their *vuuhn-vaahl*, or 'Hunter's Eye'. A successful graehl demanded all its members be expert trackers, prey-stalkers, and spear wielders — many of the skills forming the vuuhn-vaahl. The rules of the tsullee-hunt were simple: find a prey animal, the bigger the better, and get close enough to tap it with either a paw or the blunt end of the ynth.

Killing was forbidden. Only stealthy proximity mattered.

A full tide after the shraga harvest, the waters around the Oyster Shell skerry still bristled with predatory excitement. Hordes of fish, both great and small, competed for scraps from the otters' table. Armed and eager, Sleek swam through the towering kelp groves. He studied every frond for movement. Potential targets flittered back and forth in the water column. Skittish others crowded in the quavering shade of wave-jostled nooree.

Sleek set his sights on a gang of dhanda hovering at the edge of his vision. They patrolled the waters surrounding the Oyster Shell, swallowing any fish they could chase down and fit in their mouths.

Those'll do nicely, Sleek thought.

With slow, deliberate sweeps of his tail, the Lontra hunter advanced.

The confusion of current-swept kelp supplied cover. Sleek singled out a tuna floating at the rear of the school. Twice his size, the fish seemed oblivious as the young Saia stalked it through the shifting light and shadows cast by kelp and wave.

Closer. Just a little closer...

He drifted with the current, full concentration fixed upon the quarry. The target dhanda floated just out of reach, serene, its gill slits pumping rhythmically.

Sleek carefully raised his spear...

Whoosh! With a flick of its muscular tail, the dhanda, along with its fellow tuna, vanished into the Oorum like a volley of blue and emerald javelins.

"Bishq!" Sleek cursed, bobbing in the wake of their escape.

He felt grateful no peers, especially Grabber, were around to witness his failure. He gripped his ynth and prepared to give chase.

"You'll never catch them."

Sleek spun about, startled — the spear almost slipping from his paws.

Gloss floated before him, ashen pelt and stiff silvery whiskers lit by surface sunlight and her ureola's amber glow. Framed against the emerald kelp and aquamarine sea, every bit of her, from petite nose to groomed tail, bespoke elegant poise. Her beauty intoxicated Sleek.

After an awkward moment of silence, the Beta found his voice. "W-what was that?"

"The dhanda. You'll never catch them, let alone take one. Not that way."

Sleek frowned. "I wasn't trying to slay. I'm on a tsullee-hunt."

Gloss' gaze drifted to Sleek's ynth. "That's a mock hunt, right? To sharpen your skill? Improve the graehl? Make you a better hunter?"

"That's right," Sleek said, impressed. "What are you doing here?"

"I followed you."

Sleek's pulse quickened, a smile curling his mouth. He felt flattered. "Why?"

Gloss floated closer. Her proximity tugged Sleek's Aanandi-shade with undeniable strength. She reached out and touched the shaft of his spear. "I thought... maybe... we could go hunting. Together. I can show you a special technique for dhanda."

"A *special* technique? But... aren't Lutris uja forbidden to hunt?"

"I watched father show Grabber how to hunt them," Gloss replied. "I'm surprised you don't know it. You <u>are</u> a Saia, right?"

"Well... I was just fooling around," Sleek fibbed. The fur along his spine rucked with mortification. He made a mental note to ask his father about dhanda hunting as soon as they returned home.

Gloss' gold eyes flashed, full of amusement. "Of course, you were." She closed her paws over Sleek's spear once more and gave it a little tug, as if playfully contesting its ownership. "Let's see what we can hunt."

"But we've just *my* ynth."

"Yes, I'm aware of that. We'll share."

"Oh...uh...I suppose..." Sleek realized that his answer sounded far more reluctant — unwilling, even — than he'd intended. His eyes, and thoughts, were focused on the alluring contours of Gloss' hips and tail.

"It sounds like you don't want to go hunting or share your ynth with me." An undertone of hurt colored Gloss' hijna.

"W-what? No! I mean, yes. I mean... I want to hunt with you. I want to share. Here."

He held out the spear. Gloss' smile struck Sleek like a lightning bolt piercing the sea. She took the spear into her paws, holding it with an almost reverential air.

"Thanks." Gloss swam away with a graceful kick and tail swish.

Sleek watched her vanish behind a veil of trembling kelp-fronds before it dawned on him that he should follow. "Hey! Wait for me!" he called and darted after her.

The young otters swam side-by-side, exchanging flirtatious glances and coy smiles. Soon, they were spinning and rolling through the water, silvery bubbles trailing. Engaged in playful rivalry, they vied to see who could swim faster, or deeper; or who could hold their breath the longest. Kelp groves and coral hollows became their playground, swirling currents alternately pushing them closer and then pulling them apart.

While others of their cohort explored the safer shoals surrounding the Oyster Shell, Sleek and Gloss made for more remote and perilous regions. Though they recognized the heightened danger — no otter could afford to be careless, even two youths in the throes of first love — the notion of facing threats together proved too irresistible and romantic.

Besides, too many curious and disapproving eyes watched from land. Gossip would follow, drafting behind them like pesky sculpins, questions and discipline following in its wake.

Sleek and Gloss propelled themselves through the water, longing to touch. Even alone, however, they hesitated. Despite their youth and inexperience, both otters understood the granite-hard truth that stood between them.

Gloss belonged to The Raft. Sleek, to The Holt —

True, they shared Aanandic attributes, spoke communal hijna, used similar tools, swam in mutual waters, and hunted common prey. But Lontra and Lutris did not — and could not — mate. Species incompatibility aside, their societal structures and worldviews were too different. Even their deities existed in opposition.

And yet, the amorous tide of first love kept swirling, drawing them closer and closer. They couldn't halt it, nor did they want to.

Gloss floated to a stop and pointed to a spectacle at the surface. "Look there."

A flock of black-winged gulls bobbed above them on the sparkling waves, preening and jabbering their Monoic-gibberish. Bright orange, webbed feet dangled beneath white underbellies, propelling the birds about in tiny circles.

"Lhuuni." The Beta shrugged. "So?"

"Let's play *qloobuu*." Gloss took Sleek's right forepaw and kicked for the surface. "Come on. It'll be fun."

The aim of qloobuu — the 'foot-tug contest' — was to startle an individual bird without triggering the whole flock's 'flight-reflex' and send them into the sky. A lark for kits and pups, the 'foot-tug contest' taught valuable lessons in stalking prey, controlling buoyancy and breath and, greatest of all, honing patience.

From this carefree seed of play all graehl skills sprouted. In many ways, qloobuu represented the whetstone upon which the Hunter's Eye first sharpened itself.

"That's a kit's game," Sleek protested. "I thought you wanted to hunt."

"I do." Gloss' mouth twisted into a mischievous, alluring grin. "But first *I want* to play. What's wrong? Afraid you'll lose?"

Sleek scoffed. "I'll have you know I'm qloobuu champion back at The Holt."

"Really?" Gloss prodded. "Then prove it."

"I will," Sleek boasted. The two youngsters swam to within two tail-lengths of the paddling orange feet. Sleek motioned to Gloss, then to the seagulls. "You go first."

Gloss nodded graciously, knowing how Sleek honored her with that simple gesture. His Saia-rank allowed him precedence in *all* things — but he put the privilege aside. For her.

Gloss smiled and relinquished his spear. "If you insist."

She selected her target, drifted closer, and, with a steady paw, reached out and yanked the bird's foot. The gull squawked in alarm and took to the air while its flock-mates remained afloat, unperturbed.

Gloss pointed at herself, then at Sleek. "One, nothing."

"Not bad," the Beta admitted. He pushed the ynth back into her paws. "Watch this."

"I'm watching."

Sleek found his feathered mark, and, with skill refined over many tides playing with his milk-brothers, pulled the gull's foot. It screeched in a panic and flew off, trailing a squirt of white-green guano.

"One to one," Gloss winked. "Now, may the best *Lutris* win."

The competitors played in earnest. Two birds became four, then six, then eight. Gulls winged away with their skittish neighbors never realizing why. With each point scored the tension mounted. Any second, the flock would launch into the sky in a noisy mass flight.

Sleek found his focus divided between the game and Gloss. Her golden gaze, scrutinizing his every move, made him hesitate each time he tried for a point. Projecting poise and skill, when he owned little of either, proved difficult while beauty watched him.

"This sure is getting intense," Sleek said as he swam close to an oblivious gull. If he scored this twelfth point, it would tie the game. "I never had a match go this long."

Gloss offered a boastful smile. "That's because you've never played me before."

Sleek pinched the webbed foot. The gull leapt for the clouds, squawking. The Beta swam back to where Gloss floated in the lower currents. "Are all Lutris as skilled as you?"

"Not all. Grabber is, but neither of us can beat our older brother Cries Often." A smile lit Gloss' face. Sleek would consider himself the luckiest Lontra alive if he could claim that smile for himself. "I once saw him pluck twenty birds. He would've kept going but it got dark."

"Twenty?" Sleek blinked at this stout claim. "Ookl's Ink, he must be an incredible hunter." Just then, he realized that Cries Often had not accompanied the Raft to the shraga hunt. "Where is your older brother? I'd like to meet him."

"That probably won't happen," Gloss replied. "He's lame. Crippled since birth. He stays at Tanglesafe." A note of sadness colored her hijna.

Sleek's handsome snout scrunched in confusion. "And your father let him live?"

Abnormal births were uncommon among the Lontra. When they did occur a sharp bite to the neck nape while still womb-blind mercifully, and quickly, dispatched them. It was kinder than any fate The Blue might offer.

"Yes!" Gloss growled, bearing her needle-sharp teeth. "What sort of question is that?" She shoved the spear back into Sleek's arms. "My brother's caring and gentle and wonderful! He deserves to live, and if anyone ever says otherwise, I'll—"

"I'm sorry." Sleek flattened his ears against his skull. Offering a conciliatory paw, he added, "I shouldn't have said that. I'd love to hunt with Cries Often."

Gloss' eyes softened once more. "You would?"

Sleek nodded. "I'd be honored. Any otter that can pluck twenty birds in qloobuu is worth knowing. I'd gladly join his graehl any tide." He still pondered why the stern Doyen would spare a cripple's life. *If I'd been born lame, would Father have allowed me to live?* he wondered.

Abruptly, the entire flock launched into flight, frenetic wingtips slashing the water, white abdomens, and webbed orange feet bright against the hard-blue sky. Feathers rained down upon the sea's riled surface.

"So..." Sleek scratched his chin. "How do we score that?"

Gloss shrugged. "Well, I didn't do it. And neither did you."

The younglings looked into each other's eyes, hearts racing. "Equals then?"

Sleek offered a paw. At first Gloss regarded it like a snapping crab, but her eyes softened.

She slid her paw inside his — "Equals" — and with that touch, a bolt of emotion struck both otters. Sleek fought back an urge to gasp. A lungful of water and a coughing fit would have been embarrassing.

Paw-in-paw, they surfaced for breath. Sleek again offered Gloss his spear. She took it with a shy smile. Diving, tails, and hind feet moving in perfect cadence, they swam together. For this special time, their graehl-of-two shared the same burning heart.

The young otters soon came upon a vast flotilla of sea jellies drifting mindlessly in the mid-water column. Like tiny pillows of light and mucous, the jellies translucent bodies were rimmed with a skirt of delicate cilia, the white cross marking on their gelatinous bells identifying them as *floopf*.

Floopf-jellies were abundant, and a favorite toy for both kits and pups, who loved turning them upside down or knocking them about. The passive creatures went wherever the currents took them, like a lethargically pulsing constellation wandering through a syrupy firmament.

Sleek and Gloss swam amongst the school, performing summersaults and cartwheels with whimsical abandon. They joined — bellies touching, and tails entwined for an all-too-brief moment — then peeled away to meander amongst the floopf once more.

Gloss hid behind an extra-large jelly and issued a playful challenge. "If you catch me, you can kiss me."

Sleek saw one of her gold eyes wink at him through a semitransparent bell. Not for the first time on this magical day did Gloss' beauty strike his heart like a stone-sharpened ynth.

"What makes you think I want to kiss you?" he asked while skirting the jelly in pursuit. *I can't believe I just said that!* he thought. *Yurch! Don't be a fool.*

But as he moved, Gloss darted to the opposite side of the pulsating bell. "I can tell. It's as plain as the nose on your face. A cute nose, by the way."

"You think my nose is cute?" Sleek touched a clawed digit to his snout. "Really?"

"Really." Gloss giggled and plunged back through the galaxy of throbbing floopf-jellies. "Try and catch me, slowpoke!"

Sleek needed no goading. Thoughts of nibble-kissing Gloss, of even getting the chance, spurred him on.

Gloss banked and dove. She twisted and turned through the floopf-swarm more numerous than falling snowflakes. Sleek matched her, move for move. No maneuver could deter him. No mindless sea jelly would distract him. In all the tides of his young life, he desired this prey above any other.

Gloss arrowed for a current-tussled kelp bed, hoping to hide in its thick emerald tangles, but Sleek grabbed her rear right ankle before she could reach it. She aimed a half-hearted kick at his head, which failed to dislodge his grip. As he pulled her closer, she did not resist. He threw both arms around her shoulders.

"I caught you."

Gloss put up a token struggle. "Let me go."

"No. You have to kiss me," Sleek insisted. "You said."

"I did." Gloss melted into his embrace. "My Doyen says it's important to keep your word." She placed a paw on Sleek's cheek and twirled one of his whiskers with her finger. "A hunter's word is his...*her* bond. Don't you think?"

Sleek's heart thudded so fiercely he feared it might leap out of his chest and swim away. He answered with a blink, and a slow nod. "Yeah."

Gloss wrapped her arms about his waist and pulled Sleek tight, belly to belly. She snuggled closer, her petite nose a hairs-width from his. Her whiskers tickled his cheeks.

"Are you ready?"

"I, well... uhm...y-yes?"

"I've never kissed a Saia bef..." Gloss' body went rigid as she stared over Sleek's shoulder. "Deshi-Oad's Stone Teeth, what is *that*?"

Sleek turned to see, what in all The Blue had robbed him of his very first kiss.

CHAPTER 34

OLD GRUMPY MOUTH

S lowly, a shape emerged from the Oorum.

At first just a gray blob against The Blue, it steadily drew closer —
and bigger, bigger, then bigger still. Sleek watched the motley palette of
greens and ambers solidify into the contours of a giant sea bass: the biggest
he'd ever encountered. The slow back-and-forth swish of a massive tailfin
propelled the monster fish effortlessly forward.

"Uh...Sleek..." Gloss' flirtatiousness vanished. Her ambitious Hunter's
Eye had returned.

"I see it," Sleek replied. "But...may I..."

"Not now." Gloss tried to push away, but Sleek refused to release her. "Let go," she insisted. With a sharp twist of her body, she freed herself from the Beta's grip. The simple act of strength suggested to Sleek that — perhaps — he hadn't caught Gloss at all.

Maybe she allowed *herself to be captured...* he thought. *Maybe she's just toying with me.*

"It could be trouble." Gloss kicked off to reconnoiter, still clutching the spear. "Let's investigate and tell the others."

Sleek considered asking for his weapon back, but his eagerness for Gloss' affection outweighed his dismay at being unarmed. "Okay. And then after, maybe...I could get my kiss?" Gloss gave no hint that she'd heard him. "Fine," he sighed, and followed.

The younglings cautiously approached the mysterious fish until they could discern its nature. Gloss back paddled to a quick stop; her eyes now slits as she realized the truth.

"Deshi-Oad's Stone Teeth!" Her hijna sparked with both awe and excitement. "That's *Ghuruhg*, the 'Old Grumpy Mouth' itself."

The giant sea bass known as Ghuruhg surpassed five tails in length and weighed the equivalent of fifty adult Lontra. Perhaps more. The enormous fish displaced the water like a boulder of solid scale-coated muscle and bone. A school of cigar minnows accompanied Ghuruhg like royal attendants, fixed in opportunistic orbits about its cavernous mouth. Rumors of its insatiable hunger, and volatile temper, were legendary.

Sleek had heard graehl hunters speak of this mighty apex-predator while swapping stories in the Great Hollow over clamshell bowls of fermented oixrd. Its name, synonymous with tenacity and toughness, always garnered respect. It had killed numerous otters over the seasons.

"Ghuruhg... Ookl's Ink, I think you're right," Sleek said. "I never thought I'd see it."

"It swallows aorxa whole, they say. What a prize it'd make."

With one look at the fearsome creatures, its gaping, hard-plated mouth bent into a perpetual frown, Sleek believed the rumor. Any fish that could gulp down a shark could easily swallow an otter. Or two. "Maybe we should just leave it be?"

Gloss slipped off her amber wristlet and tucked it into the skin pouch under her right arm. Only a seasoned hunter wishing to remain unseen removed the ureola. "I need to get closer."

"Closer? But we only have..."

Gloss sped off before Sleek could finish his protest.

"...the one ynth." The Beta sighed. "This isn't going to end well."

He reluctantly followed Gloss as she swam a wide arc toward her target. Soon the two otters floated unseen behind the Envoric monster-fish. This closer vantage gave Sleek a chance to examine the immense sea bass. Multiple healed puncture wounds, each the telltale evidence of a painful spear thrust — and the eroded nubs of several broken ynth-shafts still protruding from its flesh — marred Ghuruhg's mottled skin.

No wonder it's called 'Grumpy,' he thought. *It must hate otters.*

Gloss sized up the great fish. "Magnificent. What a prize this would make."

Sleek watched ambition light up her golden eyes like twin pryzoa. And it worried him. "This prey is beyond us," he said. "I doubt even our fathers' combined graehls could dispatch it. We should leave it be."

"Isn't this what the tsullee-hunt is all about?" Gloss turned to face Sleek. "Just think of the praise. We'd be legends!"

"No," Sleek retorted, realizing too late Gloss meant to slay the giant bass. "The tsullee is *not* about killing. It's only about sharpening the Hunter's Eye."

"And that's exactly what I'll be doing," Gloss insisted. "Sleek, I'm going to make this kill. With or *without* your help."

Before Sleek could protest any further, Gloss turned and sped away, lance at the ready. All he could do was watch her hurtle towards disaster.

Gloss swam alongside Ghuruhg's right pectoral fin: a hard-scaled limb over twice as broad as she was long. Though filled with trepidation, Sleek could not help but admire the young female's poise. She looked and behaved like the seasoned hunter he wished to be.

Gloss chose a spot at the junction of fin and body, adjacent to the gill slit — that 'sweet spot' target that dispatched most prey-fish outright. Then, with all her might, she jabbed the flattened fishhook-tipped spear into the dense flesh. Blood gushed from the wound in a scarlet stream. A hijna-howl of agony accompanied Ghuruhg's powerful convulsion. Cigar minnows scattered as their host tried to dislodge its assailant. Displaced water pummeled Sleek from ten tails away, a testament to Ghuruhg's strength.

Gloss kept her grip on the spear, delighting in this life-and-death moment as she drove the metal barb in deeper. Thrill of the kill, and her burgeoning hunter's pride goaded her to stay and finish off the quarry, instead of receding to a safer distance to wait for blood-loss and shock to finish the job.

Ghuruhg's simple hijna refrain — "Swallow-you-up-swallow-you-up" — sounded more like a series of painful grunts than true speech. Its unblinking, bronze flecked eyes glowered with menace. Hatred enough to boil the very sea itself emanated from the creature.

This mighty fish, wanting nothing more than to be left alone, now craved something else: to fill its cavernous belly with the body of its attacker.

Gloss tugged the ynth in her attempt at a second strike. But the barbed tip would not pull free from the rock-hard muscle. The joy and pride that warmed her soul just ten heartbeats earlier morphed into cold dread, clenching her belly and turning her spine to floopf-jelly.

"Oh... no..." she moaned.

Realizing her predicament, Sleek raced to help. "Hold on, Gloss! Don't let go!"

The spear bowed nigh to breaking as Ghuruhg struggled. Though flung like a blade of seaweed in a riptide, Gloss managed to keep her grip. Old Grumpy Mouth's lifeblood filled her eyes and stained The Blue arterial red. Before Sleek could reach her, the sea bass sped for darker fathoms with a strong pump of its massive tail, trailing blood, and bubbles in its wake.

The frightened young Lutris clutched the spear for dear life.

Sleek swam after Gloss with all the strength he could muster — but it proved useless against Ghuruhg's raw power. Fear and dismay nearly overwhelmed the Saia as he fell further and further behind.

Finally, momentum and drag did what thrashing alone could not and, to Sleek's relief, the ynth pulled free. He watched as backwash from Ghuruhg's immense tailfin sent Gloss tumbling. Somehow, she kept her hold on the spear.

Any relief Grumpy Mouth felt from being freed of its anguish paled in comparison to its fiery anger. The giant reversed its pell-mell dash and bolted back towards the pesky creature that had caused it so much pain, vengeful eyes fixed Gloss.

But Sleek reached her first.

"Are you hurt?" the Saia cried, adding his grip to hers upon the spear.

Gloss' paws trembled against the shaft. "Oh, Sleek. You were right!" Her eyes flashed pure dread. "I've killed us both!"

"No. We'll survive," he insisted, trying to offer her the very courage he struggled to find within himself. "Together. Say it."

Ghuruhg was closing the distance with terrifying speed. Its wrath seemed to darken the water like a storm cloud, the cigar minnows rimming its mouth like daggers of rage.

"We'll survive..." Gloss said without conviction.

The Scare clawed at Sleek's mind, threatened to tear his Kleaa to ribbons. His limbs began to seize in fear. *No! Fight it, Sleek! You must be brave! Brave for Gloss!*

"Say it again. Believe it!" Sleek demanded, both to Gloss, and himself. A cold stiffness crept from snout to tail. He struggled to subdue the desire to flee and leave this foolish Loyc to her fate. But he could not. "We will survive! Believe it!"

"We *will* survive," Gloss finally offered. "Yes. Yes!"

Sleek's paws faltered on the spear. "Get ready!"

The young otters braced themselves. Pressed together, they appeared larger than either would alone. That, plus brandishing a formidable spear, would have deterred most predators — but Ghuruhg wasn't most predators. The monster fish hated being the target of ambitious hunters, the many ynth puncture wounds on its scaly bulk a testament to their bloody determination.

It had tasted plenty of adult otters in its time. These younglings were hardly a snack.

The colossal beast barreled towards the juvenile hunters. Its huge body seemed to fill The Blue, its gaping maw a lightless cave, its idiotic hijna-chant — "Swallow-you-up-swallow you-up-swallow-you-up" — pounding in their minds.

Sleek and Gloss hijna-roared back, and, as one, jabbed with the lance.

The ploy worked.

Ghuruhg veered off at the last second, its jaws clapping shut with lethal force. As the fish passed, its massive tail clobbered the otters, sending them into a topsy-turvy spin. A furious rush of water buffeted Sleek's eyes, filled his ears and sluiced up his nose. In the tumult, he lost touch with both Gloss and the spear.

By the time Sleek regained his bearings, Ghuruhg had targeted Gloss once again. The Beta cast about for the only thing that could deter the angry fish — his spear. After a few desperate moments, he spotted the weapon embedded on the seafloor amongst the kelp holdfasts.

His heart sank. He couldn't retrieve it *and* reach Gloss in time.

Only one real choice remained.

Sleek tugged the sea-glass acuur from his ureola and swam to Gloss' side. Though The Scare bellowed like a vengeful gale in his mind, he fought to preserve his last shreds of courage. He wouldn't let Gloss face this terrible fate alone.

The younglings embraced, limbs and tails entwining as scaly doom bore down upon them. Sleek's acuur stood as sole defense against the gaping immensity of Ghuruhg's mouth... and the dark gullet beyond.

Gloss looked deep into Sleek's eyes, whispered, "Equals", and kissed him.

Sleek's Aanandi-shade rejoiced, and The Scare went mute as his tension melted away.

And then...

...*darkness.*

CHAPTER 35

A GRAEHL OF TWO

S leek had never been swallowed whole before.

His brain needed a few heartbeats to process what had just happened. It was an altogether baffling experience.

He held up his wrist to see, revealed in the ureola's pale blue light, the disgusting, terrifying details of his surroundings. Slimed with mucous from the slide down Ghuruhg's throat, Sleek now lay in a membranous chamber awash in a foul organic slurry. He struggled to breathe the thick, humid atmosphere. The acidic miasma stung his eyes and nose.

I must be in Ghuruhg's stomach! Ookl's Ink... Gloss!

Sleek spun frantically in the fetid soup, searching, groping — and then shivered with relief. Gloss lay motionless beside him, face turned away and limbs draped at odd angles.

"Gloss..." he called with feeble hijna. But she did not answer.

He felt Ghuruhg's belly ripple. Layers of thick muscle propelled the fish towards the benthic depths. Sleek's consciousness began to fade. Darkness hemmed his vision, and a creeping numbness would soon make his limbs and fingers useless. The Scare began its insidious gibbering, filling his mind with shrieks and screams.

If he didn't act quickly, he wouldn't feel anything again.

He and Gloss would be digested, reduced to spraint... and shit into the abyss.

Come on, Sleek! Focus! He twitched his fingers. Something hard brushed his paw. *What is this?* The object's contours felt familiar. *Thank Ookl! The acuur!*

After a determined struggle to get his fingers to obey, Sleek at last seized the multi-tool. With the remaining dregs of his strength, he drew the blade across of Ghuruhg's stomach. It bit long and deep. Blood gushed from the wound, blurring Sleek's vision in a gory wash of red.

The fish convulsed as pain rippled through its body.

Inrushing seawater jarred Sleek's senses. Up and down, surface and seafloor — all became tangled, jostled nonsense.

The next thing Sleek knew, he and Gloss were paw-in-paw, kicking for the surface amidst a flurry of crimson bubbles. His empty lungs burned and his limbs almost too cold and heavy to move. The Scare still rattled his mind, but it faded as he drew closer to the surface light.

He chanced a downward glance. Much to his relief, he saw no sign of Ghuruhg, only a dissipating cloud of blood trailing down into the darkness. Old Grumpy Mouth had coughed them out, then fled for deeper waters, no doubt to recuperate.

Sorry, Ghuruhg, the Beta thought with a pinch of regret. *I'll understand if you hate me.*

The two otters broke the surface, still paw-in-paw. Both filled their oxygen-starved lungs in great, heaving gasps. Sunlight and warm sky sweetened the sensation.

With one inhale The Scare evaporated, and as the young otters floated on the waves, Sleek felt more like a hunter now than while fighting off the dhanda earlier. He had been swallowed whole, and he'd used his wits to save not just himself, but his beautiful Gloss as well.

Oh, the stories he would tell over a hearty clamshell of oixrd back at The Holt!

"We're... alive?" Gloss asked. Her bewildered eyes watched a tuft of passing cloud as if for the first time. "Shouldn't we be Swimming in Oussia?"

"Not this tide." Sleek offered the glass acuur. "And you can thank this."

Gloss fingered the shard. She shook her head. "I almost got us killed."

Sleek tucked the acuur back into his knotted wristlet. He put a reassuring paw on her shoulder. "We survived. That's all that matters."

Gloss rolled onto her back and floated in the Lutris rest position. "I just wanted to prove myself so badly. I wanted to show the Raft that I'm a skilled hunter." She pulled her ureola from her underarm pouch. Its amber light sparkled in her paws like a circlet of stars. "I need them to know that uja can hunt just as well as uju." She slipped the glowing bracelet onto her slender wrist where it contracted to a snug fit. "My gender shouldn't matter."

Sleek took hold of the now-adorned paw. "It took bravery to do what you did."

"You warned me." Gloss reclaimed her paw. "I didn't listen."

"Your mind was set on trying."

"And you saved my life. How can I *ever* repay that?"

"You could give me another kiss. I'd call us even then."

"Really?" Gloss' brow furrowed in doubt.

"Well..." Sleek hesitated. True, he'd saved their lives, but somehow wringing another kiss from Gloss seemed twice as daunting as confronting Ghuruhg. *What if she says no?* he thought. *Ookl's Ink, what if she laughs?*

To Sleek's relief, Gloss slid her arms around his neck, pulled him close, and nibble-kissed his nose again and again. With each kiss, his spine jellified, his tail curled like a sprig of kholo, and all his skin flushed beneath his fur. Closing his eyes, he allowed the euphoria —which rivaled the eating of the juiciest pryzoa — to wash over and through him.

Gloss released him. Swooning, Sleek let the waves carry him off.

Gloss giggled, grabbed his tail, and pulled him back. "And where do you think you're going?"

"No idea," Sleek replied. "I don't even know where we are. Is this Lutris territory?"

Gloss looked around. "Maybe. I've never been here before."

Sleek performed a quick somersault. "Does the water feel strange to you? Heavier, somehow," he observed. "I wonder why?"

"Yes. And that's why." Gloss pointed to a hillside covered in thick stands of cedar and old-growth pines. A stream meandered down the hillside. Its waters bubbled over smooth boulders and snaking tree roots before reaching the sea. Beyond, The Still reigned, foreign and incomprehensible; its mystery wreathed in coastal cloud. "There's a stream feeding The Blue."

"Ah-h-h. Fresh water is mixing with the salty. No wonder I don't feel as buoyant."

"Fresh water means many different types of prey." Gloss' eyes gleamed with excitement. "Let's go find some."

The juveniles nibble-kissed again, then dove to explore this new estuarial realm.

Below the gentle waves, abundant shoals of fish pecked on anemone-softened corals or hid in the towers of dense kelp swaying by the current. A rainbow of urchins, sea stars, and shelled snails colored the seabed, sharing their tranquil domain with hermit crabs, skittish shrimp, and prickly barnacles. And everywhere, sea grass and dulses blanketed each rock.

Even in an ocean filled with beauty — this place was exquisite and bountiful.

Reminding himself that he must search for and retrieve his lost spear, Sleek followed Gloss as she slipped from the creamy surf onto the flat stones rimming the shoreline. There, for a time, they sniffed through a mixed carpet of red, green, and brown seaweed, discovering where tiny invertebrates and hard-shelled mollusks hid amongst the wrack.

The two younglings loped farther up the beach, to where Gloss spotted a granite ledge. Tufts of spongy emerald and yellow moss softened its coarse surface. Surrounding the outcropping, carpets of lush ferns competed with berry brambles heavy with fruit. Sleek and Gloss clambered upon the ledge and settled side by side to watch the tiny stream below foam and gurgle as it emptied into The Blue.

The purity of this place — this *Little Mouth* estuary — filled them both with peace.

"This will be our special refuge," Gloss whispered in Sleek's ear. "This is where we'll meet, you and I, as equals. And we can't tell anyone about it. And we'll never, *ever*, hunt here."

"Equals, yes," Sleek agreed. "But no hunting? This place is teeming with prey."

Gloss shook her head. "*No* hunting, Sleek. Spilling blood will only attract more hunters. I want to keep it untouched. I want to keep it ours. Special forever. Agreed?"

"Agreed."

"But I *do* want to hunt. Only you and me. Our secret graehl of two." Gloss took Sleek's face in her paws and rubbed her whiskered cheek against his. "I will teach you and you will teach me. And we will be together."

Sleek felt a delirious sensation — as if he had just eaten a pryzoa — both intoxicating and wondrous. He closed his eyes and smiled, limbs and tail almost going limp.

Gloss slipped the sea-glass acuur from Sleek's ureola. She offered it back to him. A firm resolve set on her graceful face. "I need your help."

"Of course. Anything."

Gloss gingerly set the acuur into Sleek's paw, closed his fingers over it. "You said we're to be equals. Before Deshi-Oad and Great Ookl, you really mean it?"

"Yes."

"Then I want to wear the alcq of a hunter."

Sleek blinked at the request. "Uh-hm-m...what?"

He knew some of the tribal restrictions regarding Lutris females, had heard stories about their oppression. Merely asking for a thing as simple as an alcq-piercing tempted jeopardy. Sea otter discipline often required the maiming of their uja, and, if rumors were to be believed, this could prove deadly. Yet Sleek saw the yearning and sincerity in Gloss' beautiful gold eyes. This was no ordinary female; this was a being of will and great poise. This act would not only cast her on the tides of a proper, *if secretive*, hunter; it would unite them in a love bond sanctified with pain and the spilling of blood.

"Will you help me?" Gloss asked. "Help me become a hunter? Like you."

Sleek glanced at the acuur in his paws, then back at Gloss. "It'll hurt. But I'll be quick."

"All hunters must sometimes swim through the currents of pain to find their prey," Gloss reminded him. "Isn't that what they say?"

Sleek nodded. "Some do, yes."

"So then I must swim. And the pain will not bother me, for I will be a hunter."

Sleek shifted his grip to the blunt end of the acuur. "Close your eyes."

Gloss smiled and shook her head. "No," she said. "I'm ready."

She's brave, Sleek thought. *And determined. Ookl's Ink, I can't believe I'm doing this.*

He took Gloss' lower lip with his left paw, pulled to expose her sharp teeth and, with a quick jab of the acuur's tip, cleanly cut through the thin skin. It was done.

Gloss winced but did not cry out. She made no sound whatsoever. A drip of blood slicked the fur under her smiling mouth. "That wasn't so bad," she said.

Sleek was so impressed by her resolve that he plucked the Turritella shell from his own lip and offered it. "For you."

Gloss hesitated. She gazed at the labret with caution. "But... that's *your* alcq."

"And I want you to have it."

"You're Saia, son of *the* Den Sire. I'm just a Loyc." Gloss wiped the blood from her chin and shook her head. "The Doyen would not approve. It wouldn't be proper."

"Your father needn't know." Gloss' paw quivered as Sleek slid the alcq into it. "You've earned this more than I. Let it be a reminder of me, of this place."

"By Deshi-Oad's Stone Teeth, I promise. And I will only wear it when we're together."

"May I?" Sleek gestured to her lip. "This is also custom between hunters."

Gloss nodded. Her emotive eyes hinted at the pleasure she felt over this hard-earned achievement. "Please."

With gentle paws, Sleek slid the smooth base of the alcq into the fresh cut in Gloss' lower lip. The shell was notched and shaped to keep it in place once inserted. It hurt for only a moment.

Gloss touched the hunter's adornment and smiled. Her tongue probed the alcq and the tender tissue surrounding it. Many tides would pass before she no longer felt its presence.

"Good. Good. You look like a proper hunter." Sleek grinned. "Now, you pierce me."

Gloss's smile faltered. She tilted her head, confused. "Why? You're already a hunter. There's no need."

"Equals, remember? You shouldn't be the only one who bleeds for our graehl of two."

Gloss nodded and nibble kissed Sleek's nose. She gingerly placed the acuur's tip into the long-healed alcq-slit. Sleek closed his eyes and braced himself. "Quick, before I lose my nerve."

With the deft paw of a Lutris female who had strung hundreds of urchins on plijet needles during her life, Gloss put a clean incision into Sleek's lip, expanding the alcq-slit a whisker-width. A moment of pain, a sharp grunt, and Sleek was bleeding — just as he wanted.

The two younglings embraced, nibble-kissing the pain away. Licking clean the blood of their shared affection swept Sleek and Gloss into feelings deep and unique: the hostile made harmonious. Lontra and Lutris had never tried what they wanted to now attempt. Love, and the natural acts that followed, were reserved only for their *own* kin. Blending of blood would never, *could* never, be condoned by either tribe. Both clans' adversarial deities explicitly decreed it so.

But Sleek and Gloss didn't care. Together, this graehl of two had discovered, quite by accident, something unseen since Great Ookl, epochs earlier, had joined octopus and sea-snail to create the Ulurii: two distinct species, separated by biology and ethos, melded into *a perfect union.*

No food ever tasted so delicious. No hunt so euphoric. No pryzoa so transcendent.

At this moment, all other sensations fell away...

Only *this* uju and *this* uja, together at Little Mouth estuary, mattered. Only their reposed bodies, spent and contented, warming under the sun with limbs and tails entwined, felt real.

Gloss laid her head against Sleek's chest, a purr rising from her throat.

"Sleek, kalaayaa... I think I'm falling in love with you..."

PART FIVE

CONFLUENCE

*"A mind stretched by a new experience
can never go back to its old dimensions."*

Oliver Wendell Holmes, Jr. (1841 – 1935)

CHAPTER 36

A Fantasea Encounter

S leek awoke from the scithma-snaag with a yawn, followed by a luxurious stretch of spine, hips, and tail. The young Saia nestled into the
warm bed mound, tossing, and turning to find the elusive position that
would send him back into the embrace of the dream-remembrance.

But restless limbs resisted. They wanted to move, to run, to swim...to
hunt.

Internal pressure made the Beta groan. *Tyranny of the bladder*, he
thought.

Grumbling, Sleek crawled from bed, rubbing sleep-crust from his eyes.

His injured hind leg still ached. Sleek examined the gash, now a quarter of its original size, and edged with healthy new pink skin. The ingested pryzoa continued to work their restorative magic.

At this rate, I'll be fully healed in just a few tides. Plenty of time for Suckling Mother's weaning-day celebration, Sleek thought as he gingerly tongue-cleaned the wound.

In the corner of the den a flat stone concealed a crack between floor and wall — a privy hole that emptied into the sea far below. Only a pawfull of dens boasted such luxury. Most Lontra used the busy communal latrines rimming the Great Hollow. Sleek slid aside the stone, squatted into the cleft, and relieved himself. Rejuvenated, he returned the rock lid to its place.

A shaft of sunlight slipped through the crescent fracture window. Sleek peered out, saw puffs of tattered white cloud lacing a rich lapis sky. Across the wave-swept bay, the rocky coves and beaches — their pallet a tousled mélange of blacks, grays, and tans — sat in beautiful contrast to the rich greens and browns of timbered hills beyond. A breeze carried the rumble of crashing surf and the scent of sea salt mingled with pine and wildflower.

Tantalizing odors drew his attention to the den entrance. A tree-bark platter laden with a tiny squid, a juicy minnow, and a pile of shucked clams waited. Gentle's personal abalone shell-bowl filled with fresh, cloudy oujit rounded out the breakfast.

Sleek's stomach gurgled with hunger. He licked his lips. "Thank you, mother."

He gulped the oujit, savoring the subtle-sweet flavors of pre-chewed kholo, pulped nooree squeezings, and the faintest aftertaste of mother's milk. Gentle's dam had taught her the recipe for the curative elixir, as did her dam before her, and so on, going back generations. The oujit warmed Sleek's belly and blood. Its restorative quality would speed the healing of his wound even further.

Sleek licked the last drops of oujit from the shell, then attacked his meal, beginning with the fish, barely chewing in his haste to fill his stomach. *Why am I so hungry?* he wondered.

Just as he gobbled down the last clam, Swims Past poked his face into the den. "Nookeelee, lazy bones." The Dyah-Delta strolled in without waiting for an invitation. "It's about time you finally woke up." His whiskers twitched as he chided his friend.

"What?" Sleek discarded the empty clam shell and tucked into the squid, starting at its head "You know I sleep in late, oyster-face."

"You've been asleep for *six* tides. That's a new record, even for you."

"Six?" Sleek's eyes widened. "Quit pulling my tail."

Swims Past scratched his chin with a hind-paw. "I can tell time, bishq-for-brains. You've been motionless as a barnacle — and twice as ugly, I might add — for six tides. Except I've never heard a barnacle snore. Anyway, Ookl's Eye is fully open tonight. The hunting should be good. Grab your spear, and let's go."

Yurch! The schithma-snaag really bit me! I hope I'm not late, Sleek fretted. He swallowed the last bite of squid, snatched his ynth from beside the bed mound, and limped out the fracture-door. "Maybe later. I've something else to do now."

"You want company?" But sleek was already scampering down the corridor towards the bridge to the next den level, tardy for his rendezvous. Swims Past shrugged. "I guess not."

Sleek raced through each habitat floor and across the next spanning bridge, traveling ever downward until he reached the Great Hollow. He crossed the stony expanse, ignoring the polite greetings and whisker tug acknowledgements from otters cleaning food scraps from the floor, and continued further down towards the Holt's flooded basement. Once there, Sleek slid into the moon pool and swam off, taking no notice of the trio of otters harvesting edible, leafy kelp off the tunnel walls by ureola-light.

The lovesick Beta had no time to waste.

Gloss was waiting for him. But before he swam into deeper waters to find the xhooja that would whisk him to her, he had to fulfill his pledge to his mother.

Sleek arrowed along the submerged passage until he reached the exit, sped out from under the rock overhang shaped as a reclining otter, and then kicked hard for the sunlight above. He surfaced with barely a ripple, inhaled, sniffed the salty air, and felt rejuvenated.

Two hundred tails away, upon the rocky shore of a shallow cove safe from the ceaseless, pounding waves, lay the revered Cellum. Sleek had vowed to Suckling Mother that he would visit that sacred place and construct two ghaydn: one for healing Chaser, and a second for the safe return of his lost son, and Sleek's dear friend, Diver.

Sleek *hoped* with all his heart the ghayden would work their miracles as the romp believed... but his same practical heart *knew* the odds were nil. The exercise was pointless. The magic, if it ever existed, hinged on the good graces of Old Father Fathom.

One illusion tied to another, Sleek mused.

But a promise must be kept, especially to one's own mother.

The Saia dove again, rehearsing his observances as he swam toward the eroding shrine. He would array the crab shells, legs, and pincers of the ghaydn in the standard petition patterns, offer the requisite supplications with each inserted seagull feather, pull his whiskers, bite the tip of his tail, and then be off for his rendezvous with Gloss before anyone ever knew he...

"Oh, Sleek," the panicked hijna of Frolic, a female Delta, broke his scheming. She held the tawny paw of a newly weened, yet-unnamed kit. "Nookeelee. We're so glad you're here."

Sleek backstroked, slowing to a stop. Frolic, along with the male Epsilon's Ripple and Limber, were clearly distressed. "What's wrong? Is there a predator about?"

Frolic cast a frightened glance at the shoreline. "There's a filthy *Penuree* desecrating *our* Cellum!" she answered, pointing. "As we speak!"

"What?" The idea seemed absurd. "A Penuree? At The Cellum? Surely not."

"See for yourself," Limber said.

Sleek kicked for the surface, the other otters following. He peered across the cove...and spied a bipedal shape occupying their place of prayer.

Sleek blinked in disbelief and looked again. Yet the intrusive figure remained. "Ookl's Ink. It can't be."

The Penuree crouched on the slanted deck, its back foolishly turned from both The Blue and The Above. Only Monoic simpletons, the diseased, or those wishing to perish in the jaws or talons of a predator did such a thing. Could this Penuree be all three?

Ripple pointed at the holy site. "It destroyed our ghaydn for healing, for safety, and for Liminal's freedom. It kicked them into the water. What sort of *ptahhf* does such a thing?

"We've already rebuilt them," Limber bemoaned. "Twice. Each time they lose potency."

"That kexxing thing'll get us cursed." Frolic clutched her child close. "It could even draw out The Cruel Dweller to punish us."

That awful notion sent all three Lontra into a frightful state. They nibbled their tails in dread. "Ookl's Ink! You must do something, Sleek," Limber pleaded.

"Me? That's a Penuree monster. What am I supposed to..."

"You're Saia. And the Den Sire isn't here," Ripple reminded. "You *must* take responsibility. Drive the thing away."

Yurch, Sleek thought. *Another distraction that'll make me late for Gloss.*

As the highest-ranking Lontra present, it fell upon him to deal with this menace. Trapped by duty, Sleek weighed his options.

He could assemble a graehl, return in force, and drive the creature off. Maybe even slay it. It would take time — and time was not his ally.

Then, afterwards, he would have to make up an excuse as to why he was not returning directly to the Holt, which the others would find exceedingly odd. He couldn't very well tell them the truth! No one would question him if he did leave, but his father would hear of it, and demand answers from him upon his return. He'd be forced to lie to his father's face. Again!

No. There was only one acceptable option.

He'd deal with the human trespasser alone: just his ynth and his courage. Quicker...but potentially more dangerous. Did even Ookl ...*if he ever exi sted*... know what vile powers the Penuree brandished?

Frolic humbly took Sleek's paw, her mimicking kit doing likewise. "Please, Sleek. Please. Do it for the Holt. Do it for Old Father Fathom."

Sleek centered his Hunter's Eye and tightened the grip on his spear. "Wait here."

"Ouch." Ayana hissed as her wrist scraped a stack of crab cages.

Pain, amplified by sunburn, surged up her forearm. She mentally kicked herself for forgetting a hat in her haste to leave the house this morning. She'd shed her coat hours earlier beneath an increasingly relentless sun. Setting aside the magnifying glass she was using to scorch an image of a seahorse into the deck, Ayana pressed a finger against her arm to gauge the sunburn. The imprint lingered.

That's gonna sting later, she thought.

Ayanna shrugged. So be it. The *Fantasea* demanded a captain made of sterner stuff. She would meet the challenge.

She picked up the magnifying glass and returned to her work. The incomplete seahorse was only one of many images burned into the deck boards: random shapes, flowers, opossums, names of her favorite bands, and of course, her own name. She didn't mind decorating the ship in such a way. The *Fantasea* was a blank canvas that needed covering. And Ayana had an entire summer to adorn every inch of it with her creativity.

Sleek swam past the sentinel boulders, his purposeful hunter's-stroke arrowing him across the cove. Ynth loose and ready in his grip, the Beta approached The Cellum, his focus on the crouching Penuree. Turned away for now, it would soon be face-to-face with a mighty hunter of High Split Rock...

Craving something sweet, Ayana opened the backpack, fished out two pieces of hard toffee and popped one in her mouth. The second she set aside to warm in the sun.

She considered tasting the red-glass seashell snugged deep in her front pants pocket but decided against it: so much sensorial acceleration happening too quickly could be risky. She couldn't afford to get clumsy in the resulting euphoria. One misstep and — *snap* — a twisted ankle, sprained wrist, or something vital permanently broken.

Like my neck!

A search party would be sent to look for her and she couldn't risk anyone else finding her secret beach. She could always trip out later in the privacy of her bedroom.

Ayana rolled the toffee around in her mouth, tapped her glue drops, then focused her makeshift laser onto the deck wood until it started to scorch. As she hummed one of her favorite pop songs, the seahorse slowly took shape. She was totally unaware that, at the very same moment, a six-foot long, ashen-furred river otter with piercing golden eyes and a deadly sharp spear gripped in both paws, had slipped onto the *Fantasea's* deck behind her...

Sleek shook excess water from his pelt and advanced. He could sense Frolic and the others watching, each scrutinizing his poise and bravery. The next few moments would produce tides-worth of gossip over how the Holt's resident Saia did, or did not, deal with this intruder.

I better make a good show of it, Sleek thought.

Ayana put the finishing touches on the seahorse. Not her finest work — the anatomy looked a little off — but, still, a passable job, considering she'd had to rely on memory. Training the laser beam onto a new section of the deck, Ayana opted for a simpler project: the vessel's name. She began burning block letters into the wood, slowly pronouncing each one aloud —

"F... A..."

The Saia crept towards his prey, preparing for a quick thrust that would bury his spear in its back. He'd never been so close to a Penuree, and a part of him dreaded making contact. The creature, wrapped in colorful, decorative outer layers, remained oblivious to its peril.

Ayana smelled acidic wood smoke, her entire focus on the pinpoint of pure sunlight.

"N... T..."

Sleek gasped in horror at seeing the Penuree's foul handiwork charred into The Cellum's hallowed surface. How dare the creature desecrate that which his romp so revered? The blind, disrespectful monster!

"A..."

Sleek paused, realizing there would be no honor in killing this *thing* with a silent ynth strike. The Vuuhn-Vaahl would never condone such an attack. It demanded the Penuree acknowledge and fear Sleek's formidability. Then, and only then, would it flee The Cellum and never return.

The tip of Ayana's tongue poked from her lips as the newest letter neared completion.

"S..."

The Saia struck the base of his spear onto the deck boards, hoping to get the creatures attention. But it remained squatting, back turned, and making odd vocalizations.

"E..."

Almost there, Ayana thought. *So far, so good.*

Sleek hissed "Yurch," and delivered a second, more powerful, spear strike to the deck.

Ayana finished etching the third and final —

"A..."

— then felt the wood judder under her knees.

She turned to look...

CHAPTER 37

YURCH AND YAEEELI

Two sets of eyes — the shocked brown of a teenage human girl and the sharp gold of an Aanandic male Lontra — locked.

Ayana froze.

Sleek froze.

The world went quiet and still. No wind, no surf, no crying seagulls overhead.

Ayana couldn't process what she saw. This wasn't a person, or a seal, or a mermaid, or anything else her brain might recognize or imagine.

Oh-crap-what-is-that-thing-it's-looking-right-at-me! she thought as a rising wave of panic threatened her reason.

Sleek realized the Penuree feared him far more than he, it. This was no monster; this was easily dispatched prey. The Beta stood taller and struck an imposing posture, delighting in the anguish his presence invoked. But something about this interaction felt... off kilter.

Motion and sound abruptly returned to Ayana's world. Adrenaline crackled along each nerve, prodding her to choose either fight or flight. She let out a gasp as her predicament came into crystalline focus: a huge otter, wearing a glowing blue bracelet and holding a wicked-looking spear, now stood before her!

With a fierce countenance and needle-sharp teeth exposed, Sleek barked a challenge. The Penuree reacted just as he'd hoped, with noises that sounded more comic than alarming, and a look of shock on its hairless face that filled the Beta with confidence. He had to fight to retain his menacing stance, even as his snarl threatened to soften into a roguish smile.

It has gold eyes. WHY ARE ITS EYES GOLD? Ayana's mind screamed as she scooted away. *Is it a radioactive mutant? Is it going to chew my face off?*

Then something happened that neither girl nor otter expected.

"Don't hurt me," the hapless Penuree said... *without* using its mouth.

Sleek took a faltering step back and snorted, as if a myzee kelp-fly had just stung his nose. The Penuree hadn't vocalized those words, yet he'd perceived them.

It could only mean...

"How do you have our hijna?"

Ayana gasped as Sleek's question coalesced in her mind, as clearly as if spoken aloud. She not only discerned but *felt*, in a manner beyond her ability to explain, what the otter had said to her. "Hijna?" the frightened Penuree asked.

Sleek cautiously advanced, his gaze pinned to the trespasser's face. He sniffed, keen nose detecting the faint pryzoic scent-markers, indicative of its evolved condition. Looking into the creature's bronze-flecked eyes only confirmed the truth — this Penuree was Envoric!

Ookl's kexxing Ink! he thought. *This is impossible!*

And yet... he realized he could no longer consider the creature quarry. It was now, in the broadest sense, kindred... which afforded it all the rights and privileges of the Envoric world.

"Chookzl," Sleek cursed. "An Envoric Penuree? Cixtindi needs to hunt a word for this."

Ayana shook her head. "I don't understand."

The telepathic link felt like a pleasant tickle just behind her eyes. She didn't know whether to smile or scream. The fact she had to pee confirmed she was neither dreaming nor delusional. Everything happening at this moment was truly, shockingly, real.

For Sleek, all his assumptions about how this encounter would unfold were upended. He felt his duty should switch from hunter to ambassador, but the idea seemed absurd. He hadn't the temperament or experience for diplomacy, especially for such an unprecedented situation as first contact with an Envoric Penuree.

No. this needed handling by those much older and astute than he — like his parents.

Sleek recalled the wise words of his father: "As Aanandi we can learn the lessons others are incapable of learning, and then teach them in ways they can understand. There is no greater duty. It's what Ookl would have us do."

Sleek's hostile mien softened along with his threat-bristled pelt. *Don't spook the Penuree.* His grip loosened on the ynth. *Convince it to leave without violence. Slowly, slooooowly...*

Ayana's fear cooled as the otter crouched on the deck, as if casually idling with a friend. It didn't abandon its odd, yet clever fishing-pole spear, but she no longer felt the dread of an impending attack. Her heartbeat slowed, the urgency to urinate subsiding.

Ayana took a moment to appraise the splendid animal.

It wore a luxurious pelt of ashen fur, the irregular pattern on its chest as pale as spilled cream. Thick whiskers framed a black, dog-like nose, and its bottom lip was pierced through with a brown, spiral-shaped shell. Its lithe torso tapered into a long, muscular tail. It held the spear with what looked more like a human hand than an animal's paw, and a human-like poise informed its posture.

But the piercing gold eyes under its contemplative brow captivated Ayana the most. She recognized an inquisitiveness in that gaze. This otter was reasoning things out.

Ayana no longer wanted to flee. She wanted to engage. But how could she gain its trust?

Only one foolproof answer came to mind, one she learned from a movie about a boy and his homesick extra-terrestrial friend...

"Candy," Ayana said aloud.

She retrieved the toffee from the deck and unwrapped it. The crinkling of the cellophane made Sleek's ears twitch. He sniffed. The alien, yet enticing, fragrance drew him closer, eyes fixed on the confection.

Here's another thing Cixtindi needs to word hunt, he thought; then asked: "What is it?"

Hearing the question in her mind, Ayana nodded in rudimentary understanding. "Candy. Caaaan-dy," she replied, thinking rather than speaking the words.

This strange mode of communication felt effortless, even simpler than forming words with her lips and tongue. She couldn't fathom *how* it was happening, only that it *was*. And, lurking behind each syllable, a microsecond of sensation like the effervescent fizz of a freshly poured cola tingling her lips — much like how the red glass shell felt against her skin.

"C-aaan-dy?" Sleek cautiously moved to within a tail's-length of the Penuree, his spear still held at the ready.

"Food." Ayana offered up the sweet. She gestured her fingers to her mouth, pantomiming the taking of food. "You eat it."

An image of a famous painting flashed through her mind: an old, bearded man in white robes reaching to touch the finger of a naked man reclining on the grass.

She held her breath, trying to remain perfectly still...

Sleek took the candy, his fingers brushing Ayana's. The fleeting connection sent a jolt between them; an electric first contact between hitherto unknown worlds. They both shivered.

Ayana noticed the tiny splotches of blue fur on Sleek's outstretched arm, and he saw the spattering of white on hers. The patterns were eerily similar, like two halves of the same shell. Could this moment, instead of a chance encounter between two divergent species, be the whimsical act of a higher power?

It's just random, Ayana thought.

Sleek's view echoed his Penuree cohort. *It's merely a coincidence.*

His pink tongue licked the toffee, eyes widening in delight. Though a distant contender to pryzoa, it still tasted delicious. "Yurch, that's good."

Ayana intuitively sensed the use of a profanity as a positive expression. She felt relieved. The toffee had broken the ice between them.

"Yurch," she parroted with amusement. "I like that. Yurch, yurch, yurch..."

It made a peace gesture, Sleek thought. *I should reciprocate.*

The Saia set aside his spear and proffered his paws for inspection. He wanted to show he had nothing to hide, and that his intentions were nonviolent. The Penuree's thin smile confirmed to Sleek that it understood.

"Ucaay-yaeeeli-uraari," Sleek said, respectfully tugging his whiskers and offering the full face-saving greeting between Envoric strangers. He hoped the Penuree's whisp of Kleaa would grasp the sentiment, because he had no time for vocabulary lessons. He had to hasten this clumsy diplomacy to ensure the Penuree would leave without bloodshed.

Many Lontra eyes were certainly watching by now...and judging.

Ayana shrugged. She understood that the otter was trying to communicate something significant, but this alien language was being spoken too fast. It all sounded like gibberish.

Sleek sensed the confusion. "Yaeeeli" he tried again, motioning between himself and the Penuree. "I am me-you are you-we are equal. Equal. You. Me. *We*. Equal. Understand? Yaeeeli."

Ayana frowned in concentration. By themselves the string of words conveyed little; yet, between the otter's body language and paw gestures, she grasped the barebones of his statement. "Yaeeeli," Ayana replied, hoping she said it correctly. "Equals. Yaeeeli."

"Very good." Sleek smiled and licked the toffee treat. "Now we're getting somewhere."

Ayana grinned with the joy of achievement, and revelation. She never imagined an otter could smile or that telepathy existed. But both were true. Fantastic things were possible, after all. Even magic, flowing freely between them, like water or an electrical current. It then occurred to her that the red-glass seashell and this extraordinary otter both came from the same place.

But where?

Standing on the threshold of a strange new world made Ayana dizzy with the possibilities. She had one toe dipped in a vast enchanted ocean. One tiny push and she would splash in...and drown. The notion both thrilled and terrified her.

As Ayana watched the otter munch on the toffee, she recalled last night's bizarre dream. A humble snail peacefully grazing in a resplendent garden, she'd been rescued from a fearsome, shadowy crab-like monstrosity by a creature with a whiskered face...

Much like the one smiling at her now.

A sudden flash of insight showed her what she needed to do.

Ayana removed the sandwich bag containing the red-glass shell from her pocket and held it up so the otter could see it.

Sleek's eyes fastened on it, and he *knew*.

Yurch. Don't tell me, he thought and groaned.

"Look." Ayana dumped the shell out onto her palm. "Pretty."

Sleek realized that this unique encounter stemmed directly from his Liminal theft. The clumsy Penuree had somehow found the scrap he'd deemed fit only to be discarded, and had, for some unfathomable reason, tried to eat it!

It hadn't succeeded, obviously, but what few particles of pryzoic matter it had ingested contained enough residual potency to raise the creature from mindless to sapient, but just barely. Sleek winced at the enormity of the consequences. His love for Gloss and desire for a courtship gift had indirectly created an Envoric Penuree — something that had never happened before.

Sleek had upset the natural order of things.

Ayana saw the dismay in the otter's face, its furrowed brow. Had she insulted it with something she did... or didn't do? "You're angry?" she asked with hijna. "What is wrong?"

Sleek shook his head in shame. *Bishq. How could I have been so careless?* Panic soured his belly. He sensed thing slipping out of his control. "This is all my fault," he confessed, self-esteem withering to the size of a sand crab.

He envisioned the disappointed faces of his parents, their rightful scolding: "Returning pryzoa to the surface is aijeer for a reason, son. You don't think things through. You're rash. Now do you see what happens when you disobey? You may have put all our lives in jeopardy..."

Sleek weighed his options. He could let this thing live and drive it away from The Cellum. But that would mean loosing a sapient Penuree onto the Envoric world. Who knew what kinds of mischief it would get up to? It might even implicate him in the ensuing mayhem.

Or he could slay it, and allow The Blue to sweep its corpse away, and with it any traces of his involvement. *That's the easiest answer,* Sleek decided, with regret. *I don't like it, but I can't take any chances.*

Ayana tensed as the otter tossed aside the toffee and retrieved its spear.

This is not a good, she thought. Unease tingled along her spine as she tucked the shell back into her pocket. The need to pee surged anew. "Yaeeeli?" she hijna-asked. In her alarm she cried aloud, "Yurch! Yaeeeli!"

"I'm sorry, but I have to do this," Sleek said, raising his weapon to strike.

The Penuree cowered...

Sleek hesitated...

Within a splash of water six Lontra emerged from the sea, and in unison, leapt upon the deck. Sleek spun to face them, a guilty look on his face. Brandishing their whalebone ynths, the newcomers took the hunter-stance and advanced, wet brown and black coats glinting, the anger in their eyes sharp as their snarl-exposed teeth. Fierce growls rumbled deep in their throats.

Ayana saw the multi-colored wristlets, the pierced lips, the gold and bronze eyes — but her brain was unable to make sense of the sight. The picket of barb-tipped spears now pointed at her face eclipsed all reason. Fear contracted her world to a pinpoint.

She shrieked and scooted backwards, her boots slipping on the deck boards, throat constricting as adrenaline choked off her cry. And behind the otters' barks and growls, Ayana caught snips of terse hijna-conversation:

"Chookzl, Sleek. What're you doing?" one otter demanded.

"Why is this Penuree filth still here?" a second questioned.

"And why isn't your ynth sticking out of its belly?" a third snapped.

"I was trying to be respectful," Sleek answered. He motioned towards Ayana. "I...I didn't want to defile The Cellum with its blood."

"Then kill it in The Blue," a fourth otter growled and pointed its spear at Ayana's neck.

Kill.

Ayana perceived much of their dialogue as gibberish — but that word she understood.

KILL.

"Shiiiit!" she squeaked. *RUN NOW!* her panicked brain screamed.

Ayana groped for anything that offered a handhold. Clutching a rope bollard, she pulled herself up and scrambled for the open deck hatch. The skin between her shoulder blades tingled, as if anticipating the cruel bite of a flung spear piercing her spine. Within seconds — though it felt like hours — Ayana reached the hatch and slid down into the musty hold. She wiggled through the hull gash, scraping belly and back, and dropped to the beach.

Landing hard, she nearly toppled headlong into a tide pool. Righting herself, Ayana took off running, her boots throwing up sand and gravel with each pounding step.

And between footfalls, like a mantra swirling through her head...

How weird the world is...

Ayana ran and ran until her breath came in wheezing gasps and her sides ached.

Only when the Fantasea had shrunk to the size of a thumbtack in the distance did she dare to slow down and risk a backwards glance. No angry otters chastised her from the deck railing, no sharp spears hurtled towards her.

Frantically, she ducked behind a seaweed-coated boulder and, moments from losing complete control of her bladder, she ripped down her jeans and underwear and squatted. Ayana nearly sobbed with relief as the cruel pressure eased. With nothing on hand with which to wipe, she had no choice but to pull up everything and continue back towards home.

She had made it out alive! Exhilaration at her survival made her light-headed...

"Oh, yurch!" Ayana cursed, stumbling to a halt.

She'd left all her gear on the boat: backpack, rope, slingshot, spray-paint, magnifying glass, coat. Everything. "Yurch! Yurch!"

She had to go back. She couldn't just leave everything behind. But then, she thought of what had forced her to flee in the first place and knew she would be crazy to return. Still lightheaded, and now a little nauseous, she rested her palms on her knees. *That otter gang nearly turned me into a human pincushion! I'm never going back. Not ever.*

Ayana compulsively rubbed the white spots on her arms. The impulsive ritual soothed her fear and helped focus her thoughts. She pictured herself as a big cotton-filled tomato, stabbed with enough pins to make a porcupine envious. The idea was so absurd...

Laughter bubbled up from deep within the tender, hidden place in her soul where hot anger and cold cynicism wrestled for control. As it burst from her mouth it swept out much of the pessimism trapped within her like so many stale crumbs.

Ayana dropped to her knees in a briny puddle, unconcerned that her jeans were now soaked. Somehow, the very fact she was kneeling in seawater made everything seem funnier.

She laughed until she couldn't breathe, her whole world now contracted to the spaces between snatches of air. Tears streamed down her face, mingling with the snot from her nose. She laughed until her stomach ached; her diaphragm as hard as the stones that gouged her kneecaps. But she didn't care. At that moment, something in Ayana shifted. For the first time in what felt like an eternity, her intense desire to choke the world with smoke from her parboiled soul dimmed. A small space had opened up for something else.

She could fill this newfound void with laughter. And so, she did.

Eventually, the fit of hilarity subsided, giving way to more sober reflection.

The experience she'd just had was so strange, so far beyond anything she could've imagined, it defied explanation. Only a few minutes had passed and already the encounter felt like a dream. Ayana knew she could proclaim the truth of this bizarre day until she was blue in the face. No one would believe her in a million years.

The old saying "Silence is golden" was true. The time wasn't right for disclosure.

For now, she'd keep this entire episode to herself...

Well, I might tell Shep.

CHAPTER 38

A Prayer In The Sand

M idday found Hayley traipsing idly down the woodland paths. It felt good to stretch her legs along the verdant trails. Toppled trees, their mossy roots splayed like hundreds of frozen green serpents, beckoned from deep within the stinging nettle and bramble thickets. Horse power had its charms, but most of the time, she preferred to travel these coastal groves using the power of her own two feet.

Hayley soon reached the sundered driftwood fence. She peered over the edge of the collapsed section of sea cliff, took in the littoral chaos of the neighboring beach. It appeared inhospitable and dangerous. *I'll tell Eugene about this,* she thought. *I'll help him fix it.*

Hayley descended the rail-tie stairs rimmed with magenta ice plant. Below, the family beach waited. She stopped at the last tie, scanned the sandy crescent, and found no hint of her daughter. "Ayana?" she shouted over the noise of wind and surf. "Ayaaaana! Lunch!"

No answer. Hayley wasn't worried. Ayana could be nestled in one of the numerous cliff nooks, out of sight and earshot. Hayley slipped off her boots and socks, set them on a driftwood log, and strode towards the water. Overhead, seagulls coasted lazily on new-day thermals. At the waterline, lanky sandpipers, skittish willets, and darting plovers waltzed back and forth with the lapping waves, slender beaks probing the wet sand for tasty invertebrate morsels.

The sand between Hayley's toes felt deliciously warm until she reached the tidemark, where the sea basted it to a cold hardness. Six steps further, and the waves erased all evidence of her footprints. She turned her face into the fresh onshore wind, savoring the sensation as it caressed her cheeks and tousled her hair. The vista of natural beauty soothed on her soul.

Offshore, five familiar sea stacks, foundations perpetually wreathed in the milky froth of crashing waves, rose like a series of massive stone chess pieces from the water. One particularly large megalith, the last of the lot, dominated the others — a king among pawns. Split down the middle, it wore a single conifer tree as a living crown.

Hayley always considered that tree an odd, yet somehow fairylike, fixture. *It looks like a unicorn's horn,* she thought with a smile.

Hayley set off along the beach, leaving a trail of footprints amongst the cuneiform patters of bird claws. She found no sign of her daughter's presence. "Where is that girl?" she wondered aloud. "Ayaaaaana!" she called again, but the stiff breeze blew the sound back in her face.

Hayley headed towards the cliffs; certain she'd find Ayana in the deep fissures eroded into the rock. In happier times, they'd play *hide-and-seek* among the boulders and cervices.

As Hayley recalled those carefree days a white disc, partly buried in the wet sand, caught her eye. Tide exposed, what first looked like a Frisbee turned out, on closer inspection, to be...

"A sand dollar." Hayley picked up the echinoderm, marveling at its unusual size. She turned it over, heavy in her hands, and traced the flower-shaped pattern on its sun-bleached shell. "It's bigger than those from last year."

Hayley spotted another half-buried sand dollar, this one even larger, and reached for it...

-Mmurpt-

The sound, like a swimming pool vent sucking in water, drew Hayley's attention towards a driftwood log at the waterline. The discus sand dollar slipped from her fingers, forgotten. Hayley approached the eroded log, wondering if her tricksy daughter sat crouched behind it, ready to spring out and frighten her.

-Mmurpt-

Hayley couldn't help but smile at the wet, flatulent noise. Anxious to turn the tables on her teenage prankster, she quickened her pace. Rounding the driftwood timber, she lunged...

"Gotcha!"

Ayana wasn't there.

A tight kernel of worry knotted up in Hayley's stomach. What if...?

No. Don't be silly! She's in one of those little hidey-holes. This beach is perfectly safe.

As Hayley turned away, her eye caught a wriggle of movement. She looked back to glimpse a green-gray mass of — *something* — submerged into the water. It appeared frayed, as if trailing cords or dragging limbs. A tangle of kelp, maybe? Knots of discarded rope, perhaps?

But no. This oddity wasn't floating like wave-jostled seaweed would. It looked like it was...swimming! Hayley observed the *whatever-it-was* for only a moment before it vanished under a frothy swell. Her eyes followed the squiggly trail the 'thing' had left on shore.

A gasp lodged in her throat. "What are *those*?"

There, scrawled into the wet sand, were dozens of... images. Circles. Ellipses joined and stretched in odd unions. Curlicues looping, coiling, and wrapping around themselves like a tangle of bizarre script.

Are they... words? Hayley thought as she approached. *No. Impossible.*

Beyond English, Hayley knew just a smidgeon of Spanish. She'd seen Japanese and Chinese text before, although she couldn't begin to tell them apart. She'd even seen Sanskrit once while flipping through a National Geographic. These markings in the sand were nothing like those; in fact, they were unlike any type of script she'd ever seen.

And yet, they made those others seem simplistic in comparison.

Regardless of what they *might* be, they were beautiful, elegant even. Hayley felt certain the scribblings hadn't been formed by random tidal action. No. They seemed purposeful, deliberate, the work of a reasoning mind.

Hayley kneeled near the inscription and gently touched one. Smoothly written, it looked more like an imprint in the sand, rather than something carved by a finger or a stick. Could that thing in the water have been responsible? Questions buzzed around her brain like sandflies.

A tiny wave touched Hayley's foot, reminding her of the rising tide. The chilly water had already erased the closest marks. It would soon wipe clean all traces of the remaining inscription.

If only I had Eugene's Polaroid, Hayley thought with regret.

She had no chance of re-creating such complexity from memory. But, if she copied one of the 'verses' above the waterline, she could perhaps preserve it long enough to return and document it with a camera.

Hayley chose one section simple enough that she could do a passable transcription. With her index finger, she copied the swirling lines as best she could. Her version was more of a rough approximation. Yet she sensed, in a way she couldn't quite explain — even to herself — the importance of what she had scrawled, crude as it appeared.

Hayley stood, gazed at her handiwork for a moment, then set off along the crescent-shaped beach. She found nothing, not even a single footprint, to indicate her daughter had even been there. Certain she and Ayana had missed each other on the woodland path, Hayley returned to the driftwood tree stump, wiped the sand off her feet, slipped on her socks and boots, and headed up the trail for home.

Hayley never suspected that she was being watched... and studied.

CHAPTER 39

OFFSHORE OBSERVATIONS

F ifty yards off the Gentle Crescent, two rubbery stalks, each crowned with a billiard ball-sized ocular orb, emerged from the water. Ever curious, Uuvaloo lingered just under the surface and watched the Penuree move clumsily along the beach on its two jaunty legs.

What a hideous creature. And not nearly enough limbs, the Ulura thought. *And the noises it's making sound like a wounded luuhni. How uncouth.*

Among Holt-members Uuvaloo alone took interest in the Penuree, or, as the Vialae called them: *Heey-ou*. An admittedly dangerous fascination, as Penuree were a cruel, erratic species, quick to kill without provocation — eating more than their share and wasting more than they ate. Gross polluters, they befouled all they touched. Envorah believed them monsters, incapable of receiving, or even recognizing, Liminal and its gifts of True Speech.

Creatures forever blind and dumb. And yet... Uuvaloo had lingering doubts.

Heey-ou were awkward and noxious, true. Yet, he suspected there was more to their nature than ugliness, ignorance, and greed.

Not much more, granted. But, enough to elicit further study?

Unwilling to pass up such a rare opportunity, the octo-snail abandoned sensible caution and swam closer to the shore. His keen eyes scrutinized the Heey-ou's every move. Through his own observations, coupled with hours of discussion and debate with Envoric seabirds that frequented The Still, Uuvaloo had gleaned enough information on the species to generalize about this individual.

Its size and weight marked it as an adult. Chest protuberances suggested the teats of a breeding female. A firm stride hinted at an overall robust state of health. At least, she did not *appear* diseased or afflicted with parasites, but Uuvaloo couldn't be sure without a closer examination. The very notion of such an inspection appalled him. Yet, overall, the female was a splendid specimen — if such a horrid, bi-pedal creature could ever be thought of as *splendid*.

Uuvaloo observed the Penuree render something in the sand with one of its tiny limb-digits. *What is it...she...doing?* the octo-snail wondered.

He watched the Penuree complete her task, walk back to a driftwood log, and gather her effects. The female then ascended the trail, vanishing into the densely timbered Still — and thence, into mystery.

Pitiful Heey-ou, destined to be blind forever. Never knowing hijna, or communing with Great Ookl, or swimming in the... The thought died as

Uuvaloo's eyes alighted on a startling sight — the image the Penuree female had drawn in the sand. *Is it...could that be...* Eemsura?

The hallowed prayer-poems written upon sand were used to beseech Old Father Fathom. Waves dissolved the Eemsura into The Blue, where — hopefully — their virtuous messages would drift into the primordial gills of Great Ookl and rouse him back to awareness, and then, blessed communion.

"It can't -*mmurpt*- be," Uuvaloo gurgled with disbelief.

The flummoxed Ulura squirted seawater from a posterior siphon, propelling himself closer to the shoreline. He lingered in the wave-lapped shallows, cautious that no hungry eyes watched, either on the beach or above it. Normally, Uuvaloo wrote Eemsura under the protective cloak of darkness. But he felt his devotions had slipped into a rut: fifty thousand tides of nighttime sand prayers had not yet stirred Great Ookl, nor predicted the Glow's arrival, nor revealed the location of The Skynth. Perhaps prayers under the full light of the sun — and the heightened risk of death by tooth, beak or claw — would prove more efficacious.

Confident sand and sky were clear, the octo-snail squirmed out of the Gentle Crescent's surf and towards the mystery. His crippled limb slowed the journey, but at last he arrived, winded but fired with curiosity and trepidation.

He peered at the crude image the Heey-ou etched: '*Great Ookl dreaming in The Blue...*'

The implications of this phrase made Uuvaloo recoil from the words as if they were the pincers of Vile Chaac'Xib, itself. He nearly squirted ink in fear-reflex.

No! Impossible! It must be mimicry, the tharuuspex thought. *There's no other explanation! Penuree are incapable of True Speech!*

Uuvaloo, better than any other living being, knew the ancient dogma of how Old Father Fathom bequeathed His sacred words to the *Ulurii alone.*

No creatures were allowed to witness, let alone attempt, the making of sand prayers. For first learning, practicing, and ultimately perfecting Eemsura bestowed power — the blessed *Psimea*, the 'rare and precious pearl' — that took shape in the mind like a solid thing. And once lodged, this calcification of potential acted as both tool and ally, unique in all The Blue.

The very idea that a benighted Heey-ou would write Great Ookl's holy verse offended Uuvaloo to his devout, cartilaginous core. It made his skin itch and crawl.

And yet...here the words lay scrawled.

Uuvaloo examined the image closely. Though the Penuree's first attempt looked abysmal next to his practiced script, the rough strokes and whorls hinted at promise.

There's a potentially graceful mind here, the Ulura grudgingly admitted. But he didn't know if this was rote imitation or true inspiration. *I must know. But how? Perhaps... a test...*

With his remaining limbs, the octo-snail completed the unfinished prayer. He made the consecrated ahmijna — the most intricate glyph in all the Envoric world — with the delicate precision only ten-thousand tides of devotional practice, seven dexterous tentacles, and forty nimble finger-tendrils could impart.

"*Gitxsanimaq-Ookl-Thipuuntzn-Tyypara-Mataxiae-Haqipenxurn-Ell udeenthi...*" he recited, uttering the hallowed and utmost secret words to invoke his Deity. "...Great Ookl dreaming in The Blue, whose Ink colors the night sky..." The prayer progressed, beak-clicks stressing unique syllables for reverent effect: "...whose Eye always watches from the deep; by Your Will alone all obstacles shall be removed, and Your Garden Effulgent restored."

There. Eloquent and civilized, Uuvaloo thought with satisfaction at his issued challenge. *If the Heey-ou returns and accurately renders this prayer, then maybe it — she — really has the gift to compose Eemsura. And if that's*

the case, Ookl's Ink! We'll need to reexamine all our assumptions about the
Penuree.

The time had come to leave. Lingering under the sun had dried Uu-valoo's skin, and clinging sand scratched and irritated. Moreover, the Den Sire required his tharuuspex's augur-skill to divine the forthcoming Glow. Peering through the ceptual lenses to decipher flickering cyr and pryzoic movement would take all evening and well into tomorrow's First Tide.

Of greater urgency, if Uuvaloo remained exposed much longer he risked attack. Quith and Quiln, the mated Envoric bald eagles who ruled The Above and hunted during the day, would love nothing more than to devour one of the last two surviving Ulurii.

With a burp of relief, Uuvaloo slid into The Blue. Cool water refreshed and cleansed his parched flesh. Propelled by squirting posterior siphons, he departed for deeper fathoms. The octo-snail's boneless body squirmed over sandbars and between kelp holdfasts. His skin shifted between dark and lighter hues — in a pattern known as 'passing cloud' — intuitively matching shadow and sand fluidly and unconsciously.

Uuvaloo's tentacles, each supported by a rudimentary brain, probed seafloor nooks and fissures for food without his direct command, the suc-tion cups both touching and tasting as they did. To the octo-snail, it was if his limbs behaved of their own accord. He perceived their actions like seven different daydreams unfolding concurrently on the edges of his awareness. Not having to guide his appendages allowed Uuvaloo a chance to think. He couldn't scrub the sand-prayer created by the Heey-ou from his tri-lobed brain. No revelation from Old Father Fathom, nor any pryzoic prophecy or shraga dissection had ever hinted at such a possibility.

But aren't all things Ookl's Will? Uuvaloo wondered. The problem vexed like a biting parasite he couldn't dislodge. *Is it a test? If so, then to what end? Do I need to pray harder? Do I need to create a new word for the 'Gifted Penuree'? Are there other...*

The sharp tug and reflexive contraction of a tentacle dispelled the thought as a new imperative took over: food. Uuvaloo — without even being conscious of doing so — had just snared a *hahpah*, the delicious Dungeness crab, hiding in a coral cleft.

Ookl provides, the tharuuspex thought as his tentacles wrapped around the struggling crustacean. *Perhaps a meal will clear my head and get me thinking straight.*

Normally, Uuvaloo would dispatch the crab like his cephalopod progenitor: chitinous beak cracking open the shell, and a toothy radula-tongue rasping the food into his stomach. But the old ways often took longer than The Blue would safely allow, and time was short.

The tharuuspex turned inward, touched the *rare and precious pearl* lurking in his Aanandi-shade — and with a sharp discharge of power that cast a pulse-ripple in all directions — split the crab asunder. Death was instant, and the octo-snail leisurely ate the hahpah as he continued towards High Split Rock. Unlike his spawn-sibling Cixtindi, Uuvaloo had never mastered the art of eating and swimming simultaneously. Instead, he inched across the seafloor, texturally camouflaging the contours of his skin to mimic a small, algae-encrusted boulder.

A useful ploy to avert any hungry eye. But a hungry nose... that was another issue.

As the octo-snail enjoyed his meal and pondered the benthic mysteries of Old Father Fathom, a slim-bodied aorxa leopard shark, slightly over two-tails in length, emerged from the Oorum. It busily sniffed the sandy bottom searching for worms, fish eggs, clams, and other easily gleaned food until the current-dispersed scent of pulverized hahpah caught its nose.

The shark abruptly changed course, arrowing towards Uuvaloo. The octo-snail froze, skin now indistinguishable from the surrounding corals. The Ulura held his breath, squeezed his gill cavities shut, and instinctually restricted nearly all the electrical activity in his body. Each limb went numb as his metabolism slowed to an imperceptible crawl.

The leopard shark glided so close the prone tharuuspex could see the curved mouth set in its short, rounded snout. If not deliberately inert, he could have easily reached out and touched the pattern of black saddle-markings across its bronzy-gray back.

Dim-witted aorxa, the Ulura thought. *It's nearly as smart as the rock I'm pretending to be. Let's see if it can find me.*

And so, the predation game began...

Uuvaloo's usual emotional response to such an encounter was an experience-honed dread. He knew exactly how appetizing hungry mouths found his flesh. After the mauling from the moray eel Majah had claimed a tentacle, he'd avoid any fish larger than a lingcod without a graehl protecting him. True, the razor-sharp ceramic acuur held in a pinched suction cup near his beak gave him some reassurance. He could defend himself, if pressed.

But now Uuvaloo felt no fear. No hesitation. The riddle of the Penuree had stirred something defiant within him and he welcomed it, to the depths of his Aanandi shade.

The odor of Dungeness crab drew the leopard shark ever closer. Uuvaloo watched, W-shaped irises catching every movement of its sweeping crescent-shaped tail and triangular pectoral fins. His muscles tensed, and as the aorxa came within a half-tail's-length of discovering him, Uuvaloo discarded his hahpah-meal, awoke his frozen body, and struck.

In a burst of motion, seven powerful limbs constricted around the hapless leopard shark's body. It squirmed and bolted headlong into the kelp, trying in vain to bite whatever was clinging to its dorsal fin, frustratingly out of reach.

Uuvaloo rode the aorxa, excitement speeding his three hearts as the careening fish whisked him deeper into The Blue. But spirited recklessness, no matter how enjoyable, was not the point of this endeavor, control was.

Safely tightened around the shark's belly, Uuvaloo brazenly slid his tendril-fingers into the flared gill-slits. The invasive act caused the leopard shark to instinctively thrash, but the Ulura held tight. Uuvaloo focused, and by envisioning a fully realized Eemsura sigil, accessed his pearl of Psimea. The potency tingled down his arms, through his forty boneless digits, and wormed its way into the leopard shark's primitive mind.

Ookl's Ink compels you to obey, Uuvaloo commanded, perceiving the cognitive union as a simple knot of kholo easily untied. *Be still. Slow your panic. Ookl's Ink compels you...*

Nictating membranes over the shark's eyes fluttered as its agency drained. It soon went limp. Psimea — Great Ookl's gift to the Ulurii alone — had done its work. Uuvaloo owned the aorxa: he felt its circulation, its steady respiration, the food in its belly...even the teeth set in its mouth. Every inch of the shark now felt like an extension of his rubbery body.

Take me home, the tharuuspex commanded. *I've work to do.*

With a pump of its tail, the leopard shark veered towards High Split Rock. Uuvaloo casually guided the fish like a puppeteer. It offered no resistance, its simple brain overwhelmed. As the symbiotic pair neared the Holt, the octo-snail sensed the *precious pearl* had reduced in size. Its finite power needed replenishment, and only inscribing Eemsura could do that.

One more task to do when time allows... if it ever allows, Uuvaloo bemoaned as the thick nooree groves swathing the jagged foundations of

High Split Rock appeared. *There are never enough tides to get everything done.*

The Ulura guided the leopard shark towards the granite overhang redolent of a river otter. A shoal of foraging fish scattered into the swaying kelp fronds as the Psimea-bonded pair swam down the submerged tunnel. Ahead the Holt's moon pool sparkled in the darkness.

As soft corals and sea anemones passed by unseen, Uuvaloo's thoughts once more drifted down more obscure currents: *How do I untie the knot of the Penuree and Eemsura? Should I spill my ink as penance? Yes. That may reveal the answer...*

The octo-snail's leopard shark conveyance fell quiescent as it reached the moonpool, its journey concluded. On the water-slicked stones encircling the flooded portal, a trio of Deltas stood upright, enjoying a clamshell bowl of oixrd — a respite from their labors harvesting edible kelps growing on the moon pool's interior walls. As they sipped their fermented drinks, they chatted about plans for an upcoming hunt.

As Oovaluu's eyestalks broke the surface, his hijna interrupted their discussion. "A little assistance, if you -*mmurpt*- please."

Startled, the three Lontra dropped to all fours and respectfully tugged their whiskers. "Nookeelee, Uuvaloo. We didn't see you." They knew when the Alpha's tharuuspex asked for help, compliance was mandatory. "How can we help?"

"Dispatch this aorxa for the Great Hollow meal," Uuvaloo ordered. "And I require a *cjaalet*. The Den Sire expects me at Oussia's Puddle. Quickly now."

The Deltas leapt to obey. Two of them fetched their spears, dove into the moon pool, and delivered a killing jab into the shark's 'sweet spot' as Uuvaloo removed his fingers from its gill-slits. The aorxa convulsed, thrashed...and went limp in a thickening cloud of blood.

The octo-snail swam to the pool's edge and crawled onto the porch stones. The third Delta crouched so Uuvaloo could climb onto his back. Carrying a tharuuspex, the submissive act of cjaalet, was an honored task. Once Uuvaloo's tentacles tightened about the Lontra's abdomen, the river otter raced through the Holt's switchback tunnels, crossing the many bridges connecting the habitat levels, traveling upwards as fast as his four legs could move.

I need to discover what Ookl has planned, Uuvaloo thought as his mustelid mount arrived at the roots of Old Tree and scampered up to the threshold of Oussia's Puddle. *Because if I fail... if I don't decipher what the Old Father has planned for me, for the Holt... then I'll never find Skynthuuhrnymlex. And that may be my — our — last and only hope.*

CHAPTER 40

A Cold Reality

E lihuul was several hours away as Gloss approached the kholo partition. The braided High Polyp curtain, sensing her ureola, began to unknit. Splitting up the middle, it coiled back and away to allow her passage.

Stepping into Gwelth's innermost sanctum, Gloss paused. The spear she held fell to her side as her eyes — drawn to the forty-one burning pryzoa clinging to two floating Penuree tires — began to water. The light they cast, and the succulent-sweet odor they exuded, almost overwhelmed her.

Gloss understood her father's compulsion to always be near them. She could spend tides basking in the light of their presence, forgetting all problems, obstacles ... and ambitions.

Soft snoring pulled Gloss' attention to the tattered pile of rope and shredded life preservers where Fearless slept. Broken urchin shells and cleaned fish bones lay scattered about the royal bed. Gloss approached her father and gently sniffed his head, careful not to startle him. Fearless awoke at the tickle of her whiskers on his graying muzzle.

"Gloss?" the old Doyen mumbled. "What are you doing here?"

"I thought we might talk before Elihuul."

Fearless yawned, exposing massive teeth. "Of course. It's time I got up anyway." He scratched his fluffy cheeks and whiskers with a forepaw. "How is Cries Often?"

"Safe. Playing with the pups. They help keep him calm, which helps him sleep."

Fearless stretched one leg, then another. His bushy tail stiffened. "Good. That's good."

"He wants a ynth and to hunt with a graehl. He wants to be treated like every other uju."

Fearless nodded. He noticed the spear Gloss carried and frowned. "But he's not like others. We must keep him close. Otherwise, he'll wander off and The Blue will swallow him. Just like Grabber." The Doyen attacked an itch on his belly with a hind paw. "I want him to be healed. But we hardly ever get what we want."

"Cries Often is more capable than you realize," Gloss countered. "Maybe he'll surprise you, us, the entire Raft someday."

"That's a Diuun Dunn-sized maybe."

Gloss shook her head, weary of this old dismissal about her sibling. Time to change the subject. "Did any graehl bring back news on Grabber?"

"No."

Gloss sighed, her whiskers drooping. "I miss him."

"We all do." Fearless placed a gentle paw on his daughter's shoulder. "He was our smartest, bravest, *best* hunter. But The Blue had its own plans for him. Just as it does for all of us, Monoah, Envorah, and Aanandi alike."

"Is there no escaping it?" The idea of her life-current having already been charted, yet remaining unknown until her final breath, galled Gloss.

"There is not. Sadly." Fearless crossed to the six Orca skulls jutting from the chamber wall. He scaled them, putting himself at eye level with the pryzoa adorning the hovering, interlocked Penuree tires. "Something called to Grabber's Aanandi-shade, he swam off, and now he's gone. It's that simple. We must accept that he'll never come home. And it breaks my heart."

"Mine, too."

The Doyen squinted, studying the enchanted gastropods and their sublime movements. "Sharp Tooth spoke to me earlier. He was upset. Do you know why?"

Yurch, Gloss thought. Her tail swished in agitation. "I can only guess."

"I'm sure you can," Fearless replied, exasperation coloring his hijna. "But even more perplexing is *why* you don't listen?"

Gloss shrugged. "I like to hunt. It speaks to my Aanandi-shade. And I'm good at it."

"That's not the point. Lutris uja do not hunt. That is our way."

"Lontra uja hunt," Gloss pointed out. "They form graehls. They use the ynth and majl. They do their share to feed their kin. All I want is the same chance."

Fearless shook his head in frustration. "Why must I constantly explain this to you? We are Lutris, *not* Lontra. Our ways have superior value and set us apart from those usurpers. You should revel *in* them, not rebel *against* them." The Doyen turned his angry gaze back to the pryzoa and their cyr-flames. The orca teeth ringing the First Life dimpled his footpads. "The

Lontra are thieves. Their customs are poison. I'm more convinced of that than ever."

"Not all Lontra are bad, father."

"Hmmph. I can only assume you're referring to the Den Sire's brat."

"Sleek is honorable. He treats me as an equal."

Fearless shot his daughter a look of mingled shock and disgust. "Treating you as *his* equal diminishes *you*. You are my daughter, and far superior to any thieving Lontra."

"Father, I want to..."

"No!" Fearless dropped to the floor and stood a paw-span from his daughter. The impact of his landing reverberated through the disheveled floorboards. A fluffed pelt and flared whiskers heightened both his physical and psychological dominance. Gloss backed away in sudden fear, dropping ootith. If she'd been any other Lutris, she'd be bitten and bleeding by now.

"Understand me, uja." The Doyen's deceptively gentle hijna made his words even more frightening. "The Lontra want The Blue and everything in it for themselves. They want all Envorah under their paws. They covet Liminal, the Golden Barnacle, and The Glow. They will take everything we have if we let them. They're nearly worse than Penuree!"

Gloss made no effort to hide her sadness. "I don't believe you."

"Things are simpler when you're a child."

"I'm *not* a child!" Gloss cried. "I haven't been for a long time now."

"And yet you're *still* not mated, *still* without pups. That says 'child' to me."

Gloss growled, agitation darkening her hijna. "I do not have a mate and pups because I do not *wish* to. I have other things I want to do."

"We all have things we *wish* to do," Fearless countered. "But there comes a tide when our lives no longer belong to us. They belong to the next generation."

"This life is *my own,*" Gloss retorted. "I want to fill it with experiences and adventure before I give it away. It's that simple."

"Nothing is ever that simple. The Blue is becoming more complicated with each tide."

"Because we're making it so. Can't you find it in your heart to make peace? You always tell me to listen to my Aanandi-shade for answers. What is your shade telling you now?"

The Doyen rasped his teeth. "That time is running out."

Gloss didn't like the sound of that. She followed Fearless' gaze to the floating tires and the radiant magic they harbored.

"My pryzoa have shown glimpses of what the future currents may hold," Fearless continued. "And what I've seen isn't good. Our way of life will be destroyed unless we act. We have until this next Glow, perhaps not even that."

"*May* hold. Maybe the pryzoa are wrong. Did you ever consider that?"

Fearless huffed. "Don't be foolish. They're a gift from Oussia, sanctified by Deshi-Oad Himself. They're *never* wrong. Their guidance is not just for the here-and-now — even if it's only partially seen — but for every generation of Lutris not yet born. The Lontra hunt our waters. They take our prey. They steal our uboo. They hoard pryzoa that are ours by right. Their numbers grow unchecked, like generations of putrid myzee. That's dangerous. Even you must see that. If we wait too much longer to take back what is ours, we will not have the strength to defeat them. Then all will be lost."

"Deshi-Oad's Stone Teeth! I'm so sick of this nonsense!"

"Oh, you think it's nonsense, do you?" Fearless' golden eyes glowed with barely suppressed anger. "You'll soon learn otherwise, I promise."

"I doubt it."

Fearless' heavy paw twitched with the impulse to cuff his petulant offspring across her mouth. "As my daughter, you need to set a proper example for the other uja. And you can begin by staying away from Sleek. He's beneath you. Put him out of your mind. Cast your feelings for him to the waves. Then, you must choose a mate from among your *own* kind." The Lutris Eehr scratched his furry chin. "Consider ... Sharp Tooth, for instance."

"What about him?"

"You know very well what I mean, Gloss. Sharp Tooth is an eminently suitable mate. His father was Bravest. He's my Saia, after all, and I did not choose idly. He's honorable and courageous and will sire strong pups. True, he does have an unsightly snaggletooth, but we all have imperfections. Trust me when I say you could do much, much worse."

"I've already told you. I don't want a mate yet."

"There are those three words again: 'I-don't-want.' Have you heard nothing I've said?" Fearless stamped his foot, gratified his daughter had sense enough to flinch. "It's not about what *you* want. It's about what's best for The Raft. You must find a mate and start a family. We need strong pups, now more than ever."

"Is all I am to you a means to produce more fighters for some ridiculous war?"

"You're my daughter. You're a prize to be cherished and fought over by the Raft's best males. You deserve the grand *vouruum* a worthy uju will build for you."

"None of that matters to me. Only Sleek's love does."

"Your obsession with Sleek is unnatural." A deep growl accompanied the Doyen's hijna, his patience frayed near to breaking. "I'd hoped you'd come to your senses on your own. But I've allowed this to go on for far too long."

"You've *allowed* this?" she asked. "Explain."

Fearless sighed. "This...*attachment* of yours for the Den Sire's son is my fault. I assumed you'd tire of that scrawny uju and move on. If I'd raised you better, trained you to be a proper Lutris uja, you would have. But that was supposed to be your mother's duty. When she died, I had no choice but to assume her task. I admit I focused more on protecting The Raft than raising my pups. I could have — *should* have — done better."

Fearless' denigration and dismissal of her love for Sleek hurt Gloss as surely as if her father had shoved an urchin quill under one of her claws. She could think of no adequate reply.

The Doyen returned to his throne heap. He nudged the fluffy mass around until, pleased with its contours, he nestled in with a satisfied grunt. "Enough of my past mistakes. I plan to correct them. So, first things first. I want your ynth." He held out his wide paw expectantly.

The demand shocked Gloss. "But Grabber gave it to me. It's all I have left of him!"

"Your possession of that spear sends the wrong message to the others... that uja are equal to uju, that their place is the graehl and *not* the uboorl."

Gloss rose, stiffened her posture. Her silvery whiskers bristled. "Why is that wrong? We should all be free to choose our own currents to swim!"

"You dare to say such things to me?" Fearless' hijna shone with menace. "Disobedient uja! Your attitude invites weakness. The Lontra see it and laugh!" He bared his teeth in warning. "We Lutris do not tolerate weakness. Now do as you're told!"

Gloss bared her own teeth in response, clutching the lance to her chest like a protective mother would her threatened pup. "I will *not*!"

"Disobey..." Fearless' golden eyes glinted like lethal ice chips, "...and Cries Often dies."

Horrified, Gloss lowered the spear, nearly dropping it. "He's your last remaining son," she whispered. "Your eldest child. How could you say that?"

The Doyen shrugged. "He's an imbecile. A defective embarrassment. If Cries Often weren't my offspring, he would've been drowned at birth.

Season after season I've turned a blind eye as he drained our resources, but that's easily fixed." Fearless casually placed his paw upon the Eehrynth — and the implication of the gesture was clear. "Remember how I dealt with our Oyyan injured? Any uju who could not hold a spear or strengthen a graehl was dispatched. No exceptions. And those were warriors defending our Raft. They knew and accepted their fates."

Gloss stepped closer to her father, her golden eyes filling with pleading tears. "Cries Often is gentle and kind. His heart is full of love, for you and for all The Raft. He hurts no one, takes little more than a pup. That you'd even consider..."

"I mean to have your obedience!" Fearless snapped. "And by Deshi-Oad's Fluke, I will use *all* means at my disposal to get it. Defy me and Cries Often dies. As does Sleek."

"You're a monster."

"I am *Doyen*. I will kill Cries Often myself, mount his head on my trophy wall, and then order every graehl in The Raft to slay the Lontra brattling on sight. I care nothing for treaties. I will eat his eyes and make you wear his tail around your neck until it rots off."

Gloss' heart hammered in her chest. Her head spun and her throat constricted, stifling the moan of anguish welling up from her gut. Dark visions of Sleek and Cries Often dead and mutilated pinned her to the floor.

"You have tonight to reflect upon the foolishness of your attitude. Then, first tide tomorrow, you will return Grabber's ynth — but you'll do so before the *entire* Raft. I will also announce your intention to take a mate. Now, leave me."

Gloss turned away from her father before he saw the pooling tears spill from her eyes. She refused to grant him the satisfaction of seeing her pain. Numb from nose to tail, she left the pryzoa chamber without another word. She neither tugged her whiskers in respect nor left submissive four-legged ootith.

After all, what more could she say or do?

If Gloss must give up her spear to save her dearest brother — and her kalaayaa — then so be it. In the end it was just a tool; other ynth could be made and secreted away. If her acquiescence proved inevitable, then it would be to the letter of the demand, if not the heart of it.

Anger swelled Gloss' heart like the incoming tide, drowning her pain in the process. As she exited Gwelth for the chilly waters of Tanglesafe, she resolved to accomplish as much as possible before the next sunrise.

After Elihuul. She felt the turritella shell alcq hidden in her underarm skin-pouch. It fueled her defiance. *When all is dark, and everyone sleeps... that's when I'll make my move.*

CHAPTER 41

A BRISINGIDA IN THE BATH

"Tʜere you are!"

Ayana turned to find her mother striding up the path. The light-and-shadow dapple cast by the evergreen canopy could not hide Hayley's displeasure. Ayana could feel the simmering anger from ten paces away. Even the birds chirping in the trees fell silent, as if sensing the pending parental scolding and not wanting to interfere.

"Where on earth have you been?" Hayley huffed. A little winded from climbing, she paused to catch her breath. "I've been looking all over for you."

"At the beach..." Ayana answered, acting as casual as possible. *I'm not technically lying,* she thought; then added: "...just, you know, hangin' out and stuff."

"I didn't see you."

Ayana shrugged, tapping her glue drops. "That's weird."

"I called and called. So, again: where were you?"

"I didn't hear you. Sorry, mom. Must've been the wind. But I was at the beach. I swear."

Hayley fixed Ayana with skeptical eyes. Her motherly intuitions were acute. She knew a lie when she heard it but the wet knees and the telltale dirt stains on her shoes and pants lent credence to Ayana's story. Still, she had doubts...

The traces of Jake's face in Ayana's — the shape of her nose, the curve of her lips, the tilt of her head — blunted Hayley's anger to irritation. Ayana nervously shifted under her mother's wilting gaze. She moved a fraction into sunlight that lit her left eye and cheek.

"What's that?" Hayley asked, her irritation further softening to curiosity. She took her daughter's face into her hands. Ayana resisted, but Hayley persisted. "Stop squirming."

Hayley looked into her daughter's eyes and saw...bronze specks.

Ayana's brown irises were now peppered with them.

"You have bronze dots in your eyes."

"I do?"

"When did this happen?"

Ayana shrugged. "How should I know?"

Hayley knew something unusual had occurred. Be it a puberty side-effect or a late-onset chromosomal effect related to her vitiligo, she couldn't tell. In truth, she thought the bronze glitter haloing Ayana's pupils looked unique, almost... haunting.

But then Hayley notices something else. "Have you been crying?"

"What? No."

"Your eyes are all red and puffy. Is everything okay?" *Is everything okay? You're kidding me, right?* Ayana thought. She repressed the urge to laugh at the question on this, the most profound day of her life. She had been crying, true: but from hilarity, not pain.

"It's...just from the sun and wind. Don't worry about it."

Hayley sensed her daughter's impending emotional shutdown. If she pushed any harder, she'd never get to the truth lurking behind Ayana's blatantly false smile. She'd try finding the answer via a different path, once her daughter's emotions had cooled.

'Fine." Hayley stepped around Ayana and continued up the trail. "C'mon. We're late."

Mother and daughter trekked back to the house in silence, dry pine needles crunching beneath their boots. Spoken words risked confrontation and retreat. Each one focused on her individual mysteries, be it shells, otters, or enigmatic sand patterns.

The quiet between them lasted until they reached the three-acre pasture... and the solitary apple tree that grew within.

"Have you paid respects to your father yet?"

"Not yet." Ayana nervously *tap-tapped* her glue drops. *Crud*, she thought. With all the rival excitements of the day, she'd forgotten about the somber reflections at her father's grave.

"I hope you'll make the time soon," Hayley said softly.

Ayana stomped up the stairs. *Gross. I feel like the floor of a movie theater,* she thought.

She swept into the bathroom and shut the door behind her, harder than intended. Years earlier, Grandpa had modernized the shower stall, but that had been the extent of his remodeling. All the fixtures and the blue cast iron tub were original from when the house was built.

Probably during the Dark Ages!

Ayana turned the brass taps to start the water flowing, adjusted the temperature to just below scalding, then plugged the drain with a rubber stopper. As she waited for the tub to fill, she gazed at her reflection in the mirror. Ignoring the unripe pimple beside her right nostril, she examined her eyes.

"Bronze? Ayana said. "What the...?"

It seemed unreal. She pulled down her bottom eyelids for a better view.

Remarkably, her irises now had a dusting of metallic glitter. Could this somehow be a result of her encounter with the spear-totting otter? It had *gold eyes...*

"Hmm," she muttered. "Maybe I'm some kind of mutant now." Ayana peeled off her sweat-stained shirt. Her sunburned arms and neck were dirty from the Fantasea. A sniff of her armpits caused her to wrinkle her nose in disgust.

On the shelf next to the sink, Ayana spied an ancient box of bath salts. 'A Veritable Luxury,' proclaimed the label. *After a day like today, I could use a little luxury*, she thought. *Grandma won't mind.*

Ayana opened the box and sniffed. The contents gave off a pleasant lavender aroma, but time and humidity had consolidated the granules into a purple brick.

Ayana upended the carton over the tub. The salt hit the water with a *plop* and sank. She was forced to break up the mass by hand and swish it around until it finally dissolved.

This should get rid of my 'b-o' for the next week.

Ayana unfastened her bra, shed her dirty jeans and underwear to the green bathmat, then slipped into the tub. The hot, floral-scented water stung the reddened skin on her arms and neck at first, but soon, the pain faded, soothed to bliss. She probed the plump, self-inflicted blister on her hand and then examined the long scratch on her leg. She picked at the blister, half-tempted to nibble off a piece, but decided against it. *That'd be too gross*, she thought.

Ayana inhaled and let herself slide beneath the surface. As the water closed over her face, she shut her eyes. She decided she would try to hold her breath for a full minute. The buoyancy created by the bath salts made it harder to remain fully submerged, but by focusing all her willpower, she was able to relax as the tub continued to fill around her.

She started to count.

One Mississippi, two Mississippi, three Mississippi...

The first thirty seconds came and went easily. Tiny bubbles tickled her nose. Fifteen seconds more, and her lungs started to tingle.

Forty-six Mississippi, forty-seven Mississippi, forty-eight Mississippi...

The tingle morphed into burning pain that doubled and doubled again. The need to exhale became imperative. *This is stupid. Why am I doing this? What's the point?*

Perhaps the point was to improve even one small aspect of her otherwise unremarkable self. To reach a goal she'd set, no matter the difficulty.

She gritted her teeth and fought past the pain. *Fifty-eight Mississippi, fifty-nine Mississippi, sixty Mississippi, sixty-one Mississippi...*

Ayana surfaced with a gasp. "Yes!" She coughed and wiped water from her eyes...

...only to discover the tub had overflowed onto the yellow-tiled floor.

A hasty lunge to turn off the faucet resulted in yet more spillage. The spreading puddle soaked her heaped clothes as it crept towards the toilet and the door beyond.

"Shit!" Ayana exclaimed as she climbed out of the tub, sloshing yet more water over the brim... and promptly slipped on the slick floor, landing hard on her backside. The ice-cold tiles against her heated skin made her yelp. It felt like sitting on a popsicle.

Ayana got to her feet, took a step, and slipped again. Gritting her teeth against the pain of whacked knees and elbows, she gingerly crawled on all fours to the towel rack, only to find...

...a single pink washcloth, draped over the metal bar. "Great. Just great," she muttered.

Remembering to late that all the clean towels were in the hallway closet, Ayana set to work sopping up the spilled bathwater with her wholly inadequate tool, wringing the cloth into the tub again and again. Her skin grew cold and roughened with gooseflesh, but then, she noticed a red glow emanating from the front pocket of her jeans.

In disbelief Ayana stared, all discomfort forgotten.

What on earth is happening now? she wondered. Cautiously, she opened the wet pocket, and peered in. "Ooooh...wow!" she gasped in astonishment.

The blown-glass shell she'd found on the Fantasea, stuffed into her pocket, and forgotten in all the weirdness of the last few hours, now burned brighter than a red-hot ember. Ayana dropped her jeans and scooted away; suddenly afraid they might go up in flames. But, no, sodden denim couldn't burn...couldn't it?

Ayana stared, transfixed, hesitant to touch the shell lest it singe her fingertips. When she saw no steam, nor smelled scorching fabric, summoning her courage, she reached back into the pocket, gingerly probing, ready to withdraw instantly.

Ayana gasped again. Instead of heat, the shell felt cold to the touch.

It's glowing. Why isn't it, like, a thousand degrees? she thought. But then, glowing didn't always mean heat.

She palmed the shell. The crimson light sparked an idea. Ayana padded over to the wall switch by the door and flicked off the lights. The shell's illumination cast eerie facets across the darkened bathroom, reflecting off the sink mirror and toilet.

Yet, after a few seconds, the vibrancy faded. Chilled skin and a sudden hunch set her back into the tub, where she submerged the shell in warm water. Upon contact, it once again flared with blinding crimson radiance.

Ayana squealed. The shell slipped from her cupped hands to settle on the bottom of the tub, sinking like a speck of the sun. She shut her eyes against the light, afterimages dancing behind her lids.

After a few seconds, she cautiously reopened her eyes, and immediately scooted back from the incandescent shell, sloshing more water over the side of the tub. She stared at it, waiting, but nothing more happened. Excitement shivered up her back, conjuring fresh gooseflesh despite the warmth of the bath.

Ayana plucked the shell from the steaming water, laughing like a giddy toddler.

It's still cold! she thought. *Even after soaking in hot water!*

Ayana once again felt wedged between the hard, indifferent world she detested and another woven from the gossamers of a hundred dream-like fantasies she loved. But how close to the one realm, and how far from the other, she couldn't yet determine.

Ayana closed her hand over the shell and the bathroom fell into darkness. The glow exposed, in a palette of red and pink hues, the anatomy of her clenched fist, like when she pressed her thumb over a flashlight lens, except a thousand times more powerful. Seeing the bones and muscles of her semi-transparent hand captivated her so much she didn't hear the approaching footsteps.

The bathroom door swung open. A hand flicked on the light.

Hayley stood in the doorway.

Ayana screamed and quickly thrust her fist beneath her thigh, praying her mother wouldn't notice the red light in the bathwater. "Moooom!" she screeched. "What the hell?"

"Geesh-God!" Hayley yelped.

"What are you doing?" Ayana demanded. "Can I *please* have some privacy?!"

Hayley's shock quickly slid to puzzlement. "Why are you bathing in the dark? Why is the tub so full? And why is there water all over the floor?"

"Does it matter? I'll clean everything up. And knock next time, for cryin' out loud," Ayana hollered. "And put a fresh towel by the door. Please."

"All right, all right!" Hayley rolled her eyes and closed the door. "I'm leaving."

"Thank you."

The door clicked shut. Ayana sighed as her heartbeat slowed too normal. She opened her clenched fist. The red-glass shell still glowed like an aquatic star on her palm.

That was close, she thought. There had been several close calls on this strangest-of-all-days — slipping ropes, slippery rocks, a precariously sloping deck — and otters, alternatively hostile and friendly.

"Yaeeeli," she whispered, remembering those wondrous gold-on-gold eyes, the way the otter spoke without speaking, and the elegance of its posture. But most intriguing of all — the splotches of blue fur scattered over the otter's arm. She couldn't be certain, but Ayana had the distinct impression that they matched her own vitiligo pattern in both number and arrangement.

"Yurch," she hissed, as the terrifying memory of menacing fishing pole and bone spears came rushing back; of golden eyes darkening with aggression.

Somehow, Ayana knew that she would see those golden eyes again. And when that day came, she'd be ready. She forced the fearsome recollections to the back of her mind; she had an experiment that needed doing.

Ayana stepped out of the tub, carefully walked over to the door — locked it — then, just as carefully made her way back to the water's warm embrace. Safe for now, she put the shell to her mouth and nibbled off a sand grain-sized morsel. The sweet-savory flavor she'd anticipated swept over her tongue. She swallowed, and a jolt of electric euphoria accelerated and aligned her whole body — as if every cell now played in perfect unison, the glorious, single-note composition swelling to crescendo in her soul.

Ayana's five senses expanded with the same magical intensity.

She heard her jeans soaking up tub water. Felt the liquid inside her blister being reabsorbed back into her hand. Saw micron-sized mildew spores infesting the grout between the tiles. Tasted the fillings in her teeth like metallic candy. And smelled the myriad universe of musty-aged beauty products filling the sink drawers and medicine cabinet.

And then it ended. The universe contracted to the bathtub like a stretched rubber-band snapping back to shape. But she wasn't alone —

Something otherworldly now clung to the inner wall of the blue cast-iron tub.

Ayana yelped and scooted away, slopping more water onto the tile floor. Fear pumped adrenaline into her veins, and her heart pounded like a snare drum. The instinct to flee nearly drove her from the tub once more. But instinctual fear morphed into utter amazement when Ayana now realized she shared her bath with a...

"Starfish?"

It actually didn't look like anything she'd ever seen before, but a starfish was the closest analogy she could think of. The fantastic creature was the size of her splayed hand, with a dozen spindly limbs radiating from a delicate glassy smooth central disk. A rainbow of oscillating colors pulsed outward from its body, rippling along each ray-arm and back again in rapid succession. The invertebrate-wonder moved across the tub with unnatural speed; a small, organic neon sign buzzing with electricity, feeling its way along with an array of translucent feathery tendrils below its tube-feet.

Ayana squeezed the red-glass shell, her eyes riveted to the luminous starfish, sensing the importance of this moment: things just didn't materialize out of nothing. This *had* to be magic.

She extended an index finger and, ever so carefully, touched the starfish. Or, at least tried...

Her finger passed into the animal without resistance. She tried a second finger, then an entire hand. Still, nothing. She realized it was an illusion: a construct of textured light.

"What's going on?" Ayana whispered.

Was this encounter a side effect of her hours spent baking under a hot sun all day? Was her mind coughing up synaptic gobbledygook, playing tricks on her sense of reality? She wouldn't be surprised. Stranger things had already happened over the last twelve hours.

As Ayana stared at the starfish, she felt the seashell poking her pruning palm. It slipped from her fingers as she adjusted it and clinked to the tub floor.

The starfish vanished.

One second it was lingering by the faucet, the next: *Poof*. It simply blinked out of existence. Ayana rubbed her eyes and looked again. Still gone. She grabbed the shell and the starfish returned... right where she last saw it, crawling along, oblivious to her presence.

Ayana purposefully dropped the shell, and the starfish promptly disappeared as if someone had flicked off a switch. Retrieving the shell restored it to full visibility, in the exact location, moving at the same prior speed.

The red glass seashell cupped in her hand was the key to this miracle.

Ayana regarded it with a renewed sense of awe.

I've got a piece of real magic here, she thought. *I've got to find out where it came from.*

CHAPTER 42

THAT STILL, SMALL VOICE

It would cost Sleek a half-tide of hard swimming to reach the perennial xhooja.

And, for every tail of that journey — fighting both wave and current — the Beta fretted.

Asleep for six tides? How could I be so careless? Sleek thought. *I should've never eaten a second pryzoa. The scishma-snaag bit me. Bad. Bishq! This is what I get for being greedy.*

Only once did the Saia stop to rub the ache in his healing leg. As he did, schools of easily speared prey fish flittered below him like silvery arrowheads as they vanished into the emerald shadows of wavering seaweed.

Sleek ignored them. His desire to reach Gloss eclipsed all other concerns.

The otter inhaled, dove, and swam towards the invisible slipstream. Spying the tell-tale kelp frond deformations marking its proximity, he pierced the xhooja.

The swift current caught up the Saia, whisking him away faster than a hunting marlin.

As the quicker-water conduit sped Sleek towards the distant Oyster Shell, he found time to relax... and worry: *Why was that Penuree on The Cellum? And its hijna? Ookl's Ink, that's never happened before. And it's all my fault. I should have just killed it and left.* Sleek felt obligated to discuss his encounter with the Den Sire and Uuvaloo. *If anyone knows what to do, it'd be them*, the Beta thought. *But do I confess the part I played? Or feign ignorance?*

The Oyster Shell's algae-softened foundations finally appeared at the edges of the Oorum. Sleek exited the slipstream for slower water, backstroked to temper his momentum, and kicked for the sun-sparkled surface. All thoughts of trespassing Penuree, scattered ghaydn or the desecrated Cellum evaporated as Sleek floated on the waves.

He scanned the looming skerry for any trace of his love. He saw none.

The Beta swam towards the Oyster Shell, spear in paw. Emerging from the sea, Sleek crawled across sun-warmed stones and shook water from his fur.

"Gloss?" the young otter hijna-called, followed by a string of urgent barks and yips.

Still his kalaayaa did not answer. The Oyster Shell was deserted.

Sleek glanced at the setting sun. By its position, and the length of his shadow, he knew that swimming past the pain in his leg had paid off.

He'd arrived on time and hadn't yet missed Gloss. He moved among rocks littered with the desiccated bones and long-dried scraps of ancient fish feasts. Shading his eyes from the sun with a free paw, he gazed at the empty skerry's sloped and terraced sides. Without the co-mingled populations of Holt and Raft, dining together as kin, the Oyster Shell seemed like a sad, desolate place.

Sleek tried envisioning the last shraga hunt — all the tastes and sights and wonders — but could not. The joy and camaraderie of that long passed tide was as silent in his mind as the crenated stones now encircling him. The immediacy of his recent pryzoa-charged memory-dream had already faded, its meaning beyond recall, nothing more than an echo of an echo of an echo...

It's dead, Sleek thought. *Dead and gone. And I'm not sorry. The Oyster Shell's just a rock in The Blue. A meeting place, nothing more.*

More important concerns loomed — like food.

Gloss would be famished after her long journey from Tanglesafe. Sleek slipped back into the sea to secure a meal for them. It didn't take long to find suitable prey. A Hunter's Eye, a stealthy approach, and a precise thrust of the ynth skewered a juicy atiqah. The Beta hauled the lingcod back onto the rocks where it twitched, gasped, and went still.

Sleek vowed not to take a single bite. *I'll give Gloss first portion.*

The sun — *Celipsis* — that enigmatic ball of light and heat existing in eternal opposition to the cold gaze of Ookl's Eye, made its snail-paced journey towards the horizon. Mindful of the bald eagles Quith and Quiln, who might be lurking overhead, the Beta waited and waited for his silver-pelted kalaayaa, sharp eyes watching both the sparkling waves and the darkening sky.

He sniffed the wind to catch any hint of Gloss' alluring scent, his mind attuned to her distinct hijna. *Where could she be?* he wondered. But he wasn't worried. Not yet.

The rumble in Sleek's empty belly grew more insistent. To distract himself, the Saia reflected again on his memory-dream.

Of all the life lessons and reckless misadventures Sleek had experienced over the seasons, each one imbued with its own unique wisdom or folly, why did *those* specific memories manifest? He hadn't thought about that fateful shraga harvest since last meeting Gloss at the Oyster Shell over eighty tides earlier. For Sleek, it was simply the first time he'd *met* Gloss... or *hunted* with her... or, more to the point, *kissed* her.

Just then, something began to itch the back of his mind like a bothersome sandflea burrowing into his awareness.

...g... g... g... G...

Oh-so-faint, this still, small voice — which he'd learned from his mother was the beckoning of his Aanandi-shade — whispered a phrase he couldn't yet decipher.

...Go...

But it persisted, growing incessant like a hungry kit craving the teat of its mother. Sleek closed his eyes, slowed his breathing, and listened.

...Go... to...

Sleek frowned and glanced at the lengthening shadows cast by the skerry's numerous crags, backlit by Celipsis as it angled towards the horizon. *Go where?* he thought.

Gloss' face appeared before his mind's eye, taking the focus off the whispered warning.

"She should be here by now." He absent-mindedly jabbed the lingcod with his spear. "What's keeping her?" A twinge of alarm coursed through him.

He wondered: *Could a predator have attacked her? Is she wounded?*

Sleek knew Gloss could cast the Hunter's Eye with a skill that rivaled, and often surpassed, his own. She could slay most quarry by herself. He'd witnessed her proficiency first-paw. No, a predator attack wasn't the likely answer.

...Go to... Little...

Sleek turned a troubling notion over in his mind. *Did Fearless confine her?*

The Doyen could be a problem. Rage and hate over the Cuursuurq, and the subsequent subordinate position of the Lutris, ensnared him like tangles of ropey kelp. But Gloss possessed ample cunning to slip her father's grasp. Sneaking away from Tanglesafe was kit's-play for her.

No, Fearless' restrictions weren't the cause of Gloss' tardiness.

...Go to... Little Mouth...

Sleek pondered another possibility. *Maybe she doesn't want to come? Maybe she doesn't want to hunt?*

Gloss loved their nocturnal trysts just as much as he did — even more. At the Oyster Shell, she could open her Hunter's Eye wide and clear, allowing her to pursue prey freely, even recklessly, if she so desired. Without restraint, reservation, or apology.

No. Choosing not to come couldn't be the reason, either.

...Go to Little Mouth... Go to Little Mouth...

The phrase repeated, gaining strength and urgency, like cresting waves breaking against the rocky shore.

...Go to Little Mouth... Go to Little Mouth... Go to Little Mouth...

The incessant whisper peaked into a roaring command.

NOW!

As if struck, Sleek fell back on his haunches, eyes watering.

Gentle had always encouraged her son to heed the urging of his Aanandi-shade. "It is where the voice of Old Father Fathom rings loudest..." she claimed, "...and it will never lead you astray. So, listen and obey."

"Okay. I'm going." Sleek snatched his spear and slipped into The Blue, so determined to reach Little Mouth that he left the lingcod behind, untasted.

CHAPTER 43

A Plea In The Bubbles

"We know, dear..." Grandma's voice trailed off as she reached across the dinner table and patted Ayana's hand. "You're almost fourteen years old. We get that. You're not a child anymore, however, from now on, we want you to tell us when you're going to the beach," she said with a kindly smile.

"Before you go, if you please," Hayley interjected.

"But I left a note."

Grandpa dog-eared his page in the Sears catalog and closed it. "A note after the fact isn't enough, Ayana. And besides, what if something happened to you? What if you broke a leg? Or fell and cracked your head open? You could be swept out to sea and drown."

"Drowned?" Ayana scoffed. "Really?"

"Ayana Gail Outerbridge." Hayley leveled a firm eye at her daughter. "Don't talk back."

Grandpa scratched the spot behind Shep's ears that made his right-hind leg thump with pleasure. "The point is you don't need Grandma worrying like an old broody hen."

"Excuse me?" Grandma fixed her husband with a stern look. "*Old* hen?"

"Just a figure of speech, honey," Grandpa backtracked. "I'll shut up now."

"Good idea, Eugene." In the kitchen, the cooking timer chimed. "Saved by the bell," Grandma said. She rose from the table and shuffled off to fetch dinner.

The lima bean and lentil casserole, organic and wholesome, contained little to excite the taste buds. Hayley complimented her mother-in-law on the meal, mostly because she loved Martha and felt grateful for her, if not so much for the meal itself. And, there was always the added nicety of not having to cook.

Shep made his scrap-seeking rounds. Ayana sat picking at her food, wearing a pensive expression that Hayley felt had nothing to do with her own distaste for the dinner.

What's gotten her so turned inward? she thought. *And why is she bathing in the dark?* Hayley considered asking, then decided against it. The dinner table wasn't the proper place for such an interrogation. '*Patience,*' she heard Martha caution in her mind. '*You've all summer to coax out her pain. It's only been two days. Baby steps, Hayley. Healing by inches.*'

But then Ayana smiled, a tiny, odd quirk of her lips.

Hayley realized she'd reached the wrong conclusion. Her daughter was not so much pensive as ... enthralled.

Only the little smile she wore betrayed the tickling exhilaration Ayana felt as she nibbled at her healthy-yet-gross tasting food, secretly gripping the red-glass seashell under the table.

The pulsing rainbow starfish had returned with friends. A trio of silvery-veined sea-slugs, each the size of a cucumber, wiggled across the table towards the clay pot filled with steaming broccoli; a florescent blue sea-anemone crowned with a fluttering halo of orange and yellow tendrils grew beside Grandpa's diet soda; a cluster of electric-platinum tubeworms sprouted from the casserole dish like fleshy arrows; a brain-coral the color of bubblegum pulsated beside Hayley's dinner plate; and, scattered all around the room like hard-shelled snowflakes were dozens of mollusks and chitons, each unique with a kaleidoscope of patterns and colors. There was even one crawling in Grandma's hair!

Ayana watched with quiet amazement, taking the occasional bite of food to keep her family from getting suspicious. They continued to chat amongst themselves, but Ayana pushed the sound to the periphery of her consciousness. When a question did come her way, she still had enough presence to answer with a simple "yes" or "no", a shrug, or an "I dun'no, soon," when pressed about when she would visit her father's grave.

That seemed to keep everyone satisfied — everyone but Shep.

Drawn by the irresistible aroma of the seashell, the dog began licking Ayana's clenched fist, trying in vain to sneak a taste of the prize she held. The warm, wet tongue startled Ayana, and she nearly dropped the shell on the floor as her grip faltered, and the wondrous aquatic menagerie vanished.

That was close, Ayana thought and covertly stuck the shell back in her pants pocket.

Shep persisted, sniffing and nuzzling Ayana's pocket. "Get away. I'm eating," she said and nudged him back.

"Shep," Grandpa commanded. "Be a good boy.

Ayana offered the retriever a fat lima bean as compensation for his efforts. It was poor consolation compared to the magic flavor of the shell, but the old dog gobbled it up anyway.

After forcing down the last bites of casserole, Hayley excused herself from the table and carried her plate to the sink. She then went into the living room and opened the closet door beneath the stairway. The smells of old leather and aged polyester wafted from all the outerwear her in-laws had accrued over the decades, all crammed so tight she'd be hard-pressed to squeeze a pocket-handkerchief between them.

On the shelf above the overburdened rack, wedged among bags and parcels filled with trinkets and mementos, Hayley found the object of her search — an old shoebox with the word 'Polaroid' scrawled on it in red marker. She wiggled it free, but several other boxes fell along with it. They hit the floor with a muffled crash, spilling their contents of old Christmas lights, rubber-banded receipt bundles, and other bric-a-brac in a jumbled mess at her feet.

"Shit," Hayley muttered.

"Everything okay out there?" Grandpa called from the dining room.

"Yeah, sorry," Hayley answered. "Just knocked some boxes off the shelf getting the Polaroid." She bent to gather up the spilled articles. "I'll clean it up."

"I think there's still film in there," Grandpa added.

Hayley squeezed the clutter back into its proper place and closed the closet door. She pried opened the shoebox. Squeezed in with the one-step rainbow SX-70 Polaroid camera were two cartridges of unused color film.

"Nice." Hayley removed the brick-like camera and inspected it.

It appeared to be in working order. She pulled out a film cartridge and noticed an overturned photo stuck to the bottom of the box. She plucked it out and looked...

A snapshot. Five people looking directly at the camera, faces alight with happy smiles. Each wearing a red velvet stocking cap trimmed with faux white fur. Five people, three generations of the Outerbridge family, peering out at Hayley from the last Christmas when they'd all been together, hearts and souls filled with joy.

"Oh, God..." She covered her mouth to stifle a sob, vision blurring with tears.

That moment, that *perfect moment*, had happened five years ago when Jake's parents had come to their house for a rare holiday visit. Hayley remembered the tastes and smells of that Christmas dinner she and Jake had prepared together. She remembered the delight of exchanging presents, both great and small. The sounds of wrapping paper being ripped from boxes, the joyful squeals of their nine-year-old daughter.

The house was filled to bursting with love. And joy.

So much joy you could wrap yourself in it like a blanket.

Hayley stared at her late husband's face, at the tiny mole on his cheek, the sandy-blond hair, his loving blue eyes. She remembered his strong hands resting on her shoulders or squeezing her backside, or how the stubble on his chin tickled her cheek when he kissed it.

"I love you, Jake."

She kissed the photo and slipped it into the back pocket of her jeans. She intended to show it to Ayana. But not yet. For now, she wanted it, and those memories, to herself. Tonight, she'd set it beside the lamp. It would be there when she awoke. And when she needed light.

Sleep stubbornly refused to come. Hayley sat in bed, languidly flipping through an old *People* magazine from her in-laws' coffee table. She couldn't concentrate. Something blocked her focus, like blinders on a horse.

Instead of grinning celebrities on glossy paper, all she saw were inexplicable doodles, squiggles, and odd little curlicues etched on a sandy beach. Even the polaroid of smiling Jake beside the lamp couldn't bring the respite she wanted... or thought she wanted.

Admitting defeat, Hayley tossed the magazine aside. *Vapid trash rag,* she thought.

She slipped from the sheets, snatched a legal pad and pen from the antique desk beside the window, then bounced back onto the bed. She propped the old pillows behind her, rested the pad on her knees, and began to draw the enigmatic symbol she'd seen on the beach.

"You mean something, don't you?" Hayley asked the nascent scribbles appearing on the paper. If they answered, she didn't possess the ability to hear them. Not yet.

So, she kept drawing...

As she worked, she pondered at the sheer mystery of the squiggles. Neither random waves nor unthinking animal had rendered the image into the sand. That much she knew. And there was no room in her practical world for mermaids, sea nymphs, or water sprites. Something *real* did this.

She drew the image over, and over, and over again, getting to know each swirl, twist, and bend. She drew the shape big. She drew it small. She drew it in-between. With each successive attempt, Hayley's penmanship became more relaxed and fluid.

The hours ticked by, one lazy minute at a time. Hayley's wrist grew sore as she sketched, as did that subtle headache deep behind her eyes... like a grain of sand irritating her gray matter. By 1 AM, she'd filled both sides of a dozen pieces of paper with her efforts. But she just couldn't quite capture the image as it appeared in her mind. Each failed attempt compelled her to try again, regardless of how much her hand, or head, ached.

Hayley labored on for another hour, unsuccessful in recreating a perfect rendition of the strange and compelling image. Approximations, no matter how close, were still misses. Her eyelids finally revolted. She could keep them raised no longer.

Hayley laid pen and pad aside. Switching off the bedside lamp with the cherished Christmas Polaroid photo underneath it, she surrendered to slumber.

Hayley stands on the periphery of the beach. How did I get here? *she wonders.* Did I walk, or ride one of the horses? Why can't I remember?

The forest behind her appears out of focus, as if viewed through a Vaseline-smeared lens. Only the crescent beach and Pacific Ocean beyond are clear. Hayley moves towards the wave-kissed shore. Though she can feel the cold sand on the soles of her bare feet, it's as if she's floating rather than walking.

It builds in her — an urge to write the enigmatic calligraphy. She kneels, puts the fingers of her right hand to the wet, packed sand, and begins to draw. The alien pictograph takes shape within the grains that sparkle when disturbed, like diamond dust under the sun.

The radiant sand tickles, a tactile delight. She scrawls with both hands now and the familiar rigidity of her fingers, wrists, and arms softens and melts away. They twist and squirm like a cluster of ten agitated snakes.

This does not alarm Hayley. She realizes that her hands, as they once existed, are far too crude a tool to render the image accurately. The gracefulness of her strokes easily surpasses anything she could recreate in the waking world with her clumsy, bony digits.

Hayley finishes and steps back to admire her handiwork. Every loop, curl, and lopsided whorl is recreated with perfect clarity. The image glows, fire-bright, as if lit from below by an otherworldly spotlight. In a word, it is simply...

"Beautiful," *Hayley says, so proud of herself.* "Once more for good measure."

She puts her wet-noodle fingers back to the sand but a great, tumultuous disruption of seawater pulls her attention to a spot two hundred yards offshore. A torrent of bubbles — some the size of automobiles, others as big as a house or larger — swells into a white, effervescent hillock. They rise, jostle, divide, burst, and rise again.

Like God blowing bubbles through a straw into a glass of milk, *Hayley thinks. The absurd idea makes her smile.*

Hayley watches the frothing epicenter produce powerful waves that churn towards the shore, swell after swell, in a constant procession. They rise as

they near the beach, crash with roar, recede, and repeat. The spectacle is
fascinating.

Hayley feels no fear, just a compulsion to leave the glittering sand-callig-
raphy behind and walk to the water's edge. The waves sweep up to meet her,
but the water feels as solid and unyielding as Plexiglas. While she ponders
this oddity, a voice, like a wind carrying the dust of a long-perished prehistoric
world, emerges from the depths along with the bubbles.

"Find...me..." *it hisses. And booms.*

"Where are you?" *Hayley cries, her words drowned by the sea's din.* "I
can't see you!"

"Show me the way out..." *the drowned voice pleads,* "...before it's too
late."

"I will," *Hayley cried.* "I swear!"

She steps onto the glass-hard water to act on her promise...

— plip —

The dream burst, like one of the very bubbles within it.

Hayley opened her eyes on darkness. The digital alarm clock read
3:19AM.

She fumbled for the lamp, clicked it on and settled back onto the pillow.
Her eyes grew accustomed to the light, and then settled on the photo under
the lamp. But the smiles it conveyed offered little comfort.

Hayley sighed and rubbed her brow, wincing at the lingering headache
in her skull. She'd awakened just as the dream had gotten interesting. The
screen of her mental television had gone dark before the reveal of a vital

clue. The same compulsion Hayley experienced in the dream now forced her to sit up. Her fingers twitched with nervous energy. They wanted to keep drawing the sand-image, which really meant *she* wanted that, too. It was turning out to be the ultimate earworm ...or, rather, *brainworm*.

If only this stupid headache would clear! She'd definitely need to take some aspirin.

Hayley adjusted the covers around her legs. Still caught in the grip of her odd compulsion, she traced the squiggle-stanza with her index finger against the palm of her hand. The lines flowed effortlessly and like an electrical current through a wire, her anxiety dissipated.

That's better, Hayley thought, and kept tracing. The motion felt therapeutic. If only all stressors in her life could be removed with such easy efficiency.

Reaching for the yellow legal pad and pen on the nightstand, she instead found them scattered on the floor beside the bed. *How'd that happen?* she wondered.

Hayley retrieved her effects and set to work. Flipping past the earlier scribblings felt cathartic, as if she were trekking over familiar yet unfertile terrain towards lush pastures of promise and revelation on the next blank page.

And then...

Standing out, amongst all the other failed attempts, a *perfect* rendering of the sigil. Hayley gazed at the image, feeling lightheaded.

This is what I saw! But when did I draw it? Sometime during the night, obviously. But how could that be? I was asleep. Hayley wanted to touch the squiggle, to assure herself it was truly real on the page, but she also feared it might disappear if disturbed. *I have to know,* she thought, and brushed it lightly with her finger.

Rendered in black ink, the image remained stark and perfectly realized. Here lay a clue from beyond the realms of unconsciousness. But that also meant Hayley had drawn this perfect image in the dark while sound asleep!

Holy hell! Sleep-drawing! Who ever heard of such a thing? she wondered.

Hayley had, without a doubt, stumbled upon a mystery.

No, not stumbled — more like plunged, headlong, into the deep end of a pool. Or the sea.

This image had inexplicably linked itself to her, like a leech drawing nourishment, or, more accurately, a battery charging a radio. The bubble-dream confirmed it. Those scenes, and that benthic voice, did not belong to her subconscious.

Hayley sensed the urgency of that plea; the loneliness and longing saturating it, like the salt dissolved in seawater and indivisible from it. There was no fear in her, just a need to help.

Some part of her brain, or soul, or psyche had been challenged by that voice.

Hayley had never been one to shirk from a test. She was stubborn like that.

"I accept," she said to the flawless symbol. "And I will find you."

CHAPTER 44

A Nocturnal Rendezvous

"**M**other," Cries Often whimpered as he awoke in the darkness.

Once again, a terrifying nightmare had shattered his sleep like a sun-brittle clamshell.

Images of sharks, barracuda, and moray eels flashed behind his eyelids — a frenzy of glinting teeth rimming cavernous gullets flowing with spilt blood. Tonight, the ravenous dream-predators hadn't caught him, but sometimes they did, and the pain that would tear through him was no less for being imagined. Though Gloss' sisterly embrace could oftentimes calm him enough to tamp down his nocturnal fear, only the loving arms and sweet milk of his long-dead mother, Soothing, had ever possessed the power to banish them completely.

The young sea otter never ceased to mourn her loss. He hoped against hope that one day, Deshi-Oad would find compassion and return her to life, and back to him.

Cries Often rarely slept an entire night. Even after the splendor and release of Elihuul he struggled. While other adults slumbered on their backs, or pups on their mother's stomachs, all lashed securely in place with kelp strands, Cries Often floated, awake and fidgeting.

Although there had never been an attack inside Tangle Safe's borders within living memory, tonight's dream had planted an irrational worry in the young otter's mind. The density of the kelp and kholo forest effectively stymied any potential predator from entering. He had no logical reason to fear for his safety, nor did any Lutris, for that matter. But, as unlikely as it seemed, he still needed to see for himself.

Cries Often untied the nooree frond from his belly and tail and floated freely on the gentle ocean swells. Overhead, amidst sparse cloud cover, the Helquru night patterns twinkled their celestial hijna. Elihuul, full and resplendent, followed its predetermined course across The Above. All around Cries Often, a constellation of softly glowing ureolas bobbed in the darkness as The Raft enjoyed the restful slumber he longed to share.

The young otter rubbed his chronically irritated blind eye, fluffed his cheeks, and combed a fur patch over his left shoulder, then dove. A quick reconnoiter through the dense kelp would allay any lingering misgivings about a predator lurking somewhere below.

The Doyen's last surviving son maneuvered through the confusion of fronds, aided by the excellent night vision all members of his tribe enjoyed. Even with one good eye, Cries Often saw the forest swaying within gentle currents, its resident rock wrasse, halfmoons, lingcod, and other kelp-dwelling fish floating idly among the multitude of emerald stipes.

The Lutris broke through the thick living curtain and entered the obstruction-free central pool. Below, Gwelth, also known as *The Center of the Circle*, sat anchored to the seabed like a colossal urchin. Its impressive size filled Cries Often's field of vision as he arrowed towards the Lutris sanctum. He swam between the barnacle-encrusted timbers and whale rib bones jutting at crooked angles from its spheroid exterior. Sublime radiance from the central pryzoa chamber gushed between the slipshod junctions.

That's where Father is right now, Cries Often thought as he cavorted between shadow and light amidst his own bubbles. *I wish he didn't hate me so much. I wish he was my friend.*

But even simple-minded Cries Often realized certain things couldn't be changed by wishes alone.

He dove deeper, scattering shoals of darting fish picking at the algae carpets slicking Gwelth's exterior. Below, bigger fish and scavenging crabs gathered to nibble at the midden of discarded food scraps that ringed its kholo-buttressed foundation.

Cries Often came to the slow conclusion everything was as it should be. Nary a moray or aorxa to be found ...

Until a flash of amber light sped across his line of sight and vanished into the darkness.

Cries Often floated to a stop, sculling tail and limbs holding him in position. He knew that color denoted the rank of Loyc-Epsilon, and, therefore had to be the ureola of an unmated uja. But who? The female moved quickly, sticking to the most entwined portions of Tanglesafe so as not to be seen — just like a seasoned hunter would.

But Cries Often had seen. And seeing meant following.

Natural curiosity compelled him forward. He moved slowly, taking extra care to stay out of sight. Chasing and hiding were two of his favorite activities.

Oh, what a grand adventure this would be! So much fun to be had!

Why sleep when I can play? Cries Often thought and shadowed his quarry out to sea.

Every Lontra of hunting age knew the *exact* spot where the Lutris kingdom began.

The remains of a Penuree pier, long forgotten by its makers, marked the border. Its partially submerged wooden pillars — barnacle-encrusted and rotting in the brine — symbolized a specific peril.

Sleek approached the grisly mélange, taking in all its alarming details. Disarticulated ribs, vertebrae, and the bleached skulls of numerous Lontra and Irounga hunters adorned the timbers. Gaping shark jaws, hung by lengths of gleaned fishing line, were strung between the pillars themselves. Scattered everywhere, like giant conical dice, were the pulled teeth of slain killer whales. And the combined odors of blood and Lutris spraint, smeared on the wood as a further warning, would trigger The Scare in any trespasser, prompting them to stay away.

Dread and indecision made the young Lontra hesitate. But only for a moment.

I could skirt the Lutris' territorial waters to reach Little Mouth, but that'll mean half of Fourth Tide swimming my tail off, he thought. *And, without a graehl to watch my back, yurch... Or I could take this shortcut.*

It was a risky choice: if Sleek were caught, he could not plead ignorance. The warning ghaydn on the pier, and along the shore rocks, were displayed for all to see. Trespass invited death.

If the Lutris were inclined to mercy, a rarity, they'd dispatch him quickly upon their spears. If they felt extra nasty — a much likelier possibility than mercy — they would carve out his eyes, fill the sockets with squiq, gnaw off his tail, open his belly with a dull shark tooth and then pack it with urchin quills and spraint. All while he was still alive.

But *only* if they caught him.

Catching met chasing and chasing meant finding — and finding meant *seeing*.

I'll be a hole in The Blue, Sleek thought, now thankful he'd lost his ureola in the Winnow. Confidence swelled within him. *I'll be the invisible Lontra*.

Sleek tightened the grip on his ynth, took a steadying breath, and swam forward.

With pryzoa-heightened senses discerning every shadow and movement, the Beta crossed the gruesome barrier into enemy waters. He felt better about his decision once he'd committed himself. He hadn't seen, touched or smelled his kalaayaa since Ookl's Eye had last been fully opened so very many tides earlier.

Sleek missed Gloss with an ache no stolen pryzoa could balm. It gnawed his Aanandi-shade like the Osedax bone-eating worm that chews into the crumbling skeleton of a whale-fall.

During the times he and Gloss hunted together, since the fateful encounter with Ghuruhg so many seasons ago, their bond had only strengthened. Armed with her brother's spear, she harbored no fear. No hesitation. And absolutely no regrets.

Sleek admired her skills, which outpaced most males he knew. She made him strive to excel, to match her stroke-for-stroke. And how could it be otherwise? Gloss would never give her heart to someone she deemed inferior.

Together, they formed their own graehl-of-two.

Tonight, he'd show Gloss the depth of his devotion with the magical gift he'd squirreled away inside The Gnaarl — a prize fit for the daughter of the Lutris Doyen. The thought of Gloss' reaction when presented with the pryzoa that Sleek had risked mutilation and death to obtain, and then watching as her Kleaa sharpened to match his, filled the Saia with an almost fevered joy.

Sleek's swimming speed increased, heart racing with both exertion and anticipation. He couldn't wait to feel her passionate nibble-kisses upon his nose.

My kalaayaa, Sleek thought. *Mine. Forever.*

Truly, what he felt must be love. There could be no other word for it.

CHAPTER 45

SOME ASSEMBLY REQUIRED

The ancient television's glow warmed the den with nostalgic shadows. Black-and-white ghosts from long-dead past decades skittered over the couch, bookcase, and wall as a forgettable, late-night rerun from the Summer of Love flashed across the 24-inch screen encased in a faded yellow plastic shell.

Of the thirteen standard channels, only two chose to cooperate tonight. The remaining eleven offered nothing but a vacuum-tube generated blizzard of snow hissing across the screen at different speeds.

Ayana sat on a floral-print throw pillow at the base of the couch, her eyes fixed on, but not *seeing*, the television. She'd turned down the volume so as not to disturb her family's rest. Her ears heard the insipid jokes and ridiculous laugh-track of the show about a group of people shipwrecked on a tropical island. However, her brain did not process the sounds into anything meaningful. Images of mangy opossums and spear-wielding, telepathic otters filled her head.

After a futile attempt to fall asleep, she'd given up and made her way downstairs. She'd hoped a little mindless television would help organize her thoughts and put the day's events into focus. But, after sitting through two complete episodes of the improbable survival comedy, she was no closer to any concrete conclusions.

Ayana sighed with frustration. "Yurch," she muttered, the alien epithet falling from her lips as easily as if she'd learned it years ago, instead of yesterday. Her hopes for any clarity deflated like a pinpricked balloon.

She glanced over at Shep, who lay in his bed, seemingly half-asleep, yet his drooping eyes were fastened on her. She wondered if he could smell the magic shell secreted in her pajama pocket, even though it was sealed up in plastic.

Ayana fished out the bag and extracted the otherworldly prize. Its intoxicating odor tickled her nose, making her giddy with both hunger and joy. Shep's tail began wagging. With a gusty sigh, the retriever stood on sore joints and padded over to join her. She scratched his head and ears, eliciting a happy dog-smile. But his eyes remained fixed on the shell in her hand.

"Wanna sniff, boy?" Ayana asked and, closing her fist around it, held the shell up to the dog's nose.

Shep reacted in much the same way as he had during that day in the bathtub. Pelt bristling, whiskers as rigid as uncooked spaghetti, he smacked his tail like a jackhammer on the gray/green shag carpet as he furiously licked and nibbled her hand.

You really want to eat this, don't you? she thought, a little frown creasing her forehead.

"Okay. Stop." Ayana jerked away as the nibbling grew more forceful, worried that the old dog was about to sink his teeth deep into her flesh. "Jeez, Shep... Go back to bed."

The dog stared mournfully at her clenched fist.

"I said, go... back... to... bed." Ayana punctuated each word of the command with a jab of her forefinger towards the scruffy, hair-covered cushion.

With clear reluctance, Shep obeyed, tail drooping. As he plopped onto his doggy bed, he grunted with what sounded like bitter disappointment.

Ayana glanced down at her slobber-soaked hand. *Ugh, gross*! she thought.

She opened her fingers to reveal the shell, which, to her surprise, had escaped being slimed. Transferring it to her clean hand, she wiped the shell on her pajama top, just in case, then, with heart racing, raised it to her mouth and carefully scraped a fleck off the surface with her front teeth. No bigger than a grain of sugar, and yet, as she ground it into powder, it released all the tastes of a kingly banquet, the flavors cavorting across her tongue, raising gooseflesh on her body.

She swallowed... and her stomach crawled into her throat as if she'd been launched over a rollercoaster drop into freefall. As bright dots like distant stars stretched sensorial threads through her brain, her remaining senses expanded at lightspeed to fill the entire house.

She felt Grandpa's rattling snore like he was sleeping next to her on the couch, instead of upstairs behind a closed door. The creaks and groans of an old house settling around her sounded like pistol shots. Motes of dust lit by the television floated with the clarity of driftwood timbers in a clear pool. The not-unpleasant odor of recently bathed elderly canine — a musky mix of flowers and corn chips — flooded her nostrils.

Accepting of this delicious quickening, her eyes briefly fluttered closed, then opened.

"Oh, shit," she whispered.

Dozens, perhaps hundreds, of translucent-shelled invertebrates, pulsing in a rainbow of electric colors, now festooned every piece of furniture. Clinging to ceiling, floor, and walls, some crawled, others scuttled, while some remained rooted in place. Many had tiny, fixed shapes of multi-hued fire flickering above them — delicate coils, and curls of frozen flame.

Ayana grinned at the riotous ecosystem filling the living room. That it was most certainly an illusion did not concern her. She felt submerged inside a giant tide pool briming with living Christmas lights.

Some*thing* — an undefinable force — caused her to rise and walk towards the kitchen. Shep left his bed and followed at her heels. Even with all the lights off in the house, the sparkling shellfish produced enough radiance for Ayana to see by.

Entering the kitchen, she saw the magical mollusks had covered every surface, from stovetop to refrigerator to cupboard. But the greatest concentration was clustered on the back patio door.

Ayana sensed this accumulation as less of a random act and more of a subtle beckoning to her...

Open the door. Follow us. Come and see! Open the door...
And so, she did.

Ayana pushed the door open. She perceived a flood of brilliant, multi-colored light spilling into the kitchen, dancing over her body and glinting across her retinas.

She gasped, nearly choking with shock...

Stretching from the back steps towards the three-acre field, easily ten times the number of mollusks that had materialized in the house now formed a clearly defined path, a living Yellow Brick — no, a *Rainbow Brick* — Road, urging Ayana to journey towards some benthic Oz.

She took an excited breath. Quietly closing the door behind her so Shep couldn't follow, she descended the steps, striding barefoot over wet grass that soaked the hems of her pajama bottoms. She didn't feel the damp or the cold. The fantastical visions her bronze-flecked eyes beheld crowded out all sensations of bodily discomfort.

Diverse and colorful as flowers in any terrestrial garden, the residents of the magical biome ranged from simple starfishes and bivalves to castle-like corals branching into beautiful asymmetries. Sponges bulged like alien organs. Anemones and tubeworms the hue of precious metals pulsed while feeding. Sea lilies coiled and unspooled lacy tendril limbs, while sea fans fluttered in delicate, fractal glory — and all this life blazed with a breathtaking complexity of competing bioluminescence.

In the air above the glowing pageant, specks of plankton floated like energized fireflies, their anatomies fantastically primordial and beautifully translucent. Many darted to and fro. Others crept about as if swimming in thick syrup, ribbons of frail cilia vibrating them along.

Too much. Ayana squeezed her eyes closed. *It's too much. Too fast!*

She tapped her glue drops in distress. So much life, moving in so many competing directions made her dizzy. She fought to keep balanced as the world wobbled under her feet, threatening to topple her completely. But she dared not stop. Something tugged at her heart as well as the pit of her stomach, goading her on, daring her to take another step, conquer another yard.

All she had to do was reach the fence. Then she could stop.

"Make the fence," Ayana demanded of herself. *Make. The. Fence!*

Things got easier after thirty-or-so steps. Equilibrium returned as Ayana remembered that the power over all this illusory mayhem rested in the palm of her hand. Literally.

The harder she squeezed the red-glass shell, the more pronounced the secondary world became. When she relaxed her grip, its clarity grew fuzzy and began to fade. She decided she didn't like that. Ayana wanted to see it all, even if she got so dizzy, she puked.

Somehow, she kept the nausea at bay, and soon the fence enclosing the field came into view. Beyond the slats, the luminous trail narrowed, its edges becoming more distinct. Ten paces in, the diffuse invertebrate path condensed to the width of the second-floor hallway carpet runner. Ten more beyond that, all gaps between organisms vanished. Pressed so tightly together, one animal crawling atop the other, the track looked like a rope made of pure sunshine. It wound across the field towards the distant apple tree, the air above it aglow with a storm of shimmering zooplankton swirling like a blizzard of fiery snowflakes.

Ayana had wanted only to reach the fence. But now, as she peered past it, she felt compelled to cross.

This end point had become a starting point.

The almost fourteen-year-old slipped between the wooden slats and followed the illusory cable of light. Droves of chitinous life reacted to her footsteps, scattering if they could, withdrawing into their shells if they could not. Ayana stepped through this neon magic, but she felt nothing of it, only the cold grass on the soles of her feet. So captivated by the scene, she did not see the horse-patties dotting the field like fetid landmines... until she stepped in one.

She yelped as the ice-cold filth squished between her toes. Ayana groaned and wiped her soiled foot in the grass to clean it. An understandable reaction to stepping in shit would be to curse the universe. But now, within the grand scope of her personal miracle, a random horse-patty was just too trivial to bother for such a forceful response.

Ayana pressed on, undeterred, towards her goal.

The apple tree.

Ayana gazed up at it, mesmerized.

Each branch, bedecked with bulbous sea creatures hanging like living, fire-filled ornaments, defied rationality. Woven throughout the branches, strings of translucent amoebic lights pulsed and wiggled.

Even if she'd wanted to, Ayana couldn't look away. Every glance revealed a new detail. Her eyes darted from one unearthly sight to the next, and with each fresh discovery the smile she wore grew.

Am I going nuts? she wondered. *Is this what crazy feels like?*

Her gaze drifted down the trunk, now scabbed with radiant algae and ragged-edged, prismatic corals. At the base a starfish, the diameter of a truck tire and rimmed with a hundred squirming limbs, rested on her father's grave marker — as if guarding this hallowed resting spot from the outside world. A curlicue of flame hovered above the creature like an ornate halo.

Ayana went to her knees beside the memorial and, laying her hand on the chilly bronze, she read the partially visible inscription through the semi-transparent sea star. The words drew stinging tears to her eyes.

"Jacob Henry Outerbridge..."

Seeing the marker, feeling its cold solidity against her fingers nearly pushed her mind back towards reality, but the shell kept her partially tethered to illusion.

"Beloved son... husband... *father*..."

Things are born, things live... and things die.

Ayana grasped that much. Her soul understood the frailty of existence. It was something no poem or sad pop-song could every truly capture. But *feeling* it — and accepting the finality of what the grave marker represented — might be beyond the ability of a broken-hearted child.

"...rest in power..."

The bronze plaque beneath her hand was a tangible monument to death, but all around her swirled a private celebration of illusory life. She sensed it, tucked somewhere in the interstices, a new truth awaited discovery. The only question Ayana needed to answer: was she ready to give up the old truths to which she'd clung for nearly fourteen years?

The starfish slowly turned clockwise in place, plinking like a neon sign. At the center of its transparent body, a whirlpool of light and color agitated the air, like a heat-ripple on asphalt. This counterclockwise vortex tugged at Ayana's mind, hinting at something, igniting a compulsion to do... what?

Touch it and see. You must TOUCH IT!

Ayana plunged her hand clenching the red-glass seashell into the radiant whirlpool. Her fist thudded against the metal grave marker beneath, bruising her knuckles, but she hardly felt it. Her focus had contracted to the convulsing starfish before her, its suction-studded arms now folding inward like a closing flower.

"Give him back," she demanded to whatever power might be listening.

Death never returned what it took, at least not outside fairy tales and holy books. But the shell had created, and immersed her, in a fairy tale reality... hadn't it?

She squeezed the shell tighter and pressed her fist harder against the memorial. "Back! I want him back!" she growled.

The starfish had completely enveloped Ayana's right forearm, covering it past her nineteen vitiligo spots, its multiple limbs now adhered to her skin. The light it produced — indeed, all the light dangling in the tree and the path winding towards it — began to increase, waxing brighter and brighter, pulsing towards phosphorescent incandescence.

And then Ayana felt it...

Another hand took hold of her!

It gently squeezed, as if greeting an old friend. Ayana's heart skipped a beat. She pulled, trying to extract her arm from the sea star. But it felt trapped in liquid tar and barely moved.

Pull, her mind demanded. *Pull, damn it! Pull and pull and puuuuuuull!*

Ayana got to her feet, and with the help of her back and legs, used all the strength she could muster. Slowly, millimeter by millimeter, the sea star began to relinquish its hold. As it did, all the luminous life hanging in the tree branches migrated down the trunk, as if the act of Ayana removing her arm dragged the lights along with it, like pulling a blanket through a pipe. At the same time, the sunshine-cable of fiery creatures stretching through the pasture began rolling itself up towards the tree. Blazing, hyper-energized zooplankton swirled about Ayana like a living maelstrom, colliding against her clothes and hair.

Ayana — and the act of her pulling — had become the center of this illusory universe.

Her battle with the starfish was just as emotional as it was physical. The hot peach-pit of anger in her soul provided her with fuel instead of pain. She would not relent. Whatever this was, whatever secret revelation it sought to keep from her, she would persevere and pry it forth.

As if in response to her determination, the hand on the other side of the vortex strengthened its grip. Ayana kept pulling. Her arms and legs ached from the strain. Her right shoulder and elbow felt like they would pop out of their sockets.

With a soft pop, Ayana's arm and hand emerged from the luminous whirlpool — and she saw that another hand had clasped around hers. Rudimentary, three-fingered, it was comprised of pure light! A slender wrist, then a forearm, and then a bicep followed.

Ayana continued to pull, and as more of the arm appeared, the light from the apple tree and pasture funneled into it, as if coalescing to form the radiant limb she now grasped. The entity continued to emerge, like a newborn from the womb — shoulder, head, torso, other arm, legs...

With a final cry and burst of strength, Ayana freed the being from the sea star. It spilled onto the wet grass, slick with neon amniotic fluid.

And with its arrival, it absorbed all the light from the magical ecosystem into itself.

The three-acre field went dark.

All the light it held was now consolidated in the vaguely human-shaped *thing* lying prone at Ayana's feet. It appeared as little more than a radiant lump of clay, with two underdeveloped arms and legs, and an indistinct mass where a head should be.

For several moments, it lay unmoving, then began to stir and stretch its limbs. It made a sound, like a sighing parent being disturbed from a much-needed nap. Slowly, deliberately, it pushed itself onto wobbly knees, then with significant effort, finally stood upright.

Ayana gazed with wonder at this being that barely reached her sternum. A subtle tilt of its featureless head told Ayana that it returned her gaze... and that she was being scrutinized.

It nodded.

And began to evolve.

Brighter it became. Taller it grew, soon surpassing Hayley's height and rivaling that of Grandpa. Its edges and contours refined and clarified in a matter of seconds. It was like watching a video played at six times normal speed.

Ayana clutched her magic seashell, wanting to *tap-tap* her glue drops, but her hands refused to obey. She could not move, and her lungs resisted the urge to breathe.

The light faded as the being attained its final shape.

And there, standing before Ayana, was... her father, Jake, wearing the same clothes and hat he had on the day of his death. Smiling the same mischievous smile suggesting a perpetual desire to have fun and engage in good trouble.

Ayana knew he was dead, and, yet, somehow, *not*.

He was also no longer peripheral, a ghostly presence lurking at the edges of her vision. He stood before her, front and center, solid. And when he spoke, it was his own voice. The same one Ayana recalled now only in her dreams.

"Hello, Pipsqueak."

The world cartwheeled under Ayana's feet, the ground and sky exchanging places.

White stars flicked across her field of fading vision. Her face went numb, and her lips felt rigid like cold stone.

"...Papa?"

Ayana was unconscious before she hit the wet grass.

And when she landed the magic seashell spilled from her hand...

CHAPTER 46

Xaad!

G loss' gaze swept the darkness, her mind as cold and focused as the
waters she swam.

She held Grabber's barbed spear loose, yet ready. Piercing her lower
lip: one of two identical turritella shell alcqs she shared with Sleek. She
only wore the labret while hunting with her beloved. But tomorrow, by
her father's decree, she must relinquish the ynth before the entire Raft in
exchange for the life of her brother. She would never be allowed to hunt
again. And her alcq would be little more than a token from a once precious,
but now dead, life.

If she could only possess this cherished heirloom for one more night, then, by Deshi-Oad's Stone Teeth, she'd spend that night hunting.

The Doyen's demand constituted blatant blackmail. *So be it,* Gloss thought. *I'll make Father, and every male in the Raft, choke on my hunting skill.*

If Fearless wanted to use public shame to quell his daughter's rebellious spirit, then Gloss would make sure that disgrace cut both ways. Presenting the lance embedded in the carcass of a great prize fish — a trophy few males had the skill to dispatch alone — would send just the right message.

All it took was courage, and the will to act. Tonight, she had ample amounts of both.

The thought of spoiling her father's plan for her public humiliation spurred Gloss to swim faster. Now she just needed a suitable prize, and she knew exactly where to find one.

Little Mouth...

Less than ten tails across — hence its name — the estuary's nutrient-rich blend of salt and fresh water hosted a wide variety of game. *And with the recent storm there'll be plenty of larger quarry,* Gloss thought.

Besides the abundance of prey-fish, Little Mouth estuary was important to Gloss in another way; she and Sleek had discovered it during the last, and as it turned out, final joint shraga harvest.

There, they'd recognized themselves as equals.

They'd shared pain and blood and the first of so many kisses.

There, they'd confessed their undying love to each other.

The memory of that sweet, innocent time warmed Gloss' blood and sped her heart.

Since then, she and Sleek seldom came to Little Mouth, and only to spend time together and share affection — *never* to hunt or spill blood in its pristine waters. Killing anything there would spoil its purity. The estuary existed both as physical refuge and emotional symbol of the love they shared but could never display openly.

Tonight, all sentimentality had to be put aside. Ethics, and more importantly, personal honor, were at stake.

Sleek would have to understand. *But he'll never know. It'll be my secret.*

Gloss knew she'd entered the estuary by the change in salinity. Acoustics and buoyancy felt different. Sounds were fractionally muted and a stronger, sinking gravity took hold. In a way, crossing into the estuary felt like entering a vaguely alien world.

Gloss had come to associate this disorientation with romance. Her senses may have been askew, but the tickle it produced within her Aanandi-shade bolstered the love she held for Sleek.

Many Lutris, Fearless included, believed the Lontra's Monoic ancestors invaded The Blue via this estuary, bringing with them a predisposition for thievery and corruption. With the souring of Lontra-Lutris relations after That Scathing Tide, The Doyen even declared the area aijeer. No sea otter could hunt in, or even swim through, Little Mouth's outflow lest they pollute The Raft with whatever debasing essences had warped the Lontra.

Gloss obeyed the decree, only insofar as to keep the estuary emotionally pure. She would never endorse her father's irrational edict. The notion of Little Mouth's waters being corrupted was, to her mind, irrational nonsense.

Gloss inhaled, and with a strong swish of her graceful tail, forsook the calm surface for the mid-water column twenty tails below. There *nyoota,* the prized "silver mouth" or king salmon, gathered in skittish shoals hunting smaller fish and invertebrates among the nooree beds and seagrass carpets of Little Mouth's freshwater dilution.

These salmon were in their streamlined ocean-phase, most now larger and heavier than the young huntress. The time of their river spawn — when they underwent radical physical changes as they transitioned to a freshwater environment and became *gnyootu*, the "hooked mouth" — was still many months in the future.

Gloss stopped swimming, removed her ureola and concealed it within an underarm pouch, then tucked her limbs and tail close to her body — thus minimizing her profile. The wary salmon, whose sense of smell was so acute that each fish could identify its hatch-river by odor alone, had already marked her scent and were moving away.

Since she couldn't hide from their keen noses, she'd hide from their poor eyes.

Gloss floated amongst the lush kelp and let the currents carry her. Certain shapes, like predatory fish or quadrupeds, and sudden movements triggered the flight response of the instinctually skittish salmon. Of paramount importance, Gloss must appear as *anything* other than an animal. Fearless had taught Grabber this trick, who then trained his sister in secret; and Gloss, in turn, taught the technique to Sleek.

To dimwitted nyoota, the sea otter huntress looked no more threatening than a piece of driftwood, a tangle of kelp, or any other bit of nameless flotsam. As Gloss floated towards the prey, she braced the base of the ynth shaft against her tail and willed her heartbeat to slow.

It was important to pick the ideal time and place of her strike.

So, she waited...

The salmon school glided by in an undulating, quicksilver mass, so close to Gloss that their displaced water tickled her whiskers. An especially large nyoota floated past, believing itself safe and secure within the shoal, its attentions on food rather than peril.

This is the one, Gloss thought. She opened a single eye, took aim at the 'sweet spot', that place behind its gill slit. *Wait for it, wait for it...*

...wait...

...waaaaait...

Now!

Taut muscles exploded into action. Gloss' body spun, limbs whirling.

Like an atlatl, the tip of her lashing tail propelled the spear unerringly towards the quarry.

Startled nyoota scattered in a hundred different directions, but Gloss's target, though quick, could not escape her keratin lance. It pierced the sweet spot — a deft, killing strike.

"Got you!" Gloss hijna-cried. Her heart swelled with the visceral thrill every hunter feels when dispatching an esteemed prey.

The mortally wounded nyoota shot away, leaving a ribbon of its hot blood in the chilled sea. Every swish of its tail drove the serrated barb deeper into its scaly body. It corkscrewed through the verdant nooree groves, fleeing into deeper water.

Soon, its frenetic flight began to slow as it bled out. Gloss closed in, reached for the protruding spear shaft, and prepared to deliver the *coup de grâce.*

Without warning, a shape swooped out of the darkness, snatched both ynth and the fish impaled upon it, and swam off. Gloss recoiled and barked in surprise, exhaled bubbles rising.

"Ha, ha! I found you!" the familiar hijna-voice taunted, followed by a playful laugh.

"Cries Often!" Gloss hollered, equal parts anger and relief coloring her hijna. *He followed me from Tanglesafe without being seen*, she thought. Though annoyed, she couldn't help but also be impressed. *Maybe he has what it takes to be a hunter, after all?*

"Find me, Gloss!" Cries Often challenged as kelp and saline darkness swallowed the gleam of his Beta-blue ureola.

Gloss had no desire to play. She only wanted to reclaim her prize, revel a while in the narrow focus of her Hunter's Eye, then return to The Raft. But Cries Often's levity proved infectious. Hadn't Gloss succeeded in her quest by slaying the nyoota on this, the last night she would ever carry Grabber's spear?

So why not have some fun? she thought. "Come back here, you troublemaker," she hijna-shouted. Slipping the ureola back on her wrist, Gloss gave chase.

Brother and sister glided through the seaweed forest, agile and carefree as pups, though the nyoota carcass slowed Cries Often considerably. A stream of blood leaked from the punctured salmon, flavoring the night water with its predator-summoning salts.

Gloss caught her brother, but instead of retaking the ynth, she tickled his lame hind paw, inciting peals of laughter. Cries Often dove towards the rocky seabed and ducked behind an anemone and starfish-encrusted boulder, his giggles rising like bubbles.

Gloss made a show of snooping about the seafloor, knowing exactly where Cries Often hid, but pretending not to see him. "I know you're around here somewhere," she said while checking every rock and niche except the one that concealed. "I'll tickle you when I catch you!" she promised. "And I'll never stop."

Cries Often peeked out from among the tendrilled-crowned anemones, stifling a giggle in his furry throat. He couldn't be happier playing hide-and-seek with his younger sister. The thrill of being stalked, yet seldom found, delighted his Aanandi-shade.

"There you are." Gloss smiled and reached for him...

A serpentine shape slashed through the night Oorum like a bolt of turquoise lightning. As the massive fish barreled past the Lutris siblings its forked yellow tail painfully smacked Gloss' outstretched paw.

Xaad! her mind screamed. *It's Xaaaaaad!*

Gloss spun in the predator's violent wake. Righting herself, she instinctually kicked away, the Scare rising in her thudding heart.

Drawn to the nyoota's blood by ravenous hunger, the monstrous barracuda had come to slay. Nothing more, nothing less. Just death, the thing it loved best.

Xaad's fearsome countenance — flat, bronze-flecked eyes filled with malevolence; powerful, oversized jaws bristling with dagger-like teeth — filled Gloss with cold terror. Sinewy body gleaming in the aquatic half-light, the baleful fish looked even larger than she remembered; it stretched almost six tails in length. Unlike old Grumpy Mouth who only attacked when molested, this fiend delighted in malice and the infliction of pain.

"Bite-you-dead," Xaad declared with halting, barely intelligible hijna. It circled the two Lutris, drawing ever closer and spitting, "Dead-dead-dead", like a poisonous mantra.

Cries Often, blinking his half-blind eyes, tried to find the danger, and failed.

"Gloss!" he cried. "What is it? What's wrong?"

But before Gloss could answer, the barracuda had already changed course. With a flick of its brawny tail, it hurtled straight towards the crippled Beta.

Cries Often finally sighted the monster fish and froze in fear. "G-Gloss..."

Gloss grabbed her brother's paw and yanked, trying to snatch him from harm's way. But Xaad was already upon them, its vicious jaws opened wide to expose a hideous gullet slashed with pulsating gill slits.

"...help," Cries Often whispered as the fanged mouth clamped down... On Grabber's ynth.

Cries Often gazed into the barracuda's pitiless eyes. The terrible head thrashed, scalpel-sharp teeth rasping against the lance. Only that slender shaft of calcified baleen separated the young Lutris from a messy, agonizing death.

Cries Often shrieked as The Scare awoke and tore through him like a howling wind. He tried to release the ynth and flee, but his paws refused to obey, locked in fear-induced paralysis. All he could do was hold on as the devilfish flung him from side to side.

"Brother!" Gloss screamed, desperate to intervene but not knowing how.

The murderous barracuda shook its head one final time. Unable to break the spear, it settled for dragging the hapless otter, along with the ynth and the dead nyoota impaled upon it, into the depths.

Gloss gave chase. Images of her brother torn to bloody shreds filled her with cold horror. *I can't lose him like I lost Grabber*, she thought.

Xaad hauled his Lutris prey thirty tails before letting go. Cries Often finally released the spear. It and the salmon dropped to the seabed, forgotten. The Saia broke for the surface with frantic kicks, trailing clots of spraint from fear-spasmed bowels as the barracuda circled around for a better angle of attack, its horrid maw grinding.

Tangy nyoota blood enflamed Xaad's malice and hunger. "Bite you-tear you-eat you," it growled, relishing the thought of reducing an otter into bloody shreds. The sheer pleasure and anticipation hastened its swishing tailfin.

Cries Often's nightmare had come true. Half blind and heedless, he swam directly into a tangled seaweed thicket. The rubbery fronds snared him like a vengeful octopus. Cries Often pulled and pulled but the fronds only tightened around him. Air slipped from his lungs as his heart thundered near to bursting.

Gloss put on a burst of speed to reach her brother's side. She caught his tail. He convulsed and screamed in fright. "It's me!" she cried. "It's Gloss!"

"Xaad!" Cries Often shrieked, striking wildly at the kelp. "Save me, sister!"

Gloss seized a flailing limb and pulled her brother close. He clutched her with surprising strength. She had only a few heartbeats to free him before the barracuda returned...

Gloss tugged the acuur from her ureola and slashed at the stipes imprisoning her brother.

The razor-sharp blade made short work of the fronds. As they fell away, she pulled Cries Often clear. He threw his arms around her neck, shaking like a wounded pup.

"D-d-don't let it bite me, Gloss. No, no, don't... let... it..."

Gloss tried to offer comforting words. She could think of none.

How quickly her euphoria moldered into desperation. Grabber's ynth, the only thing that might save them, had fallen out of reach. It would take mere seconds to retrieve.

Those seconds might as well have been full tides-cycles.

She'd never make it back in time.

Xaad completed its wide arc through the water and now hung motionless, staring at its prey with wicked intent. Its fangs glinted like icicles in the dark.

As Gloss watched, mere heartbeats away from certain death, the memory of encountering Ghuruhg flashed in her mind. Instead of terror at the coming attack, she seethed with anger that she and Cries Often would die before either could prove they were capable of more than what their myopic society dictated.

But then, her anger gave way to regret. She now felt grief-stricken... and vulnerable.

She'd never see her dearest Sleek again. He would never learn of her fate. Perhaps, this was her just punishment for the offense of hunting in Little Mouth.

And my Kalaayaa will go on, Gloss thought. *He'll find another mate and have a life filled with adventure and fulfillment...and our love will be a distant memory.*

Of all the agonies to come, both real and imagined, that possibility hurt Gloss most of all.

"Bite-you-dead," Xaad hissed, every inch of its body conveying menace.

With the pump of powerful tail muscles, the grotesque barracuda hurtled at the two helpless Lutris. Overly muscled jaws opened and clamped like massive scissors in anticipation of the delicious agony to come.

"Oh, nooooo..." Cries Often moaned, turning to dead weight in the arms of his sister.

Gloss put a gentle paw over his eyes. "I love you." She squeezed her eyes shut and nibble-kissed Cries Often's cheek. "Don't look, dearest. Don't look."

Brother and sister held each other tight, and awaited death.

CHAPTER 47

THE DEEPEST CUT

"Ya-aaargh!"

The fierce hijna-cry startled Gloss out of her torpor. Her eyes flew open as a streamlined shape, sheathed in a warrior's shuuhl, arrowed out of the darkness to interpose itself between hunter and prey.

"Sleek!" Gloss' heart leapt with relief.

The Beta jabbed at the oncoming barracuda with his spear. With a flick of its tail, the monster fish veered off, narrowly avoiding the flattened barb poised to skewer it through the mouth into its brainpan.

"Leave, filth!" Sleek yelled, violently brandishing his weapon. "Begone!"

Xaad's sapience might be a mere trickle, but it recognized overwhelming odds. Two unarmed Lutris it could handle, but not while an angry, spear toting Lontra warrior interfered. Its hijna roiling with barely intelligible profanity, the rapacious beast arced away in a sinuous loop and, with a burst of unmatchable speed, vanished into the Oorum.

Sleek lowered his ynth. "I don't think Xaad's coming back...*oopf!*"

Gloss flung her arms around Sleek's neck and planted a flurry of kisses on his handsome snout. "Kalaayaa," she purred.

Sleek's heartbeat quickened. All the tension and doubt of the last few days vanished. He'd dared to listen to that still, small voice and chanced crossing into Lutris territory; now, the rewards would be his. Sleek's Aanandi-shade sparkled like a sun-kissed tide pool. "Are you okay?" he asked the sea otter siblings. "Are you hurt?"

Gloss nodded, rueful. "Just my pride."

"How about you, Cries Often? Not missing any pieces?"

"I still have my pieces." Cries Often's hijna sounded shaky. He checked his arms, legs, and tail. "Wait...no... yup. Thanks."

Sleek glanced at Gloss' empty paws. "Where's your ynth?"

"I know! I know where it is!" Cries Often replied. "I'll get it." With an exuberant somersault he dove towards the sandy bottom.

Sleek and Gloss, paw-in-paw, kicked for the surface for a much-needed breath. Floating on gentle waves, the reunited kalaayaa's embraced, their hearts bursting with joy. Whiskers intertwined as they nibble-kissed, their tails rubbing and tangling affectionately. Above, the stars watched the young couple like silent, celestial chaperones, their twinkling light a sign they approved of the love they witnessed.

"I couldn't stand being away from you," Sleek confessed. "I couldn't stop thinking about you. I thought this night would never come."

Gloss nuzzled Sleek's cheek, nibbled his ear. "But how did you know I'd be here?"

"I waited at the Oyster Shell as usual but when you didn't arrive, I listened to my Aanandi-shade. It guided me here."

"I'm glad you listened. If you hadn't..." Gloss shivered. "It doesn't matter. You came, you saved my brother, and me. Again."

"I should swim into The Raft right now and declare my love for you. Take my chances."

"You'd get a dozen spears in the belly," Gloss reminded him.

"But I'd gladly risk it. That's how much you mean to me."

Gloss stroked Sleek's whiskers. "That's the sweetest thing anyone's ever said to me."

The young lovers nibble-kissed again, but Gloss was the first to push away. Her nose twitched at the telltale scent. "You... ate a pryzoa." Her eyes bored into Sleek's. Her tone, while not accusatory, held touches of disapproval but also admiration. "How...?"

Before Sleek could answer, Cries Often broke the surface. Giggling, he hoisted the lance above the water, the dead salmon still impaled on the tip. "Hey, look! Gloss slew this nyoota. Here in Little Mouth. Isn't it big and pretty?"

Sleek frowned at seeing the skewered fish. He turned to Gloss, confused. "Yes. Very."

Not to be deflected, Gloss gripped Sleek's shoulders. "How did you come by a pryzoa?" Her eyes grew wide. "You...you didn't..."

"I did."

"Deshi-Oad's Fluke! The Garden is aijeer. Vile Chaac'Xib could've killed..."

"It didn't." Sleek kissed Gloss' paw and pulled her close. "I'm too clever and too quick. I got in, took what I wanted and got out before The Voracious could untangle its legs." Sleek disliked lying to his kalaayaa, but the entire truth would upset her too much.

Besides, it was a *half*-lie. Half was truth, and that part was all that mattered now.

Gloss slid her paw from Sleek's, took the calcified baleen shaft from her brother and, with a quick tug, yanked the tip from the nyoota carcass. "We need to talk, but not here. There's too much blood in the water. Let's go ashore. Bring the nyoota, Cries Often."

"Sure thing," her brother enthusiastically replied. "Sure, sure."

The three otters swam for the shore, Cries Often dutifully lugging the dead nyoota by the tail. The growing pink sliver of dawn softened the edges of the night horizon.

Only the gurgle of Little Mouth emptying into The Blue disturbed the silence. The trio reached the rocky inlet and slipped out of the estuarial water. A blanket of coastal fog smothered the looming Still, its evergreen topography wrapped in a nocturnal hush. It smelt of pine sap and a thick understory of ferns and berry brambles.

Gloss helped her brother drag the fat, silvery salmon onto a flat, algae-slicked stone. Sleek offered assistance but she waved him away. "We've got this, thank you."

He winced at the snap in her hijna. "You're angry with me, aren't you?"

"Why should I be angry? You only risked death to prove how quick and clever you are."

I risked death to bring back a gift for you, Sleek thought. Gloss' unyielding tone kindled his own anger. He glanced at the dead salmon, its silvered eye fixed and sightless. Sleek looked at Gloss crouched over her kill, her brother's lance by her side. *Her kill...*

The realization drove all thoughts of what he'd done in Liminal away. "Kalaayaa? You were hunting here in Little Mouth. Why?"

"Sleek, I..." Gloss began, but Sleek refused to let her interrupt his self-righteous tirade.

"This is our secret spot, *ours,* the only place in all The Blue where we can come to be alone. We're supposed to hunt *anywhere else* but here. To preserve its purity. It was *your* idea."

"Sleek..."

"You took prey here. That's what brought Xaad. And it nearly killed you both."

"Sleek, *stop!*" Gloss barked aloud and stood upright in full challenge posture, her golden eyes blazing. "Be *quiet* and let me explain!"

Shocked into silence by her fierce command, Sleek rocked back onto his haunches. He took several deep breaths to calm himself and nodded. Gloss *did* deserve a chance to explain — as a hunter, a peer, and his love. "I'm listening."

Gloss' anger ebbed. Sleek only pointed out what she already knew deep in her Aanandi-shade; in the rush to prove her worth, she'd broken the one rule that truly mattered most. Her aggressive posture softened.

"I'm sorry, kalaayaa." Gloss let out a heartfelt sigh. "You're right. We made a promise, and I went back on it. But things have changed." She held out her ynth as if it were a corpse of a loved one. "Father is forcing me to give up my spear. Tomorrow. In front of the entire Raft."

Sleek recoiled in dismay. Of all the things she could've said, *this* was entirely unexpected. "Grabber gave it to you before he vanished. You can't just give it up."

"My father is Doyen. He can make me do whatever he wants," Gloss replied with a bitter snort. "And what he wants most is to make me a *proper* uja. 'And uja don't carry spears'," she added, mocking her father's authoritative hijna. "We're never allowed to cast the Hunter's Eye."

"Ookl's Ink," Sleek murmured, heartsick.

"Oops, oops. You said the 'O' word." Cries Often bit the tip of his tail to ward off bad luck. "Father'll be angry. He forbids us to ever speak that name. It's hee-ret-i-cal."

"Your father doesn't rule me," Sleek growled. "I'm Lontra."

Cries Often flinched as if struck. He whimpered, eyes filling with tears.

Sleek regretted his harsh tone. He never wanted to distress Gloss' simple brother. "I'm sorry." He gave the young Lutris a friendly, reassuring pat on the shoulder and turned to Gloss. "What're you going to do?" he asked, careful to keep his hijna neutral.

"What I must. I'll give up the ynth. But I'll also give my father the nyoota I took with it. He may have the authority to stop me from hunting, but he won't be able to deny that I'm the equal of *any* uju." Gloss proudly stabbed the spear back into the salmon's belly. It wobbled in the fresh wound.

Sleek took Gloss' paw in his. "You are *my* equal. In every way." Their golden eyes locked, noses almost touching. "And I'm sorry I scolded you without waiting for you to explain first." He nibble-kissed her. "I have something special for you, something that'll show you what I *truly* feel. It'll take away all fear and doubt. Set us on new tides."

"You do? What is it?"

Sleek smiled and winked. "A surprise."

"Oh, oh!" Cries Often pushed his way between the sweethearts, his good eye alight with playful excitement. "I love surprises. What is it, Sleek? Tell me!"

"Deshi-Oad's Fluke, Cries Often. Remember your manners!" Gloss chided.

Sleek restrained the urge to inflict a disciplinary bite on the dull-witted Lutris, Gloss' brother or no. "If I told you, then it wouldn't be a surprise, would it?"

"Uhm... errr..." Cries Often thought long and hard. Finally, he shrugged. "You like Gloss, so she gets her surprise."

"Yes." Sleek lowered his hijna. "It'd be dangerous if your brother knew."

Gloss frowned. "Why? What harm could it do?"

"That's not what I meant," Sleek cautioned. "It'd be dangerous *for him to know about*. But not for you...What I have for you is... complicated." Sleek kissed Gloss' paw, then pulled her towards the water. "Come with me to The Gnaarl, kalaayaa."

A mix of emotions flowed through Gloss — intense longing, anger, worry, and sadness. "No," she murmured, and pulled free of Sleek's grasp once more. "I can't."

Sleek stared at her, confused. Then, with a flash of comprehension, he said: "You're afraid to leave your brother alone."

Gloss nodded, wary of eye contact. "But that's not all. Father has forbidden me from seeing you. He says my feelings for you are a mistake."

"You told him you won't obey, right?"

"He refuses to listen. I'm just a 'lowly uja,' never mind that I'm his daughter."

"Then I'll appeal to him directly. Pijper can open a diplomatic channel to..."

"It won't work. Father's mind is closed." Gloss shook her head. "After That Scathing Tide, he hates the Lontra. He hates your father, your mother. And he hates you most of all. He's convinced there'll be war between our tribes. He wants war, no matter the cost. He *craves* it, like the aorxa craves blood."

Sleek went rigid with anger. *If Fearless thinks he can keep us apart, then by Ookl's Ink, let him try!* "All I know is how I *feel* when I'm with you." He gazed into Gloss' golden eyes. "Nothing else matters. Leave with me. Tonight. We'll make our own way. We'll start our own Holt somewhere else."

"Oh, Sleek." Gloss closed her eyes. When they opened, pain simmered within. "You know my father would send every graehl in The Raft to bring me back."

"Even if you don't want to return?"

"What I want doesn't matter. The Doyen's authority is supreme. My whole life I've dared to challenge it again and again. But..." Gloss paused, her heart breaking. "I've taken my disobedience as far as I can."

Gloss fell silent. Sleek sensed she had more to tell, the weight of the confession tearing her up inside.

"Tomorrow, when I relinquish my spear, Father will..." Gloss' hijna hovered on the verge of sobs. "...announce my courtship eligibility to The Raft. He will decree I take... a mate."

"*What?*" Though he'd braced himself, Gloss' pronouncement shocked Sleek to his core. He fought to keep his legs from buckling. "Ookl's Ink! You must refuse!"

"I can't. All the Raft's eligible uju will compete. The winner will be allowed to court me in the old way. There's nothing I can do."

Upset and confused by his sister's distress, and Sleek's utterance of the forbidden 'O'-word, Cries Often's whimpers grew. Gloss draped her arm around his neck, and his agitation subsided, though his confusion remained.

"Then I'll compete!" Sleek declared. "I'm Saia. It's my right. I'll force the issue. If that's what it'll take, then so be it."

"You're Lontra. Father won't allow it. He'd kill you first."

"I'd like to see him try!" Sleek retrieved his spear. The pryzoic potency coursing through his bloodstream fueled his bravado — and his mounting anger. "I'll fight him. I won't let him come between us."

"No, Sleek. I won't let you to get hurt because of me."

"I'll be hurt more *without* you, Gloss."

"You'll get over it. In time, you'll move on."

"No, I won't!" Sleek insisted. "I love you. I can't learn to *un*love you. I need you."

Gloss took Sleek's face between her paws and wiped away a tear gathering in the corner of his eye. "I'd rather have you live *without* me than die *for* me," she said, fighting to keep her hijna steady even as her Aanandi-shade screamed in agony.

She had to be strong — for both of them. Only by slaying their love now could she protect Sleek from his own impetuousness, and an ugly death at the paws of the Doyen.

"What we had was so beautiful... while it lasted." Gloss' eyes stung with sorrow. She yanked her lance from the nyoota's belly. "We swam together. Hunted together. You showed me respect and love, more than I've ever known. But now it's time I obeyed my Doyen. I won't risk your blood for my pride."

Sleek shook his head vehemently, refusing to accept her words. "No-n o..."

Abruptly, Gloss spun on him, ynth raised, her body in attack posture. "Yes! It *must* end. Now. Tonight."

Stunned, Sleek lowered his ears and whiskers in submission. "Don't you still love me?"

The answer she longed to give him remained sealed behind many barriers of hatred — for the customs of The Raft and her father's enforcement of them; for the pryzoa and the implacable inter-tribal rivalry their scarcity instigated; for her brother, who'd chosen to follow her on this of all nights, and who didn't deserve her hatred; for Xaad, who certainly did.

But mostly, she hated herself for what she must do.

And that pain would be the last to fade. If it ever did.

Gloss hardened her heart into stone. In response, her Aanandi-shade cracked as if struck by it. "No," she whispered. The lie burned her throat like acrid smoke.

Sleek staggered back, as if all his pryzoa-enhanced vitality had suddenly drained away.

"I can't ever see you again," Gloss barked, baring her sharp teeth. "Ever! Do you hear me?" She growled and, punctuating each word with a jab of her spear added , "It. Is. Over!"

Cries Often crouched by the nyoota, his slight body wracked with sobs. Never had his sister projected such naked aggression. It terrified him. "Gloss? Sister, why are you so mad?" When she didn't answer, he turned, slunk back to the gently lapping water, and slipped below the surface to wait for her amongst the swaying kelp.

Gloss skewered her ynth into the salmon a third time. "I'm leaving." She yanked out the alcq Sleek had given her, tearing her lip, and cast it at the heartbroken Beta's feet. Blood dribbled from her mouth and down her chest, the spreading crimson symbolizing her necessary fatalism. "*Don't follow me.*"

Gloss didn't look back as she dragged the salmon over the wet stones and into the water. Sleek lacked the will to stop her. He could only watch the love of his life swim away, leaving nothing but a ripple of dissipating nyoota blood to mark her passing.

"Kalaayaa..." Sleek moaned.

The act of speaking that cherished word drained the last of his strength.

Desperate, he turned his teary gaze skyward, to where the enigmatic Helquru glimmered beyond the fog. He wanted, *needed*, guidance on what to do next. But their celestial voices remained mute, as ever.

Just like Ookl had always been, and like his Aanandi-shade had now become.

Sleek had never felt so lonely — so utterly *alone* — in his entire life.

The heart-crushed Beta sat stonelike upon the shore throughout the night, not moving a whisker even as dawn's amber light softened the sky. He refused to swat away the myzee kelp flies that buzzed around his eyes to drink his tears. He did not feel the sharp barnacles dimpling his footpads, nor the itch of his healing leg-wound.

Sleek simply stared at the heaving ocean, numb from head to paw, his soul in pieces.

So many bloody pieces...

When at last the warmth of the new-risen sun evaporated the coastal fog, Sleek began to stir. Even turning his head was an effort. He saw Gloss' alcq — his original love token — lying at his feet. He picked up the shell, paw weak with grief, and pressed a thumb against the tip until it stung. The pain banished his lethargy.

At that moment Sleek wanted to hurl the love symbol into The Blue and be rid of it forever. He reared back his arm...

But he couldn't let go.

True, he felt acute emotional pain. It pulsed through his body, surely as his heartbeat.

Yet, his love for Gloss remained buried deep inside him. A single spark of warmth encased in a thick shell of ice. It must wait patiently for a warmer season to dawn. Only then could the ice melt, and the spark re-emerge.

Only Ookl knew if that season would ever come.

Sleek tucked the alcq into his ureola, retrieved his spear, and slipped into the cold ocean.

The swim back to The Holt would be the longest of his life.

-- To Be Continued --

GLOSSARY

Aanandi: The 'Garden Blessed.' An animal that ingests pryzoa within the boundaries of The Garden and undergoes the highest level of evolutionary awareness as a result. The magic contained within Liminal heightens bodily and mental attributes to a far greater degree than the random pryzoic ingestion responsible for creating a common Envorah. The eyes of an Aanandic creature burn bright gold (a secondary side effect of Aanandic attainment). 2% of all enlightened animals are Aanandi and are considered the 'elites' of the Envoric community. Much resentment exists between the evolved 'classes' as a result.

Aanandi-shade: The aspect of a Garden-evolved animals' psyche (or *soul*) that can intuitively leap beyond logic and into the realm of abstractions. It is the 'still, small voice' guiding the Envoric animal to inspiration, artistic expression, mathematics, and the rudimentary understanding of many sophisticated concepts, including deity recognition, existence of higher dimensions, and various after-life concepts.

Aanandic: The quality of being Aanandi, i.e.: the highest state of awareness beyond Envorah. All Envoric physical and mental augmentations are even more pronounced.

Acuur: Multi-tools employed by the Lutris and Lontra. Made of stone, bone, sea-glass, scrap plastic, or shark teeth, and rimmed with various notches, gouges, and pits for different tasks. Acuur are used to open shellfish, cut meat, kelp, or softer materials, whittle implements, a last resort melee weapon, etc., and are usually sheathed in the ureola.

Ahmijna: 'The Enduring Voice.' A crude petroglyph and pictogram writing system, scratched into rocks, shell, bone, or wood, that conveys everything from premonitions and Garden-related esoterica, to lineages, birth and death records, and mythological events. Originally created by Ulurii to chronicle their divinations and conversations with Great Ookl.

Aijeer: Something forbidden by Envoric law. Depending on the subject, punishment for aijeer transgression can be anything from a painful ear or nose bite, up to banishment — or even death.

Alcq: A labret piercing through the lower lip, used as a secondary rank identifier among both Lontra genders (turritella shells, collectively) and Lutris males (shark teeth, specifically). Usually assigned after a successful first kill, or during the naming day ceremony. Alcq have ceremonial, cultural, and cosmetic uses, and are often swapped out during major life events or achievements.

Aorxa: The 'blood drawn.' The blanket Envoric term of all species of shark. Since larger sharks are considered prestige quarry, there is a great amount of respect placed on the aorxa name.

Atiqah: The green-speckled lingcod (*Ophiodon elongatus*), or 'hungry thief.' Known for stealing freshly dispatched prey fish, they are considered pests.

Bishq: An Envorah expletive, generally pertaining to excrement.

Bitten: Northern Elephant seal servants of the Envoric Southern Elephant seal monarch, Diuun Dunn. Bite marks incised on their necks identify them as his chosen agents who personally carry out the Irounga lords bidding. As a youth, Diuun Dunn was likewise bitten by the great white shark Nolurrah, who, legend states, had been bitten by the Whitest Whale, Deshi-Oad.

Celimner: Name for the sacramental act of devouring a pryzoa slowly and reverently over the course of one or more tides. A deeply personal ritual where each animal expresses themselves with ghaydn mounds, prayer, and meditation. Each bite is slow and purposeful, with the intention focused on sharping the Kleaa instead of simply filling the belly.

Celipsis: The Lontra word for the sun. Believed by some to be a giant pryzoa, while others contend it is a portal leading to Oussia itself.

Ceptual: Lens employed by the Lontra during omen-diving. Harvested from animals with the keenest eyesight (Colossal squid (*Mesonychoteuthis hamiltoni*); benthic dwelling seed shrimp (*Gigantocypris*); blue whale (*Balaenoptera musculus*); Indo-Pacific blue marlin (*Makaira mazara*); (*Sphyrna mokarran*), the hammerhead shark). Used individually or together to observe finer movements, anatomical fluctuations, and subtle cyr-expressions of pryzoa not normally perceived. Preserved by pryzoic energy, they are held in an intricately weaved kholo latticework draping the hovering stones in Oussia's Puddle.

Chlooq: An obscure Lontra expletive, exact meaning unknown.

Chookzl: An Ulurii expletive. Its meaning lands somewhere between 'uboo (urchin) offal' and 'infected ink bladder'.

Cjaalet: 'Swift mount.' The act of a Lontra carrying a Ulurii on their back. Slowest of all Holt inhabitants, the octo-snails regularly need conveyance from the flooded basement of High Split Rock to the uppermost level of Oussia's Puddle and the very trunk of Old Tree. A cjaalet can do in minutes what would normally take an Ulurii many hours. Being tasked as a cjaalet is considered a great honor among the Lontra.

Cuursuurq: 'That Scathing Tide.' The Cuursuurq was a failed joint Lontra and Lutris campaign to drive The Cruel Dweller from Liminal by force. The monstrous crab proved far too formidable, and the ensuing rout claimed many river and sea otter lives. The scores that were maimed later became known as Oyyan, the 'honored injured.' Over the years, the Cuursuurq acquired an evil and cursed connotation, and the prime source of resentment between the two Envoric otter tribes.

Cyr: Tiny sigils and halos of bioluminescent light emanated by pryzoa. Cyr flicker over the bodies of these creatures like cold flame, and are believed to reflect their mood, state of health, and prescient glimpses. Envorah and Ulurii interpret cyr for divination purposes.

Deshi-Oad: The divine 'Whitest Whale' of Lutris mythology. The primordial Lutris creation deity believed by the sea otters to be an ancient snow-white sperm whale, and eternal opponent of Great Ookl, the patron cephalopod deity of the rival Lontra. "Deshi-Oad's Stone Teeth," "Deshi-Oad's Spume" and "Deshi-Oad's Fluke," are common Lutris sayings. May (or may not be) another name for infamous *Moby Dick*.

Dhanda: The Pacific blue-fin tuna (*Thunnus orientalis*). Known as the 'ever hungry,' the warm blooded dhanda are powerful, opportunistic hunters that often hunt in great schools. All muscle and bone, they are hard to catch and harder to kill. A prestige prey-fish for any hunter.

Doyen: The Alpha of the Lutris Raft. In power and influence, the Doyen is second only to the Lutris Den Sire. The Doyen wields the ancient Eehrynth spear as a symbol of power.

Eehrynth: The 'Alpha's Lance.' Believed to be the first tool, or weapon, ever fashioned by a non-Ulurii. Rumored to be carved from a rib bone of Deshi-Oad itself, the Eehrynth is the ceremonial spear of the Lutris Doyen.

Eemsura: Ulurii sand-prayers to Old Father Fathom. A sacred ahmijna, they are scrawled in wet sand and are delivered to the deity when wave action erases them. The complex sigil-language of Eemsura, indecipherable to most other creatures, is believed to impart power into the minds of those who fashion them enough times, allowing one to have visions, manipulate seawater, or project kinetic energy (*see*: Psimeaa).

Ehlmajl: When the Lontra and Lutris come together to hunt for common purpose, they create an aggregate majl-net, transitioning from the singular 'hunters weave' to the collective 'kinship weave' benefiting both species. The ehlmajl is not just a practical invention to harvest shraga and other fish shoals, but also a symbolic peace gesture between the tribes.

Elihuul: Among the Lutris, Deshi-Oad is known as 'The Divine Impetus,' subduing the cosmos in its capacity as an unstoppable force. In this way, Deshi-Oad's connection to the moon, and its nightly course through the heavens where it outshines all the stars, is established. Veneration of this phenomenon, when the entire Raft joins in singing praise to Deshi-Oad and submerged Gwelth is exposed to the sky, is known as Elihuul.

Envorah: 'We Who Speak,' those animals who have eaten pryzoa (from the smallest morsel to an entire animal) and achieved a level of physical augmentation and mental enlightenment as a result. Spontaneous spindle cell and neocortex advancement in the brain allow Envorah to communicate telepathically (*see*: hijna) and permit the rudiments of culture and higher cognition to begin. The eyes of an Envorah are a burnished bronze color (a secondary side effect of pryzoic ingestion) of varying sheen reflecting their individual level of evolution. Envorah are not governed by breeding cycles (they choose if and when to have offspring), and most enjoy metaturnality — they remain active both during the day and at night.

Envoric: The state or condition of being Envorah. Envorah are endowed with heightened mental and physical attributes, setting them above the common, unaware animals. 98% of all enlightened animals are Envoric.

Etcax: The common Atka mackerel (*Pleurogrammus monopterygius*). A readily available prey fish hunted by the Lontra. Growing nearly two feet in length, their yellowish bodies are slashed with five black stripes.

Floopf: The mindless white-cross jellyfish (*Staurophora mertensii*).

Gayathri: Deity of all Envoric seabirds, the Vialae. Gayathri manifests as a great, bird-shaped storm cloud crossing the sky, its mighty wings vast across the entire horizon.

Gayathri's Egg: The Vialae name for the moon.

Ghaydn: Envoric banishment talismans, believed to hold supernatural powers that compel a specific target to leave or enter a location; or as symbolic prayer mounds. Comprised of the materials related to the entity being banished (crab shells, eagle feathers, shark teeth, fish bones, etc.), they are arranged in stacks and patterns unique to the animal initiating the banishment or sanctioning the prayer. Ghaydn are also used as warning markers to delineate Lontra, Lutris and Irounga territorial waters.

Ghezzi-ghez: A common expletive used by the Lutris and Lontra. The meaning lands somewhere between "Your worth is less than a squirt of urine" and "Go copulate with a moldering sea slug."

Ghossn: The driftwood carryall, used primarily by the Lutris while harvesting urchins at the uboorl-mass, but employed by other species as well. Lashed together with kelp, kholo, or scavenged fishing line.

Graehl: Lontra or Lutris hunting party. Graehl are assembled to dispatch larger or more dangerous prey than a single otter could dispatch on its own. The highest-ranking animals, descending to lowest rank, are often how Graehl's are formed and dictate swimming formation. Lutris Graehl's are exclusively male, while Lontra Graehl's are both male and female.

Gribn: The common Great Sculpin (*Myoxocephalus polyacanthocephalus*). A bony, unappetizing predatory fish, it is also quite opportunistic, and is known to brazenly steal prey-fish off the spears of graehl hunters. Considered a pest among the Lontra and Lutris.

Gwelth: 'The Center of the Circle.' The Lutris sanctum constructed in the middle of Tanglesafe, made of driftwood, whale bone, kholo, and scrap plastic. Resembles a gigantic sea urchin. Gwelth is exposed nightly during Elihuul and houses the Lutris' forty-one pryzoa deep within.

Hahpah: The Dungeness crab (*Metacarcinus magister*). Considered easily harvested 'shallows-meat' and a common foodstuff for the Ulurii, Lontra, Lutris and Irounga.

Heeqoo: An Ulurii word suggesting an action or quest where an unshelled, sub-adult octo-snail searches The Blue to locate a suitable shell. A dangerous and vulnerable time that matures the Ulurii and prepares some of them for joining the Oumuo quorum in study of Great Ookl.

Heey-ou: Another Envoric word to describe Humans (*see*: Penuree). Added to the lexicon by Vialae overhearing the phrase "Hey, you..." from human conversations.

Helquru: The 'Night Patterns,' or stellar constellations and imparted with certain prophetic and mystical abilities. These patterns are named after mythic Envoric animals, like the sea hawk, the spiny lobster, or the dolphin.

High Split Rock: The Lontra home and physical seat of their power. A colossal megalith over two hundred feet tall and crowned with an ancient conifer tree, it resides across the water from both the Gentle Crescent and The Cellum. High Split Rock is honeycombed with caverns, tunnels, and numerous smaller chambers.

Hijna: 'The Shared Voice,' a form of inter-species telepathy, or 'direct knowing.' The level of hijna an animal possesses reflects their Envoric state: the greater the vocabulary, the higher the evolution — lower the vocabulary, the lesser the degree. Hijna partially refers to the common Envoric language-pool created by the Ulurii (*see*: Uraacheth.) This telepathic lexicon is constantly evolving to account for a greater range of experience and descriptions of the natural (and supernatural) world.

Holt: A single word used to describe both the collective Lontra population (the *romp*), and their physical residence (*High Split Rock*.)

Honeaa: The 'Carryover Essence' of Envoric potential granted at conception, maintained in the womb during gestation, and supplemented by colostrum. The Lontra's Suckling Mother offers her milk, imbued with an unusually high concentration of Honeaa, to those chosen kits deemed fit to become future leaders for the romp.

Irounga: The 'Free Swimmers' comprising all disparate species of seal and pinniped. This amalgamate tribe competes with both the Lutris and Lontra from an isolated island rookery and is ruled by the colossal Envoric Southern Elephant seal, Diuun Dunn.

Jaarjoora: The 'Naming Day', when those young Lutris or Lontra transition between the non-statuses of childhood into the full-fledged rights, and responsibilities, of breeding adulthood. Their first name is bestowed by the Den Dire or Doyen, but after a few seasons of gained rank-wisdom, the name may change to something more fitting of their personality and liking.

Kalaayaa: A composite word that means "Beloved," "Dearest," and "For you I'll gladly submit." A term of affection and love among Lutris and Lontra.

Keerth: the opalescent inshore squid (*Doryteuthis opalescens*), and one of the primary food sources of the Lontra and Irounga. Eaten to a lesser degree by the Lutris, who prefer sea urchins.

Kex: An Envoric expletive, exact meaning unknown. Also, 'kexxing.' Both very vulgar.

Kholo: 'High Polyps.' A feathery, soft coral-like life that spontaneously grow in proximity to wherever pryzoa are present. A magically transitional organism, they exist slightly closer to the energy-rich state of pryzoa then terrestrial life, and can produce light, conduct pryzoic magic, have high tensile strength, and offer a host of nutritional properties. Kholo can grow in long, ropy strands like kelp, or in clusters, bushes, blooms, bells, and thickets. They are used to construct nets, produce light within a den, weave the rank-identifying ureola, and other uses.

Khooradn: The 'Many moving as one' instinct of shraga, and other species of prey-fish, as they withdraw into a bait-ball when faced with predation. Exploiting this khooradn-instinct allows the Lutris and Lontra to catch them employing nets and bubbles.

Kleaa: The 'Tides of Awareness.' This ebb and flow of sapience rests directly on regular pryzoa-ingestion. After a prolonged absence of Liminal's vitalizing energy, manifest as pryzoa in our dimension, the animal's cognitive functions recede like the tide. Clarity and comprehension of language (see: *Hijna*) is a prime indicator on an animal's Kleaa-level.

Kooarii: Respect greeting used by lower ranking Lontra and Lutris when addressing an Alpha. A composite word that includes "Let peaceful tides find you", "May your pelt shine apart from ours," and "We hear and obey your commands." Often accompanied by a polite whisker-tug and four-legged posture.

Liminal: Called by Envorah either The Garden, The Garden Effulgent, and by the Ulurii as *Liminal Gheelindreeliah* (translated as "Life by Liquid by Light") it is a magical, high-energy ecosystem growing outside an inter-dimensional aperture linking The All-Light Ocean of Oussia, and our material universe. In our lower-dimensional realm, this rift manifests as the fabled Golden Barnacle. The physics of Liminal are alien to terrestrial life:

direction does not exist, gravity is subjective, light often condenses into liquid, and life — in the form of pryzoa — can appear from this liquid spontaneously.

Liminal Pact: A treaty between the Lontra and Lutris forbidding entry into Liminal with the purpose of returning pryzoa to the surface. Animals may enter The Garden for Aanandic upgrade, to enhance their Kleaa, to practice Celimner rituals, but little more. The Liminal Pact was intended to bring peace to the Envoric world by removing the temptation of recovering pryzoa, and the injury or death that would follow at the pincers of Vile Chaac'Xib. Instead, the Pact fomented Lutris resentment for being unable to challenge for species supremacy, as pryzoa possession is the only means to hold power in the Envoric world.

Lontra: The intelligent North American river otters (Monoic progenitor *Lontra canadensis pacifica*) residing in High Split Rock. Their Den Sire is High Eehr over all Envorah, with 42 pryzoa anchoring their power base. Their society is egalitarian, with graehl and child-rearing duties spread equally among genders. Young are called kits. The Lontra protect the last two remaining Ulurii octo-snails, who supply them with knots and esoteric wisdom. Lutris worship the colossal, hidden cephalopod, Great Ookl, *aka* Old Father Fathom.

Lutris: The intelligent sea otters (Monoic progenitor *Enhydra lutris kenyoni*) living in the dense kelp forest of Tanglesafe, and its submerged capital, Gwelth. Their Doyen is the second most powerful individual in the Envoric world, with 41 pryzoa at his command. The Lutris enforce a rigid social structure built on oppressive male dominance. Graehls are for males only. Young are called pups. Females derive their rank from their mate and are relegated to urchin harvesting and pup-rearing. Lutris can be aggressive and warlike. Larger and heavier than the Lontra, they consider river otters outsiders and usurpers. They worship the Whitest Whale, Deshi-Oad.

Majhee: A composite word for "Begin," "Commence," and "Together as one."

Majl: the net, or 'hunting weave.' The most technologically advanced items owned by the Lontra and Lutris. Made from kelp, scavenged twine, rope, and fishing line, they hold 'shallows-meat' of fish, squid, and other prey animals. Majl nets are prized for their complexity. The skill to fabricate them are nearly forgotten, save for a handful of older otters and the last two Ulurii.

Meta-Oorum: Whereas the Oorum acts as a perceptive threshold in the sea, hovering on the very edge of mystery, the Meta-Oorum behaves in the same fashion, offering a tableau of premonitions and prescient glimpses. 'Omen Diving' is the act of using the light cast from pryzoa, sometimes reflected by mirrors, to enter the Meta-Oorum and foresee the future. The more pryzoa one possesses, the further, clearer, and more accurate, the premonition will be.

Monoah: The 'Unaware' or 'Garden blind' animals, or, animals in their natural state that have never been exposed to pryzoa or Liminal. 99.9999 99998% of all animals in The Blue, The Still, and The Above are Monoah, including humans. Monoic animals are considered 'trapped' within a narrow predation-procreation worldview due to limited sensory inputs and simplistic instincts.

Monoic: The state or quality of being Monoah, i.e.: trapped, limited, or confined to a base 'hunter versus hunted' paradigm. Being called "Monoic" is a hurtful insult among Envorah.

Myzee: The catch all name for all species of biting, bothersome shore flies, with extra emphasis on the ubiquitous kelp fly (family *Coelopid*) that infests the coastal kelp-wrack zone.

Nataaq: Envoric expletive comparing the genitals of a male to a dead jellyfish, or pulpy bit of chewed matter. Used by females to berate or emasculate troublesome (or insubordinate) males.

Nookeelee: A composite phrase incorporating "Hello," "Welcome Home," "Good health to you," and "May keen eyes watch over you."

Nooree: The Envoric blanket-term for all disparate species of coastal kelp, seaweed, dulse, large algae, sea grass and other leafy, soft-bodied growths.

Nyoota: 'Silver Mouth.' The King, or Chinook, Salmon (*Oncorhynchus tshawytscha*) still in its morphological distinct ocean phase. Strong, quick, agile, and very skittish. A difficult prey fish to catch and dispatch. Considered a delicacy to Lutris and Lontra for this reason. When they undergo the physiological changes heralding their freshwater spawning phase, they are called *Gnyootu*, the 'Hooked Mouth' due to the pronounced curve of their jaws, called a kype.

Oixrd: An alcoholic beverage, the equivalent of Envoric liquor, which produces the same intoxicating effects. Made by masticating kholo and leaving the resulting pulp and saliva mixture to ferment in a cool, dark place for several days or weeks in giant clamshells. Often kept in the lower chambers of High Split Rock and Gwelth. Oixrd is usually reserved for adults but can be shared by all age groups during special occasions.

Ookl's Eye: The Lontra name for the moon. The waxing and waning phases of the moon are equated with the opening and closing of Ookl's Eye: A full moon means the Eye is fully open, while an eclipse means its fully closed.

Ookl's Ink: A common Lontra expression. Used in both a religious context, "May Ookl's Ink keep you safe in times of danger," and in a general vexation, "Ookl's Ink, don't be so foolish."

Oorum: An optical vanishing point, where light and water turbidity diffuse all objects into nonexistence. Not merely a tactical threshold for hunting or everyday life in the sea, many religious or supernatural attributes are also assigned to the Oorum.

Ootith: The submissive, four-legged stance used to show respect to those of higher rank. For many animals, it is easier to move ootith, as it is closer to their natural state. Envoric etiquette calls for all animals to drop Ootith to the Den Sire, Suckling Mother and Doyen.

Oujit: Universal cure-all made by pulping kholo and combining it with other medicinal ingredients, including certain kelp extracts, ground seeds, the Suckling Mother's Honeaa-rich breastmilk, and occasionally Pryzoa-infusion. Presents as a milky, salty, and sweet beverage.

Oumuo: The ruling class of Ulurii, exclusively devoted to worshiping Old Father Fathom and tasked with rousing the Deity back to awareness and interaction with the Envoric world. Usually, the oldest and most intelligent octo-snails join the Oumuo, but shell-less acolytes can also join.

Oussia: 'The All-Light Ocean,' the Envoric concept of Heaven. In truth, Oussia is a dimension of pure light and life-giving energy. The substance of Oussia leeks into our world via an aperture taking the shape of a giant Golden Barnacle in our reality. This 'liquid-light' periodically gushes into the ocean to renew its life-giving potential in an event known as The Glow. The high-energy ecosystem surrounding the Golden Barnacle aperture is called Liminal, The Garden Effulgent.

Oussia's Puddle: The stone sanctum within High Split Rock that house the Lontra's 42 pryzoa and adorning ceptual lenses. The second most holy location in the Lontra's worldview, it is, in many ways, a miniature version of Liminal: rocks saturated with energy, prodigious kholo growths, and the corresponding atmospheric/gravitational/perceptive distortions.

Oyyan: The 'Honored injured' among the Lontra and Lutris that took place in the disastrous Cuursuurq. Among the Lontra, these maimed veterans are honored for their sacrifice and wisdom. The Lutris killed their Oyyan, believing that keeping them alive would weaken the Raft and lower moral among the warriors as a visual reminder of the Cuursuurq's failure.

Penuree: 'Vulgar wasters.' A pejorative term that referrers to Humans and their society. All humans are considered Monoah, as they are not Garden-aware. Penuree, also called 'Heey-ou' from their common greeting, are considered the boogey men of the Envoric world and a source of misery and begrudging fascination.

Plijet: 'Affixer.' This multitool, used principally by Lutris females to harvest urchins, is a length of fishing line with a sharpened tip attached to one end and brace on the other. Different plijet variants exist: net and ghossn repair, hunting spindles and, in severe cases, a torture device.

Pryzoa: The 'Blessed Life' or Garden organism. Analogous to aquatic flora and invertebrate species, whose organizing principles are based on light and magic instead of water and carbon. Ingesting even the smallest portion of a pryzoa evolves a creature into Envorah, while eating them in Liminal-proper raises the animal to rarified Aanandi. Pryzoa, due to their predictive properties and ability to manipulate seawater (and other capabilities) in large groups, form the basis of Envoric power structure between species.

Psimea: The 'Rare and Precious Pearl.' Eemsura sand-prayers are purposefully designed to impart a modicum of psionic energy within the synapsis of the composing animal. This energy accretes with each sigil transcribed, much like a pearl forming around a grain of sand. Over time a threshold is reached where the stored energy can be projected outward, enabling the animal to interact with the material world without physically touching it. For Ulurii, this psionic action is utilized primarily in water, which acts as a superior conductor medium. Psimea can be projected as blunt force (to dispatch prey animals and self-defense), to manipulate seawater (counteracting or redirecting currents), and to override the central nervous systems of other animals. The use of Psimea in other animals is not yet know, as only octo-snails have enjoyed its potential.

Ptahhf: An Envoric expletive. Exact meaning unknown, but vulgar.

Qloobuu: The 'foot-tugging contest' played by Lontra kits and Lutris pups. The aim of qloobuu is to startle an individual bird, usually a seagull, without triggering the collective 'flight-instinct' and scattering the entire flock. It teaches valuable lessons in stalking prey, controlling buoyancy and breath, and the greatest of all, honing patience. From this simple child's-play, deadlier graehl-skills comprising the Hunter's Eye, like the Tsullee-hunt, are honed.

Raft: Both the name of the Lutris community, and their habit of the entire population to float among the surface kelp fronds of Tanglesafe day and night. Lutris tie themselves into these fronds for safety and anchor against wave motion and tide.

Ranks: Hierarchies in the Lontra and Lutris clans, like most Monoic animals, is primarily derived from a 'might makes right' model, i.e., physical strength and aggression decides the leader. However, Envorah also use alliance building skills, social efforts, intelligence, bravery, and breeding potential to determine rank. Ureola color marks the rank and can be adjusted when promotion or demotion occurs. Rank names and kholo colors as follows:

Alpha = *Eehr*, violet ureola

Beta = *Saia*, blue ureola

Gamma = *Vlis*, green ureola

Delta = *Dyah*, yellow ureola

Epsilon = *Loyc*, orange/amber ureola

Omega = *Nihl*, red ureola

Scithma-snaag: The Ulurii term for a 'Sharp bite of sudden memory' that overwhelms the mind after eating two or more pryzoa. One ingested pryzoa can elevate the Kleaa of most animals to their upper limits, especially in The Garden-proper. More risks supercharging the mind, and though great euphoria and clarity follows, oftentimes the animal suffers traumatic memory-echoes of crucial or dangerous past events that can often prove crippling. On occasion prescient information can be gleaned from the 'dream visions' that help the animal solve a problem or reconcile a difficult situation.

Shisslaaq: The developmental stage between squirtling and adult in the Ulurii lifecycle. Unshelled and vulnerable, an octo-snail can remain a shisslaaq for years, even decades, before finally achieving adulthood. It is a clumsy stage of life, with many Ulurii dying due to foolishness and inexperience. It is because of this tendency that shisslaaq is often used as a pejorative among octo-snails.

Shraga: The 'Sunset fish' that rise from the depths every four years to spawn. Milky white in the benthic regions, where they are believed to nibble the wounds of either Great Ookl or Deshi-Oad. Their colors change to dazzling teals, vivid reds striations, and opalescent highlights at the surface. All species consider their flesh and roe a delicacy. Harvesting shraga is extremely difficult and is one of the few times all Envorah work together for common purpose. Ulurii use the entrails of shraga to divine the future.

Shuuhl: That natural sheen of trapped air clinging to Lutris and Lontra fur when freshly submerged. Over time, this air is shed as a trail of bubbles. Envoric otters consider shuuhl to be an expression of the Aanandi-shade, or some other personality abstraction attributed to Old Father Fathom or Deshi-Oad.

Skoraa: 'Oath biter,' or lawbreaker. Someone not to be trusted. A pejorative term for those dishonorable Envorah who have willingly betrayed a friend or broken a law.

Spraint: Otter excrement with odors ranging from freshly mown hay to putrefied fish.

Squiq: Lontra and Lutris anal sac secretions. An embarrassing remnant of their primitive Monoic state, and seldom used due to its musky aroma.

Besides marking a den or other territory, squiq is used to categorize an otter as ill or injured, receptive to sexual advances, or prone to violence.

Squirtling: A freshly hatched octo-snail, still in its larval form. Tiny, transparent, and birthed by the thousands, only a tiny fraction reaches adulthood.

Tail-length: Measurement unit of the Lontra and Lutris. The average length of an adult's tail, or two feet. So: one tail equals two feet; ten tails equal twenty feet; twenty tails equal forty feet, etc.

Tanglesafe: Incredibly thick kelp forest where the Lutris Raft is found. Pryzoic energy radiating from Gwelth keeps the kelp ultra-lush and healthy. Kelp density within Tanglesafe is so great that subsurface attacks from sharks, orca, or barracuda have not occurred in many generations. Numerous species of crab, shellfish, jellies, and smaller prey thrive within Tanglesafe.

Tender nacre: Catchall name for all species of abalone, but mostly red abalone (*Haliotis rufescens*.) A delicacy for Lontra and Lutris. The greatest concentration of abalone is found in the lush kelp cathedral of Abundance, but that location is aijeer by blood-treaty.

Tharuuspex: Ulurii cleric of Great Ookl. They assist the Lontra Den Sire in omen-diving, deciphering pryzoic movement and cyr sigils into prescient hypothesis, diving the will of Great Ook through Shraga entrail examination, and providing esoteric and religious instruction to the Holt specifically, and the wider Envoric world in general.

The Above: The sky. Home of the Vialae, the Envoric seabirds. Domain of the sun Celipsis and the Helquru night-patterns. Dwelling place of the deity Gayathri and the Lutris' Elihuul-concept.

The Blue: The sea. The aquatic world for most Envorah and Aanandi.

The Cave: The tunnel connecting the Winnow to the outside world. Consisting of a long passage to the sea, and a deep subterranean decline leading into the Winnow. Vile Chaac'Xib blocked the passage section with a large boulder.

The Cellum: *aka* the 'Place of prayer.' The wreckage of a Penuree fishing boat (the 'Deep See' and later the 'Fantasea') believed wedged into The Cave opening by Old Father Fathom. Over the decades, The Cellum became a sacred site to the Lontra, who place banishment ghaydn on its deck to drive Vile Chaac'Xib from Liminal and other prayer requests to Great Ookl.

The Gentle Crescent: A patch of rock-free beach, curve shaped, directly across the bay from High Split Rock. Flat and smooth of sand, oversized sea-dollars can be found there. Uuvaloo scrawls Eemsura sand prayers upon the Gentle Crescent.

The Glow: A periodic co-mingling of the energetic substance of Oussia, The All-Light Ocean, and the sea. This magical efflux, exhibiting traits as both liquid and light, gushes out of Liminal, through The Winnow, exiting The Cave, and into the hydrosphere where it is dispersed globally. The Glow is a sacred, life-giving event, and is the greatest of all religious occasions in the Envoric world. Much study and pryzoic-contemplation are invested in predicting the exact time of its appearance. Any animal caught in The Glow is converted to Aanandi. Many ceremonies and societal events coincide with The Glow (see: *The Hasten.*)

The Gnaarl: or 'Ookl's Knot.' A mighty redwood tree stump and root tangle that spent decades floating in the ocean before being deposited on a beach and sand locked. Massive in size, it is believed to be of divine origin and endowed with miraculous traits, The Gnaarl is a sacred sight and place of refuge and worship to the Lontra.

The Hasten: A high-stakes contest used to 'reset' the Envoric power base and occupancy of High Split Rock. Challenges to supplant the High Eehr are usually settled by tooth-and-claw, employing the 'might-makes-right' strategy. But, in cases of unexpended death, incapac-

itating injury, abdication, or lack of hereditary successor, The Hasten is
used. The rules are simple: the first animal to enter Liminal and, under their
own power, return to High Split Rock with a living pryzoa placed at the
roots of Old Tree, wins. During the highly symbolic Glow, the High Eehr,
even in good health and standing, must compete if challenged. Animals
then must 'swim' through the high-energy effluence and return a pryzoa
to win.

The Scare: The instinctual 'Fight or Flight' reaction of Monoic animals but centered mostly on the flight impulse. Envorah traumatized
by The Scare can lose all mental faculties and total reduction of Kleaa,
and by extension, the ability of hijna. "Scared" Envorah are shunned (as
the condition is wrongly thought to be contagious) and believed beyond
rehabilitation.

The Skynth: Truncation of the Ulurii concept *Skynthuuhrnymlex*,
broadly translated as: "Wielding the Cleaving Ynth and Shuuhl of Oussia."
A fabled power granted to a chosen Envorah. The predetermined animal
taps directly into the unlimited energy of Oussia. Possibly bestowed during
The Glow. Foretold for generations, but never seen, no Envorah knows
exactly what powers a Skynthed individual owns, but they are believed to
be limitless.

The Still: Solid, dry land that exists beyond the shoreline. Named as
such because it never moves. Home of the Penuree, and a place of mysteries.

The Winnow: A transforming maze interstitial between The Cave and
The Garden. This subterranean labyrinth occasionally rearranges its passages in great earthen tumults. Envorah believe its complexity is designed
to weed out unworthy animals from discovering Liminal.

Tide-time cycles: The Envoric 'day' is predicated on four 6-hour tides:
two high, two low. First Tide, Second Tide, Third Tide, and Fourth Tide
can be further subdivided into early, mid, and late, i.e.: early Second Tide,
mid-Third Tide, late-First Tide. Time scales smaller than this are a source

of argument and are often tied to the movement of shadows throughout the day.

Tsullee-hunt: The 'blunt spear touch.' A mock hunt used to hone a hunter's stalking and stealth skill. The prey animal must be tapped with a spear or paw, but not injured. Much like 'Counting Coup' with Native Americans. One of the martial skills comprising the Hunter's Eye.

Uboo: The red sea urchin: *Mesocentrotus franciscanus*; and purple sea urchin: *Strongylocentrotus purpuratus*. The primary foodstuff of sea otters (both Monoic and Envoric.)

Uboorl: Sea urchin masses. Uboorl are harvested by Lutris females, low-ranking males, and pups of both genders. Left unchecked, uboorl can reproduce out of control. When it reaches a density of 300 urchins per square yard, it creates a plague-front that grinds everything in its path. This destroys entire kelp forests by devouring their holdfasts and sending them adrift.

Uhlee: The privilege of walking upright. Used by Lutris and Lontra of higher ranks over those of lower rank.

Uja, uju, uji: A group of pronouns used by Lutris and Lontra to express gender in casual speech: female (*uja*), male (*uju*), and neutral (*uji*).

Ulura / Ulurii: *Ulura* (singular); *Ulurii* (plural). Wise octo-snails. Considered sages of the sea who worship Great Ookl. Eldest of all Envoric species, extremely long lived and slow to mature, they are creators of the shared hijna-lexicon, tool making, kholo usage, and all foundational philosophies, i.e.: the nature of Oussia, Liminal communion, pryzoa harvesting and omen-diving. Freshly hatched octo-snails are squirtlings; sub-adults shisslaaq; and finally, Ulura when fully matured. Tri-lobed brains allows them to utilize Psimea (see: *Psimea*). Each of their eight limbs uses a supplemental rudiment-brain to aid with touch and finger-filament dexterity. They can rapidly, and with great expression, not only change skin color using pigment-bearing chromatophore cells, but also alter the size of *papillae* (vascular skin protuberances holding tactile corpuscles), allowing them to mimic rocks, corals, and other objects. They combine these traits for defensive, artistic, and religious practices. The tying and untying of knots fascinate them. Octo-snail flesh is considered a delicacy; the hunger for which nearly brought the species to the brink of extinction. The last two known remaining Ulurii are protected by the Lontra within High Split Rock.

Uraacheth: 'Naming Hunts' periodically undertaken by octo-snails when compelled to discover and name new objects and/or concepts. As the progenitors of the common hijna-language, Ulurii engage in uraacheth to increase their vocabulary. Friendly animals, usually the Lontra and Lutris, adopt and disseminate these lexiconic additions to others. Ulurii fixate over sounds, phrases, and symbols. They often mimic natural noises (cawing of birds, sloshing of waves, hissing of the wind over the sand) when devising a new word or phrase. Words with multiple meanings (*see*: Nookeelee, The Skynth, Yaeeeli) are also quite common.

Ureola: Knotted wristlets worn by Lontra and Lutris. Made from kho-lo, they are often knot-woven by the Ulurii, and glow a specific color per the rank of the individual adorning them. Ureola's are given to newly named otters during the Jaarjoora naming ceremony to cement their new identities. Hunters use the ureola bioluminescence to attract prey fish, and often remove them when they wish to remain unseen.

Vialae: 'Winged Allies.' The word to describe all Envoric seabirds, regardless of species. Often used as messengers and diplomats by other Envorah. Also employed for prey-spotting, for the right price. All Monoic seabird species are collectively called *Luuhni*, or the 'Skittish Ones.'

Vile Chaac'Xib: An immense crab of devious intelligence and rapacious appetite claiming Liminal as its own territory. The perpetual light and power of The Garden as bled nearly all color from the shell, pincers, and organs of this monster. Its viscera glow red-hot when it feeds, is attacking, or anticipates a meal. Known by many names, VCX has killed numerous Lutris and Lontra attempting to access Liminal over the years and has strangled nearly all the magical interaction between The Garden and the outside world. Saying the name Vile Chaac'Xib is considered a wicked thing that will bring bad luck to the speaker.

Vouruum: The courtship cairn, made of rocks, driftwood, or shell, and decorated in a manner to show the affection of the suitor and their creative spirit. Used by both Lontra and Lutris to initiate courtship negotiations, concluding with betrothal and mating. Usually, an offering from the male to the female, but not always. Considered by many to be an archaic and old-fashioned custom.

Vuuhn-Vaahl: The Ulurii word for the 'Hunter's Eye.' A catchall term addressing the skills and prowess that individuals, and graehl's, need to be successful hunters. All aggregate martial traits, from making and wielding spears, to stalking, stealth, buoyancy, tooth-and-nail fighting, and breath control are qualities of the Vuuhn-vaahl.

Xhooja: 'Quicker-water.' Those submarine slipstream currents created by differentials in salinity, temperature, seafloor topography and water density, that function as speedways through the ocean. Employed by Envorah to cross great distances much faster than mere swim-speed could accomplish. Xhooja are hard to find, but some established, perennial currents are extensively used by Lontra and Lutris graehl's.

Yaeeeli: First contact between Envorah is dangerous when innocent remarks or gestures are misconstrued as hostility, especially between animals of disparate hijna-vocabularies (see: *Kleaa*). By offering 'Yaeeeli,' both animals commit to a common equality that saves face and prevents bloodshed, unless an Alpha is involved. A truncation of the Ulurii greeting: *Ucaay-yaeeeli-uraari-omaweera:* "I am me-you are you-we are equal-I am you-you are me-equal are we."

Ynth: Spear or lance. Made from sharpened whalebone, calcified baleen of Envoric whales shorn of whiskers and stone sharpened, or, for the elites, scavenged and repurposed human fishing-poles tipped with flattened fish-hooks or other sharp objects. Otters place the base of the spear against the tip of their tail, and, like a human *atlatl*, hurl the weapon with great accuracy and lethality with a combination of body-twist and tails-slash.

Yurch: A common otter explicative. Considered as the height of profanity among Lontra and Lutris. Exact meaning unknown, but *very* vulgar.